The Guest of Night

Lucy Underwood-Healy

Sorrow is but the guest of night . . .

En Route Books & Media, LLC
St. Louis, MO

Make the time

En Route Books and Media, LLC

5705 Rhodes Avenue

St. Louis, MO 63109

Cover credit: Dr. Sebastian Mahfood, OP

Contact us at contactus@enroutebooksandmedia.com

ISBN-13: 978-1-952464-84-3

Library of Congress Control Number: 2021940406

Acknowledgements

I am grateful to those who encouraged my writing, especially Fiorella de Maria, Nick Warburton and Frank Cottrell Boyce, and to all have taught me history, beginning with my father. I would also like to thank Sebastian Mahfood and his team at En Route Books & Media. I am grateful to my parents, who taught me to value both truth and creativity, to my husband for his patience, and to the Catholics of Elizabethan England for providing plot material.

Dedication

For Malcolm Underwood

I

'And that, then, we are to take as your answer?'

The prisoner raised his head. 'I regret so.'

'I think you should consider how we will be forced to regard your refusal, under the circumstances.'

'I have considered. I have no more to say but that I cannot accept your favour on these conditions.' He looked down again at the table, and then up at his examiners. 'I am sorry I cannot satisfy you further, my lords.'

'You will have to satisfy us further, sir.' The Lord Lieutenant's irritation was ice-sharp. 'You know, Mr Branton, that there are matters concerning which we must have answers. Since you reject that obedience we partly hoped to find in you, we have no choice but to proceed with this examination according to the information laid against you.'

The prisoner said nothing. His two examiners glanced at their notes, and at each other, while the secretary seated at the end of the table filled his pen with ink.

'What have you to say, Branton, to the accusation that not only do you possess unlawful and seditious writings, but that you have acted in concert with one Lockwood, innkeeper of Merford, to spread them abroad, to the danger of Her Majesty and the realm?'

'I have no dealings in sedition, my lords, nor to my knowledge has Lockwood.'

'This is in addition to your persistent receiving of traitors in your house and fostering friendship with notorious enemies of your Queen.'

'I do not harbour traitors.'

'Were you acquainted with the traitor known as Rowsham who was executed last summer?'

'No.' The prisoner said flatly.

'And yet you were present at that execution.'

'So were a good many people.'

'What were your dealings with one Will Lampley, a glover in Gloucester?'

'I have now and then been known to purchase gloves.'

'You were seen speaking to him on the day of that execution, there is more than one witness. And Lampley was loud in his defence of that traitor.'

As the prisoner hesitated, the scratch of the secretary's pen seemed almost to echo against the stone walls. 'I wished him well, and I advised him to keep from speaking of what had happened that day. And if I had treason to plot, sirs, please believe that I would not do it in the Gloucester market-place.'

'Then you knew of his seditious speeches?'

'I say nothing of his speeches. My lord, to what does all this tend? You speak of Lockwood and Lampley, as though rumours among tradesmen and ale-sellers were aught to me. I, and divers other gentlemen, have been held since the spring with no reason given but that the realm is at war, and we – however honourable our station or long our families' service – are held untrustworthy. Why do you now strain to make matter against me out of such stuff?'

'Because the sedition of little men is fed at the hands of greater malcontents, just as those men have patrons of their own.' Lord Lieutenant Chandos retorted. 'But we shall show you better *stuff*, Mr Branton, if you wish. We have further questions about Lockwood's inn; and about how Lampley learned his disaffected opinions; and also about a servant of yours, a Ralph Hale.'

The prisoner made no reply, and the lord lieutenant continued. 'Hale, who seems to have more names than any honest man needs. And to make more journeys than the affairs of Branton could ever, surely, require.'

Still the prisoner did not respond. 'Your sedition till now may not have been open, but your disaffection is well-known. Therefore, we will have answers to these questions, and we will credit reports against you unless you give us good reason not to do so. And if we are obliged to refer the matter to their Lordships of the Privy Council, they may not be in haste to set you at liberty.'

Then the bishop spoke, leaning forward across the table. 'We do not seek to pry into your soul. But you see, we must have some demonstration of loyalty, of obedience –'

'Indeed, none of this means you cannot now reconsider.' Lord Chandos added. 'You may leave this place either for a London prison, or your home, as you choose, Mr Branton.'

The prisoner rose. The Lord Lieutenant made as if to stop him, but he only walked to the window and stood, looking out of it. There was nothing but walls and court-yards immediately outside, but beyond was the city, and beyond that – many miles and a day's journey beyond – there was a village among the hills and woods that was his to tend, with its spired and arched and carven church dwarfing the huddled cottages. A house of old greying stone and new pale stone that rang with the feet and voices and tears of children, and a woman with green-grey eyes and long, quick hands and a laugh like the dancing of summer rain on a glass window. But one could not keep thinking of these things. One must not.

He turned back to the room, and the examiners, and the questions, and the weary fight of answering them.

II

Hugh Branton leaned against the schoolyard wall, ignoring their conversation as he talked to Stephen Bourne and the other gentlemen's sons; but his hand, clenched into a fist at his side, betrayed him. Jem caught Taylor's eye and nodded toward Branton, but Taylor was absorbed by the latest gossip about the tattered flight of the Spanish ships. They had heard most of it before, but it was no penance to hear it again.

Branton's way of ignoring the war news reminded Jem Carter of his habit of coming into school seldom late, but never early, as though hurrying for school were beneath Hugh Branton. He headed the class rather as though that were beneath him, too, not boasting but as if it were hardly worth boasting about. Jem himself was far from stupid, and he worked – every evening and some mornings, knowing that each farthing paid to the grammar school was taken from somewhere else and must not be wasted. Sometimes he defeated Branton, who would look mildly surprised and, if he remembered, say well done as school broke up, rather as though he were giving alms. And Branton's silence during catechism lessons was deafening, the look on his face worth a dozen blasphemies. Master Lee let him get away with it because however much he disapproved of popery in general, the school was founded partly on Branton endowments.

The Queen, ran the latest reports, was to hold a thanksgiving service at St Paul's this next month, near to Accession Day. That meant the famous invasion was well and truly over.

'And the papists may be let loose soon as well,' Lane said. 'They're protesting their loyalty and pleading conscience for all it's worth.'

'Oh, they'll swear twenty loyal oaths, take your clemency and turn traitor next day. My brother used to say that English papists are worse than Spaniards, because they're traitors to boot.' Jem did not have to remind his schoolmates that his brother had fought the Spaniards in the Netherlands until he was captured out there. He glanced at Branton. 'What are you scowling at?'

Branton did not answer, still talking breezily to Bourne and clenching his fist. Taylor said, 'Not all papists are like that... and besides, if the invasion is all over...'

Jem was still looking at Branton. 'Taylor's your advocate, anyway. He'd take the papists' word for it they're as loyal as any of us.'

'Shut up.' Hugh Branton said, and now his teeth were clenched as well, although he had not deigned to turn round.

'Why should I?' Jem found his voice rising. 'Although truly it ought to be a sore point, having a Spaniard-loving traitor for a father –'

Hugh felt his knuckles smash against Jem Carter's jaw-bone as his fist swung out. Carter staggered back and then sprang forward. 'Oh, we're fighting, are we?'

Hugh hit again as he sprang aside from Carter's return blow. He kept hitting, dodging the other boy's heavy fists and trying to land his own where they were not expected, the muddy ground churned up beneath their feet and the smell of sweat and anger filling the air. And all the time hearing his own thoughts – Fool. Idiot. Childish fool – and not knowing which of them it was. But every time his fists struck Carter something in him stopped aching for a moment and burned instead. Stephen Bourne all-but had to drag him back as the dinner-hour ended and the school-master appeared in the doorway. Hugh ducked past to his seat praying Master Lee would not ask what the fight was about, but still seething.

*　　*　　*

'Hugh?'

Hugh turned, realising from the tone that it must have been the third or fourth time Stephen had spoken. His road home and Stephen Bourne's ran the same way, so they usually rode it together.

'I said, the boys are talking about a ball game at noon-time tomorrow, will you join?'

'I suppose so.'

Stephen sighed but knew there was no point trying to talk now. His friendship with Hugh depended more on judicious silences than either would have admitted. This one held until they reached the turning to Branton Hall, when it was broken by a voice calling from behind them on the road.

'Good day, Master Hugh!'

Both boys turned. Two horsemen had come up after them and also halted at the corner. Hugh answered, 'Good day, Mr Lister.'

Stephen Bourne repeated Hugh's greeting. John Lister asked after his daughter. Hugh replied, 'I think Bridget is well, sir' and smiled politely when John Lister asked if she were not giving Mistress Isabel more trouble than all the little Brantons together. But he was looking at the other man. He knew him, and he was sure that if he had not seen him with John Lister he would not have recognised him. Only he could not place him.

Hugh knew better than to ask questions about a stranger in front of outsiders. He also knew that Mr Lister and his guest would probably want to get safely into the Hall before it became necessary to answer questions about the stranger, though not so quickly as to seem rude. So, he said cheerfully to Stephen Bourne, 'Goodbye. See you tomorrow,' and pulled his horse round.

'My mother will be pleased to see you,' he said to John Lister, but with a glance which tried to include the stranger as a familiar acquaintance. Stephen said goodbye and turned toward his home, and as the three of them rode up towards Branton Hall, Hugh asked the stranger, 'What should I call you, sir?'

'I am travelling as Woodhill at present, Master Hugh'. And then Hugh knew him, but before he could say so a young girl had run out of the great door of the Hall, leaving it swinging wide behind her, and then stopped still, looking up at the stranger. Joy and disbelief and a shadow of fear chased each other through her eyes, and when she spoke it was quietly, almost with a glance over her shoulder.

'Richard?' Bridget Lister said.

Richard Lister swung himself down from his horse, smiling, and then she threw her arms round him. 'You've grown, little sister,' he said. 'You're too tall now for me to lift onto my horse.'

Wat had appeared to fetch the horses into the stables. Hugh went ahead into the house to tell Mother.

It was stranger than he could have thought, having Richard Lister come back. Hugh had knowingly seen priests at home a few times before; they came and went, but they talked very little about themselves, and you did not ask questions. It was just odd to hear one asking after his mother and saying his sister had grown, to know that he had sat in the same schoolroom as Hugh and dreaded the same master. And then gone to Rheims and come back a priest, his life now forfeit.

Mother had, as usual, sent Hugh to the library to task Harry on his Latin. As usual, Harry was not in the library. Hugh wandered over the house, half-heartedly searching for him. He could hear Marian, who was only a year old, wailing about something somewhere, but no sign of the others. Eventually, he found Harry with the younger children in the leaf-strewn orchard, throwing sticks for the spaniel and getting muddy, damp and, surely, cold as the autumn light faded – but with no particular desire to come inside and con Latin.

After a quarter of an hour spent getting Harry into the house and to his books, and a far worse hour trying to get some of the contents of the books into Harry's head, Hugh was glad to release him. He said nothing to Harry about Richard Lister: he did not really know what Mother's plans were for the morning, let alone how much she wanted Harry told. Hugh put his own schoolbooks out in front of him. There was time to study a little before supper.

Hugh remembered the first time he had known a priest was at the Hall. It was the time the raid happened, three years ago. He remembered that it had been early in the morning – not before anyone was awake, but while people were still dressing. The knocking on the great door fit to break it, calls to open in the Queen's name; he had still been too sleepy to be properly afraid, but he remembered Father's voice saying, 'For God's sake, what time is it?' before he started going downstairs. Hugh heard him say to Mother, 'I can give it a minute or two before I open. Use the hiding-place, of course. The house will be surrounded.' Those last words had frightened him, making home suddenly feel like a trap.

They had insisted on everyone's coming down into the great hall. Some of the men had come upstairs, shouting orders and opening chamber doors. Hugh remembered going to the hall, and the children stumbling downstairs in various stages of being dressed. Aunt Isabel had not a button out of place, but her black hair was flying loose. She had thrust an armful of clothes and shoes at Hugh with one hand while she tried to keep hold of one of the twins (who had been babies then) under the other arm. The servants came in, too, Jenufer furious over a pan of stock that had been left over the lit fire in the rush.

They clustered around the high table at the parlour end of the great hall. Mr Claydon – Hugh recognised him, the justice of the peace who must have ordered the search – told some of his men to stand guard, and himself led the others off to search the house. Hugh did not know, now, why he had not been more frightened. He had known, after all, that Mr Martin was a priest.

One of the twins started screaming. Aunt Isabel stopped putting George's shoes on him and began rocking the baby and shushing. Everyone else stood still, trying to listen over the noise to the sound of the men searching through the house, listening for they dared not think what. At one point Father, seeming to hear something, rose abruptly from his chair and strode through the open parlour door before the men could stop him. They heard his voice going towards the library. 'Mr Claydon, if you must search my evidence-chest, I have the key. I would really rather you did not break it open.'

Mother took the screaming twin and managed to quieten him. Then the other started up until Hugh wanted to clap his hand over its mouth and swear. That was all he really remembered about the rest of the morning: the tireless screaming, the wooden faces around him, and his eyes aching with sleepiness.

An hour after they had gone, when everyone had got properly dressed, and Jenufer had made clear her feelings over the stockpan (which was completely burnt out), and Mother had begun directing the maids to tidy up, Hugh saw his father going towards the parlour, and he followed him. Father went about halfway up the parlour stairs, which led to the east end of the gallery. Hugh stood at the bottom, unsure if his father knew he was there. He watched him lift up the top of the step in front of him like a lid and whisper something. Then he reached down, and Hugh saw Mr

Martin emerge, helped out by his father. He was dusty and looked rather white and tired.

'All clear?' he asked.

'Yes.' Hugh's father said. 'I had Robson and Hale watch to make sure they had left in good earnest. We gave them about an hour.'

'All well with you?'

'All well. Nothing found that they could take exception to. Thank God and a good carpenter.'

They started to come down the stairs and saw Hugh. Neither of them said anything. Hugh looked up awkwardly. 'Good morning, Mr Martin.'

Father, reaching the foot of the staircase, took Hugh by the shoulder. 'Hugh, listen.' But Hugh darted past him, up to the open hole, and peered into it. Then he ran back down the steps and stared at the wall beside the staircase. He even reached out and knocked on it, but it did not sound hollow. Both men laughed a little. 'Thank God and a good carpenter,' echoed the priest.

Father came over. 'Hugh. You do know, do you not, what would have followed if they had found that place?'

Hugh whispered, 'Yes, sir.'

'That must never happen.'

'No, sir.'

Mr Martin said, 'I should be gone soon.' He took out a handkerchief and wiped the dust off his face. 'You might ask Mrs Branton to take a broom to that hole, if it's no trouble.'

The priesthole in the parlour wall had not been used since, to Hugh's knowledge, but the parlour was never the same again. He had had to train himself not to look that way when he went in, or to tread extra carefully on the eighth step of the stairs. There had been another search, this spring. That had not mattered so much because there had been no-one to find, but Mother had been quietly furious. She and Father were both tight-lipped afterwards, and then two days later Mr Bourne had arrived at the Hall with an arrest warrant and a reluctant determination to carry it out. Hugh had not seen it happen; he had been at school. It was simply not a time when you could afford to have that kind of attention drawn to you, Mother had said afterwards. The Spanish fleet might be on the seas any day, and Her Grace's Council could not have all these recusant gentlemen at large when an invasion was threatened. Papist traitors, you see. Spaniard-loving traitors. Father might have been a Spanish captain in disguise.

Of course, it had to be Stephen Bourne's father. It had taken all of Stephen's tact and perseverance to prevent the silence between himself and Hugh from becoming permanent in the days that followed. You could not deny that Stephen's was no light kind of friendship.

There was a knock at the library door, and one of the maids appeared to tell him it was the supper hour. Hugh got up, put his unopened books back in the book-press, and went to the great hall.

*   *   *

After supper that evening, Bridget Lister sat near the parlour window, paying fitful attention to her sewing and listening to the grown-ups' conversation. The little ones had been sent to bed long ago, but she and Hugh stayed in the parlour with Mrs Branton, Mistress Isabel and the guests, where the talk turned to the things one only talked about when one was sure of one's company. Richard was on his way back from London to the North, where he was working. He would not say much, only that it had been a hard summer for Catholics in London, the Spanish fleet making the mob fearful and the judges severe. Hangings were to be expected; there had been many in July and August, but it was to be hoped the worst would be over with the Spanish threat. And the threat of the fleet was surely over now.

'I heard the Jesuits were printing again in London.' Mother said.

'I would not know aught of that.'

'It would be the first time this side the sea since the press they had near Henley.'

'That did not last six months.' John Lister said. 'Three tracts they printed, and by summer '81, they'd been caught.'

'Though only after the Oxford commencement,' his stepson put in. Bridget saw that he smiled, and so did Mrs Branton.

'What happened in Oxford?' Hugh asked.

'Why, that story went round every Catholic in England,' his mother said. 'But you were rather young then. It was – no, you tell this, Mr Woodhill.'

Richard Lister leaned forward a moment and stirred the fire. 'Well. Campion the Jesuit – and the man could write if ever anyone could – made a book he called the *Rationes Decem*, ten reasons, in defence of the Catholic faith. But he wanted it read, and by Protestants, you understand, and he could not sell it to them in Paul's yard. So, a priest in Oxford made his way one night into St Mary Virgin's – the University church – and, to cut the tale short, when we students trooped in to see the candidates for degrees awarded their honours, well, *Rationes Decem* was strewn down every pew.'

He laughed as he said it, and the others did also. Bridget said, 'What then? What did – ?'

'No-one knew quite what to do. It was not noticed all at once, of course. One person after another saw the thing, picked it up, grasped what it was... Some were furious, others pleased, but you see none could resist reading just a little of it. So, for several minutes there was very little up-roar – in fact I think there has seldom been such breathless silence during the opening address of the Academic Act.'

'But something must have happened?' Hugh said.

'Oh yes. When the zealous among us had recovered from their shock, and their curiosity, all Hell broke loose... But they did not seize all the books – I got one back to my lodging, and I know I was not the only one.' He turned to his stepfather. 'Now I think of it, it may be somewhere about the house, for I remember I brought it home that summer.'

John Lister shook his head. 'I do not know – but I remember well enough your telling us that story.'

Hugh asked, 'Did they take him, sir?'

'Not then. He was taken a month later, and I daresay no tempers were sweetened by the Oxford affair... but Edmund Campion was never going to be released alive.'

'I meant whoever put the books in the church.'

'Oh – Hartley was banished from the country a few years later. But he must have returned, for I heard he was hanged this year.'

Soon after that, Mrs Branton rose and said it was late. 'And we must be rising betimes. Hugh, I will knock at your door in the morning, and I do not want to have to keep the horses waiting while you get out of bed, understand?' She smiled as she took up her candle. 'If we cannot quite keep All Hallows, we'll at least meet to serve God the same week.' And then to Richard, 'I know not how many will come out to the old grange, but I have sent messages.'

John Lister turned. 'Messages? Tonight?'

'Yes.'

'To whom, Mrs Branton? And by whom?'

Mrs Branton's voice was ever so slightly sharp. 'To those we can trust, and by those we can trust. Does that trouble you?'

'That there are half-a-dozen messages being run all over Merford tonight with information about tomorrow morning? That it need only one of your messengers seen by the wrong person, one fool heard leaving in the morning, and we're all trapped, and will not know it until – oh no, I'm only a little troubled.'

'Master Lister, I am well apprised of the dangers, and I was not born yesterday. But it is good to hear your frank counsel.' Which meant, how dare he address her in that manner.

Bridget's father's tone as he replied showed he had understood as much. 'Your pardon, Mrs Branton. I mean only that we did not plan for anything tomorrow; and it's these unplanned ventures that most oft miscarry. Even here in Merford a little prudence would not go amiss, just at present. To begin with, have you met that charming new minister yet?'

'Mr Hall of St Martin's? I've heard something of him.'

Mistress Isabel said, 'I heard he'd been here four weeks and preached two sermons against papists.'

'You heard correctly. You may be glad you did not hear the sermons!' John Lister replied.

Mrs Branton said, drily, glancing at Richard, 'You see, father, I simply would not have the patience to be a church-papist.'

John Lister continued as though he had not heard her. 'What matters more is these enquiries into church-going. He was at my house the other week asking questions about my wife's not being at service, and he has been at others besides…'

'That has very little to do with tomorrow morning. Let's see if he does bite as well as bark before we start running, shall we? At least, I'm sure no-one will convict you for recusancy, Mr Lister.'

Bridget had not met Mr Hall, but she had heard about his sermons. The new laws were a goodly knife to cut out a canker, if only they were properly used. God's mercy in scattering the Spaniards should not be requited by allowing the pope's minions to infest the country. She also knew, though she was not supposed to, that when Mr Hall had left her father's house, her mother had been in tears.

With that knowledge in her head, Bridget looked up at her father. But before he replied, Mistress Isabel interposed. 'Well, I do not think we can alter any plans now. Mr Woodhill, Mr Lister, let me show you to the guest-chamber. Bridget, if you are going home with your father and Mr Woodhill tomorrow morning, you had better pack some things tonight. There'll be no time come the morning.'

'Yes, Mistress Isabel.'

As they rose to leave, murmuring slightly strained goodnights, Bridget wondered if anyone else had noticed that Richard had taken no part in the dispute at all.

She lingered in the parlour after the others, putting away the sewing she had hardly touched, and then slowly went toward the chamber she shared with Mistress Isabel. Too much had been said that evening to take in all at once; so, she let her thoughts fill with Richard's coming. With the oddness of hearing him called by a different name, the way in which his face and manner and voice were strange and yet not – it was as though she had never met him before, and at the same time as though he had never left.

On the stairs, she turned suddenly. Behind her was the sound of a side-door door opening and shutting, and quiet footsteps entering from the courtyard. It was too dark to see very well, but holding her candle out Bridget glimpsed a tall young man with tumbling sand-coloured hair, a wide, thin mouth and some freckles.

'Ralph Hale!' And she ran back down the stairs, almost tripping as she tried to hold her skirts up and guard her candle-flame with the same hand. She knew Ralph Hale, although she did not often see him. He was – if anyone asked – a servant in Giles Branton's household; but that household rarely saw him, for he was very taken up with numerous journeys of which Mrs Branton did not ask the details, unless there were news or goods she particularly wanted.

'Hush, Mistress Bridget.' He said at once. 'I thought you would be all abed.'

'No, they are only just gone upstairs. Tell me what's the matter, Ralph.'

'It is nothing really. There are… I shall be gone again by morning.'

'I will tell Mrs Branton you are here.' And Bridget went, running, toward the great chamber. Mrs Branton silently put her comb down, pinned up her hair again, and came.

'Come into the library and shut the door, if you please. Bridget, go to bed. Now.'

Bridget stayed a moment, staring at the door Ralph Hale had closed behind them. Then she went slowly and carefully up the stairs.

In the library, Mrs Branton set her candle down on the table before she spoke.

'I did not know you were bringing stuff here, Ralph. We did not expect you this month.'

'Some books, madam, that I was taking to Lockwood's. I thought I was being followed and I did not want to be seen going into the inn and make suspicions…'

'So, you stopped here instead?'

'Turn into Branton Hall and I'm a servant returning home. Go anywhere else, and I'm a suspect traveller carrying a suspect load. I have left them in the stables. I would not trust all the servants in this house.'

'No.' She was silent a moment. 'I suppose, Hale, if you think you are watched, you had best not take them on. I shall ask Robson. Robson I do trust.'

'Thank you, Mrs Branton.'

'I shall send him come the morning. And now good-night.'

But as the young man opened the door for her she pushed it shut again and turned back to him.

'One night. That is all. You know what was agreed about this. I would not have them find now what they were hunting for last spring.'

'No, madam. Thank you.'

'Never do this to me again.'

III

Late the next evening, Mrs Lister went up to the room that was now, usually, used as a guest chamber, and knocked at the door. Her son was seated on the edge of the bed, a book open in his hand.

'Richard?'

He shut his office-book, marking the page for Compline as he did so, and looked up. 'Mother.'

She saw her own grey-brown eyes smiling from the face of the father Richard did not remember. 'I came to ask if there were any clothes you wanted me to have washed for you.'

'I - suppose so. I don't know...'

She sighed as much as to say she had expected no more. 'There are things that want mending too, I'll be bound. When did you last think to see to that?'

'I cannot remember.'

'And there are your boots.'

'What about my boots?' He had almost laughed.

'They are about to fall to pieces.'

'I'm sorry. I do not often have time to look in a glass.'

'You do not need to look in a glass, just at your feet.' She had begun folding the cloak he had slung over the end of the bed. 'I'll see to it before you leave… look at the hem on this. What else shall I take?'

'I shall look through it all and give you them tomorrow.'

She folded the cloak over her arm. 'It will be only the family at – here – when we serve God – tomorrow morning. My husband does not wish to be imprudent.'

'Good.'

'It – he – this is the first time he has permitted such a thing, I mean in this house.'

'I see.'

'I've told the servants you are a business acquaintance of your father's. I hope that was right. They are new-come since you left and will not know you, except Joan, who of course we can trust.'

'Yes, I've been to greet Joan.' Joan had served his mother longer than Richard could remember, since before her marriage to John Lister. 'Richard, how long will you stay?'

He hesitated. Strictly speaking, he was not staying at all. He had never stopped more than a day or two in any place on his journey back north. 'I will stay until the end of the week.'

She smiled. 'It has been a long time.'

'I know. And I know I've not sent much news either. But you understand…'

'I do. But now you are here, we cannot be begrudged half a week, I think.'

Silence overtook them; there was too much to say. 'Goodnight, Richard.'

'Goodnight, Mother.'

*   *   *

'Well,' Bridget's father said. 'It seems quite strange to have both of you back at this table.'

They were breaking their fast after Mass. Father spoke quietly, but Bridget's mother glanced uneasily towards the servants, who were intent enough on their own meal. Richard merely smiled pleasantly, and said rather more audibly, 'Indeed, you told me your daughter was living away from home at present.'

'She has been at Branton Hall a few months now. The hope is that it will improve Bridget's education. It will certainly improve Mistress Isabel's patience, if it does not drive her to distraction. We are grateful to Mrs Branton for her kindness.'

'And how do you like Branton Hall, mistress?' Richard spoke with a smile, with exactly the mixture of condescension and courtesy one would use to the not-yet-grown-up daughter of an acquaintance. Bridget only said, 'Very well, thank you.' She could not get used to the ease with which he played the stranger in his parents' house.

When the servants had cleared the dishes and gone, Mother sighed as though she had been holding her breath.

'I ought to be going now, if I may excuse myself.' Richard said. 'There is someone in Branton sick I promised to see.'

'You'll be in for dinner?'

'I think so. But I must go over and speak to – there are people I need to visit in Merford this afternoon.'

He rose, murmured a grace quickly, and left the room. Bridget looked at her mother and asked, 'How long am I staying?'

'Richard said he will stay until the end of the week.'

'So can I… ?'

'If you want to,' her father said. 'Mary, do you mind if there is company to dinner tomorrow?'

'Of course, I mind. We do not want people here asking questions. For God's sake put them off,' she replied, her voice a sharp whisper. And then, less quietly, 'Bridget, if you are going to be here, there is a deal of mending you can help me to catch up with.'

And then Richard came back into the room, wearing his hat and cloak.

'Bridget, I had almost forgot. I bought this for you – when I was in Rome. It would be a shame not to give it to you after I've carried it all this time and not lost it!'

He put a small package into her hand. She looked at it, and then up at him.

'In Rome?'

'No less. I made pilgrimage there – the Easter before I was made priest.'

Bridget unwrapped it slowly. There were so many things she would have liked to ask about Rome that she did not know what to say. The package held a small silver cross, hung from a riband so that it could be worn round the neck. The light from the window of the hall made it shine in her palm. She reached and touched it with her other finger, savouring its soft cold gleam. Then she looked back up at him, wordless but smiling. Her mother was looking over Bridget's shoulder. 'Are you going to thank your brother?'

'Thank you, Richard.' Then she said, 'Is it blessed?'

'I blessed it myself.' He smiled.

'Oh – yes.'

Mother was looking over Bridget's shoulder at the silver cross. 'Put it away safe, Bridget. You'll lose it before you know it. No, not just in your pocket. Here, take it upstairs to the little coffer in my chamber. Now, child. It's too fine to have lost.'

'Yes, mother,' and Bridget turned to go upstairs, her mother's voice following. '… Wrap it carefully and make sure you lock the coffer properly…' Bridget caught a smile in her brother's eye which said, some things never change. Then he kissed his mother and went out.

He seemed to be out more often than not in the days that followed. Bridget went with her mother about the house, helping with whatever work was in hand, running errands, keeping up with her lessons and snatching the free hours she could in the meantime. The day before Richard would leave and she would go back to Branton, Bridget went upstairs with some clothes Mother had mended and knocked at her brother's door. She heard his voice answering and pushed it open. He was kneeling near the closet, busy with the cords around the large pack in front of him. There was a smaller bundle beside him on the floor. He turned quickly at her step.

'Bridget!'

She put the clothes down on the chest at the foot of the bed. 'What are you doing?'

'Business.'

'What kind of answer is that?'

'All you're going to get. Look, Bridget, I'm busy –'

'Well, if it's such a secret why did you say I could come in? I knocked and you said come in.'

'I said who's there.'

'You did not.'

He shrugged, which was most unsatisfactory.

'What's in those bundles?'

Her brother sighed. 'Church stuff, Madam Inquisitor.'

'Things you brought?'

'Yes.' He sat back, having secured the cords.

'What are you going to do with them?'

'Give them to people whose names you're not going to be told.'

'Are those rosary beads?' She went over and began to open the small pack, which had not yet been tied. He made a gesture of protest, but Bridget was already absorbed. She drew out a bundle of rosary beads, some squares of slate she knew were altar-stones, a little sheaf of printed pictures of haloed figures, and then a bundle of books. They were mostly slim octavos, cheaply printed, and without bindings. Mass-books, rosary meditations. Books such as her mother had and she knew well – only she had never really thought about where they came from, more precisely than 'across the sea.'

'Oh!' She had found some volumes tied together, bearing the same long title: *A True, Sincere and Modest Defence of English Catholics that suffer for their Faith both at Home and Abroad; against a False, Seditious and Slanderous Libel Entitled: The Execution of Justice in England.*

'What?' He looked at the title. 'You know Allen's book?'

'They have it at Branton…' She had in fact found the book when Mistress Isabel sent her to put some Mass-books away and had begun to read it. But the next time she went to the cabinet, it was no longer there. 'You had best not show it to Mother, though. She does not like it.'

'Oh, why is that?' He said lightly, though he could guess.

'I'm not sure. When I told her about it, she fussed with her coif, you know how she does when she won't admit something's wrong, and she said something like – why would anyone keep more dangers lying in his closet than he had to? And then she told the maid off for finishing the downstairs cleaning too quickly.'

'Well, I'll not mention it then.' He smiled. 'Thanks, Bridget.' His mother would know, of course, that the priest Alfield had been hanged for distributing this book the year it came out. Bridget clearly did not, and need not. It had been a risk, really, to bring those copies along with the rest. Going down to London this autumn had been a risk too, but he needed the church stuff. He started sorting the smaller pack before tying it up. He would leave Merford tomorrow, and he must also write that letter before he left. Doing it here was harder rather than easier, but it could not be put off any longer.

'Can I have it?'

His sister was still there, poring over one of the books from the bundle. 'Bridget, I thought you'd gone.'

'Can I?'

'Yes, if you must.' It must be done and sent before he went further north. He had not done it before because he had been busy. It would be stupid to be afraid of writing the report, after he had stood through seeing it happen. 'Just take care with it, Bridget.'

'Of course,' she replied with dignity, slipping her prize under her apron as she left the room.

*   *   *

She wanted it to be there on Sunday. It would infuriate him at any time, but Sunday morning when he went to start the service would be best. But that meant waiting until as late as possible, or else the sexton would just find it when he was making things ready, and that would simply not be the same. On the other hand, she was going back to Branton on Saturday afternoon.

Bridget knew, for she had seen him many times, that Toby Mason was in the habit of setting out the chancel in readiness for Sunday late on Saturday morning. She had seen him go in and out, always at the same hour he had kept for twenty years, and he was not about to change his ways. It might work. All she had to do was wait.

All through Friday Bridget waited, and on Saturday morning Mother asked her to go to the market with her, and she had to plead a headache. But then that was all to the good; Mother was safely away, and Bridget's chamber window gave a good view of the church. She waited until Mason came, and until he left; waited a little longer to be sure; and then slipped out of the back door with the *Defence* hidden under her winter cloak.

Around the back of the church, there was a point at which the churchyard wall was almost completely broken down, so that you could step across it without having to climb. And that point was scarcely six yards in a straight line from the little postern door which opened into the old Lady chapel, just to the side of the chancel. There was no reason why Bridget Lister should not walk into her own parish church (was that not what they were always wanting everyone to do?), but nevertheless she glanced behind her as she pushed open the door. There was no-one else inside. The church stood empty, a shadowy, bare place. It was cold too; every breath she took hung in the air for several seconds. She could see the pews beyond the chancel, and the cobwebs among the carven rafters. Joan used to talk about how colourful it had been before: not only the statues, and the great crucifix where the royal coat of arms was now, and the windows filled with coloured glass, but even the walls covered in paintings. Now they were pale with whitewash, broken here and there by lines of Scripture painted on in black.

The Lady chapel itself was the emptiest. The niche for the Blessed Virgin's statue dominated it, but a broken pedestal was all that was left there. You could see, too, the scar on the wall where the altar had been ripped away. Funny to think that Mass had once been said in here, every single day. Her father must have gone to Mass here when he was her age. Bridget slipped through the arch between the Lady chapel and the chancel and went over to the lectern. Mason had done his task. The prayer book lay there, marked in the right places. She stopped still, looking at it, and wondered for a moment if she dared. Then she thought of Mr Hall's face, took the Book of Common Prayer out of its place and laid Allen's *True, Sincere and Modest Defense of English Catholics* where it had been, open on the page she had chosen yesterday.

She was not quite sure what to do with the prayer book. In the end. she found a kind of crevice beneath the steps of the pulpit and hid it there. She stepped back a little, and looked into the chancel from the aisle, to make sure you couldn't see from there what was on the lectern. Then she left, but on her way out she turned back suddenly, and walked, almost on tiptoe, up to the far east end of the chancel. There she put out her hand and touched the place where the high altar had stood.

It was close to the dinner-hour when she ran up to the parlour. Joan had said the master was out, but the young master was here. She knocked at the door and asked aloud 'May I come in?', so that there should be no argument. He was sitting at the writing table in the corner. Bridget went over to the window seat in the opposite corner and took out her sewing.

'I thought you were gone with Mother to the market.'

'I told her I had a headache and she said I might stay here and see if I could do some mending instead.'

'Did she believe you?' He had caught the laugh in her eye.

'Well, she let me stay.'

'How's it done? She never used to believe me.'

He turned back to his writing as though he did not intend to speak further. Bridget threaded her needle. Despite all her care of secrecy, she found herself burning to pour out the whole story. She wanted him to share the joke; Richard would see it even if Mother would not have. He would surely agree that nothing would come of it even if Mr Hall could ever know who was responsible. But it was difficult to begin to talk when he was being like this. And today he was going away, and she would not be able to talk to him about this or anything else until Heaven knew when. She stabbed the needle into the cloth and began to stitch.

'Richard?'

'Yes?' He did not look up.

'Where are you going now?'

'Northwards.'

She fell silent and tried to concentrate on mending a sheet while he continued to write. Her mother frequently said that Richard wrote a fine hand, swift and neat, far different from Bridget's scrawls, which (said Mother) disgraced even an unschooled maid. His pen moved quickly across the page, an even line of lettering following it. Then it would stop a second in mid-air as though he were thinking what to write, and then again continue. Only once the pen dripped a little and she heard him exclaim quietly as he tried to remedy it. There was a slight frown on his face as though he were thinking, trying to remember something, and yet at the same time he looked as people do when something better not thought on intrudes into their mind. His lips were set in a thin line. Nothing moved except his pen and the hand that held it.

Suddenly Bridget dropped her gaze and stared at her linen, beginning to sew in earnest. Richard had laid his pen down altogether and sat gazing hard and unseeing at the wall, biting his lower lip. Then she had seen him suddenly close his eyes a moment and turn his head slightly, pushing away what he was staring at through the golden-brown wainscot of the parlour wall, while something like a groan slipped from his lips. He had forgotten she was there, and it felt like spying to look at him. She sat still, unbearably aware of the pain in his face, and sewed as quickly and finely as she could, trying to fill her mind with her task and not with whatever was clawing at his. She would have left the room, but she did not want him to hear her and realise she had seen.

A noise made her look up. Richard had pushed his stool back and risen. He seemed to be looking for something. Then he went quickly out of the room, shutting the door, and she heard his footsteps going toward his bedchamber. Perhaps his pen had broken and he could not find a penknife. Bridget looked at the paper, lying all innocent-looking on the table. She could not read it from here. With the doubly discomforting sense that she neither wanted to nor should look at that paper, Bridget quietly put down her needle, rose and crossed the room.

She did not touch the paper but leant on Richard's chair and bent over it. His carefully-formed hand was easily read. Two lines at the top of the page were written slightly larger and underlined as though they formed a title: *A True Report of the Holy Martyr, Christopher Buxton, Priest, put to death at Canterbury in Kent in the year of Grace 1588. With the reverend priests Robson Wilcox and Edward Campion, and Master Robert Widmerpool. Writ truly and fully by one who witnessed his death.*

'The Blessed Martyr was made priest in the year of Grace 1585, at Rheims…' A hand came down on the paper in front of her. She turned and looked up into her brother's face. She could not tell if he were angry with her. She was staring up at him, her chin trembling. She could see every line of his face and yet it was terribly far away and she could not begin to discern the expression of it.

'I'm sorry, Richard,' she said finally.

'No matter.'

She said again, 'Richard!' and this time it was a strangled cry, and she grasped his arm as though to hold him there. He removed her hand, not ungently, turned back to the desk and began to sharpen his pen.

'Do not read such things if it frightens you.'

Bridget stared again at the paper on the table. 'I've seen things like it before. Only I – never quite thought – of someone writing them.' There was a pause. 'Then – you were there?'

'Someone had to be.'

'Who was he?'

He spoke in between strokes as he sharpened the pen. 'He was at Rheims when I was – we were made priests the same day. I – knew him quite well then – but our paths did not cross in England until I went to London – and found he was on the point of being brought to trial. They sent him down to Kent for – for the sentence because he had been arrested there. There were the four – died in Canterbury – the same day. I agreed to – well, someone had to.'

He looked at her again, put pen and penknife down and placed his hands on her shoulders. 'Bridget. Let's not lose our wits in fear. There were, what, twelve priests sent to England from Rheims last year. That – is one of us. The worst will not happen to all of us. Not even to most of us. I know, this year was – but it is almost over, and I am safe here, am I not? Well, at least for...'

His voice tailed off as Bridget, for reply, put her arms round him and buried her face against his shoulder. He laid a hand awkwardly on her head and wished he did not have to be there, or that he could find something better to say. He did not know how to convey to her the thoughts he used to keep his own head clear. When she looked up again there were tears on her face, and she looked for a moment like the child he remembered from five years ago. But she was not, and he could not stop her tears by mending a doll or laughing at her nightmares.

'Bridget, don't cry.'

She swallowed and he felt her arms tighten round him at the same time. 'Richard, please…' she said, and got no further. He stood there, holding her gently and helplessly. He was ashamed that when he had stood by the scaffold in Canterbury a month ago, watching his classmate follow three other men up to the gallows and then into the butcher's hands, that had been his chief prayer. *Please not…* Sweet Jesus, if Bridget was frightened just reading what he had written – he felt that his fear twisted through every neat line of writing, rose from the page like a vapour that anyone who read it would sense. He could not have allowed her to look at it any longer.

'Why must you?' she was saying now. 'Oh, why?'

'You know why. My dearest, you know.' She said no more, because both of them did know, without his preaching a sermon on the subject. But her tears were falling against his shoulder in mute accusation, like the tears his mother would not shed as long as he was in the house, and the words his stepfather would not now say. At last, he managed to put her from him a little and meet her eyes. 'Have a hope, Bridget. Or at least have some courage. Come, you can do better than this!'

She drew her sleeve across her face. 'Yes, Richard.'

'Good. Now – I have to finish writing and you, little sister, had better make a start on that mending before Mother returns.'

She made a dogged effort to return his smile and went back to the windowsill. He turned again to the writing table.

Immediately after dinner Richard left. Mother said nothing beyond the formalities of goodbye and Godspeed, but she was harassed and absent all the rest of the day. Bridget escaped as soon as she could and went back to Branton, her father's man Cooper accompanying her. They met Hugh and Stephen Bourne on the way, riding back from school, and Bridget listened to their talk about Latin translations and Lee the schoolmaster. Nothing more had been said about the paper, and nothing either about the matter of Allen's book and Mr Hall. Richard could not say whether or when he would be in the neighbourhood again.

*　　*　　*

John Lister woke in the dark that night. Mary's face was turned away, and she was not stirring, but he knew she was awake. He reached over and touched her shoulder gently. 'Mary?'

'John? You are awake?'

'Yes. What's the matter, Mary?'

She was still not looking at him. 'Richard.'

He had guessed aright, of course.

'I keep dreaming.' she said softly. 'Dreaming that – Oh, God...'

He was silent, holding her hand, wondering what to say. He had always known that Richard meant more to her than any other person. It was mostly for her son's sake that Mistress Hanley had considered his proposal of marriage at all. Not that that had troubled him – after all, he had asked her partly because he did not want Elizabeth to grow up motherless. And he had liked the boy: only four years old then, a little younger than Bess, but bright for his age and pleasant. Perhaps he had been fonder of him because there had been no sons (not that lived) by either of his marriages. Indeed, he and Mary had all but given up the thought of having any more children at all when Bridget was born. At all events, Richard had grown up using John Lister's name, and had called him father, and John had meant to will him a share of his property. But all the same Richard was not John Lister's son; and he had realised it when the young man had announced his intention of leaving England for the seminary at Rheims, and he had nothing with which to hold him. It was not that they had quarreled and failed to make peace. It was just that neither of them had anything left to say to the other. Perhaps the young man's ears had been ringing with fiery exhortations, with the clarion call of

Heaven, but all he had been able to hear was Mary's smothered weeping.

He could hear it now, falling softly into the dark, and did not know what could make it cease.

IV

On Tuesday afternoon, Bridget was in the parlour practising at the virginals with Agnes. It was November now, and one could feel it. Both girls were wrapped in shawls, and the keys of the instrument were cold to the touch. They could hear Mrs Branton and Mistress Isabel in the hall, talking about the household and how much fuel they needed for the winter. Mistress Isabel had been to town.

'Have you heard what happened at St Martin's on Sunday?' Mistress Isabel said suddenly, and Bridget's fingers came down jerkily onto the wrong chord.

'No. What did happen?'

'I had it from Mary Wilson, and she had it from her father, who was there.'

'He often is.'

'Yes. Well, it seems Mr Hall stepped up to the lectern to open the prayer book and begin the service, and the book was not there.'

'Was not – ?'

'No. And what was worse, where it should have been, there was a copy of Dr Allen's *True, Sincere and Modest Defense.*'

'No! Isabel, what did Mr Hall – ?' Bridget tried to find her place again in the music, which had suddenly become incomprehensible.

'Oh, he was enraged, of course. There was a great deal of bluster, I understand, and he was swearing he would find out who was responsible. Pointing the finger at the church-papists first. But perhaps he has been persuaded to use discretion this time, for there have been no enquiries as yet.'

'He is quite right. It does but make him look a fool; much better try to let people forget it.'

'Let us hope he does.'

There was a pause. And then Mrs Branton spoke again. 'Ah, do not look at me so wise and grave, little sister. You are thinking precisely the same as I.'

'And what might that be?'

'That the practise of church-papistry must have its moments of sheer bliss.'

It had been a stupid, unnecessary thing to do. She knew that. But she thought of Mr Thomas Hall blustering and raging at the lectern, and inside she laughed. And Hugh's mother had laughed too.

Mrs Lister did not laugh. Her daughter heard her thoughts on the matter a week later, when she and Bridget's father came up to the Hall to make arrangements for Christmas Masses with Mrs Branton. She told Mrs Branton that it had been a fool's trick, and what was more the kind of fool's trick which put other people in danger. That if Mr

Hall did find out who it was, they would be in trouble indeed; and if he did not, he would merely hold it against all the Catholics, and there would be that much more harrying over fines and the rest. Bridget, sitting near the window with a book that was not quite absorbing her, said 'I don't understand how it was so very dangerous...' and immediately regretted it.

'Indeed? And what would you know of it?'

'Nothing, madam.' Bridget said rather too quickly.

And Mother looked at her, and Bridget wondered if she was reckoning the dates in her mind; if she was remembering how close St Martin's was to home; and if she had known about the books in Richard's baggage. 'Of course, I would not keep a book like that in the house. It would be foolhardy. And I'd not have anyone supposing I do, you understand?'

'Yes, madam.'

'Bridget – Bridget, have you any understanding of the world at all? Do you not know that you cannot play with fire?'

Bridget opened her mouth to say she was sorry, and then did not. Mother did not know, exactly. And most certainly Bridget was not going to tell her what she had done, still less that it was Richard who –

Mother looked hard at her for another second, as though she meant to ask another question; and then she too did not do so. Mrs Branton and Mother went upstairs to fetch some Mass-books which Mother and Father were to take home, and though Bridget was sure the squire's wife threw her a glance as she passed, nothing was said. And then Father spoke.

'Bridget, had you something to say?'

She looked up, and then back down. 'No, sir.'

'Did you have aught to do with that affair, Bridget?'

She fidgeted with the edges of a page in her book and said, 'Why do you think I had?'

'Bridget, answer me.'

She could not lie to him, even without meeting his eye. 'Yes, sir.' There was dead silence. At last Bridget raised her head slowly, forcing herself to look at her father. 'I did not think –'

'Well, that much is clear. At least, I hope you are not so half-witted that you could do such a thing at all if you had thought about it for three seconds together. For heaven's sake!' Bridget looked away again and wondered what he was going to do. 'You got the thing from your brother, I take it?' He had stood up and so did she.

'Yes.' Well, if he was determined to know.

'And he did not know any of this?'

'No.' He was furious now.

'If I thought it would do any good, I would beat you senseless for this piece of tomfoolery. But a girl who still knows no better at thirteen than to play such tricks I daresay will never learn.'

'I am sorry.' She said, lamely. No, he was not in a fury – or at least not the way he usually was. She almost wished he would beat her instead of looking at her like that. No whipping she had ever had seemed as bad now as that cold contempt, the crushing rebuke in his eyes.

'You had better be sorry. You have not only put yourself at risk, but your mother and myself, and indeed anyone who comes into question if Mr Hall does pursue this business. You have caused a disturbance to increase the troubles of every Catholic in Merford for months yet, as though we have not cares enough. And your brother, who goes in danger of hanging as it is – whose position I should have thought you would have remembered if you forgot all else – well, if anyone had begun asking about that book while he was still here –' Bridget's face was set as stone; she was trying to stop up her mind against his words, for otherwise she would not be able to bear them. But each one was merely an echo from within herself, like an arrow piercing twice into its target.

There were voices outside; the others were coming back in. Father released her from his gaze at last. 'You two will bleed her soul to death between you,' she heard him say as he turned away.

Nothing would come of it. Mr Hall had dropped the matter. And even if they could trace it to her, they could not trace it to Richard. Because no-one knew that he had been here. No-one knew about the things he had carried.

*   *   *

Mrs Branton sat before the fire in her chamber watching the book burn. It had been foolish to keep Allen's book in the house, although both she and Giles had really rather wanted to read it, and she was honestly not sorry she had. But to keep the thing was unnecessarily dangerous. That was why she had taken it even from the locked cabinet where she kept other forbidden books and hidden it more securely up here with some of the Mass things. But now, if there were any consequences from that foolery in St Martin's... no, it was better to get rid of it completely. She slipped to her knees in front of the fire and gazed at the flames. Giles would have said the same. It was seven months since he had been gone now, and there was no reason to expect him home any day soon.

It was pointless to wonder how long she could keep this up alone. As long as it took. And it was equally pointless to try to guess how long that would be.

She kept reminding herself of both these considerations, as the winter set in and the days grew ever colder and shorter. Hugh rode to and from school in the dark, and at home everyone stayed close to the fire whenever they could. Jenufer was heard to observe that whereas all summer the maidservants had been always busy when meals wanted cooking, suddenly they were jostling to be tasked with turning the spit or stirring the broth. It snowed heavily, and once or twice Hugh turned back before he was through the village, arguing that it was simply impossible to get to school. Mrs Branton gave in and allowed him and Stephen Bourne to make a pretence at studying in the parlour (the library was like an ice-house now).

But if Branton Hall grew cold in winter, the old grange was colder. They had one Mass during Advent, smaller than usual because the snow kept some at home. Those that came stood packed close together as far from the cracks in the walls as might be. Mrs Branton could see that Hugh, who served, was chafing his hands all during the gospel, suddenly terrified that they would go so numb he would drop the vessels at the offertory. On the way home, Isabel remarked that she wondered if they were not running a greater risk of freezing to death in the old grange than they would of being caught at home. Her sister smiled wrily and did not reply.

Halfway through December, Hugh came into the parlour and found her with a letter in her hand. Her chair was drawn up close to the fireplace and the grey parlour cat purred around her skirts while she read, and then re-read, the pages. She looked up, suddenly aware that she was properly smiling for the first time in some weeks. 'Hugh, here is a letter from your father.'

'From Father?'

'Aye. I had not thought to have one before Christmas, what with the snows and the roads… but he has got it here after all.'

'What does he say?'

'I shall read some of it to you later, perhaps. He is well.' She spoke quite easily, and it was less of an effort than usual to do so.

'Does he say aught about coming home?'

'No.'

She knew that he knew it was no pleasanter to say that than to hear it, but Hugh would not leave it there. He looked down and kicked a stray piece of charcoal back into the fire, ashes powdering over his foot. 'It's all over now, anyway, the invasion. As good as. Why can't they just – ?'

'How should I know? He would be home tomorrow if it were left to me. No' – and she gave a short laugh – 'if it were left to me he would not have gone.'

'Does he say nothing then?'

And now her voice was sharp and strained again. 'Hugh, when there is aught he should tell me, he will tell it. And there is no cause to ruin your shoes. Will you find Harry and go over his lessons? Now, please.'

'I'm sorry, madam.'

Hugh turned to go, looking as resentfully miserable as she felt. As he passed the table, he saw a package laid on it. 'What is that?'

The whisper of a smile returned briefly to her face. 'It came with the letter; he wrote that it was why he was anxious to send it at once. It is a New Year's gift for me.'

*   *   *

He walked fast down Clink Street, for sleet was starting to fall, the sharp white flakes melting into the half-frozen mud and muck of the road. He knocked on the heavy prison door, and at last a porter opened it with the words, 'Mr Branton. I was looking for you.'

'My leave's until five of the clock, and 'tis hardly four.'

'You've a visitor. Lawyer fellow. I've sent him upstairs. And while you're here, the rent for your chamber is three days late…'

But he had already gone, crossing the yard quickly and running up the stairs, which protested dangerously at such treatment. 'Well?' He said as soon as he reached the chamber door.

His friend rose. 'I am afraid your petition is not going to succeed.'

For a moment Giles Branton stood still. Then he slowly took off his cloak and hat and hung them on a nail in the door. He sat down on a stool and gestured his visitor to the other. 'Well, I am grateful to you for the attempt. Can you tell me any more?'

'Very little. It should not have been difficult. The invasion's over, and the recusants confined last summer are being released. But – I think you have been spoken against.'

The other man looked up. 'I knew *that* at Michaelmas, when they sent me up here.'

'But, Branton, one vicious report should not be an obstacle still. Someone – or more than one – who sits on the Commission of the Peace in your county is keeping this thing alive... I can get no precise information as yet, but it seems their Lordships are quite convinced that you are a dangerously obstinate popish recusant.'

'So, he is taking that line.'

'You know who this is?'

'Oh, I think we both do.'

'To be frank, my friend, he is telling little more than the truth. You *are* the most obstinate papist I know, and you have been ever since we were students for the Bar at Gray's Inn.'

Giles Branton laughed. 'Well. I must wait awhile, and try again, that is all.' And then he was silent a little before turning the talk to the weather, and his visitor's family, and the latest news from Gray's Inn.

V

As Christmas drew closer, the Hall filled with preparations. There was cooking to be done, and New Year's gifts to be made ready. Jenufer had the maidservants scrubbing and cleaning with double effort, and Mother, with Bridget helping, went over all the altar-linen, to make sure it was spotless and the trimming perfect for the great feast. Mrs Lister came to sew with them one afternoon and carried a pack of forbidden vestments home with her, to store secretly with the Mass-books and the altar vessels Ralph Hale had brought. Hugh did not know what had made John Lister agree to that in the end, and nor did Bridget when he asked her. Aunt Isabel began playing Christmas carols on the virginals. She had got a new book of music that year, and in the dark afternoons when the family crowded into the parlour she had them practise the parts. By the day before Christmas eve, even Hugh admitted to himself that it sounded well. 'Although it is very awkward,' Aunt Isabel said, 'without any tenor or bass voices,' and Hugh said, 'we've never had a bass.' She shut the lid of the virginals and did not mention that Hugh's father used to sing the tenor part. Hugh's voice was not reliably anything at present, but

Aunt Isabel had nevertheless marshalled him in to turn pages.

The priest came to Branton Hall on Christmas Eve, to say Mass the next morning; and on St Stephen's day he would say it at the Listers'. He came as the four eldest children were hanging greenery around the great hall and laughed at the sight. Later, he helped them to finish it. It was Bridget who led that undertaking, her eyes like fireflies and leaves clinging all over her dark-gold hair and her dress as though she were some strange elf.

* * *

Stephen shut his chamber door rather quietly behind him and headed for the stairs. But before he reached them, his father called to him from the great chamber. Quelling impatience and a certain unease (it was not as though he meant to do anything wrong), he went over. His father had the fire alight and was writing at the little table. 'Stephen, if you are going downstairs, will you fetch me some ink from the writing-desk in the parlour?'

'Yes, sir.' His father did not ask where he was going. Stephen simply meant to walk very quickly over to Branton Hall and be back before the supper hour. There was not much snow around; it would be an easy walk even if he cut across the fields.

Standing in the chilly parlour, fumbling in the writing-desk for the ink-pot, Stephen's hand knocked a little bundle wrapped in a handkerchief. He thought he had spilled whatever was in it, coins perhaps, but when he drew it out, the kerchief was wrapped around a string of beads. Wooden beads strung in lengths of ten with a cross attached – papist beads. He knew they were papist beads, and they were not his father's. They were certainly not his grandmother's.

Stephen's mother had been a papist. Stephen knew that, although he did not remember his mother; he had heard it spoken of by the servants, not that anyone actually used that word. He did not know she had had beads. Had held them; had used them perhaps, in some unknown popish way. She had died before Stephen was three, and his father had wrapped the beads in her handkerchief and kept them hidden, even though they were popish trumpery and Henry Bourne was a Justice of the Peace. Stephen let his hand close round his mother's beads for a moment, and then he wrapped them up again and put them away out of sight. He found the ink, took it to his father, and then pulled on his boots and cloak and left the house without saying anything.

The early dusk had already fallen when Stephen knocked at the door of Branton Hall. He stepped awkward-ly in when it was opened and asked for Hugh. The servant, never taking her eyes off him, told Stephen to wait, and she would see if Master Hugh could be found.

The door to the hall was open, and the screens passage was cold. He had not been told to wait exactly where he was.

Stephen slipped into the hall and saw in the firelight that it was hung with ivy and holly and mistletoe, wreaths of it, twisted around the fireplace and the tables set out for the morrow, draped along the tapestry hangings and even the railings of the gallery. Grandmother would not have such things about at home; she said it was blasphemy to profane the Saviour's birth with trappings of pagan worship.

Hugh still had not come. Stephen could hear no footsteps either. But, listening, he thought he heard singing – or rather chanting. Coming from the parlour beyond, or perhaps above it... a man's voice. Stephen could not make out the words, but he was sure they were not English ones. He was walking up the hall toward the parlour door, and as he pushed it open the voice came clearer. It was Latin he was singing: Stephen caught the word *Patris*. The parlour, hung with greenery like the hall, was empty too; but just in front of him was a door, hanging a little ajar, and through the door a staircase.

The words were *Magnificat anima mea Dominum, Et exultavit spiritus meus...* On the sixth step up he bumped into Hugh coming down. They stared at one another for a single moment, and then somehow they were back in the parlour and Hugh was pulling the staircase door shut behind him. 'Stephen, what are you doing here?'

Stephen was still looking at the closed door. 'Is it Mass?' he whispered.

'No.' And Stephen thought there was a certain relief in Hugh's face as he said it. He recollected himself and took out the package he had brought with him.

'I – I have a New Year's gift for you. And I remembered you said you would be from home at New Year…'

'Yes. I have one for you somewhere… But why now? It is Christmas Eve!'

'I – I do not know.' But he did know. 'I had better go home. A merry Christmas to all of you.'

'You, likewise. Thank you.'

'Will I see you tomorrow?'

'Tomorrow? I – perhaps, but Christmas is so busy.'

'I suppose it is.' And then he had to go, but not without looking again at the hall all covered in its beauty of pagan decoration. Not without a small backward glance at the door with the staircase behind it.

Hugh felt a little guilty as he went back up the stairs to hear the end of Vespers. The priest was finishing the final Magnificat antiphon as he knelt once more at the back of the room. Of course, it was not his fault Stephen had arrived like that, and it was not he who had left the door ajar, either. And if he had been a little impatient with Stephen, he could hardly be blamed for that, given the situation. There was really no need for Stephen to look quite so much like a stray puppy asking to be let in.

It was not until later that he wondered why the only thing he had not been uneasy about was that Stephen would not have to think very hard to deduce that there was a priest spending Christmas at Branton Hall.

* * *

Hugh woke on Christmas morning to the sound of the shutters rattling in a biting wind and thought for two minutes about staying in bed. Then Mother knocked at his chamber door, and he got up to dress for Mass. The old grange was every bit as cold as he had known it would be. At least, being Christmas, there were plenty of people, and they stood and knelt in each other's warmth, though Hugh was sure he could still hear teeth chattering behind him. As he watched the priest, Hugh found himself thinking of Richard Lister again, and glancing at Bridget he wondered if she was thinking of him, too. That made him think of his father, and he wondered if he had found a Christmas Mass. Priests in gaol did say Mass: they could hardly be arrested for it. The priest raised the Host above his head, and Hugh tried to remember the prayers he meant to offer for himself and others, as he had been taught. But again, he suddenly wondered what the priest, whose face he could not quite see, was feeling and fearing and asking for; and he thought of Christ, being born and being executed.

Dawn was beginning to break, the light streaking the snow so that it glistened almost too much to look at, as they rode back up to Branton Hall and went in to break their fast.

The rest of Christmas Day was as Christmas usually was, or almost, and they tried not to notice too much the voice that was missing from the singing, and the face that was not at the head of the high table. Mrs Branton presided, stately in her best gown with its wide, decorated skirts and her fine lace-edged ruff. The children were dressed in their best too, Hugh stiff in a new doublet and with one of his father's swords at his side, the first occasion he had worn one. Most of the Mass-goers and some of the tenants were there to receive the hall's hospitality, and Hugh went to stand beside his mother as she greeted each one. Geoffrey Lockwood came but left very soon: the inn would not run itself just because it was Christmas.

'Was that Lampley the glover I saw gathered with us this morning, madam?' he asked as he was taking his leave.

'Yes. He did not stay though. It's a long ride back to Gloucester.'

'He rode all the way from the city, in this?'

Mrs Branton smiled. 'I believe they in the city were disappointed of keeping Christmas at the last moment – as one sometimes is. Verily burning with zeal, that young man. Convert, of course.'

The innkeeper grunted. 'I'll say. The last time he was at the Raven, he sat in the common room settling the question of the royal supremacy with a crowd of strangers.'

Mrs Branton laughed.

'It's no jest,' Lockwood said. 'I had to go over and tell him to hold his peace in the end. I cannot afford to have people committing treason in my inn.'

'You think they would prosecute a tradesman to the death for disputing the Queen's head of the Church over the ale-mugs?'

'Given that they were my ale-mugs, I don't care to find out. But that lad is going to get himself into trouble.'

'He'll learn prudence as he grows older.'

'Or he'll not grow much older. But I must be going: good day to you, madam, and my thanks. And a merry Christmas.'

After dinner, the children begged permission to go outside in the snow for a little, and Mrs Branton consented on condition that they came in before the sun set. With the dogs bounding after them, they ran right down through the meadow to the stream, frozen thick and clearly made to be slid and played upon. Hugh and Harry took turns at carrying Marian, so bundled up in cloak and shawls and hood that she seemed hardly to have any limbs at all, but she was determined not to be left behind. It was while he and Harry were trying to mould something like arms onto the snowman they had sculpted that Hugh heard his name called. Stephen had come slipping down his side of the bank and across the frozen stream where George and the twins were sliding up and down.

'Hugh! I thought you might be out here. Is it not a good chance it is fine today?'

'Aye. Take care coming up this side. Tree roots.'

'Thanks.' Stephen came up and looked at their snow-man. 'Your work, Hugh?'

'Mine and Harry's.'

Stephen took off his hat and set it over the snowman's eyes, and then picked up a stray stick of willow and stuck it under one of its arms. 'Bourne,' he quoted in a menacing growl, 'If I have to correct your use of the ablative absolute once more...'

Hugh laughed aloud. The snowman did make him think of Mr Lee. Harry said 'Ah – so that is the man Hugh takes his tone by.' So, Hugh threw a fistful of snow at him, and battle was joined. It ended only when the shadows lengthened and Stephen realised with a start that it was almost time for prayers.

His grandmother looked up from the bible in front of her as he ran, still dripping with snow, into the parlour at home. For a moment he thought he was late, but she smiled at him as she passed the book to his father to read and knelt down.

'...I bring you glad tidings of great joy, that shall be to all the people. That is, that unto you is born this day in the city of David, a Saviour, which is Christ the Lord. And this shall be a sign to you, Ye shall find the babe swaddled...'

Stephen thought of something else from the parlour at Branton Hall, something that was not usually to be seen there. Among the wreaths of ivy, a statue of a woman and a baby. The child was held on the lap of the woman, who was swathed in a blue-painted plaster robe, with a gilt crown on her head, and the child was also crowned, but his short, round baby fingers were raised in a blessing.

'...So, they came with haste, and found both Mary and Joseph, and the babe laid in the cratch...'

He looked up at Grandam, perfectly still on her knees, her eyes closed, unconscious and uncaring of his gaze or of anything but the words which made their echoes in her soul. Stephen closed his eyes again.

'...But Mary kept all those sayings, and pondered them in her heart...'

*   *   *

Bridget had never been to the great house at Norton Court before. She had secretly hoped that she might be allowed to join the party that went up from Branton Hall for New Year's, but still she was pleasantly surprised when it was agreed upon. And here she was, riding next to Hugh behind Mistress Isabel and Mrs Branton, with the best of her gowns folded carefully into her pack, on a fiercely bright morning four days after St Stephen's. It was cold, but had not snowed any more for several days, and the sky was clear. Still, it would be heavy going, and they would not reach Norton Court much before sunset.

Bridget did not care. The sunlight was dancing on the snow that stretched across the frost-swollen earth, making it gleam – if possible – even whiter; you had to squint to look at it. The snow on the trees glittered like jewels against the black branches, and even her and Hugh's frozen breath seemed to glisten for the minute that it lingered in the air. She could hear Hugh whistling a Christmas carol and began softly singing the words until she could not remember any more. Then she gave up and whistled, too. When they fell silent, she asked, 'Have you been to Norton Court before?'

'A few times. Her ladyship is my godmother – she is kin to Mother, you know.'

'My mother and Mistress Isabel *both* said they feared I should disgrace them. I shall have to mind my manners for my life as long as we are there.'

'What, *all* the time? Have you prayed to St Jude of Desperate Causes?' Hugh said, and Bridget laughed.

There was dancing on New Year's Eve, in the great hall filled with guests, and music played from the high gallery. Hugh joined in, knowing what Aunt Isabel would have to say if he failed to do what was proper, but he felt rather awkward among so brilliant a company, especially dancing with girls he did not know, and he hardly knew more than two, apart from Bridget.

But three dances were enough for courtesy, and then he withdrew to one of the window-alcoves and watched. He could see Aunt Isabel, dancing as she did everything, precisely, exactly as it ought to be done. He thought he could see her glancing over at her charge every now and then, to make sure she did not go too much amiss, although nothing could make her steps as graceful as Mistress Isabel's... But when Bridget danced, everything about her danced, even her eyes. Especially her eyes.

In the morning there was Mass, and after dinner music-making. Halfway through the long afternoon, Bridget rose quietly from her seat, with a sideways glance to see that Mrs Branton and Mistress Isabel were not looking at her. Mistress Catherine, the eldest daughter of the house, had shown Bridget her commonplace book that morning, copied full of everything from prayers to poems to receipts, and even said she could copy out anything she wanted for her own book. And there was something... surely no-one would mind if she went just to the writing-table in the corner...

She found ink and paper and the page she wanted. *Edmund Campion, of the Society of Jesus, Sancti Martyr. A Letter to the Lords of Her Majesty's Privy Council.*

It seemed longer in the copying than when she had read it this morning. After several minutes she had got no further than the first half-page. Across the room the music was still going on, and the others showed no sign of growing weary of it. She went on, only hoping they would not finish before she had done.

'What are you doing, Bridget?'

Bridget looked up. Hugh had also left the group by the fireside and wandered over. 'I am copying this from Mistress Catherine's commonplace book. She said I might.'

Hugh looked over her shoulder to see. 'Edmund Campion's letter.'

'Yes.' And she bent again over her writing.

'Well,' Hugh said, 'One of you has mistaken the case ending of *sancti*. It ought to be nominative singular, agreeing with the noun.' And he took the pen out of Bridget's hand and corrected it on her copy.

She snatched it back. 'Hugh, shut up or go away.'

He preferred to shut up and stood reading Edmund Campion's famed challenge to the Queen's divines over Bridget's shoulder.

'Hugh! I am not done copying yet, stop turning the pages.'

'Sorry. I wanted to read the beginning.'

'You can have it presently; I am nearly done.'

At last, she laid down her pen, and began reading over what she had written. Hugh was looking over her shoulder again. If he makes any more corrections, I shall hit him, she thought. But he said nothing.

'…are determined never to give you over, but either to win you heaven, or to die upon your pikes… cheerfully to carry the cross you shall lay upon us, and never to despair your recovery, while we have a man left to enjoy your Tyburn, or to be racked with your torments, or consumed with your prisons. The expense is reckoned, the enterprise is begun; it is of God, it cannot be withstood…' Almost without realising it, she had begun reading the words aloud, softly, and her heart rose with the passion of them.

Hugh said, 'And they did hang him. At Tyburn.'

Bridget nodded and replaced the lid on the inkstand. 'Hugh, they've stopped playing. We had better go. It must be time for supper.'

As they followed the others out of the room, Bridget saw that Mrs Branton had not been singing either; she was standing with Sir Christopher by the far window.

'I think you do wisely, cousin.' Sir Christopher was saying. 'You already do your duty and more… And with Mr Branton's position at present…'

'Don't,' she said. 'But tell your man he must go straight to Lockwood's. There is to be nothing at Branton.'

'Lockwood's a good man. Come, no more of this now. Let us go.' And he offered her his arm as they went down to the hall.

VI

One morning halfway through Lent, Jem Carter was on his way to school. It was raining, a cold, miserable February rain that drained away your faith that spring would ever come. Just as he was crossing the market square, a man stopped him and asked if Jem could tell him his way.

Jem looked up. 'That depends where you're trying to go, sir.' He was not sure from the man's appearance whether he needed to take off his cap to him, but it was raining so hard that he gave himself the benefit of the doubt.

'Well, I'm looking for the Widow Carter's home.'

Jem stared in surprise. 'What did you want to see her for?

'I've a message to deliver.'

'It's just she's my mother. I'm Jem Carter.'

The man stared in his turn. 'You're her son?' But he did not say any more about his message, or ask Jem to take it for him.

'It's – we live back that way. It's the cordwainer's shop. Third house on the right after the Raven inn.'

'I thank you... You'll be going on home to your mother soon, lad?'

'After school.'

'Ah.' And the man pulled his hat down further over his ears and tramped off, his footsteps making little splashes as he crossed the muddy square. Jem turned and headed for school. He could see a thin curl of smoke rising from the chimney of the schoolhouse, which meant that Lee had permitted the fire to be lit, and that Jem would have to hurry if he wanted to get anywhere near it.

He had barely joined the group of damp, sneezing scholars jostling round the hearth – Stephen Bourne moved over slightly to let Jem squeeze in – when Lee marched up to his chair, called the school to order, and, when prayers had been said, began to lecture the upper forms on the precepts of religion.

Stephen never knew exactly what the words were that did it. But then, he was not listening like that at the time. Mr Lee's subject was the Lord's Supper. Hugh, beside Stephen, was leaning back against the wall as always when Lee taught religion, and had another book – Sallust, Stephen thought – open where in theory the schoolmaster could not see it. But he must have been hearing in spite of himself, because Stephen sensed him stiffen the first time Lee said something about 'popery'... it was inevitable that Lee should refute the Romish doctrine in the course of the lesson, and it was at least likely that he would not be terribly courteous about it. That he would not spare to impress upon his pupils the absurdity as well as the iniquity of such rites...

There was a snap as Sallust's history shut; and the next thing Stephen knew, Hugh was halfway toward the door, his mouth set in a thin line. Mr Lee, from his desk, stared in outrage, and shouted, 'Branton, where do you think you are going?'

The only answer was the bang of the door behind Hugh. For a moment it looked as though Lee would go after him, but he thought better of it; and after a moment's silence, resumed the lesson. But Stephen heard quite distinctly the sound of a stone being thrown heavily against a wall outside, followed by two more, and then quiet.

When school broke at noon, he went outside, not sure what to expect; and found Hugh sitting on the schoolyard wall, still damp from the morning's rain, swinging his feet, the volume in his hands as though construing Sallust were of all-consuming significance.

'Hugh?' he said hesitantly.

The other looked up. 'Is it the dinner-hour?'

'I had thought you'd gone.'

'Where?'

'I don't know. Home.'

'No point.'

'Lee'll beat you if you come back in.'

'Had I gone home he'd have beaten me tomorrow. It's not going to hurt more today.' Hugh jumped off the wall. 'Come on. I'm hungry.'

When the school had reassembled for the afternoon, Mr Lee called Hugh Branton up to his desk and took up his rod. 'Untie your points.'

Hugh had known he would be beaten; no master could allow a pupil to get away with such outright defiance. But before he could obey, something caught inside him and he heard himself say, 'Why? Because I thought the time would be better spent reading my Roman history than listening to foul-mouthed lies?'

The schoolroom gasped, and Stephen wondered if anyone else had noticed that Hugh's hands were clenched so tight by his sides that the knuckles were white.

The master seized Hugh's collar and fairly threw him against the desk. 'You will do as you're told, you impudent papist.' The voice suddenly ordering him to take off his doublet was hardly recognisable, and Hugh found that his hands were shaking because he realised it was no longer a question of discipline, but of sheer rage. As the blows cracked across his shoulders it was like the difference between target practice and shooting to kill. In the end he gave in and cried aloud, although one did not do that in school.

He got back to his place, dimly aware through a hundred searing aches that Stephen had risen to his feet and put out a hand to stop him from falling, and sank onto the bench. When school had finished – Hugh was never quite sure how – he and Stephen went and fetched their horses as they always did. As they were bringing them out, Robert Wilson caught up with them, calling Hugh's name.

Hugh turned. He knew Robert; they had served Mass together at least once. Now he looked at him and said, 'I suppose you think that was foolish.'

'No, I – I think it was brave of you.'

'Truly? You think I was right to have done it?'

'Yes…'

'Then why do you not admit straight that you're a coward?'

Stephen took in his breath sharply. Robert Wilson reddened. Then he bit his lip and walked away. Hugh swung himself into the saddle, wincing as he did so, and dug his heels into Gilian's sides. Stephen rode after him.

'Why did you do that, Hugh?' They were almost home before he dared say it.

'Why do you think?'

Stephen tried again. 'I only meant that Lee teaches religion every week…and it's not as though – '

'No. But – he was making a mock of the Blessed Sacrament.'

'The – ?'

'The Blessed Sacrament. Eucharist, Holy Communion, whichever name you use.'

'And that made all the difference?'

'What do you mean, made the difference? It is as if – as if the soldiers were spitting in Christ's face, and I stood and… I could not sit there. I do not know if it was brave, or… I just couldn't, that's all.'

'But – ' He was thrown by the passion in Hugh's voice. 'I've heard of – the Mass and all that, but it's not as if – I mean –'

'It is precisely *as if*. Christ makes himself as bread for our sake, and Lee stands there – and *mocks*.' Hugh spat the word. His mouth had set again, and his eyes were blazing.

'But you cannot verily believe that Christ is –'

'Why, do you imagine we risk our necks going to Mass for the sport?'

'No – '

'Well then.'

Stephen said no more. He felt as though he had almost grasped the key to a door which had over and over again been closed politely in his face. He wanted to ask another question. But they had reached the lane which led to Branton Hall, and Hugh had gone.

*   *   *

Bridget shut the door of the library softly behind her and sighed with relief. So far as Mrs Branton was concerned, the purpose of Lent – apart from monotonous fast-ing – was spring cleaning. Bridget felt she had not understood how big Branton Hall was until this week. She and Mistress Isabel had gone through every shred of linen and hanging cloth to be found, looking for things to be mended or cleaned or replaced. Whole cakes of beeswax had been consumed in polishing the parlour furniture, whose shine now competed with the walls, where the panelling – put in a year ago – still held its new-carven sharpness, and new-painted fierceness of colour. And besides there were the children and sewing to keep up with, and Mistress Isabel still insisted on one hour of lessons each day at least.

Today, the hour had been spent in the still-room, bent over the medicine-book and the graters and knives and little bunches of leaf. Lessons in the still-room were not bad; it was quiet in there, and smelt of herbs and salves and cordials, and it fascinated Bridget to learn how things were made. But the endless precision, the counting of each clove, the cutting of piles of leaves into tiny, even pieces, grew tedious, especially when she was tired. And the sheer maddening constancy of the drip – drip – drip of a cordial through the straining-cloth had made her want to scream.

But there was a good half-hour before supper now, and for the time she had no task set, though doubtless that would be remedied as soon as anyone noticed it. The library, however, was not being cleaned today, and no-one was likely to come in here at present... She stood in front of one of the book-presses, stretching the fingers that had cramped themselves round the handle of a knife in the still-room.

The book she took at last was the King Arthur book – *La Morte Darthur*, it was called. She spread it on her knees in the window-seat, with the table between her and the door, and breathed in the smell of leather and paper. *La Morte* was long, and the writing old-fashioned, but at least it was in no possible sense a lesson-book. Indeed, she was not sure whether Mistress Isabel would like her to read it. She was deep in Launcelot du Lac's agonies of honour and love when the sound of the door opening made her look up. But it was only Hugh, putting his schoolbooks away. She watched him bend down to take the books out of the satchel, then straighten rather carefully and open the book-press. 'Hugh?' She said at last. 'Is something wrong?'

'Bridget! I did not see you there.' He replaced his Roman history next to his Greek grammar, and then stood there fastening the straps of the now-empty satchel.

'What is wrong?'

'Nothing. How do you, Bridget?'

She shrugged. 'Oh, well enough, but if I so much as see one more basket of linen, I shall run mad.'

'At least you don't have to put up with Master Lee.'

'Would you change places?' she said, and Hugh laughed. He went out of the library, and she watched him go. After a minute, she closed *La Morte Darthur*, put it back in its place, and left the room, too.

Hugh went up to his chamber and eased off his doublet. The ride home had not only jolted the pain back into life, but also made his doublet rub against his shirt, chafing places where the skin was broken so that they bled. He could feel it through the linen as he twisted his hand round, gingerly, to touch his back.

There was a knock at the door and Bridget put her head round it. 'Hugh – Mother of God!' He had turned round as the door opened, but not quick enough. 'Hugh, tell me what happened.'

'Nothing. I did something Lee did not like and he took a rod to me.'

She had come right in and closed the door. 'Does your shirt always look like a butcher's apron after he's taken a rod to you?'

'It isn't that bad.' And then suddenly he wanted to tell her – tell someone who would understand. 'Mr Lee was teaching religion. And he was mocking the Blessed Sacrament.'

Bridget answered with a couple of words that would probably have earned her a whipping had Mrs Branton or Mistress Isabel overheard them. Hugh smiled. 'Quite. And I was angry, and so I – left the schoolroom.'

'You left? Walked out?'

'Yes.'

'And then he did that to you?'

'He – called me up after dinner and – well, I did not ask his pardon.'

Bridget was silent a moment. 'Your mother'll be in a fury when she hears of this,' she said at last. Hugh looked up.

'Don't tell her.'

'What do you mean?'

'I had rather you did not, that's all. She – she cannot do aught about it in any case. It would only trouble her.' And besides, what anyone whose parent – certainly whose *mother* – went and berated the schoolmaster on his behalf would hear in the schoolyard, probably forever, did not bear thinking about.

'Very well,' Bridget said, 'but you'll have a task explaining that shirt.'

He hesitated. 'I could say I was in a fight.' But she did not have to tell him how lame that sounded.

'Give it me and I'll wash it. I'll not tell, you have my word.'

He gave it to her, careful not to turn round as he took it off in case she saw. Bridget scrunched it up under her arm as she went out so it would not be seen.

Mother asked him when he came in for supper if anything was amiss, but when he said no she did not say any more. As they went up to bed, Bridget whispered, 'Hugh, your shirt is drying in the laundry.' And then, 'you were right, you know. You were quite right.'

The Guest of Night

*   *   *

When Jem Carter got home from school that evening, he found there was a visitor. He came in through the shop, past the lasts and half-made shoes and the heavy smell of leather, into the kitchen, and saw a man sitting by the fireplace. He sat in the seat Jem's mother only gave to important guests, but he was quite a stranger, and he wore very ordinary, travel-stained clothes. No, not quite a stranger: he was the same man who had stopped Jem in the market square that morning. Jem hung up his hat and cloak, hoping someone would tell him who the visitor was.

His mother was sitting near the table, sharpening some awls from the shop, but the strokes on the whetstone sounded ragged, without her usual steadiness. His older sister, Jane, was there, though Jem's brother-in-law Hudson was not with her. Jane's small daughter was annoying Jem's younger sister, who was sitting the other side of the fireplace shelling peas, and the maid was standing over the wash-tub, trying to scour a pot silently.

'There you are, Jem.'

He looked at his mother as she spoke and saw that she had been crying. 'What's wrong?'

She shook her head. 'It's quite all right, Jem. You should go and wash – and you've time to get some studying done before supper, if you'd like to.'

'What has happened?'

'We'll talk about it after we've eaten.'

Jem glanced at the stranger. 'I want to know now.'

'It's Tom.' Jane said.

'There's news from Tom?' Jem asked, though it clearly was not going to be good news.

'About Tom.' Jane said. She had been crying as well. 'He's dead.'

Jem turned to the stranger, wordless.

'You knew he was taken prisoner, did you not?' the man said. 'I – I came to bring you word, and I'm sorry to have to do it, that he had died.'

'How come?'

'He fell sick. People do, especially in prisons.'

'How do you know?'

'I was there, lad. We fought in the same company, and we were in the Spaniards' gaol together too. When I got back to England, I set out to find you... there was a little money of his, and some things he wanted you to have. I'm sorry I did not come sooner, but travelling is costly, and I never have much to live on. This country's not always kind to her old soldiers.'

Jem did not say anything but dropped his satchel in the corner. He knew suddenly that every day since Tom had left, until this day, his mother had dreamed of opening the door to Tom, and seating him in his father's chair by the hearth. Jem went over and took the awl and the whetstone out of her hands. 'I'll do that.'

VII

'But it makes no sense!' Stephen said, in a tone almost of desperation. They had stopped on the way home from school, to linger in the first light evening and mild weather that spring and were sitting now by the stream some dozen yards from the road. There was a place where a steep bank gave way to a small flat space between it and the water's edge, under the shadow of a willow tree. It had become, over the course of several summers, their particular haunt. Hugh had fallen in easily with Stephen's suggestion to go down there today.

But Stephen felt rather aggrieved. It had taken him three weeks to find a way of bringing the conversation round to this subject, and a half hour of desperately careful questioning to get Hugh to explain it properly, without putting him into a rage again. And, after all, the key was a trick and the door opened onto a wall. 'It cannot make sense.'

'It makes perfect sense that if Christ says the bread becomes his body, then it does.'

'So, you say, but I do not understand how –'

'He never asked us to understand. It is a mystery.'

'That,' Stephen said, 'is not an answer.'

'Do you understand the Trinity?'

'No –'

'The Incarnation?'

'No –'

'Eternity?'

'No –'

'But you believe in them.'

'Yes.'

'Well then.'

'Well then nothing. Hugh, it does not follow that your Mass is true because other things I cannot understand are true.'

'I did not say it did. I say that it does *not* follow that the Mass is *not* true because you do not understand it.'

Stephen sensed a point of stalemate. He thought of Christmas Eve and the voice chanting Latin in the chamber above the parlour. He wondered whether his mother had ever knelt among them and received their Eucharist. And suddenly he thought of his grandmother, and what she would say if she knew.

'No.' He said at last. 'It would still be all wrong –'

'Wrong?'

'It – suppose it were true. Suppose that were God, that piece of bread – anything could happen. Suppose mice ate it. Suppose it were trampled underfoot. Suppose – it would be blasphemy, Hugh.'

Hugh glanced at him and then away. 'Yes, it is blasphemy,' he said quietly. 'That is the depth of Christ's humility... it is how much he craves our closeness.' And then, with an edge to his voice, 'Not that it means aught to you.'

'To me?'

'Well, there'd be no blasphemy if you did not commit it, would there?' As Hugh turned, Stephen saw that his face was taut again.

'If I – ?'

'If you did not trample the Blessed Sacrament under your feet, if you did not set up lewd mockeries and masques... If you did not rip the altar stones from the churches and make hog-troughs of them, if your precious reformers did not tear the Sacrament itself from the tabernacle to kick it down the aisles of his own cathedrals – what do you think you're proving? Do you think Christ's enemies proved he was not God because they could kill him? Do you think – ?'

'Why do you keep saying me?'

'Why not?' Hugh shouted. Stephen stared, speechless, not at Hugh's anger – he had seen him angry before – but at the way his voice almost broke on the words as he flung them out.

He said rather lamely, 'Hugh, please – there is no need to –'

'Is there not?' Hugh said, only a little more quietly. 'It is – it is – Oh, I cannot make you understand. You haven't seen, you haven't –'

'Show me then.' It slipped out of his mouth, and it was only as Hugh stopped in mid-torrent and stared speechless in his turn that Stephen quite realised what he had said. 'Well, arguing is getting us nowhere, is it?' He went on recklessly. 'Show me then. Show me your Mass.' And then, he thought, perhaps I will know. He suddenly wanted badly just to *know*.

'Are you in earnest?' Hugh said.

'Are you?'

'I will think about it.' Hugh answered at last. It was not going to be enough. He met Stephen's eye. 'I will try.'

And then suddenly they both turned away at the same moment, retrieved their school satchels, went scrambling back to where they had tethered their horses, and rode their separate ways home without exchanging another word or glance.

Over the course of his life, Hugh had at various times been dared to climb onto the schoolhouse roof, smuggle marchpane into the nursery and eat it under the covers, catapult acorns at the schoolmaster from behind the hedge, swim to the very bottom of the river at risk of strangling himself on the weeds and bring up a stone as proof that he had done it, or undertake any number of other more or less pointless actions most often in defiance of one authority or another. He had usually done them; he had been watching his parents court disaster and avoid it as a matter of course ever since he could remember.

But no-one had ever asked him to do anything like this before. He had no notion how or when he was to do it, or whether he would enlist Mother's help (on consideration he thought not; it would be difficult to explain, and it might be easier on Stephen if he did not tell anyone else). Perhaps Stephen would think better of it. For heaven's sake, his father was a magistrate, he could not really go about – Well, he would see, Hugh told himself as he reached home. If Stephen was in earnest, then so was he. That had been the promise. Hugh left Gilian in the stables and went to put his schoolbooks away, resolved to think no more of it unless he was asked to.

And it appeared that he would not be asked. Hugh meant to wait for Stephen to bring the matter up, and that Stephen never quite did, although he seemed several times to be on the verge of it. So, it was past Easter, and past Whitsun, before anything more was said.

In April, both Agnes and Kit were sick with a fever; Mother spent her time either in the sickroom or in the still-room preparing physic, leaving Aunt Isabel much occupied with the household, and the other children mostly to the nursemaid. Bridget tried to help in the nursery, Hugh and Harry crept around trying to stay out of the way, and

Stephen could not visit. When they were better, Mother herself grew ill and after two days had to admit it and go to bed. That was an especially wretched week. It was not until mid-May that Branton Hall seemed really itself again.

On the Saturday after Whitsun, Mrs Branton was in the herb-garden with Isabel, inspecting the beds of marigold and sorrel. The pale yellow stones of the house were bright with sunshine, and the springtime voices of sheep and lambs reached them from the hillsides beyond the Hall.

'You had a letter from London last week, did you not?' Isabel asked.

'Yes,' she said, and sighed. 'The fever kept me from going up there after Easter, as I had meant to. And now I must be on hand until shearing is done and the wool sales settled and all.'

'Afterwards?'

'He does not want me to go to London in the summer. The city stinks with sickness in the hot weather, he says, and I'd best wait until Michaelmas. Unless, of course, he is home himself before then,' she added, in a tone that did not convey high hopes. She heard herself called and turned. 'What is it, Hugh?'

He had come to say that he and Stephen Bourne wanted to study together in the library. She said of course they could and wondered as she looked after him whether he had cracked a book during all the Whitsun holiday until today, its very end, and if she should have been stricter with him.

When Hugh and Stephen went into the library to wrestle together with the long Greek reading Lee had set before Whitsun, someone who had not been thinking had left a string of rosary beads on the table. Hugh reached out to hide them and met Stephen's eyes. 'I suppose I had better put those away,' he said awkwardly, and added, almost in excuse, 'or someone else might chance to come in and see them.'

Stephen only nodded. Once, years ago, his grandmother had taken him with her on an errand to one of the cottages where someone was sick. He remembered following Grandam with her basket into a small, low room that smelled of smoke and old thatch and more than a little of dirt, pulling back from her hand just slightly, and feeling her clamp it all the tighter. Grandmother did not believe in shirking. The sick woman was in a tiny back room, just visible through an open doorway through which a voice was coming. It did not sound like a peasant's voice though, nor did it sound sick. The voice was praying; Stephen could not make out the words, but he knew they were prayers. Grandam walked to the doorway and stopped there; and Mrs Branton looked up from her seat beside the bed. Stephen could not see much from behind Grandam, but he saw that Mrs Branton had one hand on the blanket which covered the patient, and that hand held a string of beads from which a wooden cross hung; and the sick woman's eyes were fixed on those beads as she moved her lips with Mrs Branton's prayers.

Grandam said nothing. The face of the sick woman did not change, but suddenly it was uneasy. Mrs Branton rose. 'Good e'en, Mrs Bourne.'

'Good e'en.'

Then Mrs Branton picked up her empty basket and turned to the patient to say goodbye.

The woman thanked her landlord's mother respectfully for the visit and the provisions she had brought, then said her grandson was a bonny child, and was most grateful. But the look of unease never quite left her eyes.

When they were outside, Stephen asked, 'Why was Mrs Branton there?'

Grandam's lips tightened. She was not so petty as to resent the squire's wife giving alms to a sick woman who happened to be a tenant of Henry Bourne's, and not the squire's; there was something else. 'Because widow Brett is a papist, and so are they.'

'They?'

'The squire and Mrs Branton.'

Stephen had not known at the time that those strings of beads with the crosses were called rosaries and that all papists used them to pray. But he had somehow known that as he and Grandam walked away, the woman was quietly fishing the beads out from under her blanket and praying as the squire's wife had done.

'Stephen?' Hugh's voice dragged him back to the present. 'Are we doing this Greek or not?'

He shook himself out of his thoughts and looked for his page. 'Yes. Your pardon.'

They did not talk further, except about Greek grammar, until they had finished. Then Stephen spoke. 'Hugh, do you remember what you promised that time in Lent?'

Hugh did not look up, but his fingers tightened on the page he had just turned to close. 'You mean – about Mass?'

'Yes.'

There was a moment when he thought Hugh was going to be angry. Then he said, in a low, even whisper, 'We are hoping to have Mass on Corpus Christi day. If you want to come, I will take you. Just this once. But you must not tell anyone.'

'I know that.'

'It is – it is against the law, you know.'

'I'm coming.'

'Meet me in the hollow in the copse on the common, then. Two hours after midnight on Corpus Christi day.'

'Yes.'

*　　　*　　　*

Robert Claydon was relieved when he saw the Bournes ride up to his front gate, and recognised Hudson riding behind them. He did not know that he could not trust Henry Bourne's other servants, but he did know that with Hudson there all was certainly well. Quite possibly Hudson had arranged to attend his master that day.

Claydon went down to the main hall to greet his guests, thanked them for coming so far, asked after Mr Bourne's young son (what was the boy's name? Simon? Stephen?), and received his compliments on the handsome new gatehouse for which Claydon had just about finished paying the mason.

Dinner passed in fairly trivial talk. Afterwards, the women discreetly withdrew as soon as they could. Claydon had intimated, when he asked Henry Bourne to dine with him and stay the night (since Branton was a longish ride to make twice in a day), that he wished to discuss some business concerning the forthcoming Quarter Sessions, and both Mrs Bourne and Ursula knew that, too. His young wife stood in admiration and a little fear of Mrs Deborah Bourne. She had been in something of a fidget all morning, after coming down late for breakfast with a book of devotion still in her hand. When they gathered again for supper later on, Claydon was sure the women had been talking religion and were probably at their devotions together upstairs. Ursula had that excited and yet awed look about her.

It was not until after supper, when Ursula and Mrs Bourne had gone up to bed, that Claydon drew his chair in

towards the hearth (it was chilly for May, and he had had a
fire lit in the parlour, disregarding Ursula's half-murmurs
about the cost) and said quietly, 'Bourne, there is somewhat
else of which I must speak with you.'

Bourne glanced behind him, as though wondering on
whose account Claydon was lowering his voice. 'What is it?'

'There is an urgent matter in which I shall require your
help; a matter important to the Queen's service.'

'Is there?'

'I have received information from – from a member of
the Council of the Marches – that papist priests are haunt-
ing this district.'

Henry Bourne looked relieved. 'Yes, it is a regrettable
state of affairs.'

'I mean particular information. They have learned,
from one who has cause to know well, a place where papists
are wont to hold Masses. They have since, through the eyes
and ears of an honest man who lives close by, understood
that it is very likely that men shall gather there early tomorrow – it being Corpus Christi.'

'And you mean to surprise them?'

'I mean to try. I can collect men and raise sufficient
arms. To examine prisoners – if need be – I would ask you
to join with me.'

'Where is this place?'

'In Branton parish, some mile or two from your house, I
think. They meet in the buildings of an ancient grange, it

seems, in the open land between Branton village and Merford town.'

Henry Bourne's face had frozen still. At last, he said, 'Are you sure of this? I had no – '

'As sure as a man can be... and the advice from the Council is very clear.'

'I see.' He ran his hand quickly over his face. 'Well, we must go out and see what we find, then.'

'Since you are the Justice resident nearest the place, will you sign the warrant to make search?'

'What need a warrant, if we're there?'

'That the men may act without us, if search has to be made in several places.'

'You have the warrant already drawn up, I think.'

'Well, yes.'

'Let's have it then.'

Claydon fetched the paper, together with pen and inkpot. Bourne spread it on the table, and said, 'What's this of Branton Hall, and another house in Merford?'

'These are the known papist houses of the district.'

'You did not say you meant to raid Branton Hall!'

'We must take precautions for whatever may be necessary.'

Henry Bourne signed the warrant. Claydon watched him lay the pen down and then said, 'Bourne, we should settle our plans for tonight.'

'Tonight?'

'Forgive me, but it is several hours' ride, and these papists will meet early if they meet at all. With the warrant, the men can search without our presence if need arise, but you and I must be at hand, if there are prisoners to be examined, and so forth. And – I hope you will not take it amiss – but the most convenient place for the bringing of them is your house.'

'My house?'

'Well, there is no prison closer than Gloucester Castle, and how shall we know whom to commit there and for what, if we cannot make enquiry at first?'

'I see.'

'Are we agreed?'

Henry Bourne straightened abruptly. 'You know I will do my duty. My house is at your disposal. It might be as well if my housekeeper knew to expect it, particularly with myself and my mother both absent.'

'Perhaps if your servant Hudson were to set out now…'

'Yes. Do you wish me to explain matters to Mrs Bourne? Or is the undertaking of too great import for that?'

Claydon replied, a little frostily, 'I have not discussed the matter with Mrs Claydon, nor with any but those of part in it.'

'I hope someone will be able to give them some account come the morning? If we have both left during the night?'

'Well, yes.'

'When do you wish to set out?'

'About midnight.'

'So. Then I think I had as well take some rest in the meantime.' He went to the door, turned and bowed stiffly. 'Goodnight.'

'Goodnight.'

Claydon did not know how much his visitor guessed. He had told no lies, but he had certainly wished Bourne to understand that this business had only just arisen, that he had received his instructions in the last day or two. Bourne might take it as an insult to have been informed so late of an undertaking in his home parish that had been planned for weeks, if not months. But if he had told Bourne earlier... Giles Branton was Bourne's neighbour, and while Henry Bourne's zeal for Queen and Church was real, so was his sense of what was owed between neighbours and gentlemen.

VIII

Hugh tightened his hand around the bark and cautiously shifted his weight. His left ankle had had the worst of the half-crouching position he had taken up against the tree whose roots reached into the hollow. He had chosen the place because it was not too visible, and yet distinctive enough to find if you were looking for it. And when he got there, he had curled into the shadow of the tree-roots and tried to breathe noiselessly.

If he thought about it, no-one was likely to be looking for him or anyone else in the copse, but he was instinctively, tensely cautious... If only Stephen would come soon. He did not want to be late for Mass and cause more comment than was inevitable.

He had not told Mother. However sure he was that it was safe, he could not quite imagine how he would tell her. So, he had said yesterday that Gilian had got lame, that it was not bad, but he would not ride her for a day or two. She need not trouble to rearrange who should come to Mass or how they would ride, he insisted earnestly – he could walk quite easily. And so, he had an excuse to leave the house alone and before everyone else and wait for Stephen in the copse. If only he came on time and could find the place in the dark... with luck there'd be no questions asked and he would not have to debate the issue with Mother or anyone else. But if Stephen was not here soon, he would have to give him up and leave...

He heard a footfall. At last. It did not sound like the normal rustlings of the night; almost certainly a human step, followed by another. Hugh stood up cautiously. He did not want Stephen to miss the place. He was peering in the direction of the sound, through the black tangle of branches. Perhaps he had better call.

Hugh froze. A shaft of moonlight had caught a glint of grey among the black tree trunks and lit up the shadowy form it belonged to. Not Stephen, but a man, wearing a helmet and with a sword at his side, stood barely three yards away in the copse.

For a moment Hugh could not think. He had no clear idea what the man was doing there, but an armed man was a soldier or an official and therefore an enemy. If he had been able to move, he would have run, as far and as fast as he could. He would have run back to the others, who did not know there were pursuivants about... And then another sound stopped his breath again. A second man was approaching the copse.

'You there?' came a voice.

'Aye.'

Hugh strained his eyes to see the other soldier in whose path he might be standing, stilling his breathing in the effort to hear which way the footsteps would go, but he could not move away lest he make a noise. When they stopped, another shape was standing next to the one with the ominous glint.

'Well?' said the glinting shape.

'Hall surrounded,' replied the newcomer.

'Good. My men are ready to close on the old grange as soon as we've seen them all in.'

Hugh's hand curled around a knot on the trunk of the tree. He was flattened against it, every nerve tight.

The first man was speaking again. 'Did you count them out?'

'Aye, just a few minutes back. They went by the road after all. Need hardly have watched the whole place! Hudson, you certain you don't want those men up at the grange?'

'No. Keep the Hall watched in case any slip through the net and make to return there. And the priest?'

'Not sure. At least one man as well as the squire's wife and some children. May have been servants.'

'Hm. And he may have come from the Lister place in any case. But Bales is watching that.'

Keep the Hall watched. Lister. The priest. What else had they said?

'Now what, sir?' asked the second man.

The first soldier turned to go. 'Move to the road and watch it against any escape. I shall be needed at the grange.'

There was a pause and then, in a whisper like a dark smile, the man said, 'We have them, Carson. We have them.'

Hugh had to run. The thought pierced the numb dread which had spread through him as he listened. He had to run away, faster than they could, and warn the others. Suddenly his heart, which had seemed to stop, was beating again, so fast his head throbbed. He forced himself to wait, to see which way the grey glint moved, strained his ears to hear where the steps went, rustling so quietly he could hardly be sure he recognised them.

He uncurled his hand very slowly and moved his foot, with a sound that seemed loud as a shout. He must move slowly, creep, until he reached the open. But he could not see the underbrush before he trod upon it, the twigs which snapped like pistols firing at each step. He was breathing slowly, stumblingly, trying to calm the throbbing in his temples.

In front of him the copse fell away into the shadowy ocean of the common. Around him as he glanced about were the tangles of trees, the little shadows and shapes that could be the soldiers. He pressed himself against a large tree at the edge of the copse and held his breath. There was no sound of footsteps, and the thin moonlight lit up no glinting shapes. It caught what might be a bird diving through the trees onto its prey, and the odd shrub or tree out on the common. He could hear no more voices.

The others would be on the road. Soon they would turn off it and cut across the common to the old grange. If he missed them, he would never find them in the dark. They would reach the old grange, Mass would begin, the trap would be sprung and there would be a hanging in Gloucester. He could not wait any longer. Hugh ran. He left the cover of the trees and was running across the common, scrambling up and down its slopes, his mouth full of the taste of fear and his feet pounding, trying to breathe, trying to see where he was going, trying to run silently because he did not know where the pursuivants might be. He must reach the road before it was too late. He ran, tripped on tussocks, fell, ran again, dodged trees and bushes that he almost crashed into, his shirt sticking to his back and the words of that exchange pounding in his head. *Oh God, God...* Ahead was the road, the tree that marked the turn-off. He could not see any horses. He was too late. *God...* He would have to try to find them on the common. No, there they were, not ten yards from the oak... Hugh almost fell into the road and grabbed the bridle of his mother's horse.

'My God!' And then 'Hugh?'

'Mother – stop – we must not – we – they – '

'Hugh. Find your breath and then tell me what has happened.' Her voice was steady, but sharp with alarm.

Hugh hung onto the bridle and tried to pull enough air into his lungs to speak. 'Pursuivants. They've surrounded the old grange. They're watching our house and the Listers'.

They saw you all come out – I do not know if they saw me. I think they saw Mr Foster but they are not certain he is – '

'How do you know?' The priest's voice was quick but deliberate.

'I heard two of them talking in the copse.'

'They are watching the house as well?'

'Yes.'

'It seems we can neither go forward nor back. But we must do one of them.' Mother again. She paused, and Hugh's gasping breaths filled the darkness until she spoke once more. 'We will let them think as long as possible that they have succeeded. We will go on. But you, sir, should turn aside now and try to get out of the neighbourhood. You know Norton Court?'

'I have been there once.'

'Mother – the road may be watched... Should not he go cross-country?

'Perhaps… '

'I think I can find the way on foot.'

For a moment his mother hesitated, and then said, 'Very well. You will take Mr Foster.'

'As you wish,' said the priest. 'But, madam, you do realise that you are riding straight into a trap?'

'None of us is in your danger. Indeed, without you we are in no danger. No priest, no Mass - no Mass, no crime. For God's sake go quickly!'

He had already dismounted. 'Take the altar things,' she continued. 'No need to give them those. Harry, take Mr Foster's horse; Agnes can ride alone if you keep close to her.' Harry slipped down and helped Agnes take the reins of their horse, before swinging up into the empty saddle. 'Isabel, you ride round to the road from town and warn anyone you meet except the Listers to turn back. Fast, Isabel. Agnes and Harry will have to stay with me.' She shook her reins. 'Godspeed.'

Hugh and the priest turned and ran.

*   *   *

They did not run for long. As the blackness of the common closed around them, they slowed to a walk, trying to hush their footsteps to silence, straining their eyes. Out of the dark they heard all the common noises of the night, but magnified because each one might be the sound they dreaded. The air was cold against Hugh's sweat-damp face, and the frantic race from the copse had given him a stitch. His hands were clammy, too. The pursuivants were around the hall and the old grange and the Listers' house, not across the fields and the woods. But Hugh's ears were straining for the whispers of voices or the fall of horses' hooves, his eyes suspecting every shadow. His imagination kept throwing him into the hands of their pursuers, and he found himself feverishly wondering what in God's name he would say if they were caught.

What would Mother say? Mother, riding impervious into a trap. There was no story they could tell, only hide the truth... It would take one person. One frightened child... and Agnes was only nine... He shook the thought off, and at that instant a soft footfall just behind stopped both of them in their tracks. Hugh looked at Mr Foster. It was too dark to see his face clearly, but his breath was held as he too listened, and his chin jutted a little as though his teeth were set beneath it. The footsteps rustled, padded past them and faded. No voices came with them. An animal; a badger or a fox. Cautiously, they moved forward again. But to reach the stream Hugh meant to follow towards Norton Court they would have to cross the road – the road which led from the old grange. It was close to dawn when they came to it. 'We cross here,' Hugh whispered. 'And then follow more or less the line of the stream to meet the road up to Norton Court further on.' The priest nodded silently and put a finger to his lips. And then suddenly he flung himself down by the verge, jerking Hugh down beside him. Horses' hooves – many of them – could be heard around a bend in the road.

Neither of them moved; only the blades of grass in front of their faces quivered a little as they breathed. Hugh could just see the priest out of the corner of his eye. He was looking up the road.

The horsemen came round the bend, and there were many of them. They were, in fact, the whole troop of pursuivants and soldiers returning from the grange. With them were the Mass-goers they had found there.

Silent and breathless, Hugh and Mr Foster watched the cavalcade ride past. They could see the faces well enough now in the increasing light and could only hope their own were still concealed behind the grass and weeds of the roadside. There might have been two dozen prisoners, men and women, some on horseback, others walking. Hugh had known, of course, that anyone found at the old grange was likely to be arrested, but – He gasped suddenly and would have cried out, but the priest grasped his wrist to silence him. At last, they had gone past. When the sound of the hooves had all but died away, Hugh and Mr Foster rose, crossed the road swiftly and silently, and continued on their way.

At last Hugh spoke. 'Sir – did you see?'

'I saw.'

'What do we do?'

'We keep walking.'

'But they – my mother – the children – did you not see?' His voice had risen.

'Hush.' The priest stopped short, took Hugh's elbow, and looked into his desperate face. 'Hush. Who would we help by turning back?'

His voice was sharp and his face, dim in the greyness, was strained. Hugh turned silently away, and they kept walking, doing the only thing they could, hollowly ashamed of doing it.

Hugh fixed his mind on finding the right course. They must follow more or less the line of the stream for two or three miles and keep parallel with the road, but not on it. Not on it. Better go by lanes or even fields and find some explanation for anyone they met if they needed to than risk meeting the pursuivants on the roads. They would surely think of Norton Court once they found Branton empty.

'Hugh.' The priest said.

'Yes, sir?'

'If we meet anyone, I had rather you said nothing, do you hear? I will answer any questions. And if the pursuivants do catch up and stop us, the moment I tell you to, you run, is that clear?'

'Yes, sir.' Hugh said. He swallowed and tried to walk faster, for the danger grew with the light and diminished with every yard they put between themselves and Branton. 'How long have we got, do you think, sir?' he asked at last.

'Until they've questioned every man at the grange and made certain none of them is a priest – which may or may not take long.'

But it seemed they had been in time. Once or twice, they turned off their path to avoid other travellers, but met no-one. At last, even Hugh stopped turning his head at every rustle of a leaf and breath of wind. The sun was climbing high when he said, 'I think we've crossed the county border now.'

'Good.' The priest stopped a moment to look back down the path they had come, and then asked, 'You said they were watching two houses and the old grange?'

'Yes, sir.'

'They must have used a small army on this night's work,' he said thoughtfully. 'They do not do that on a sudden because someone runs with a tale that a priest's in the neighbourhood.'

'What do you mean, sir?'

'Only that I think someone must have been wanting to raid the Catholics of Merford for some time. They carefully watched us ride past their spies...'

'I wondered why they did that.'

'They wanted us to reach the old grange and make the proof as good as they could get. They could arrest the priest; they could charge whoever they chose for Mass-going, even the church-papists. They would have evidence of priest-harbouring at the Hall. And they could search it...They will almost certainly search it –' He turned to Hugh. 'Do you know if your mother still – ?' and then he stopped. 'No. No, you most likely would not.'

Hugh said, 'They will question everyone who was there about this.'

'I am afraid they will. And the place cannot be used again... but with no priest they cannot really charge anyone.'

They were almost within sight of the great house when Hugh said suddenly, 'Who told them?'

'Who? God knows. Some Catholic under questioning, an apostate priest, an informer who made his way into Mass – it happens.' There was a silence. And then a thought occurred to Hugh so terrible he almost stopped dead. He pushed it away as reasonably as he could. It was not just that Stephen was not the kind of person who would do that... he had not in any case even known where Mass was... But he had known the day and the hour – and if someone else had already... Well, of course, it was not impossible. One could not reason it out of the equation. One simply refused to think it because it was not true.

*   *   *

Mrs Bourne met her grandson when he came in from school. He looked exhausted, and rather strained; all the disturbance early that morning must have woken him, too. She herself had set out for home almost as soon as, on rising, she received the message Henry had left. Whatever came to pass with this business, the servants should not be left to manage it alone.

Stephen greeted her dutifully and asked if she had had a good journey.

'Well enough.' She told him. 'Stephen, you are to sleep in your father's chamber tonight.'

'I... why? I mean, yes, madam, but what has – ?'

'I have already given Mr Claydon the guest chamber. I've asked Mrs Branton to sleep in mine, but there is nowhere except your chamber where I can conveniently put John Lister.'

'What has happened?'

'You know what passed this morning?'

'Yes... the maids said...'

'Well. It seems they did not arrest a priest, or at least they have not yet. So, most of those who were at the old grange have been sent home. No Mass, nothing to make charges with. But Mr Claydon and your father have not released Mrs Branton, nor yet John Lister.'

'W – why?'

'That is not your concern or mine. But I believe they found a great deal of unlawful stuff – popish Massing stuff – at the Hall and at Lister's house. I cannot say what will happen later, but for this night both of them are held here.'

Stephen said, 'So – so, can I fetch my clothes from my chamber?'

'Yes, but please knock before you go in.' Lister, she recalled, had gone up to Stephen's chamber some time ago, while the squire's wife remained in the parlour. Mr Claydon had made something of a fuss about not leaving his prisoners alone together.

Claydon had dispersed most of his men after the business of searching and questioning was done with, but he had retained eight of them, presumably to keep some sort of watch through the night. That meant, in all, ten people to find sleeping-room for, ten more people to feed at supper. And it was not going to be the most convivial of meals either.

Predictably, when they sat down at table, Henry set himself to keep up a desperate courtesy, to which Mrs Branton responded in kind. John Lister spoke about half a dozen words in all, though those were irreproachable. Robert Claydon was occupied with showing himself at ease and kept engaging Mrs Bourne in conversation, but her mind was only half in the present, and it was an effort to answer him. She did notice, though, that Stephen – listening to his elders – was uneasy; indeed, she almost thought he seemed frightened. When they rose from table and Henry announced prayers, Mrs Branton said, 'I think I shall go upstairs now, if you do not mind.'

Henry Bourne nodded, Claydon glanced sideways at Mrs Bourne, and Mrs Branton and John Lister left the hall. One of Claydon's men followed at a discreet distance.

When Deborah Bourne entered her chamber that evening, Mrs Branton was seated at the table by the window, staring into the night. She had neither closed the shutters, nor lit a candle as it grew dark. Mrs Bourne put the candle she carried down on the dresser and crossed the room.

'Shall I put up the shutters?'

Mrs Branton turned her head. 'Yes.' She rose to move out of the way. 'Excuse me.'

'Do you want to borrow a night-shift?'

'Thank you.'

Mrs Bourne opened her linen-chest and found a clean night-gown and cap. In silence, the two women washed, undressed, and changed. When Mrs Bourne took up the book of psalms that lay on the table and knelt down, she was aware that across the chamber the other woman had also knelt down, silently crossing herself.

When she closed her psalter, the other woman rose at the same moment, and they both climbed into bed. Mrs Bourne blew out the candle, set it on the stool, and pulled the curtain shut. 'Goodnight.'

'Goodnight.'

Fear tastes like vomit, and a little like hunger. It sounds like the hollow thuds which are your heart beating crazily, and it feels like the sweat on your skin from running. You start running in your mind long before you run with your feet and your limbs. Fear is a dark night, and the feel of the leaves of a shrub and the smell of candles and of precious, dangerous books and the sharp half-whisper giving the alarm and faces on which the tautness of fear gives way to the certainty of dread, and a room which shrinks around you as you hear the sounds which tell you that they have come.

She was filled with fear, a memory of fear strong as the thing itself, pounding through her head until fear and memory were one. She was crouching in the shadow of a yew-tree, watching through a broken fence to be sure the yard in front of her was empty and no window upon it was open, and she could run across it to the garden door which led into a street where she thought - hoped - feared - no armed men would be.

The sounds from the house still reached her through the hammering of her heart, sounds pulling her back and driving her forward. Then she thought she heard a door open behind her - the door into the yard - and there was no time for any more watching and she ran, scrambling through the broken fence and across the next-door neighbour's yard. And then she was tugging at the bolts until the garden door opened, and then running again, running and hoping and fearing that she had not been seen and was not followed.

How far in truth did she run? Not very far, not more than half a mile through the still-sleeping city to the lodging where her husband was lying in bed wishing she would not take such risks. But when it came back, that night, that fear, she was always running, eternally running, with the voices and the dark and the glint of pikes and handcuffs and the light of flames in her head. Running with her father's face before her eyes, turning to her – at once, unmistakably to her – as the cry came, *they're here,* and then the tramping feet.

There were so few seconds. Seconds to thrust the bibles out of sight. Seconds to decide whether to lie or to hide. Seconds to remember that she knew her father's house like the back of her hand, and that behind the yew-tree the fence between its yard and that of the house next door was broken down; and because the next house stood on a corner, it had a garden door which opened onto a lane, which the watchmen and pursuivants might not know to watch.

Half a second to turn away from her father's face and run. Other people were running too... there was a chance of hiding in the rooms of the house. There was a faint chance that if everyone tried, one or two might get past the men and out the front door and down the street, and with fifteen prisoners to hold, would they pursue two or three? Deborah Bourne ran for the yew tree and the garden door.

She did not see what happened. She did not see the pursuivants entering the house, the searching and the hiding and the chaos; she did not see them lay hands on her father, nor shackle him and take him away. She did not even know for sure, as she ran, that he had been seized. But she saw it over and over before her eyes.

Her husband promised that he would find out what had happened to her father. He promised too that he would take care of her mother, who had been watching with a neighbour in childbed the night of the prayer-meeting, and so had not been there either to flee or to stay. He made Deborah go home. Go home to the children; go as soon as the day has begun; go home and go quietly. So, she went, and all the long ride home was still running from the memory of the things she had not seen.

There were no prayer-meetings in Branton parish to go to or flee from. She went to Mass very little. They used to tell the priest that her daughter was unwell and needed nursing, which was frequently at least half true; Grace Bourne was sick for probably more than six of the eleven years of her life, in all. Parson Russell was a convinced papist, but he had laid up his own memories of cowardice over the last ten years and did not usually press her. Deborah Bourne sat in the nursery with Grace, hearing the church bell and murmuring English psalms from memory. Another way of running.

The sitting still and the keeping quiet, the fearing and the hoping and the waiting for news, seemed always a part of that night of fleeing through the dark. She was running and falling and rising and running again, sick with dread, her hands scratched from the fence and each breath ripping her lungs and every muscle aching and her father's face before her...

'Mrs Bourne? Are you unwell?'

She opened her eyes to the calm darkness of her bed and the voice of the other woman lying in it and wondered what noise she had made. She unclenched her fists and slowly let her knotted muscles slacken.

'No, there is nothing wrong.' She answered. 'I am sorry to have woken you.'

'You did not.'

IX

It was drawing towards evening when Hugh returned to Branton Hall. When they reached Norton Court, he had been urged to rest and ride home the next morning, but he could not have slept without knowing what had happened. He had borrowed a horse and left almost at once.

Branton Hall had been searched. It was all over by the time Hugh came home. Aunt Isabel was there, pale and worried that Agnes and Harry had been terribly frightened, but relieved to see Hugh. Bridget, it seemed, had gone home with Mrs Lister.

Mother was not there. She had not been released when most of the others had been; nor had John Lister. Aunt Isabel did not know any more, only that they had been questioned, and at last she and the children had been sent home without seeing Mrs Branton and had found the house as the searchers had left it.

They had done the work thoroughly. Bedclothes had been ripped as they searched through mattresses, some of the pots in the kitchen were smashed, chairs were broken and tables chipped and scratched. The lock on the press where some of the books were kept had been forced, the doors swung crooked on broken hinges and all the Catholic works had been taken. Aunt Isabel's virginals still stood in their place, but some of the keys were broken. Hanging cloths were ripped. Even in the nursery the children's toys were scattered on the floor and some had been trodden on. The once-new-panelled parlour had, to judge from the damage, come under the strongest scrutiny. And it had paid off. The priesthole lay bare to see, robbed of its contents, as did the little hidden cupboard in the great chamber. But they had not found the priest. Surely without that they had not evidence to charge anybody.

There was nothing to be said or done about that. What could be done was to tidy, sweep, pick things up that had been scattered. It was difficult to know what to do about smashed panelling and torn hangings. It was difficult to know what to say to big-eyed children, after you had told them to put their toys back in the chest. As evening fell, they were eating supper – of a sort – in the hall, too tired and too numb to talk much, the table seeming empty with neither the squire nor his wife to sit at its head. The smaller children had gone to sleep eventually on the strength of reckless promises from Isabel that Mother would surely be home tomorrow. She and the elder boys went straight to bed; the parlour was unusable for the present in any case.

'Did you get there, then?' Harry asked, when they were sitting on the bed in Hugh's chamber, talking in whispers.

'Yes.'

'Did they go after you?'

'I don't know.'

'What did they say? At Norton Court?'

'That it was a narrow escape, God be thanked it was no worse, and I should ride home on one of their horses.' He looked at Harry. 'What happened here?'

'They arrested everyone, and took us to Mr Bourne's house, and asked a lot of questions.'

'To Mr Bourne's?' To Stephen's house. Stephen must have heard... seen...

'Yes. And they searched here and the Listers' house.'

'Were you – were you here when they came?'

Harry had turned away. 'We did not know until we came home.'

'Were you questioned, Harry?'

'Of course. Everyone was. Children especially. They think if you're younger you cannot lie.'

'Agnes too?'

'Of course.'

'I'm sorry, Harry.' Hugh said. And then, 'What did you say?'

'I'm not an idiot... Agnes started screaming and tried to run out of the room. Then she bit the man who was trying to hold her.'

'Bit him?'

Harry nodded, and then said, 'Mother's still there.'

'She'll be home.' Hugh said. 'They – I mean nothing bad can happen. They did not find a priest. Mother will be home tomorrow.'

There was a silence, during which Hugh felt the conviction drain out of his confident words. Then Harry asked, 'Hugh, how come you knew? How did you know what was going to happen?'

'I overheard them.'

'Yes, you said, but how come?'

'I told you, I was walking across the common and I overheard two of them talking. Harry, we should go to bed now.'

*　　*　　*

Mrs Branton stood quite still in the parlour doorway. Indeed, it would have been difficult to go any further. The new panelling lay in heaps around the floor, much of it broken. The walls stood bare and dusty. Several of the windowpanes had been smashed. And what had once been a hiding-place was a gaping hollow by the parlour stairs.

'Damn.'

Damage was not the word; that would imply the possibility of repair. Destruction. And certainly she could not afford to replace it. She would have to tell Giles.

'Damn!' She threw the word down into the shattered room like a gauntlet. There was a sudden sob behind her, and she turned guiltily. Agnes had come in after her. The child darted past her into the room and pulled a piece of broken, blue-painted plaster from under a panel. Crying now, she dug out the head of the Infant Jesus, and part of the Virgin's hand. Mrs Branton looked at it for a long moment and saw again the damaged statue standing on the table in Henry Bourne's parlour with Claydon's grimly pleased face behind it. She looked back at Agnes, and finally said, 'It is only a statue.'

'But Mother – '

She pulled the little girl to her feet and put an arm round her. 'I know. I know... But it is still only a statue.' She looked about her. 'And it is only a room.'

Hugh wanted to ask her what had happened, but somehow there was no time. She went all round the house, commended Isabel for her efforts at restoring order, reassured the little ones, spoke to the servants. Before dinner she had dispatched Robson to hire some men to clean up the parlour. The panelling was a thing of the past, but one could at least have the broken wood carted away and the stripped walls whitewashed. In the evening, after she had been to the nursery, she went into the library to try to make sense of the now-scattered papers which contained all the business of the estate.

After half an hour spent in his chamber staring dutifully and uncomprehendingly at his schoolbooks, Hugh went downstairs and knocked at the library door. 'Mother? I came to ask if I could help.'

She looked up. 'Why, thank you. Yes, come in.' He sat on a stool and watched her sorting sheets of paper into piles, of letters, accounts books, legal papers, records of letters sent, and unused paper. Among them lay scattered sealing wax, quills and one spilt bottle of ink. 'Nothing of importance seems to be missing, thank God. Here, take these and sort them into order. I think they are all dated.'

They worked in near silence for some time before Hugh asked, 'Mother, what happened?'

'They found the Mass-stuff in the house and questioned me over it.'

'But they... all will be well?'

'I am here, am I not?'

'Please, Mother.'

She laid the papers she was reading on the table. 'They found there was no priest among us, but none of our evasions, or flat lies, were going to make them think we had not gathered at the old grange for Mass. It was then, I think, that they searched here and the Lister house. When the men brought in the vestments and things, they called Mr Lister and me and asked if we recognised them.'

'What did you say?'

'Well, not that I had made them and kept them in my house two and a half years.'

Hugh sighed. 'And then?'

'I thought I was safe from the grave charge – they'd found no priest. But, as Mr Claydon pointed out, there are other laws one can break. Enough rosary beads and Agnus Deis in that hole to make half-a-dozen indictments. More, it was evidence that priests have entered Branton Hall even if none were actually found. I told them, of course, that they'd need a name and a date if they meant to frame an indictment and proof of both if they meant to win the case. But – well, it could have been dangerous.'

'How come – Mother?'

She shrugged. 'I know not whether they would have tried to bring it to court. But it was made clear to me I'd be in Gloucester gaol by tomorrow morning if I gave them reason, and not just for the night neither.'

'Gave them reason?' Hugh echoed.

'They offered to take, instead, my bond to go no further than ten miles from Branton without licence for six months hence, if I gave them a promise of conformity.' His mother was not looking at him, and he could read no expression in her voice.

'What did – ?'

'So, I gave it them and came home. I'll betake myself to church like a law-abiding subject, and they'll drop the charges.'

'Will you go then? This Sunday?'

'I swore I would. Besides they bound me to appear in a month, and they'll take the parson as witness.'

Hugh was silent for several seconds, staring down at the hand which clutched the edges of the papers in his lap. He loosened it slowly and smoothed the crushed corners with his thumb. Then he heard himself say, 'do you want me to come with you?'

'Come with me? Why?'

'I don't know.'

'Most certainly not.'

Her son turned back to the papers he was trying to sort. Among them was a notice detailing his father's and mother's conviction for recusancy, dated 1583, and declaring them liable for fines of £60 that quarter. Suddenly he remembered something and asked, 'Mother? What of Mr Lister?'

'He is in gaol.'

'Why? Did they make him an offer? Will he be charged?'

'I know nothing of that. I hope there'll be no charge – they've no more evidence against him than against us. As to the other...' She laughed shortly. 'Perhaps they now know precisely what John Lister's conformity means.'

At last, she dismissed Hugh to bed. Just as he was leaving she asked suddenly, 'Hugh, what happened about school?'

Hugh turned in the doorway 'Nothing. I told Mr Lee there'd been a raid on this place. He was not pleased, but he could hardly say that was my doing.'

Mrs Branton sat still in the library for some time after Hugh had gone. The contempt of one's children was almost harder to bear than one's own. No, not contempt; that was unfair. Hugh was only shocked. Shocked; surprised; unable to understand. How could he understand? How could she explain to a boy of fourteen, whom she had taught to believe that one stayed away from Protestant services as one did from mortal sin, that there were moments when one had to compromise? He could not understand the long night she had spent, fearing what could happen to Giles and perhaps to her if they brought a charge of priest-harbouring; wondering what other charges they had, how much they knew of Branton Hall's secrets; thinking of what would become of the children if she let them send her to gaol. He could not understand the weight that had been lifted when Henry Bourne, muttering something about clemency and her husband being already in prison, had quietly proposed his bargain… Hugh did not need to know these things. And yet some part of her wanted to call him back and explain. It was not only that she was afraid to lose his trust; it was as though she wanted to warn him. But of what exactly, she did not know.

She sighed and picked up her quill and a blank sheet of paper. She must write to Giles, and she would have to explain to him what had happened, and that she could not come to London in the autumn either. He would probably be writing soon; it was two months and eleven days since the last letter from him. He must surely write soon. If only there could be some good news to exchange.

*   *   *

The sound jerked Hugh awake. A sharp crack, coming from outside and yet seeming startlingly close. He sat up, staring into the darkness, his heart beating fast while his brain was still half in sleep. At last, he parted the bedcurtains cautiously and peered out. The second time the sound came he recognised it for what it was, a pebble being thrown against a pane of glass, and crossed the room to the window.

Standing outside the house, Stephen sighed with relief when the window opened. He dared not call out, but he looked up at Hugh and beckoned. A moment passed, and the figure at the window disappeared. He waited, hoping and fearing, and at last there was the sound of a door shutting, and then Hugh stepping softly towards him.

'What are you doing here?'

'Hugh, I heard what happened.'

'You did?'

'Is all well?'

'Let's see. To the good, you captured a great lot of Massing-stuff and frightened the hell out of every papist in

Merford. On the other hand, it seems you've not got a priest, and can make no priest-harbouring charges either.'

'Hugh, stop it.'

Hugh folded his arms.

'Hugh, why? Why were you not speaking to me today? You did not wait to ride together this morning – and then you did not speak to me all day.'

Hugh did not answer.

'And why – Hugh, why did you not wait in the copse?'

'What?'

'Why did you not wait in the copse? I watched nigh on an hour. I was not later than you could have stayed for if you'd cared to. I waited until it was almost too late to get back home without being seen... I did not hear what happened until later. And I'm sorry. And I'm glad no-one is - is in serious trouble. And I think my father is too.'

'I think I don't care very much how your father feels.'

'Hugh, you are not listening. Why did you not wait? If you do not trust me, why did you not say so in the first place? Or is that what you call a jest?'

His voice had risen, and Hugh glanced behind him. Stephen's sudden anger took him by surprise. 'Well, because – ' he began, and then stopped. Now Stephen was there, the terrifying thoughts he had been trying to push away only showed their absurdity. There was no need even to ask. And yet he found he could not speak.

'Why?'

Hugh opened his mouth to tell Stephen about hearing the men in the copse, dodging like a hunted animal across the dark common. About watching the soldiers take Mother and the children away, about the long, uneasy walk to Norton Court, and the choking, blinding fear. 'Well,' he said, 'it would have been somewhat awkward if I had.'

Stephen was still looking at him, maddeningly uncomprehending.

'I daresay your father would not have needed to ask your name.' And he turned and disappeared into the house.

In the morning he woke early and began to dress. At some point, for no reason he knew, he began to hurry. By the time he was pulling on his shoes he was in such haste he could hardly fasten them, and as he saddled Gilian he knew for definite that he must reach the road that led from Stephen's house before Stephen did. He had the mare cantering almost before they were out of the stableyard and was pounding up the lane. At the corner he pulled up, breathless and hot, and waited. There was no sign of Stephen. He might not be here yet. He might have come and gone on to school. Surely, he could not have passed by already. But as the minutes passed, as the sun climbed higher and Hugh strained his eyes up the road, he began to worry. Perhaps he was too late. He could not stay much longer if he wanted to reach school on time. Perhaps he was too late.

And then Stephen arrived, riding his horse at a trot because there was not too much time to spare. He drew up in surprise.

'Hugh?'

'What are you trying to do, Stephen, get us beaten for being late?'

Stephen laughed, and both of them spurred their horses down the road to town. Nothing more was said about the previous night, or about the raid.

X

It was past Midsummer when Mother set about replacing the things which had been taken in the search. Nothing had been said at first about that particular loss; it had seemed a little pointless, when they almost certainly could not have Mass at the old grange again, at least in a long while. All the small damages that could be mended had been, the household otherwise went about its business much as usual, and even the children stopped talking and asking about what had happened. One evening in late June, Mrs Branton and her sister discussed the denuded parlour walls. 'We could put damask paper over the whitewash, just for now.' Aunt Isabel said. 'There's plenty left of what I used for the upper walls of my chamber – mine and Bridget's.'

'Isabel, I'm not putting damask paper up in my best parlour!' Mrs Branton looked around the room again. 'We could move some tapestries from the guest chamber – that would cover some of the walls – and hang the guest chamber with the old painted cloths that are stored away. For the time being.' She sighed. 'It'll do.'

She had sat silent over her work for a little while, and then said, 'the other things – the things they found – I had best ask Hale.'

Bridget and Hugh, playing chess at the small table, looked up and then at each other. Isabel said, 'Is that… necessary? I mean, we cannot use the old grange again for…'

'Then we will find somewhere else.' Mrs Branton said, sharply.

'But…'

'Well, what else is to be done? I do not intend – since it seems necessary, let me make clear that I do not intend that no-one at Branton should hear a Mass again.'

'Of course not, sister,' Isabel said, and was silent. Hugh absently moved his king into check and Bridget forgot to say so. One did not often speak of *Mass* by name like that, even in private.

Isabel changed the subject to preserving strawberries, which were particularly abundant that year, and Mrs Branton's voice as she replied was even again. But there had been anger under her voice ever since the raid. It was not only the search itself, and the damage done: she did not usually smoulder quite so long over such things. She had gone to church as agreed the Sunday following, and the one after that too, and no-one had said one word on the matter, before or after. Mr Bennett, so Hugh understood, duly reported that the squire's wife had conformed, apparently choosing to ignore the rosary beads she took with her to the service. Perhaps Mother was worried, too, that there was still no letter from Father.

John Lister was in gaol in Gloucester. No-one really knew whether charges would be brought, or what they would be if they were. He had said nothing about that when he wrote to his wife, a long list of instructions about how things were to be ordered in his absence, including that Bridget should return to Branton Hall if Mrs Branton would have her. Of this last, Agnes had been especially glad, and Hugh found that he was too.

*   *   *

Stephen had done something very wicked. He was not sure how wicked. He was not even sure what it was, or why he had done it.

It had begun this morning. Hugh had been thinking about something else all the way to school; it was quite clear that he was, but when Stephen asked, he was told sharply that it was nothing. Hugh had asked pardon a few moments later and made a half-credible effort at ordinary talk. But Stephen could not make himself ignore Hugh's preoccupation. He could not stop wanting to know what it was. There was no need for Hugh to be rude, anyway, even if he could not tell. And there was no good reason for him not to tell. How long had they been friends now? What more could he do to make Hugh his friend? He would have thought that conversation in the spring would have shown Hugh enough.

What was he up to? Were they having Masses again? There could not be much harm in just saying that to Stephen. Hugh ought to know that. Stephen's mind went back to that night at the Hall. 'You caught a lot of Massing-stuff...' And he noticed the empty pannier Hugh's horse was carrying for no clear reason and wondered whether that was it - if they were trying to get new Massing-stuff. He had still no clear idea what that was. What exactly was Mass, come to that? What did they do there that was so wrong it had to be attacked with armed men? Grandmother would say it was a superstition that damned men's souls. Father would say the Queen's peace must be kept. And Hugh would get himself flogged because he could not hear it mocked.

As they came out of the Raven's stables, Hugh said 'I have to speak a word to Lockwood. You need not wait,' and darted into the inn. Stephen looked after him, started to leave, stopped, and at last set off down the road to school, walking fast and biting his lip. He had seen that Hugh had taken the empty pannier with him. Hugh caught up with him at the school door, with a grin but without explanation. Only as lessons were starting, Hugh whispered, 'I've forgotten my book. May I share yours?' Stephen shifted his book so they could both see it, and they went on working like that. But if Hugh thought Stephen was so blind he had not noticed that Hugh's satchel was in point of fact more full than it had been before they reached the Raven, he was stupid. Hugh was stupid anyway, if he thought that he could trust Stephen to lend him a book, but not with the reason he had to ask.

After school, they went back to fetch their horses together, Hugh now quite zealously pretending he was not pre-occupied, and that was when it happened. Stephen attended to his own horse, and as he turned to lead her out, saw that Hugh's pannier was now full too. But he said nothing. Only then Hugh put his satchel down as he bent to check a loose shoe on the mare, and Stephen put his hand into the satchel, pulled something out, and stuffed it into his own.

Books. He had felt the edges of the pages. Of course, popish books. That was what Hugh would not tell. What he had done did not sink into Stephen until they were out of Merford. Hugh smiled at him suddenly in the midst of some inconsequential remark, a frank smile such as he seldom gave, and Stephen realised what that sudden, crazy act had meant, and simultaneously that he could not possibly explain now.

When he got home, Stephen climbed the stairs to his chamber slowly, trying not to think about what he ought to do when he got there.

'Mind where you go, son!'

He looked up into his father's face. 'Oh! Your pardon, sir.'

'What are you day-dreaming of, to be knocking your father down the stairs? I hope it is not mischief.'

'No – no sir. I am only tired.'

'Ah. And not done with your books yet, I see.'

'No. I – I thought I would take them to my chamber.'

'Aye. Rather think you in your chamber at your books than running wild. Your grandmother says that of late she knows not where you are except when you're at meat.'

Stephen smiled tentatively. He was not sure whether he was being teased or reproved. 'Sorry,' he said.

His father continued downstairs. 'Well, good luck with Virgil. I am tired myself. A long day it has been.'

After he had shut his chamber door firmly, Stephen put the satchel on the floor with the bed between him and the door, and carefully opened it.

A small, slim volume, bound. He could still put it back unopened, and perhaps tomorrow... the title page read, *Rationes Decem: quibus fretus, certamen aduersariis obtulit in causa Fidei, Edmundus Campianus e Societate Nominis Iesu Presbyter: allegatae ad clarissimos viros, nostrates Academicos.*

Edmund Campion. There was no printer named on the title-page, but Stephen remembered a story of its being printed secretly in a house in England, not in papist countries overseas. This was the book that a string of scholars had refuted, that corrupted minds and traduced the Queen and sowed popery. There was another small book in his satchel that was not a Latin reader. He lifted that one out too. '*A brief directory and plain way how to say the rosary of our blessed Lady...*'. Stephen's eyes widened. He remembered the string of beads in his father's desk; the woman in the cottage and Mrs Branton years ago. It had never occurred to him that rosary-beads were things one could write books about. He began turning the pages, just to see. Someone had set the type for these books, perhaps in that very house in Oxfordshire where Campion had lain. Someone – some papist – had placed these very pages Stephen now held in the press, looking over his shoulder the while, breathing a popish prayer perhaps, in case the magistrates...

Stephen shut the book and sat back on his heels. These books were a crime. Hugh had committed a crime. Geoffrey Lockwood was trading in crime. And he, Stephen, had to go downstairs and show these things to his father and tell him where they came from, or he had to commit a crime, too.

He got up, suddenly hurried. He could shove them in among his schoolbooks – hide a leaf in a forest – or under his mattress, only he did not want the maids finding them when they made the bed. At last, he put them right at the bottom of his linen chest; neither Grandam nor the maids were likely to look there. Then he went down to supper and tried to eat.

He had stolen something from Hugh. He had concealed seditious literature from his father. Hugh would be furious if he knew, and what his father would feel he could not begin to think. All he knew was that tonight he was going to take those books out of his linen chest, set his candle by his bedside, and start to read them.

*   *   *

Neither Hugh nor Bridget had heard the question of future Masses debated again, but the next time Ralph Hale returned to the Hall, Mrs Branton had given him a commission to find some new altar-vessels, and one altar crucifix, and a few small ones if he could, and some beads. It would be a shame, she said, that those people she had promised to give things to should not get them. Hugh was in the library copying a letter for her when she made the list out.

'I must send Robson to Lockwood to see about books,' she said. 'Missals we must have. And my New Testament is gone, and I had a copy of Southwell's book that I was keeping for your father, and then there was Vaux's Catechism, three of them...'

'Mother, need you send Robson? I could go on my way to school. I could bring the things home after, too.'

'Could you? Yes, I suppose you could. Well, I shall give you my list tomorrow evening, and let you take it in the morning. I do not know what Lockwood will have, of course, or be able to get. It may take time.' She sighed impatiently. 'It is such a bother, to do all over again.'

Geoffrey Lockwood was cautiously sanguine when Hugh gave him Mrs Branton's list. 'Aye. Missals I have.' he said slowly, as though counting in his mind. 'New Testaments I can do. Vaux – I hope I'll have more of them soon. The others I shall try, but I cannot promise anything. Give me ten days before you come back.' He rolled up the paper, walked over and put it in the fire. Then he turned back, smiling at Hugh's face. 'Never keep things like that longer than it takes you to put them to memory, Master Hugh.'

When Hugh went back ten days later to collect the books, he found Lockwood talking to a young man, a tradesman from his clothes, whom Hugh vaguely recognised. Both of them looked round sharply as Hugh entered, and then Lockwood nodded to him. The young man was putting a book into his pack. 'My thanks,' he said. 'I've been trying to get that for so long.'

'No trouble.' Lockwood said. 'You will take care with them, will you not?

'Of course.'

'Lampley, I mean that. I've started to hear things about you – and not only from Catholics. When casual customers in my inn are saying what a zealous papist that young glover back in town is, you are drawing too much attention to yourself.'

'I will be careful.'

'Why did you want two copies of this?'

Lampley smiled. 'There's a couple of people I'd like to give it to.'

'It may be a costly gift.'

'Costly?'

'You know what I mean.'

'What price do you put on the truth?' With which remark he was gone, leaving Lockwood to shake his head after him. He turned to Hugh.

'Master Hugh. I have what you sent for.'

'Thank you.' Hugh looked at the volume on top of the pile and suppressed a smile. He had read Mother's list, too, and been rather excited when he saw *Rationes Decem* on it. He had not known Mother and Father ever owned that book, but here was Mother asking Lockwood to replace it. He meant to read it this time. He also had a half-thought that he would like to show it to Stephen.

He gave Lockwood the money Mother had given him and began putting the books into the pannier he had brought. He had to put some into his satchel as well, so it was lucky he had left some of his schoolbooks at home this morning to make room. He realised he could not take the pack to school; Lockwood said his son Jake would leave it in the stable just before Hugh got there. Lockwood himself would be too busy in the inn by that time to deal with this sort of thing. At school, he shared Stephen's book so that the absence of his own did not matter, and after school he found the pack in Gilian's stall as promised and took the whole lot home to give Mother.

*   *   *

'It is not Hugh's fault, I suppose it is mine for letting him do it,' Mrs Branton said 'The real point is what happened – whether someone found the things and – '

'You have asked Hugh?' Isabel said. 'What did he say?'

'I did not want to frighten him. But he was quite sure he did exactly as I had told him, that Lockwood did not say there was anything missing, and that no-one had seen him.' She sighed. 'He had some of them with him in his school satchel, but he says he was certain it was closed.'

'He's sure?'

'Y-yes.' She glanced up. 'He said if Master Lee had seen anything, he would have made sure Hugh knew that he had.'

'Sister, a spy would not have alerted us by taking anything. He would simply have informed that we had them. Perhaps Lockwood mistook. You have sent to him to make sure?'

'Yes, I have. He is certain he did not.'

'Could not Hugh have mislaid them in his chamber or something?'

'Let us hope so.' Mrs Branton got up. 'It is not Hugh's fault. He is hardly more than a child.'

That evening, Mrs Branton burned Lockwood's brief answer to her message at the candle in her chamber and tried not to worry. As Isabel had said, an informer would not have stolen the things. Perhaps she would have a look in Hugh's chamber tomorrow. She did not intend to worry him by mentioning it: she should not have brought him into this in the first place. At all events, she and Isabel, and also Jenufer and Robson, would keep their eyes and ears open. And she would ask Hale when next he came if he thought she had any cause for fear.

She resisted the temptation to call Hugh in and ask him about it again when he knocked on her chamber door to say goodnight. He did that sometimes, last thing before going to sleep himself, although of course he, like the others, had bid her goodnight properly when she sent him upstairs. It was comforting somehow to hear his knock as she was sitting alone thinking it was time she went to bed. Her eldest son had always taken after herself in looks, but tonight as he stood in the candlelight, the ever-untidy tan-coloured curls falling over his forehead and those earnest eyes that could never hide anything, she had noticed that Hugh had something of his father's mouth. That, and how very young he was, and how hard he was trying to be grown up.

Mrs Branton untwisted her hand from the folds of her skirt, stood up and began to unpin her hair. It was ridiculous, the way she seemed to lose herself when something was gnawing at her – as though the faster her heart was beating and her thoughts racing, the more her body froze still. Giles was the reverse. He moved faster when he was afraid, worked faster at whatever he was doing. Talked faster too, though never loudly, and seldom about whatever was frightening him.

She lay awake some time after she had said her prayers and blown out the candle. It had perhaps been foolish to try to replace the *Rationes Decem*. Giles had acquired and read it after it first came out, and she had read parts of it with him (it was in scholars' Latin, with bits of Greek). That had been risky in the first place, and replacing the book was pushing her luck, after the magistrates had found it among various other contraband in Giles' library. And after Henry Bourne had agreed to ignore her possession of Edmund Campion's polemic along with all the rest, for the price of a token conformity neither of them had believed in even at the time. She had no explanation for that other than that he was Henry Bourne.

Certainly foolhardy, asking Lockwood for it twice. These things did not grow on trees, and when you'd got it, it was just another on your list of potential dangers. And who at the Hall was going to peruse it now? Giles would understand, had it been the kind of thing one could say in a letter, that these things did get seized, and frankly they had come out of this in credit, since no real trouble had followed.

But she remembered when Giles had brought home that book. He had shown her how the men who made it had worked in secret with what equipment they could lay hands on. They had not had any Greek letters: Campion's Greek quotations had to appear in Roman alphabet. And they had been in short supply of one or two letters, using substitutes or a different fount. Marks of shoddy work if it had been printed in any shop. Evidence of the crazy heroism of the secret printers at Stonor Park, who indeed had been caught only weeks after the author himself, their press broken, and the printers taken to prison. She and Giles had glanced at each other over the book and the baby's head – she had been rocking a wakeful child at the time, it must have been Harry or Agnes. There was in Giles' face the gravity of the prudent master and husband and father who must not take too many risks, but there was also the spark of – of what made him take some.

Hell, she had *wanted* to get that book again. It was as though the chill loneliness, the weary impatient fear which occupied more and more of her, was broken a moment. And a fire burst through, that had burned in her before she knew Giles, and which each of them had seen in the other and kindled to. She wrapped her arms close around herself, curling her legs up toward her chest, and closed her eyes.

XI

A man came to the door of the chamber and said quietly, 'someone is going to catch the Gloucester carrier now. He could take letters.'

The gaoler, who was just coming out, said, 'I am afraid he will not be able to – '

'Perhaps I could write something for him – to let them know – if he can tell me where they should be sent on from Gloucester.'

'No.' The weakened voice was insistent, and both men turned as he half-succeeded in sitting up. 'No – no need. It will only trouble them. I would not have her made anxious. I will be able to write soon enough. By the time the summer's over – '

And the other prisoner had to leave him alone, muttering as he went back to the common room, 'he could be *dead*, and he wouldn't write so as not to trouble them…'

*　　*　　*

One night in July, Hugh sat awake in bed, thinking hard. He had read the note Mother had written to Lockwood a week ago, because he had half-guessed what it was about. He had heard a couple of words between Aunt Isabel and Jenufer by which he knew that Mother had alerted the servants she trusted but told them not to frighten 'the children.' He had also heard the strain in his mother's voice as she told Aunt Isabel it was her own fault really for sending a child on such an errand. All they could do now, she had gone on to say, was wait and see if anything came of it. And pray nothing did. It was not as though Hugh would have preferred her to be angry with him, but still his ears burned.

Perhaps that was why tonight he sat here thinking of it, although it was also hot and stuffy and fretting often took the place of the sleep one could not get on such a night. Hugh screwed his eyes up tight, remembering every detail of that day.

Suddenly he leapt from the bed, his feet hitting the floor fiercely before he collected himself and began hunting for his clothes as noiselessly as he could. But he was still breathing hard.

Stephen woke up and lay listening, trying not to be afraid. Someone was in his room. He had heard footsteps and a breathing not his own. The obvious answer was that it was Grandam or someone, and he should call out and they would call back. But he was instinctively afraid. The footsteps were carefully quiet, not with the caution of someone considerately trying not to wake the sleeper, but *stealthy*. The footsteps of someone afraid to be heard. They moved around the room, their owner invisible beyond the bedcurtains. He must be feeling his way about by the patchy moonlight, looking for - what? The footsteps never headed towards the door and the rest of the house. Then they stumbled close to Stephen's linen chest. He sat up, his temples beginning to throb, listening to the muffled sounds of the chest being opened and searched. And then the stranger was close to the bed, fumbling, Stephen realised, for the light. He heard the flint and tinder struck, saw the flash of the candle-flame as it was lit. What kind of robber lit a candle? Stephen parted the bedcurtains and stared into Hugh's white-hot eyes.

For a moment Hugh stared back. Then he put down the candle which he had held over the title-page of *Rationes Decem* and leapt at Stephen. 'You *thief*.'

Stephen did not feel very safe with one of Hugh's fists in his chest pushing him backwards and the other grasping the neck of his nightshirt, so he put all his strength into regaining his balance and forced Hugh off him. 'Hugh, listen -'

'What is there to say?' Hugh's voice was strained to breaking point with pain and rage and fear. 'You thieving, treacherous Judas - '

'I like *that* from a papist.'

And then Hugh hit Stephen in earnest. He did not just hit him once but tore into him with all his might. It was daft: Stephen knew there was no denying that he was in the wrong this time round, and he had not meant those words even while he said them, but he had to defend himself or have his bones broken. So, they fought, furiously, silently, all over the room. They fought clumsily in the dim light, the only sounds whispered groans as they hit each other or stumbled against things. Some of Stephen's clothes had ended up on the floor as Hugh went through his linen chest, which did not help matters. It was Stephen who tripped, knocked the candle over and shrieked like a girl, as Hugh said afterwards.

The crash of the stool her grandson had tripped on and the shriek brought Mrs Bourne. Luckily, she and Stephen's father did not find the chamber on fire because Hugh had managed to smother the flames fairly quickly with the coverlet from the bed. But the burnt end of the bed-curtain was visible in the light from her candle, and the smell hung in the air. 'Stephen?' they heard her call as she came, and then as she opened the door, 'Hugh Branton?'

They stared back at her. Stephen had a bruise on his cheek, and Hugh a cut lip. Stephen hoped that the books were hidden by the coverlet that was now on the floor but did not dare move to make sure.

Mr Bourne appeared, pulling on his gown, and so did one of the servants. 'What the hell is going on? Hugh Branton, what on earth are you doing here?'

Neither boy answered. They stood side by side, not looking at each other and not quite looking at the grown-ups.

'Have you been fighting?'

No answer.

'How did the bed catch fire? Who did that?'

'I knocked the candle over.' Stephen muttered.

'How?'

'Tripped.'

'Who started the fight?'

Silence. Again, Mr Bourne asked, 'Hugh, why are you here? It is the middle of the night! How did you get in? Stephen? How did – ?'

Mrs Bourne, who had been looking quietly about the room, broke in. 'The window-catch has been forced. He climbed in.' She looked at Hugh. 'Do you not know that breaking and entering another man's house is a crime?'

'I will handle this, Mrs Bourne.' Mr Bourne turned to the boys. 'Stephen, did you let Hugh Branton in?'

'Sort of.'

'What were you fighting about?'

Hugh half-glanced at Stephen. But Stephen, like himself, made no reply.

'For the last time, is either of you going to tell me what happened?' The boys looked down. 'Very well. You must understand that I cannot have you two attacking each other in my house in the middle of the night, disturbing the household and causing fires.' He turned to the servant. 'Find a fresh coverlet, please. The rest can wait. I see no reason for anyone else to lose any more sleep over this.'

Mrs Bourne said, 'There are clothes all over the floor. This chamber is chaos.'

'Yes. You two will pick up everything you have scattered, and then you will come downstairs with me.'

*   *   *

A little while later, Hugh and Stephen were lying on their stomachs side by side in Stephen's bed, Hugh wearing a spare nightshirt of Stephen's. The books which had caused all the trouble were back in Stephen's linen-chest. Stephen had contrived to kick them under the bed while they were tidying up, but when they got back upstairs the chest had seemed the safest place to keep them until morning.

'Hugh, I'm sorry.' Stephen whispered.

Hugh said, 'I suppose I started the fight.'

'I knocked the candle.' Stephen replied. 'I'm sorry you got in trouble too.'

'Well, it would have been hardly fair if you had and I had not, and there's no-one to beat me at home.' Hugh said, and then laughed. 'Every cloud.'

Then there was silence, until Hugh broke it. 'You did not tell.'

'No.'

'You could have got out of that nicely by telling them what it was about – how we had those things and you took them off me.'

'Hugh, of course I did not! Why would… Oh, I'm sorry for the whole thing. But I could not see why you were so very secret about it. I guessed you were getting books from Lockwood – but I could not see why you would not just tell me. I suppose that made me angry.'

'Stephen, why do you think I was secret about it?' Hugh had raised himself on his elbows. 'It is breaking the law! It is – '

'Hugh, please do not wake them up again – '

' – people get arrested, hanged even, for trading in this stuff. Of course, you cannot go around telling people who are not – who it is not to do with.'

'But are we not friends?'

'That is not the point.' And then he said, more quietly, 'I did not tell you for the same reason you did not tell your father.'

Stephen had no answer to that. It was what he had been trying not to think all along. 'You forgive me though?' he said finally.

There was a pause. 'Yes.' Hugh whispered. 'But I do not understand what you thought you were doing.'

'Me, neither.'

∗   ∗   ∗

'So, you are not going to tell me?'

'I am sorry, madam.'

'As you please.' Mother picked up her sewing again. 'Hugh, I do not greatly care what you and your schoolmates fight about, or how you choose to make peace. But I do want to know that nothing of the sort will happen again. Ever. Is that clear?'

'Yes, madam.'

'Good grief, what did you expect me to think when you were not here this morning? And then Henry Bourne's servant arrives with a message to the effect that he found you breaking into his house and fighting like a small savage with his son! What do you think your father would have said, if he were here?'

Hugh bit his lip. 'I'm sorry.'

'I cannot - I *cannot* have you disgracing us like this.' She threaded her needle and then looked up again. 'Well, you can go.'

Hugh went. He did not give the books back to Mother straight away. It would have looked suspicious. He waited nearly a week, and then said that he had found them in his chamber. They had become mixed up with his schoolbooks and then mislaid. It was a thin story, he thought, but it seemed to work, probably because the truth was too unlikely for her to guess. The main point, which he was careful to stress, was that the books had been safe at home all the time. No-one had found about them.

XII

'Is that Lockwood from the inn?' Stephen asked.

'Could be.' Hugh said lazily. 'Where?'

'Coming into your kitchen yard.'

'Oh.' Hugh rolled over onto his stomach and found a piece of grass to chew. They were lying on the slope that rose behind the Hall's orchard, warm in the sunshine and tired from wandering up and down the stream for half an afternoon. From the hillside you could see the trees growing heavy with fruit in the orchard, the buildings of the hall, and the beds and carefully-patterned hedges of the knot garden Mrs Branton was rather proud of. Bridget, sitting just beside Hugh, should have been copying some receipts Mistress Isabel had taught her and finishing some sewing, but she had spent quite a number of afternoons when she should have been sewing rather as she was spending this one.

Hugh had gone down through the paddock to the stream a couple of days after Bridget had come back to Branton and found her there under the willow. She had some mending with her and was making a reasonably credible gesture towards working on it. Hugh had barely seen her since Corpus Christi, and suddenly found he did not know what to say to her. He felt he ought to ask after her father, but he did not know how. And then, as she replied to some awkwardly polite remark of his, Bridget looked up and caught his eye; and he saw all his own thoughts and fears looking back at him, and nothing needed to be said. When Stephen came at last, Hugh did not after all suggest going up towards the swimming place, and in the end they had stayed at the willow-flat with Bridget, doing nothing much, until it was time to go indoors. After that, Bridget was very often with Hugh and Stephen if they were hanging around Branton, sometimes bringing with her a piece of sewing or a book that she largely ignored. Now she looked up from the grass-stain she was trying to rub out of her dress and agreed that it was Lockwood.

'I wonder what he wants.' Stephen said. 'He must have come over from Merford.'

'He does sometimes.' Bridget shrugged, turning back to her grass-stain.

'What's it to you what he wants here anyway?' Hugh said with sudden sharpness.

Stephen looked from him to Bridget and said, 'Nothing. I was just saying – by God, Hugh, you aren't half –'

'What?'

'Nothing.'

*   *   *

Mistress Isabel fastened the dressing carefully, and then turned to tidy away the jars and lengths of bandage. 'The burn is nearly healed,' she told the maid. 'Mrs Branton said to keep the dressing until she can look at it tomorrow.'

'Yes, mistress.'

'Is your brother-in-law any better? Is he still taking the physic?'

'Yes. Mrs Branton said it should be taken for five days.'

'Good. Don't lift anything heavy with that hand yet, and you can tell Jenufer I said so.'

'Yes, mistress. Thank you.'

Mistress Isabel closed up the still room and went towards the parlour. Her sister was there. Mrs Branton had sat down at the table and was staring at it rather blankly. She looked up at Isabel's step, and as she did so noticed a long, white piece of half-hemmed cloth lying on the table with a needle stuck in it. 'Isabel, is this what I think it is?'

'Why, it is the stole for – Bridget was finishing it.'

'And left it out here in plain sight of anyone?'

'I'll put it away.' Isabel took the Mass vestment up and carefully folded it. 'I'm sure there's no harm done.'

Her sister pressed her fingers against her forehead. 'You do not just leave these things lying around! For God's sake – '

'What did Lockwood have to say?' Isabel asked.

Mrs Branton sighed. 'We will keep Assumption Day here, God willing.'

'I'll try to get the sewing done in time. I let Bridget help because I'd got so behindhand, but of course if you think better not...'

'Also, Will Lampley's dead.'

'That young lad from Gloucester?' Mistress Isabel crossed herself. 'God rest him. When?'

'At the summer Assizes.'

Isabel sat down. 'At the - ? What happened?'

'What do you think happened? They did what Assizes do.' Mrs Branton leaned forward against the table and ran a hand across her forehead. 'He was charged under the Act of 1581, for persuading Her Majesty's subjects to be reconciled to the Church of Rome. The Assize jury convicted him, and the judge sentenced him as a traitor.'

'For persuading?'

'That's what I said.' She was silent a moment. 'Lockwood told me that his... his friends tried very hard to get him to conform and have his life. They failed. And when he was meant to die, when he was waiting to go out, you understand, in the church nearby they rang the passing-bell. Will Lampley heard it: they told him it was for him.'

'Did they?'

'And he yet would not conform, and went out and was hanged, drawn and quartered, according to sentence. Lockwood saw it. He says Lampley bought his passage to Heaven with as much pain as have any.'

'Poor soul.' Isabel said, and 'God reward him.' Then she shook her head. 'But what made them call up Will Lampley? And why now?'

'The first should be but too evident; the second, well, we could discuss it all day.'

'Did they question him?'

'I daresay.'

Isabel looked down at the folded cloth in her hands, not saying what they were both thinking. Not only of the young glover, but of what might have led to his death, and could perhaps follow it; of what other dangerous questions were now being asked and might be answered. Mrs Branton said aloud, 'I will not have this mentioned to the children, if you please. Some of them are old enough to be frightened. Please put that stole away now.'

Bridget and Hugh ran the last part of the way after they left Stephen, and came in, racing each other, by way of the kitchen yard. They had stopped briefly at the well to splash water over their faces and made it into the great hall just as Mrs Branton was about to say grace. She looked askance at both of them as they took their places but did not seem really angry; Bridget always felt somehow that she understood why no-one would want to come inside from a summer's day as long as there was any of it left.

'Hugh and Bridget, you were both of you absent from prayers.' Mrs Branton said when they went into the parlour that evening.

'I am sorry, madam,' Hugh said. 'We did not mark how the time was passing.'

'Bridget?'

'I am sorry, madam.'

'You also left your sewing unfinished, and you did not put it away.'

'I beg pardon, madam. I'll not do it again.'

'I hope not. It is not only undutiful, but also foolishly dangerous to leave such things where they might be found by anyone. Have you forgotten what happened at Corpus Christi?'

Bridget's mouth tightened a little. 'No, madam.'

'Take care you do not. You are old enough that you ought to be able to be trusted with such things, but certainly I cannot take risks with such heedlessness.'

'No, madam. I will be careful, madam, I promise.'

'Well. We will say no more of it now.' She sat down and took out a piece of sewing rather carefully, and Hugh and Bridget waited for her to go on. At length she said, 'Ralph Hale tells me there is a good man who could come to Branton Hall next week.'

'Next week?' Hugh said.

'The fifteenth is Our Lady's Assumption, had you forgot?'

154

'And he will - we will be serving God here?'

'Of course.' She bent over her cloth and painstakingly righted a pin that had been placed crooked. 'Mr Lister's house is impossible at present, and we cannot use the old grange neither, so – so, we will keep the feast on the fifteenth here at the Hall. There will be confessions heard on the eve, and I hope the good man may stay some days.'

Bridget glanced at where the priesthole had once been, and said, 'is that safe?'

Mrs Branton threaded her needle. 'No. It is the most foolhardy thing I have ever done in my life.'

But it seemed luck was with them, for the fifteenth passed without incident; and as September drew in, there was even talk of a Mass at Michaelmas or near it. But Hugh did not think Mother really meant to take a second risk like that in six weeks. It did not help that the last news from Ralph Hale was that he had been arrested over in Worcestershire. No grave charges had been made, as far as anyone knew, but one still feared.

Late one afternoon, just after school had begun again in the autumn, Hugh went down to the willow-flat to meet Stephen. When he reached the bank, Bridget was standing at the water's edge, throwing ducks and drakes. She turned at Hugh's step. 'Hugh – I thought you were at your books.'

'Came here to meet Stephen. He has not come?'

'No. Mistress Isabel gave me some sewing, but I came down here with it.' She gestured vaguely toward a small pile of linen with a needle stuck in it heaped by the big tree, and then spun her stone at the water. 'Two – three – four – and it's sunk. Four!'

Hugh threw a pebble after Bridget's, and watched it hit the water midstream and sink.

'You have to spin it.' Bridget said. 'Look.' And she sent another disc-shaped pebble skimming across the brown ripples.

There was a cry from the other side of the stream, and both of them looked up to see Stephen running toward the opposite bank, calling urgently as he scrambled down it.

'Stephen, what's amiss? And why do you not go round by the bridge?'

Stephen was making his way across by means of the fallen tree which almost bridged the stream. He made a long step from its nearest end and came up on the edge of the willow flat. 'Hugh – Bridget – they're going to arrest Geoffrey Lockwood.'

'What? How do you know? What for?'

'I – overheard. I was in the garden and the man Hudson was talking to my father in the parlour. Someone had left the window open.'

'But you're sure?'

'Oh yes. I heard the name quite clear – and then Hudson spoke of popish books, do you see, and I knew that – '

'Yes.' said Hugh. He stared across the stream for a minute. 'When did they mean to do it?'

'Tomorrow. Before noon.'

'Tomorrow?' Hugh's voice sharpened. 'What precisely did you hear, Stephen?'

'What I said, that Lockwood – '

'Can you not remember the words?'

Stephen paused. 'Well – the man Hudson said "I'll stake my hat there is enough popish writing in that inn to..." Then my father interrupted, he asked what precisely Hudson proposed; and Hudson said, search the place tomorrow and arrest Geoffrey Lockwood.'

'That is all?'

'Then I think my father said "Very well" or something like that, and then Hudson was talking again – I did not catch it – but there was something about "bring him in by tomorrow noon." Then I came here.'

Bridget said, 'Someone should warn them.'

'And that quickly.' Hugh turned and scrambled up the bank. 'Say nothing about this to anyone, Bridget.'

'I am not a fool.'

And he disappeared. Stephen and Bridget looked at one another. 'What is he going to do?' Stephen asked.

'You know what he is going to do. Why else did you come?' And she gathered up her sewing, said farewell and left the willow-flat.

When Hugh reached the town, he did not go to the front entrance of the inn but rode round the lane to the back, where he dismounted and slipped in the sidegate, looking for Jake.

'Master Hugh! What's stirring to bring you to our backyard?'

'Jake, call your father. I have to be quick.'

Geoffrey Lockwood refused to appear ruffled by the news. He listened to Hugh's breathless explanation, and then asked him a question or two. Hugh repeated the conversation as Stephen had overheard it. The innkeeper nodded. He laughed at his wife's suggestion that he should leave home and be out of distance of their warrant by the morning. 'Nay, no need. We'll get the stuff away and they'll have no evidence. To run away is as good as write a confession. Besides, we should not make it quite so clear that we have a counter-informer.' He looked at Hugh. 'And this information is trustworthy?'

'Yes.' Hugh said.

'Well. There's over two hundred books to get away before tomorrow noon, and we cannot shift them in daylight.'

'Where will we take them?' Mrs Lockwood asked.

'That's the point needs thought. The place I've used once or twice before is no longer safe. Norton Court is too far... there's Branton Hall, if the mistress will agree.' He swung round to Hugh. 'Can you be here tonight, 'twixt twelve and one? You and any one of the Hall folk you trust.'

'I could do that.'

'Good. They'll look in vain for their papistical books this time at least. And my thanks to you – it was well done.'

Hugh reached home just before the supper hour. He went to the library and knocked. There was a kind of fear he could not have explained in the thought of telling Mother about this, but it was clearly what he ought to do. She was there with the steward Robson and the month's accounts.

'What is it, Hugh?'

'It is Geoffrey Lockwood, Mother. I think they mean to arrest him.'

'What? What has happened?'

'Someone has warned Lockwood,' Hugh began carefully. He found he did not want to name Stephen; it was easier on him, and somehow on everyone. So, he only said briefly that Lockwood wanted to move the Catholic books stored in his house before tomorrow noon, so that he would not be taken with them on the premises.

'And he wishes to move them here.' Mother said.

'I – suppose so.' Hugh said. There was a tone to her voice that he did not quite understand. Not quite fear; not quite anger; but something –

'Can we do that, madam?' Robson asked.

Mrs Branton turned. 'There is not time to think of anywhere else. Lockwood will be in grave danger if we do not. Of course, they must bring them here. And this is nonsense about you going, Hugh. You'll go to bed and stay there. Robson, you are willing to go?'

'Yes, Mrs Branton.'

'Good, then. Hugh, go and wash yourself before supper; you are covered in dust.'

*   *   *

Hugh went to bed at the usual hour as bidden, but he could not stay there. Lying awake with the curtains of his bed half-open, staring at the moonlight on the floor, he heard the door of the great chamber open late in the night. He thought he caught the faint sounds of a horse coming round from the stables, and even a voice that must be Robson's. He rolled over and tried to quell the unease that had come from nowhere. Mother and Robson would hide the books in the Hall. Lockwood would not be arrested. Stephen's part in it need not be known. It would all pass.

Two hours later he was still lying awake. Somewhere outside a couple of the cats were engaged in a border war. The bedclothes felt twisted and smothering. He thought there were sounds downstairs again, perhaps the great door opening, and then he heard a footstep going past his chamber.

Hugh got out of bed and went on tiptoe out towards the staircase. Then he ran swiftly, quietly along the gallery and crept down the parlour stairs. By the window that looked out in front of the house, a nightgowned figure was standing, peering out. She turned at his step. 'Could not you sleep either?' Bridget whispered.

Hugh came to stand beside her. 'They've come back?'

She nodded. They both stood, peering through the diamond-panes into the darkness. They could dimly see a cart before the door of the house, two men side by side behind the horses, and in the back the dark shapes of the load they had brought.

'Where's Mother?'

'That is her standing in the porch. She must have been waiting for them.'

One of the men climbed down, and a woman stepped out of the shadow of the great door to speak to him. 'Could we open the window?' Bridget said.

'They are taking them round to the stables.' Hugh whispered. 'I wonder why. I thought the hiding-holes were all in the house.'

'They found the hiding-holes last spring, Hugh.'

The cart, with three passengers now, disappeared round the corner of the house towards the stableyard, and the shadowy sound of the wheels and hooves shrank into the night. But they still stood there, the floor cold under their feet and neither of them saying a word, until Geoffrey

Lockwood drove the empty cart back past the house and away, and Mrs Branton and Robson went quietly inside.

'So. All done.' Bridget whispered. 'I am so glad we could warn them.'

'Yes.' Hugh said. Then they heard a door creak as Mrs Branton came back through the great hall and ran out of the parlour and back up to their respective bedchambers.

But Bridget did not at once slip back under the covers beside Mistress Isabel. She risked opening the shutter a crack and stood by the window a few minutes. Over there were the stables, the stream, and beyond that the road winding past Stephen's house. She found herself wondering if he were awake too.

*   *   *

Stephen lay in bed, listening to the sounds of the night outside, and wondered. He wondered what they would do about the warning he had given; hide the stuff, he guessed, but where? Perhaps Branton Hall.

But much more, he wondered why he had given it. At the time he had not thought at all. The sound of footsteps coming toward the window had made him retreat so as not to be caught listening, and then he had found himself running down to the willow-flat, thinking *what will Hugh say?* Perhaps it had been the guilty knowledge of the two volumes he had once hidden under his linen, which had come from Geoffrey Lockwood: that he knew that once he had guessed their secrets and kept them he was, whether he liked it or not – 'I am not on anyone's side,' he said aloud, and realised at once how foolish that was.

Or perhaps it had been the weariness in his father's voice as he said, 'and why do you want me to arrest Geoffrey Lockwood?' Then there had been Hudson talking, fast and quiet and insistent, and his father saying very little. And as the informer finished at last, a long silence out of which came his father's voice, with an impatience Stephen knew, 'oh, very well.' As though he were conceding a point on which he would have preferred not to yield.

Well, they would not be arresting Geoffrey Lockwood, because there was going to be nothing to arrest him for. And Hudson was going to look very foolish by the end of tomorrow's search. Stephen grinned to himself as he drew the covers around him and shut his eyes.

XIII

Hugh was late next morning, so late Stephen had not been able to wait, and Hugh had to ride hard to reach the schoolhouse before Lee called prayers. As he came in, Stephen looked as if he wanted to ask a question but said nothing. As they poured out into the schoolyard after dinner, Stephen muttered 'is all well?' and Hugh whispered, 'yes.' They found no chance to get away and talk during the whole noon hour, until it was almost time for the scholars who had gone home to eat to return and lessons to begin again. The rest would have to wait for the road home.

'Guess what has happened in town?'

Every head turned at the shout. Jack Taylor was panting into the yard, face flushed, brimming with the importance of a sensation to share. 'They have arrested Geoffrey Lockwood!'

Hugh and Stephen stopped still. Around them a babble of questions and exclamations broke out, and Taylor waited for the effect of his entrance to pass before telling his story. 'The magistrates, Mr Claydon and Mr Bourne, they came to The Raven this morning and raided the place. They were still at it when I was going home for dinner. All the guests were turned out, and Claydon made a great ado of taking the names of all those he did not know. And they turned the whole inn upside down searching it, you could hear the other side of the market.'

'Were they looking for priests?' someone said.

'No, popish books. I heard someone saying. Why, Geoffrey Lockwood's been doing a great trade in them for years, they say. Half the town going to his inn, and all the time Jesuit poison hid all over the place – '

'But did they find any?' Stephen asked.

Taylor shook his head. 'No. They must have been well hid.'

'Perhaps Branton knows where he keeps them.' That was Carter, of course.

Stephen said, 'But how? How can they arrest him if there was nothing there? You said they did not find any books.'

Jack Taylor shrugged. 'They must still think he's guilty. I suppose they cannot make charges until they find the stuff. But it is certain he had it. Why, it's all over the town...' The bell rang then, and the boys went inside, still happily scandalised as they made their way to their forms. Hugh and Stephen said nothing to each other; there was nothing to say.

The afternoon did pass. Hugh sat in his place, trying to think and not to think, occasionally catching hold of his attention and dragging it back to the schoolroom. He made mistakes he had not made since the third form, and Mr Lee reprimanded with increasing impatience. Hugh begged pardon and tried to pull himself together, and the schoolmaster turned his attention to Stephen, who, he said, seemed to have caught the contagion from his neighbour... Hugh bent his head over his book. He knew Carter was looking at him; not that he really feared there was anything behind his remark more than the usual malice, but he could not let Carter see him lose his nerve.

The Raven was quiet when Hugh and Stephen got there after school. Quieter, indeed, than it should ever have been at that hour. They did not go straight to the stables, but into the great common-room of the inn. Hugh stood awkwardly in the disordered room, Stephen silent and pale at his shoulder, and called softly.

Jake Lockwood came in. 'Master Hugh. We thought you might be along presently.'

'Is your mother here?'

He nodded. Stephen said, 'But Jake, what happened? Hugh said – '

Jake shook his head. 'Not here. Come into the back. Perhaps my mother will speak to you.'

'I meant, how came it they still arrested him? The boys at school said they had not found anything.'

'Well, they still suspect him, I suppose. Come through, if you will.'

Stephen turned to go, and Hugh followed Jake to where Mrs Lockwood was standing at a table in the great kitchen, trying to sort out what was left of the crockery. She smiled at Hugh, and thanked him for coming, but her face was strained and her eyes had the look that tears leave behind. He said awkwardly, 'I am sorry. We thought – that is we hoped – '

'Well, it would have been a good deal worse had you not come. My husband is safer than he would be if the justices had found the stuff. We are grateful.'

'I hope the books will be safe at the Hall.' Hugh said.

'They will have to be, for we've nowhere else to put them. Nay, I am sure it will be well. And do not you fear: they will ask Lockwood where they are, no doubt, but they will not find out, not from him.' She looked down at the table suddenly, and Jake put his arm about her.

Hugh asked, 'What will happen to the inn?'

Mrs Lockwood raised her head and spoke briskly again. 'Why, Jake and I will run it. We must expect to lose some custom, at least for a while.'

'We'll do well enough until my father comes home.' Jake said.

Hugh picked up his satchel. 'Goodbye. You will send to Branton Hall if there is anything we can do to help, will you not?'

Mrs Lockwood nodded. 'I shall. And – ' she smiled wryly, how Hugh did not know, 'tell Mrs Branton I am sorry not to be able to get her her *Epistle of Comfort* for the present.'

Hugh could only nod in response. At the door he turned and added, 'You will all be in our prayers, Mrs Lockwood.'

*   *   *

'Well,' Robert Claydon said. 'What do you propose to do now?'

They had eaten a delayed dinner at Henry Bourne's house, after which Claydon rather seemed to assume that he would stay to discuss the morning's business. So, they were now alone in the parlour, mellow with the late afternoon sun. Henry Bourne shrugged his shoulders.

'I cannot see what there is to be done now. We have not found evidence of seditious trading at Lockwood's inn. Of course, he remains gravely suspect, but…'

'You do not suppose we did not find the stuff because Lockwood did not have it?'

'No, as I said, we cannot cease to suspect him… I mean you were quite right this morning, that Lockwood should be committed to prison, and he must be examined again. We shall see what comes of that.'

Claydon rose and shut the parlour window. 'Bourne, my question's this: where the Hell are those popish books?

And my observation's this: Lockwood will not be telling us soon or easily.'

Henry Bourne was a little nettled. 'Perhaps my information was mistaken.'

'I doubt it. Hudson's neither a liar nor a fool.' Claydon spoke as though he knew Henry Bourne's servants better than their master himself did. 'The books were not at Lockwood's. Therefore, they must be somewhere else, unless our papist friends can conjure.'

'You want to comb the county for a few dozen superstitious tracts?'

'No, combing Branton Hall should suffice.'

Henry Bourne's eyes snapped up to meet Claydon's. 'What?'

'Bourne, it is the likeliest place for them to have been taken.' Claydon said, relentlessly matter-of-fact. 'We have the men still on call, and we can be there by nightfall.'

'This is mere supposition – '

'Then we shall be able to put that family out of our suspicions, when we have found the Hall empty.'

'I cannot consent to this!'

'No? Bourne, I know that you consider yourself a friend of Giles Branton, and I know too of the standing of that house in this parish and district. Which, by-the-by, makes Branton's disaffection all the less to be tolerated. But I hoped, Mr Bourne, that you would not allow your regard for a neighbour to weigh heavier than your duty to Her Majesty and to the realm?'

'Mr Claydon, I do not need teaching my duty. I acted properly, I think, on the information I had, and I shall continue to do so. Only I decline to act on information I do *not* have.'

'We have plenty of information that Giles Branton – and his wife – and the most part of his bloody household – are obstinate, fanatical and shameless papists!'

'I did not think *that* was under debate. Mr Claydon, I thank you for your counsel, but I do not find grounds for pursuing this affair at present. When I do, you may be assured I shall honour my duty.'

'You would refuse, then, to assist me in searching Branton for this stuff?'

'For goodness sake...' Henry Bourne turned away under the other's gaze.

Finally, Claydon spoke, as though he had carefully re-considered the question. 'Well. Perhaps I will have to proceed as I can, alone.'

'Mr Claydon, the search you propose to pursue is in *my* parish, and I am the nearest justice, who ought to deal with the matter – '

'Indeed, but if you will not – I suppose I will have to explain to our fellow-justices your reluctance to pursue information against popery that has come to your hands –

the Council at Ludlow, I may say, is much concerned at present by the spread of papistry in this part of the realm – '

'The Council of the Marches can confine its attention to the Marches. I am sworn to the keeping of the peace in Gloucestershire.'

'Gloucester county is not beyond the Council's authority, Bourne, especially when there are webs of sedition reaching into…' And then he stopped himself, as though there were a great deal more he thought better not to say. 'Look, Bourne, if you will not pursue this case – well, I intend to. With or without your goodwill.'

Henry Bourne turned back to his companion and was silent in his turn. Then he said, slowly, 'I am not sure that is a prudent thing to do.'

Claydon stared. 'How so?'

'How shall I put it? You promised we should find a seminary priest at Branton last Corpus Christi, and we did not. You proposed, I understand, that there should be stores of papistical books there last year, and we found none. Lord Chandos had us take Branton into custody anyway, the Spanish fleet being on the seas, but… Are you sure you wish to hazard another wild goose chase?'

'Bourne, this is why we cannot have them slip away this time!'

'Yet you have given neither me nor anyone else good reason to pursue the matter. One more of these unlucky failures, and people might begin to think that your – your zeal was, at best, misplaced.'

Claydon said nothing.

'After all, what happened last summer? We arrested a crop of papists, searched Mrs Branton's home, found nothing to make an indictment of – and Mrs Branton conformed. Nothing to complain of in *her* conduct there.'

The other man almost snorted. 'Conformed! I do not suppose she has the certificate to show it?'

'No, I do not know that she has certified her conformity before the bishop as yet, but then it's but a short time ago, and these things are a little cumbersome, with the affairs of the diocese in such disarray.' He almost added, Mrs Branton will conform the day Bishop Bullingham makes peace with his archdeacon, but that might have been a piece of wit too far. Claydon was still saying nothing. Henry Bourne could not tell if his desperate shots were hitting home or not, but he went on.

'It might even be said, though I would not put it so strongly myself, that Mrs Branton's credit stands higher than yours, just now. And, if you stage any more of these arduous pursuits against that house and have nothing to show them necessary to keeping Her Majesty's peace – well, as I said, people – whether in Gloucester, Ludlow or London – might wonder whether your information were to be relied on. They might even recall that you and Giles Branton have been suing the shirts off each other's backs for the last ten years, and think that – ' He stopped, as though wondering how to continue without discourtesy.

'Bourne, that has nothing to do with – '

'And such a thing would be a pity, for it would hinder you and I both, in striving to serve Her Majesty in this county.'

There was a silence, after which Claydon rose and explained that it was time he set off home. He had said scarcely ten words more by the time he rode out of Henry Bourne's gate. As he passed through Branton village and came on to the road toward Merford, a man stepped out from the side of the road. Claydon pulled up his horse.

'Hudson.'

Hudson pulled off his hat. 'Good e'en, sir. If I may ask, sir, what is the news?'

'Bourne will not play.'

'And you, sir? Shall we – ?'

Claydon narrowed his eyes, looking up the road. 'If I do this in Bourne's parish without his goodwill, I'll have to give the Lord Lieutenant a reason. And then Bourne will have to defend himself by speaking against me… But if I wait to make sure of Chandos' approving it – if that stuff *was* there, Hudson, it will not be there by this time tomorrow.'

'So, what should we do, sir?'

'Keep watching. We need to find something no-one can deny. But when we do – when we have them, we shall have them well and truly.' And then the magistrate added, more sharply, 'and the next time you have a piece of important news, make sure you come directly to me.'

XIV

Jake Lockwood came to the Hall late the next afternoon. Bridget, sewing by the parlour window, saw him walking up to the house and round towards the kitchen yard, and called to Hugh.

'Perhaps there is news of his father.'

'Perhaps.' Hugh said, with more dread than zest.

A few minutes later, they heard Jake and one of the servants come in the side-door from the courtyard. 'Mother's in the library, I think.' Hugh said.

They left the parlour. Suddenly Bridget grabbed Hugh's sleeve. 'Still-room' She whispered. 'No-one'll be there.'

She headed there at a run, and he followed her. By standing right up against the wall and listening shamelessly, one could just about hear a conversation in the library closet on the other side, where Mrs Branton often withdrew when there were Catholic affairs to be discussed. Sure enough, she and Jake Lockwood were talking quietly there now.

'There have been no charges made yet, madam,' Jake was saying. 'But he is in prison, and like to remain there.'

'Please tell your mother how sorry I am, and that if there is any more help we can give, she is to send.'

'I will, madam, thank you. And I must thank you again for – for what you have done. If they had found that stuff at the Raven, my father –'

'I could not in conscience have done aught else, Jake,' the squire's wife said crisply. 'But it is of that that I must speak with you.' There was a pause, and then Mrs Branton's voice again. 'They will not give up because they have found nothing at the Raven; and we both know, Jake, that this place will be the next to be searched. I'd put a wager Claydon will be here by the end of the week.'

'I know it is a risk you have taken, Mistress Branton.'

'And I tell you I do not begrudge it. But the point is, the stuff cannot remain here. It is a fruitless danger, for it will only be found, to all our harm.'

'I see, madam. But there is nowhere else – my father would not have brought it if –'

'I know, Jake. We cannot have them find it, and we cannot move it. So, I think we must dispose of it.'

Jake's voice was puzzled. 'But there is no time. We cannot possibly distribute the books to – And it would be far too dangerous.'

'I know.' Her voice was both sharp and low. 'I meant –'

'*We* are to destroy Catholic books?' Hugh and Bridget could not see Jake's face, but each thought he must look as astounded as they felt.

'I never thought to hear myself say that, either.' Mrs Branton said. 'But what else can be done?'

'I – I understand you.'

There was a pause. 'Look, Jake. Rashness helps no cause. What good do we do by handing our best men to the enemy? Say we must sacrifice this load, which otherwise will almost certainly be taken; we make a good chance that the work can go on again later.'

Again silence. 'I will do as you say, madam.'

'Very well. I shall speak to Robson.'

'No need. I will come tonight. It will all be gone by the morning. Good day, Mrs Branton. Thank you for your help.'

'Good day, Jake.'

They waited until Jake's footsteps trailed away, and then without quite knowing why, Hugh went after him and met him coming out of the kitchen yard.

'Jake?'

'Master Hugh.'

He did not want to admit to having listened. 'What – what is to happen now, Jake?'

'To my father? Nothing, I hope.'

Hugh tried to form a question and failed. 'Jake, I heard.'

Jake said, 'You should not have been listening,' but did not manage a frown. Hugh was suddenly aware that Jake was not many years older than he was. 'The mistress is quite right, of course. It is too dangerous here, and there is nowhere else.' He looked away. 'But – I wish all my father's trouble need not be in vain.'

Hugh was silent. Then Jake shrugged his shoulders. 'Good day to you, Master Hugh. Thank you for asking after my father.'

And he went. Hugh watched him go, and as Jake disappeared there was a step and the rustle of a skirt, and Bridget's voice said, 'it is a shame, though.'

'Mother was right. There is nowhere – ' and then, 'yes, it is.'

Bridget was scuffing at a small stone on the ground. 'I can think of a place. At least –'

'Where?'

'In the woods north of the town. There is an old cottage – I do not know how long it has been empty... Agnes and I found it last summer. We were just cutting through on our way to my parents' from the Wilsons'. They would not search it because they do not know it is there. It might be Branton land – I am not sure – but it is not anyone's house.'

Hugh was still staring in the direction Jake Lockwood had gone. 'He is coming back tonight.'

'Yes.'

'If I went after him now, I might catch him and speak with him...'

'Yes, you might.'

'We cannot tell anyone, Bridget. Mother will be furious if she finds out we were – '

'Eavesdropping. I know.'

'It does no harm to ask.'

'No.'

Hugh stood still for one more second. And then suddenly he walked away in the direction Jake had gone, and Bridget saw him break into a run as he neared the gatehouse. She did not see Hugh again until the evening, but she felt him grasp her hand as they passed out of the parlour after prayers and knew that he wanted to speak to her. Hugh went to his chamber straight after supper, saying he was tired, and she waited a few minutes and then followed.

As soon as she had shut the door behind her, he said, 'Bridget, can you get out of your chamber without waking Aunt Isabel?'

'Of course,' she said. 'What are we going to do?'

'What you said. Take the books to the old cottage in the woods. If you can remember where it is.'

'I think I can find it again.'

'It is most likely the safest thing, after all.' Hugh said. 'It is what Mother would probably have done if she had known that – '

'Yes. Are we going to tell her?'

He met her eye for a moment, and she saw in him the same sense of guilt and half-formed unease that was nagging at her. Then he looked down again and said, 'No. There is no need. I mean it would be dangerous – '

'Of course.' She said again, quickly. 'What time are we going?'

'Midnight. Home before two, I hope.'

Bridget was awake when Hugh tapped against the door. She had not been to sleep; she had been lying in bed listening to Mistress Isabel's breathing and trying to convince herself that her stomach was not tied in knots of apprehension, or that if it was there was no need, not really. She wondered if every one of Richard's days and nights were like this, and how long it took before you stopped being afraid. And she wondered what Mother and Father would say if they ever found out... but this was not tomfoolery, not playing with fire. This was different; it had to be done.

Then she heard Hugh's knock and climbed, carefully, out of bed. She dragged her gown on over her night shift, stuffed her hair into her cap and picked up her shoes – there was no time to dress properly. Hugh had not undressed at all, but he did not share his bedchamber. On tiptoe and holding their breath through the nursery; breathing slightly more easily through the long gallery; pattering quietly but quickly down the stairs and out the garden door.

Jake was in the stableyard, and just outside the gate was his cart. None of them spoke. Jake walked over into the empty stall at the far end, and they followed. They had used the lofts, of course. There was a place where new floorboards had been put in not long ago; Jake shifted some old sacking and lifted a couple of boards, and there were the books in a hollow between the new floor and the old one. It took all three of them some time to get the packages down, Jake at the hole, Hugh half-way down the ladder, and Bridget at the bottom. One of the floorboards slipped as Jake replaced it, and Bridget was sure every animal in the place stirred at the sound. Hugh went back once it was all loaded and fetched Gilian to ride home on.

And then they were trotting swiftly through the clear chill of the autumn night. Bridget, sitting beside Jake at the front of the cart, could feel her heart leaping and pounding swifter than the horses' hooves. The woods in the middle of the night were a different matter from a summer's after-noon. Bridget strained her eyes all the way for the tree that marked the place where you left the lane to find the old cot, and had begun to think she had missed it when a chance moonbeam showed the branch that hung over the path in a queer v-shape, as though it had started to arch down over it and then changed its mind. They could not get the cart any further, and there she climbed down and, with Hugh at her heels, tried to find again the path she and Agnes had traced for themselves among the trees and undergrowth. As soon as she saw the stained white of the walls, she whispered to Hugh, 'it's here' and they turned back at once, and began unloading the packs from the cart and carrying them to the cot. Her skirts were soaked with the night-time dew (please God they would dry before Mistress Isabel asked about it in the morning), and their swishing and rustling seemed loud in the darkness. The only other sounds were the breath-light movements of beasts and the calls of night-birds. Jake looked all round the place, and felt the walls and up toward the roof, and said he thought it would do. Once they had got all the books there in manageable bundles, they went back for a pair of wooden chests Jake had brought for better safe-keeping against damp and rats, and laid the books in close, packet by packet, bolting down the lids at the end.

Then they left, dragging the rot-softened door shut behind them – it was still on its hinges, although the bolts were gone. Gilian whinnied as they reached the road, and Hugh hushed her. Jake climbed into the wagon seat, brought the cart round and was gone. Bridget mounted behind Hugh and they rode home. As they left the woods she began to shiver; she did not know whether it was cold or fear or just weariness. She said nothing, but Hugh must have felt it, because he unclasped his cloak before she could stop him, reached round and draped it over her. 'You mustn't. It's my own fault for not bringing mine.'

'I'm not cold.'

'Nonsense. Same wind.'

'I'm older than you.'

'By two months,' she said, but gave in. Wrapped in the cloak, gently carried by Gilian away from the woods and towards home, Bridget ceased to shiver and realised how tired she was. She could almost have dropped her head against Hugh's shoulder and slept.

At Branton Hall, they stabled Gilian in silence and crept back upstairs. After Bridget had given him back his cloak and gone, Hugh shut his chamber door behind him, climbed into bed and tried to feel relieved. They had gone, they had got back safely, it was over. Mother and the Lockwoods and everyone were quite safe. Bridget was probably already asleep.

But there was something he had not told Bridget. It had been as they were fetching the chests from the cart while Bridget waited in the hut. He had whispered suddenly, 'do you think they'll be safe here?'

'I hope so, Master Hugh,' Jake had replied just as softly. 'Unless someone stumbles on the place by chance.'

'How long can we keep them here?'

'I do not know. To my mind they'd be safest if we could disperse them – give them to the Catholics they were meant for, that is. But we cannot. Have you got that other end, Master Hugh?'

'I think so.'

And they had gone back to the hut in silence. But as they were dragging the second chest from the cart, Hugh again found himself whispering, 'do you know who they were meant for?'

'I – some of them,' Jake said. 'But my father never wrote down things like that, and it is only this last year he'd let me have much to do with any of it.'

'But you know?'

'Master Hugh, we have agreed already it cannot be done now!' Jake only just remembered to speak under his breath. 'Why, they will be watching like hawks.'

'They may be watching you.'

Jake looked sharply at him. 'That's enough for now. Let's get this damned job done and get home in one piece.'

Hugh picked up his end of the wooden chest. 'Could you tell me when I came by in the morning?'

He still did not know quite why he had said it. It was not as though he were planning anything. But it could not be denied that as each thought rose to his lips, it was possible. One could do it if one chose. If one was careful. If Jake took him as earnest and gave him the names. But they were only thoughts. Probably he would do nothing. There was no harm done in asking. Probably it was all over, and probably the books were safe enough where they were. It was merely a pity and not a danger that they could not be dispersed.

But still Hugh could not sleep. He tried praying Aves in thanksgiving that the errand was safely done, but lying to the Blessed Virgin was even more pointless than lying to oneself.

*   *   *

Jake was not there when Hugh brought Gilian into the stables at The Raven next morning. He was alone, because

Stephen no longer came there, going to the stables at the Unicorn instead; Hugh was fairly sure that was his grandmother's doing rather than Mr Bourne's. But they still rode together, parting at the market cross and meeting there later to go home.

Just as Hugh was about to give up and leave, Jake came quickly across the courtyard and entered the stable.

'Well?' Hugh said.

'Hush. Well, I have made out this –' and he held out a paper. 'But, Master Hugh, I cannot see how we can risk this now. I tell you they'll be down like a ton of bricks if I give any cause. The danger of leaving them where they are is most likely much less...'

'They may be watching you. But not me.'

'Branton Hall's under enough suspicion too. Your parents – '

'But we need not take anything to the Hall. Listen, Jake, if you tell me, I might be able to do something if you and my mother cannot.'

'You're too young for this.'

'That's the point. Nobody'll be spying on a schoolboy.' He took the paper from Jake's hand and tucked it into his doublet. 'I'll wait a bit. Perhaps after a few weeks it will be safe to go back and – and do something. If it is not, well, we can leave it.'

'Have it as you will.' Jake sighed. 'But hearken to this, Master Hugh – you are not to do anything without you tell me first. You do not understand the dangers…'

'Yes, Jake. Goodbye.'

All day Hugh felt the paper hidden in his shirt, scratching against his skin, and tried not to wonder too much what was in it. He did not mention it to Stephen, nor even Bridget. He wanted to read it first. But when finally he was in his chamber, he found he could not. He took the thing out and looked at it, but he could not unfold it. There was a queer feeling that once he had read it there would be no going back; he would have to go through with it. And he was not sure what 'it' was. At last, he folded the paper as small as he could and hid it within the mattress of his bed. He could not do anything with it now in any case: they had agreed it was safer to wait. Perhaps the whole thing would be impossible anyway. He would wait and see.

Meanwhile he kept the paper carefully.

*   *   *

Giles Branton slammed the letter onto the table. 'Why does it never rain but it pours? Hardly a day after I manage to leave my chamber, and damned Robert Claydon chooses this moment to sue for a piece of land I cannot afford to lose.'

'Why don't you sit down?' The other man looked at the paper. 'I was wondering what had kept you. I suppose now you'll have to pay some lawyer a king's ransom to argue the matter?'

'I hope not, being a lawyer by training myself, though I ceased to practice when my older brother died... I'm sorry. It's a dispute so old it's grey in the beard, but he has certainly timed this bout of it well.'

'You'll get leave from here to go to court?'

'Oh, yes, they'll just about concede that.' He sighed. 'And yet there's more than one iron in this fire. If I win this case, I'm still a recusant convict, and Claydon's still a magistrate, with a heavy interest in my fines being demanded. Which amount to more than the worth of the land we're arguing over, and more than I can happily take out of my coffers. A seizure of my lands in lieu of payment would serve Claydon's turn very well. But, hell, I believe it would suit him best of all to get me hanged and sue for the entire forfeiture.'

His companion caught something under the bitter laughter and lowered his voice. This part of the common room was not bad for discreet talk: from it one could see any possible eavesdroppers, and yet it was less obviously clandestine than one's chamber. 'Do they have anything against you that could do that?'

'They could have. Priest-harbouring, if a witness could be persuaded. They almost caught us with a shop's worth of books a year and a half ago. We've had naught to do with that since, but – ' He looked up. 'Father, I am – I am troubled.'

The priest smiled. 'I promise I will not repeat it if you say you are afraid.'

XV

It seemed the matter of the Raven and the Catholic books was closed. Hugh did not ask Jake or Mrs Lockwood for news of Lockwood after the first couple of weeks. He knew they would all hear it if there was any. But when he saw Jake or his little brother Francis, a look would pass between them of kinship, and not only for a secret shared; it was as it had been with Bridget, after they arrested John Lister during the Corpus Christi raid. Francis was still in the Grammar, where he had started just after Easter, and Hugh used to see his rather pale little face, quiet among the whispering younger scholars near the back of the room. There was another Catholic boy who was new too, a boarder whose parents apparently lived in another county, and whose name was Westby. Hugh knew he was Catholic, because he had heard other boarders talk about how Westby was heading for trouble over not going to church. It seemed he swung between acquiescence, excuses such as sickness (never easy to pass off on Mr Lee), and the risk of outright refusal.

But Hugh did not forget what had happened at the Raven. At first it was plain fear. Geoffrey Lockwood could keep his counsel if anyone could, but what if someone found the books? What if he and Bridget, or Stephen, had been seen? As the days became weeks the fear faded, but still he could not get the memory out of his mind. The smell of the bundles of books, a mingling of ink and paper and the roads... Douai-Rheims New Testaments, Lawrence Vaux's *Catechism*, Campion's *Rationes Decem*, Southwell's *Epistle of Comfort*... Books of a kind Hugh had known all his life, and never thought – or never dared – to ask where they came from. And always, every time he went to bed, there was the knowledge of the paper hidden in the mattress. The knowledge that if he only dared, he could go back to that hidden treasure of cheap paper and do with it what it had been meant for.

There was still no letter from Hugh's father. Any number of reasons might explain that; and Hugh thought Mother was counting them, when she sat silent over her sewing, or seemed to scold the little ones without hearing herself or sighed impatiently over the papers spread out on the library table.

It was on an afternoon in early October that, as Hugh was leaving the Raven to go home, he heard his name called. Mrs Lockwood was leaning out of the window, and she was holding something. 'I had almost missed you, Master Hugh. A letter for your mother. From London.'

The direction was written rather faintly. It was only when Hugh looked at the seal that he recognised his father's hand. He thrust it into his doublet and made for his horse, calling his thanks. He waited for Stephen by the market cross as he had promised, but it was all he could do to keep his patience. As soon as the other boy came up he said, briefly, 'I have to get home fast today' and dug his heels into Gilian's sides. At home he rode up the lane calling for Wat, left him to stable Gilian, and ran into the house, shouting his news. Mother was not in the parlour, nor the library; he found her at last in the long gallery, with the children and Aunt Isabel, where some game designed to tire the smaller boys out before bedtime was being played.

'Mother! Letter –' He had to shout above the children's feet and voices. 'Letter from London!'

She stopped still in the midst of swinging Tom above her head, put him down, and took the letter without a word. Hugh heard the sigh of relief that was at the same time a choke of apprehension as she looked at the seal, and then she left the gallery. The door of the great chamber shut behind her. Hugh looked at Aunt Isabel.

'I hope all is well.'

'So, do I. It has been a long time since we heard.'

The little ones were crowding up with questions of their own. Aunt Isabel shushed them, saying their mother would tell them later. Hugh went to his own chamber to take his cloak and boots off, trailed by Harry, wanting, as ever, to know. After some time they heard Mother's door open; she called Aunt Isabel's name, and then they were both going downstairs. The boys, staring at each other across the room, could not hear any more.

'Hugh, something bad has happened. I know it has.'

'We don't *know* anything.'

'What was in the letter? Why has she called Aunt Isabel? She is afraid, you heard her!'

'Harry, shut up. I'm going to put my books away. Don't come down after me.' And he went out and down the stairs.

The door of the library was closed, but not quite completely. Hugh stood at the bottom of the stairs, his hand on the banister, unsure whether to go in or not.

'Isabel, it is not here.' Mother's voice was sharp, higher than usual.

'It must be. Here, let me look.'

Then the sound of papers being turned slowly, methodically, as Aunt Isabel looked through them. Hugh stood outside, his hand tightening over the banisters. Then Mother moving over to the library closet, searching through the coffer, someone rummaging in one of the book-presses. He stood and listened to the sounds of the search speeding up until even Isabel, it seemed, was outwardly worried. Finally, Mother's voice again. 'Is it not there either?'

'No. I am sorry, sister.'

There was silence. And then Mother spoke again, suddenly. 'Isabel –' Her voice was certainly frightened now. 'Isabel, they searched this room. You remember; you remember the mess it was in after the raid last spring. Claydon's a magistrate. He ordered the search –'

'You do not think –'

'We can look as long as we like. We will not find that paper.'

Isabel was silent a moment. 'I suppose it is possible.'

'Possible? Given Claydon, it is almost probable. And now what do I tell Giles? That I could not take care of the household, and he had better cede his case?'

'It is not your care that's at fault – not if your guess is correct, I mean. But – oh, perhaps we have not looked hard enough. Perhaps it is in your chamber?'

'Well, I will not wear myself out with looking for evidences Claydon has stolen.'

Aunt Isabel spoke again. 'Are not some of his deeds and papers in Gloucester?'

'Yes, they are still in the keeping of Casham, who helped us with that case at *nisi prius,* last Assizes but two. But Giles says clearly that this one is at home.'

'In any case, Casham may be able to advise. Can we write to him?'

'No, I think, if need be, I will go myself.'

'You'll have to get Bourne's licence for that, will you not?'

'Yes. Yes, thanks to that same damn raid. Well, I'll get it. I can send to him at once.'

'Very well. You have the other papers Mr Branton wanted? Come, there is nothing more we can do at present.'

And as Aunt Isabel, behind the door, rose and shook out her skirts, Hugh ran forward and knocked on it before it could open. 'Mother, may I come in? I need to put my books away.'

'Yes, Hugh.' He replaced his books silently, unable to frame a suitable question. Mother watched him but said nothing. He did not go upstairs again in case Harry was waiting. Instead, having seen Mother head toward the still-room and Aunt Isabel back up to the nursery, he wandered through the corridor to the parlour, wondering if Bridget were there – he had not seen her upstairs.

She was there. He saw her as soon as he opened the door, though she was not curled into the windowsill with a book or her sewing, but on her knees beside it, head resting on the edge. She glanced up at his step.

'Oh – I am sorry.'

Bridget stood up. 'I have just done.' She wound her rosary beads into a little knot as she spoke and tucked them into her bodice. 'I thought I would tell my beads while I had the chance… I have neglected them of late.'

Hugh said, 'there's a letter from my father. I brought it home just now.'

'Oh good! At last. He – is well?'

'I do not know; Mother has not said anything… but she is worried.'

'And you are worried, too, Hugh.'

'Well, yes.'

'Why do not you ask her what is wrong?'

'She will tell us if she wants to.'

Bridget nodded. 'Well, there's been precious little news for my mother either, if 'tis any comfort. But what there is is good, I suppose.'

'Is it?'

'There have been no charges laid, is about the sum.' She sighed. 'It all seems to be happening to everyone, does it not? And we thought we had survived pretty well, after last year and the Spaniards and everything. How do the Lockwoods?'

Hugh said only, 'I think as well as anyone can expect.'

Mother spent most of the evening in the library. She told them only briefly that Father had sent a letter, that he was well and sent them all his love, that she was going to Gloucester on business tomorrow, and they were all under special instructions to behave themselves in her absence. On his way to bed, Hugh knocked on her door, thinking he must bid goodnight at least. But when she had blessed him, he said, 'Mother, was there bad news?'

She said, 'Why do you think so?'

'We – we were all grown worried; he had not written for so long.'

'He has been sick.'

'Oh.'

'He did not want to write until he was mending again,' she added, 'for fear of troubling me.'

'Why must you go to Gloucester?'

Mother sighed. 'There are some papers your father wants in London. There is a law-case.'

'Law-case?'

'To do with some land – a dispute about some land. Don't look like that, my darling!' She held him close for a moment. 'And now go to bed.' She smoothed her hand across his forehead. 'That ancient look does not belong on your face.'

*   *   *

All the next day Hugh was angry. At Claydon, and what he might have done. Angry because he had been able to do it. He was no longer afraid – in all honesty, some adult wrangle over who owned a couple of fields or whatever it might be did not interest him. It was only the sense that Claydon could cheat and his father should be playing, and know he was playing, against loaded dice.

But that was not all of it. There was another anger: that he – that all of them – should be so easily worried. That they should walk in fear of such men, and live to avoid their wrath. Hugh was furiously angry with himself, because he did not dare to do things that should be done.

It was all he could do to be civil to Stephen on the way home, not to let the waves of anger break in unjust words. By the time he reached Branton Hall, he had decided to find Bridget and tell her about the paper Jake Lockwood had written. Further than that he did not try to think.

But she was in the nursery with Agnes, trying to get all the little ones washed for supper. When she saw Hugh, she only called out that Harry was in the library with his grammar – or at least that Mistress Isabel had sent him there. Hugh went and found Harry unusually docile; perhaps he had taken Mother's injunctions to heart. Afterwards there was no time to talk either, for Bridget was taken up with the children while Aunt Isabel oversaw the supper. Hugh muttered as they went into the hall that he wanted to talk to her, but they spent the evening sitting in the parlour, and he could not find any excuse to get away. When at last they went to bed, he did not undress at once, hoping she would come. He said prayers, and when he had finished sat there, holding the paper in his hand, wondering...

The clock had just struck ten when he heard the knock at his door, very quiet. When he opened it, she was standing there, in her gown but with her hair falling loose out of her nightcap and her feet bare. He let her in, glancing past her as he did so, but there was no sign that anyone had seen. When he had shut the door, she said, 'I am sorry – Mistress Isabel did not sleep for hours... I think she is anxious too, about whatever it is Mrs Branton has gone to Gloucester over. What is it, Hugh?'

He held out the paper. 'When we hid those books, I asked Jake Lockwood how long we could leave them there… and what was meant to happen to them. And –'

'And he gave you this? Oh Hugh, I am so glad.' She put out her hand, apparently ready to seize the letter and devour the contents forthwith.

'Yes.' Hugh took the paper over to the table, where the candle stood. 'He said it was impossible to do anything just then, and the books were better left in the hiding-place, but we were agreed it would be safest in the long run if we could disperse them. So, I thought if I waited a bit…'

'Come, Hugh, read it.'

And they read it, Bridget looking over his shoulder. Names. A list of names… 'John Crowe a pedlar sometimes brings books and sometimes takes others on… Mrs Katherine Wilson, the packet of Vaux catechism and the Magdalen's tears, she has a servant that she sends… Fowler servant at Norton Court the three packets marked with a holly leaf drawn, for his master… Southwell's epistle of Comfort for Mrs Branton and one of the same for Norton Court… the New Testament, these: Mrs Wilson, Mrs Lister (by her servant Joan)…'

Hugh and Bridget looked at each other. 'What do we do?' he said.

'Well, we go back to the hiding-place, find the books, and give them to the people on the list.'

'How? When? Do we even know them all?'

'Most of them, I think.'

Hugh looked back at the paper. 'Crowe must be the pedlar Jake brought to Mass once. Remember him? Dark hair, and big hands. But how can we know when he is like to come?'

'Wait. There is more, here... "Crowe knows which books are for him to take, we expect him at The Raven before the end of November, Fowler also. The others my father makes shift to meet in course of business." There you are.'

Hugh said, 'I suppose we can try.'

'We ought to destroy the paper.' Bridget said.

Hugh looked up, suddenly aware of how long he had already kept it. 'Tonight. We must have it by heart.'

She took the paper from him. 'Suppose I remember the first half and you the second, then we'll have it between us. And then we can burn it.'

So, they did that, poring over the sheet with a candle, hearing each other in whispers by turns. Hugh sat on the stool, and Bridget perched on the edge of the bed, knees drawn up to her chin and bare feet tucked under her long skirts; she sat very still, her face frowning a little in con-centration, moving only when she leaned forward to take the paper from him or pass it back, or reached up to tuck back a lock of hair which had slipped forward. She was quietly intent on the task in hand, as though it were a schoolroom lesson.

Above their own whispered words, Hugh's ears were straining for any sound which might mean they were caught. They could not explain about Jake's letter to Mother, Aunt Isabel or indeed anyone... He did not really want to think clearly about why, but of course they could not. Once he saw Bridget, sitting on his bed, glance up sharply as though she too were listening. As she caught Hugh's eye, she looked back down at the paper in her hand, flushing a little. Neither of them spoke at all about what would be said if anyone found her in his chamber.

At last Bridget left and went back to bed, and Hugh crept down to the kitchen fire with the precious, perilous paper curled in his hand. As he watched it burn, he seemed to feel a flame rise within himself: the ugly smouldering rage he had felt had broken into fire, dancing and golden, hot and glowing with fierce light.

And he remembered something else Jake had said. Do not do anything without you tell me first. But he already had; he had spoken to Bridget. Hugh knelt beside the fire. Perhaps he should ask Jake before... but they were watching the Raven. No-one was watching Hugh Branton or Bridget Lister. It was safer this way. And Jake would not forbid it if he did not know.

There was a knot in his stomach as he crept back up to his room, but he had expected that. After all it was only a little thing. A few books, and then the hut would be safely empty, and it would be over. Hugh put on his nightshirt and, exhausted as he was, went to sleep.

*   *   *

Some of it proved easy enough. Bridget pointed out that most of the people on the list came to Mass either at Branton Hall or at the Listers', and there was a priest due at Branton Hall within two days. So, they had only to fetch the named books and give them to him to distribute. Packets of several books might be more difficult. Hugh could not think how he was to get them to the Wilsons', or to Norton Court. And if the priest's coming solved part of the problem, it left very little time: the errand would have to be done at once.

The next night, Hugh crept out of bed and downstairs in stockinged feet as he had done with Bridget nearly a month before. He had to take two panniers from the stables – last time they had gone to the old cot laden and left empty-handed. The road to the woods he knew well enough, though it was harder going without a lantern. All the way along the track he was muttering what Bridget had told him as to how he would find the hut. Even under the trees he did not quite dare show a light, although when he thought about it he realised that if anyone did come this way Gilian's hoofbeats would betray them, and being lanternless would merely be another thing to explain. Once in the cot, he fumbled to light the lantern, its wavering beams when they finally shone sending wood mice scurrying and alarming a sleeping bird. The bolts seemed to screech rather than squeak as he opened the chests, but who was there to hear? The mice could hardly inform on him. He worked as quickly as possible, glancing over his shoulder at every movement of the lantern-beams as though it might be a shadow appearing. Once he heard a movement outside the door and froze, but nothing followed. He supposed it was some animal.

He found the packet of New Testaments first, extracted the copies he wanted, fumbled through the rest of the hoard muttering under his breath the list of titles he had memorised. When he had done, the packs were heavy to carry; Hugh dropped them to rest his arms as he stopped on the way back to the road to check his path. He looked back at the hut, a dim shape in the darkness, with its moss-grown thatch straggling over the eaves. He could just make out the dark patch of the door through the brambles and undergrowth which surrounded the place, seemingly unvisited for years... Gilian was stamping her feet as he came up; he hushed her softly, and as he mounted felt the horse's muscles taut beneath him. But, he thought wryly, she could scarcely have been more frightened tethered by the road than he had been in the old cot.

He had meant to come in quietly, without waking anyone, but when he reached the stables Bridget was there, wrapped in her cloak.

'What are you doing here?'

'I could not sleep. I saw you coming from the window and came down. You have got them then?'

'Yes.' He began unstrapping one of the panniers while she set to work on the other.

'Where shall we keep them until tomorrow? Your chamber?'

'I had thought so.' He was putting away Gilian's bridle, patting her gently, thinking how fortunate it was that she could not talk.

'What are you going to tell the – the good man?'

Hugh gave the mare a final pat. 'I think just that they came by a Catholic near here... He can tell those who come that he has the books, and those who want to can take one. I have brought a fair few. There are dozens in there. I mean, Jake did not say we could only give them to people he named, and it will save having to go through the business with the list.'

'What about paying for them?'

'Let people hand whatever they give to the good man and I'll get it to Jake.' That was the only thing to do; and as the errand would be safely done by then, Jake would hardly mind.

'Does Jake know about this?' Bridget asked.

'He gave me the paper,' Hugh said. And then, 'No, he does not know that I went out tonight.'

Bridget said, 'Oh. Perhaps that was safest.'

Between them they got the packs inside and upstairs. Hugh was yawning by the time they had finished hiding the books at the bottom of his linen-chest. 'I suppose I had best put the packs back in the stable before they are missed.'

'You go to bed. I'll see to it.' Bridget said. And she picked them up and went. As he looked after her, she put her head back round the half-closed door to say goodnight. Her face was serious, even grave; but in the candlelight her eyes were dancing.

*   *   *

Bridget took off one of her shoes, moved it against the door so that she would have warning if anyone tried to come in, and carefully opened the pannier. It was All Hallows Eve, and she was at home in Merford. Home was pleasanter than it had been for some time, because Father was back and Mother was smiling again. He had come home quietly last week, saying only that no charges about the priest-harbouring had been made in the end, and after all not even Claydon could claim that John Lister was an obstinate recusant. He had said nothing about whether they would have priests in the house again, but he had not turned away the one who had arrived in Merford yesterday. And now Bridget had come home for a day or two, and there was to be Mass tomorrow morning.

She took out her night shift and her comb, and then, glancing once more at the door, she lifted out the packet of books, unwrapped it and counted them once again. She knew what she was going to do. Hugh had managed it three weeks ago at the Hall, and she herself had given two other books to Mrs Wilson two weeks ago without anyone guessing anything. She would give them to the priest in the morning and explain that they came from the Lockwoods; that a few of the books had been salvaged before the raid. That was all anyone need know she knew. Then Hugh would pass the money for all the books to Jake Lockwood quietly, and that would be that. Bridget pushed the books back into the bag, stowed the bag in her clothes chest, and went down for supper.

She went up to the garret early next morning. Father was there with the priest, preparing the room for Mass. Bridget walked over. 'Father –' They both turned, and she said, 'I – I wanted to give you these.'

Her father looked at the books, and then back at her, sharply. 'How on earth did you come by these, Bridget?'

The priest said, 'do you know who they are for?'

'I think they are for – the people who come to Mass,' she said, as innocent as she could make it.

'But where did you get them from?' Father would not let it be.

'The Brantons had them from Lockwood's, I think. They must have managed to save a few from the raid, you know.' And she looked up and met his eye. 'It was not wrong to bring them, was it?'

'No – no,' her father said. 'But not a word of this to any-one, you understand? And if you hear any more of this sort of thing, ask me about it.'

'No, sir. Yes, of course sir.' And she had done it. He had believed her. He and Mother would not be worried, and no-one need know that she knew any more.

She had done it. She had lied to him.

*   *   *

He looked up from the letter and stared blankly at the damp-stained plaster on the wall opposite. The door creaked open, and the other occupant of the chamber returned. 'Something amiss, Branton?'

But Giles Branton did not seem to hear. He turned his eyes back to the page. It was an old letter, it had been delayed; she had not read his about the lawsuit when she wrote this over six weeks ago. '...Lockwood's apprehension has troubled his family. Nothing being discovered in his house, we are in hope he will not be charged, though certainly he will be examined of these matters…' The carefully brief, non-committal sentences, laden with unspoken fear. And it must be replied to in the same way. He could not write the questions he needed to ask, could not commit to paper the warnings he wanted to give. 'I need to go home,' he said aloud.

His companion grinned drily. 'Don't we all?'

XVI

As far as Stephen knew, nothing more had happened about the popish books Geoffrey Lockwood had been arrested for not having in his house. Hugh and Bridget had managed to hide them somewhere, and no-one could be charged with their possession. The matter had really ended there.

Except that it had not. He was sure it had not, though he could not have said why. Hugh did not say anything more about it, and there was no reason why, when he was late meeting Stephen on the way to school and struggled to keep awake all day it should mean any more than that he had stayed up later than usual the night before, or at the most had gone to Mass that morning. Or why, when Stephen came down to the willow-flat once and found him in earnest conference with Bridget, which they broke off when they saw Stephen, it should have aught to do with unlawful books. And when, one day at the beginning of November, he asked Hugh casually if they would meet at the market cross, and Hugh said no, wait for him at the Unicorn, he would come there, it was certainly not usual; but again, there was more than one possible reason for it.

Stephen had already brought his horse round from the stables to the main yard of the inn to wait when, peering into the gathering dusk, he saw Hugh riding up on Gilian. As he reached the entrance to the Unicorn he dismounted. But he did not come straight up to Stephen; he loitered under the archway for a few seconds as though he were looking for someone. And sure enough, a man – a servant from his clothes – came out of a side door. Hugh reached into the saddlebag slung by his horse's side and gave the man a packet. Then the man touched his cap and went back inside, and Hugh waved to Stephen, calling cheerfully.

Stephen did not say anything; he did not know what to say. But there were two burning questions in his mind. The first was why Hugh would not tell him, given that Stephen was hardly in a position to give him away after what he – Stephen – had done in September, and the second was how on earth he had not noticed this morning that Hugh had had more than his school satchel with him.

*   *   *

Hugh came into the Raven's stable and saw Jake talking to a small, dark man who was unharnessing a packhorse. The man turned his head sharply at Hugh's step. Jake said, 'Good morrow, Master Hugh,' and to the dark man, 'he's safe.'

Hugh led Gilian into the stall next to the man's packhorse, and as he came closer recognised him. Jake had brought him to Mass once: he was the pedlar called John Crowe.

'So,' Jake said. 'There is nothing we can do at present.'

'Aye. I shall pray for your father... but the goods were not found?'

'They were not. Thanks in no small part to this young gentleman.' And Jake smiled at Hugh. 'But I must go; we should not talk thus too long.'

He went. Hugh began unharnessing Gilian, and John Crowe unhurriedly rubbed down his horse. 'I am Hugh Branton,' Hugh said at last.

The pedlar looked up. 'Are you so?'

'Are you – you are the pedlar who sometimes brings books here and takes others on, are you not?'

'Why would you think so?'

'I have seen you at Mass. I have heard your name from Jake – I mean in secret.'

'What would you have to say to me, if I were?'

Hugh hesitated. He did not want to drag the Raven back into it; Jake was probably right about it being watched. 'Would you meet me at the Unicorn this afternoon?'

The man did not answer. He looked at Hugh for a long time, with a gaze so wary and so piercing it was almost frightening. Hugh met his eyes for as long as he could, and then turned away, muttering that it was not safe to talk any more now. He kept wondering all day why he had done it. Perhaps he had been flushed with his success in recognising Sir Christopher's man, Fowler, and getting the packets marked for Norton Court to him last week; perhaps he was just foolhardy.

He was cleverer this time. Rather than ask Stephen to meet him at the Unicorn, he said nothing, but raced back to the Raven, fetched Gilian, and waited at the edge of the market. When he saw Stephen ride up, he dodged round and rode back to the Unicorn almost sure Stephen had not seen him. He left Gilian in the yard and went straight to the stables, slipping in when no-one was looking, and sure enough the pedlar was there, in one of the stalls at the far end apparently tending his horse. Hugh went over. 'John Crowe?'

'Aye.' The man straightened and looked at him, expressionless. 'What have you to tell me?'

Hugh hesitated. 'Only that – I know where the stuff is – if you want to fetch it.'

'And you could tell me?'

'Meet me at the crossroads. Where the left fork goes into the woods north of the town. You know the place?'

'Aye. When?'

'An hour before midnight.'

'Very well.'

Hugh turned to go. And Crowe said, 'one thing, lad –'

'Yes?'

'You'd best learn not to give out your name so easily.'

It was not until Hugh was halfway to the door that he saw Stephen standing in the doorway, one hand on his horse's bridle, looking at him.

They were well out of the town and on the road home, the horses picking their way slowly in the dark, before either of them spoke about it. Then Stephen said, 'Hugh, if you are going to carry on popish plotting at the Unicorn, you had better be a little more careful.'

Hugh turned, unable to find a suitable reply. Stephen went on. 'That man Hudson was watching when you went into the stable after the pedlar. And he started crossing the yard towards the door.'

'Stephen – '

'I don't know if he would have gone in, but when I went and stood in the doorway he stopped. I suppose he could not have slipped in quietly with me there.'

Hugh was silent after that, and so Stephen knew he had understood. But he could not quite leave it there.

'Hugh – what kind of books are they? That Lockwood was hiding. That that pedlar…'

'Stephen, speak softer for heaven's sake. Catholic books, of course.'

'The law forbids the keeping and selling of seditious books.'

'It also forbids the Mass, because that is *seditious*.' Hugh said with contempt. 'Oh, come, Stephen. Remember the ones you had from me? Not precisely stirring rebellion, were they?'

'No, but that does not mean –'

'The New Testament in English. The *Magdalen's tears*. Mass books. The *Christian Directory* – '

'For God's sake, Robson Persons wrote that!'

'So?'

'Oh, come. That Jesuit's guilty of enough sedition to be hanged six times over. He just does it outside England.'

'There's no sedition in the *Christian Directory*.'

'But – can you part the two things? The men who make these books, what kind of men are they? *Can* you be a Papist – a Catholic – and not be caught up in – '

'Yes.' Hugh said curtly, staring straight ahead into the dark. 'Or you could if the damned laws would allow it.'

They rode the rest of the way home in silence, neither of them quite sure whether what had been said amounted to a quarrel. When Stephen came in, Grandmother and Father were talking in the parlour. He did not mean to listen, but Grandam's words as he passed the door stopped him. 'Do you know where Stephen is? He should be home by this.'

'No,' came his father's reply. 'Perhaps he is over at the Hall. It is not very late as yet.'

'I'll wager he's at the Hall,' Grandam said, a frown in her voice. 'He is at the Hall far too often.'

'What do you mean?' But Father knew what she meant, and so did Stephen. And he felt something like anger rise inside him, on behalf of Hugh and Bridget and all of them, and yet at the same time knew that his grandmother's fears were perfectly well-founded.

'I mean that I would not have him influenced to his harm,' Grandmother was saying quietly.

'For heaven's sake, Mother, they are our nearest neighbours. And for myself, I would count Giles Branton among my friends rather than my enemies.'

'I wonder if he returns the compliment,' Grandam said drily.

'Well, you'll never stop a pair of boys playing together, no more now than you could when –'

'You may not remember my father, but I will never forget him.'

And then there was a silence. A silence heavy with unease on his father's part and grief on his grandmother's. Stephen held his breath, suddenly aware that he should not have been listening and unable to creep away now. Grandam spoke again.

'It was this month. This month, two-and-thirty years since, that he was arrested in the night on charges of heresy, and my mother never saw him again. Your father found out that he had died in prison three weeks after it happened, and I told that news to my mother, here in this room. And yet that was easier to tell than what might have come to pass – that he had gone, like some of his friends, to the stake and the fire.'

Again the silence, filled with a grief so old and so deep that it thickened the air as you breathed. Father spoke again.

'That was not the fault of the Brantons.'

'That is not what I am saying, and you know it. He died for the sake of the Gospel's truth. Let that be the measure, and do not have your son slip away from it without even knowing.'

Father said, 'I do not think you have talked much with Stephen of this – I mean of your father's death.'

'I am not minded to, at present.'

'Why is that?'

'It is the Gospel I would have him keep faith with, not his great-grandfather's memory; God I would have him fear, not wounding me.'

Stephen heard his father stand and cross the room to her. 'Mother, I am sure you make too much of a small matter. There'll be no slipping. You have taught him too well for that.'

Stephen managed to shrink into the shadows just as his father opened the door and came out. As soon as the coast was clear he fled to his chamber and closed the door. He slipped to the floor beside the bed and sat there for a long time, his grandmother's words echoing in his ears, clashing against other words and other thoughts which yet would not quite be drowned out. Her words and her grief accusing Hugh and everything he did; accusing him, Stephen, and everything he quietly connived at. And before his closed eyes, suddenly, inescapably, there was a memory of which he had never told Hugh or Bridget or anyone. A memory he had carefully buried, but which needed no digging for.

It was summer, the summer after the Queen of Scots had been executed at Fotheringhay. The Spanish fleet came the year after, but it was on the horizon and in the news on the streets of Gloucester. The Assizes were happening. Stephen would not usually have been anywhere near the city at that time, and his father not always. But this year some kinsmen of his father's were to be in Gloucester a few days, Father had to see them over some business, and Grandam wanted to see them, so in the end they all three took lodgings in Gloucester when Mr Bourne went up to attend the Assizes.

Stephen did not know exactly how it all happened. He had spent a lot of time playing with the cousins from Worcester, often through the streets and market of the city, or down at the docks watching the boats come up the river. Grandmother did not, he felt, entirely approve of this, or of the cousins. Or at least not of Matthew and Jeremy: their parents were undeniably godly but could not always swear to what their sons were up to. Stephen enjoyed watching the judges come in for the Assizes and felt rather proud to see (and have the others see) his father among the county justices. They did not crowd into the church to hear the Assize sermon but wandered over towards the Boothall where preparations for the sitting of the judges were being finished. Matthew rather wanted to watch the court in session, but Jeremy said no, it would be dull and Matthew knew it. 'When you're grown and a lawyer you can have all the trials you want.' They asked Stephen where and when the hangings would be, but he did not know and felt ignorant in his own county.

It was Jeremy who picked up the gossip next day about the priest. There was a popish priest in the gaol right now, due for trial. Matthew explained that as he was a papist priest, that would be a treason trial and a treason execution. The thieves would be hanged, but the priest would be cut down alive and drawn and quartered. Also, they'd drag him to the gallows tied on a hurdle, they would not have him walk with the felons. Stephen mentioned casually that of course they had hanged and quartered a priest in Gloucester last year as well, but when they asked had he seen it he had to say no. Matthew explained that they could convict any papist priest of treason, as soon as they had proof he was a priest, the new Act of '84 said that. 'And high time too,' he added in the voice people used when they were quoting their elders (most likely Matthew's father, Stephen thought).

Then Jeremy said there were some people who thought that law was over-harsh, and then the talk went to the Spaniards, and the Queen of Scots' plot, which 'just proved it,' and then the Dutch war, and why we must win it, and

Stephen pointed out the place where Bishop Hooper had been burnt to death for the Gospel thirty years ago in Queen Mary's reign, and somewhere along the line the French and the massacre of St Bartholomew were mentioned too. They had been kicking about the town for much of the morning, but they had missed seeing the judges arrive at the Boothall for the second day of the Assizes. In the afternoon, Jeremy was agitating to go and watch the prisoners leaving at the end, and near the Boothall they found other boys just out of school, waiting for much the same reason. Matthew impressed everyone with his description of a regiment he had once seen embarking for Flanders. And then again it was the papists, and the particular papist on trial in the Boothall now. A popish priest, one of those who would fight for the pope and the Spanish when they came, who taught their most trusted friends that the Queen ought to be killed, who said Masses, mumming in silken robes, worshipping their wheaten god. This priest had been mumbling his Masses all over Gloucestershire, no-one knew all the places. 'Could have been anywhere,' Jeremy said. 'Any papist's house at least.' Stephen thought with a sudden jolt that that meant the man could have been in Hugh Branton's house. But he did not want to think of Hugh – with whom he played and fought and rode to school – as part of all this.

As they chattered, a few men joined the talk. One seemed to know quite a bit about the Assizes, and the priest. He said when they pressed questions that yes, he did know the man. In fact, he had helped to take him. Matthew's eyes widened, and the questions were beginning to pour out, but the man said quietly that he was sorry, but perhaps he had better not say any more. Matthew and the other boys fell silent at once and looked even more impressed. Jeremy ventured, 'he's in there now, is he not?'

'Aye. The trial's well over, but they're all in there – all the guilty prisoners – for the sentencing. You'll see them come out.'

Another man said, 'The priest – his name is Rowsham, by the way – will be the one walking last, with the double guard. They're devious, seminarists. Not easy to catch, nor to keep when you've caught 'em. And dangerous, too, God knows.'

'And this was as devious as any,' added the first man, 'twas no easy matter catching up with him, that I may tell you. Obstinate, too. They've done their best to bring him to conform, and even after today they might get him a pardon if he would but have done with popery. But I think he'll rather spit at the Queen's clemency and die.'

His companion had turned away slightly and was looking down the road. Now he said, 'if you want to see better, come along a little way where there's less of a crowd. You'll get a good view of the whole lot as they come towards us.'

Matthew saw what he meant at once. 'Yes, let's.' And he followed the man eagerly, the other boys falling in behind them. As they stood at the corner where a lane ran out into the high street, sweating in the heat and unpleasantly aware of the dungheap just near them, waiting impatiently for the spectacle to appear, one of the men – the one who had helped take the priest – said, 'it's not a pretty business, bringing a traitor to justice. But this country's the safer without men like him.'

And then the prisoners came. There was a little group of felons who had received the benefit and been branded, who came forth free men, but with fresh marks on their ears or thumbs which you could see as they drew closer and passed by. Then there was a weary column of ten men and four women, all with irons on their feet, chained in pairs, and surrounded by guards. They were not all to die. Some would be vagrants to be whipped or convicted only of petty larceny and the like. But some were marked for the gallows, and Stephen thought you could tell which ones from the look in their eyes – a look as though they were watching everything from a great distance and did not belong here anymore. And behind the column, the priest. He was walking shackled, like the others, and four guards surrounded him. He was a little man, with grey in his hair, and he walked with a limp, and was slightly hunchbacked – his right shoulder was distinctly higher than his left. He walked staring straight ahead, looking neither to right nor left, as though he were setting his mind very hard on some all-important task.

The prisoners drew almost level with the boys. The priest was going to pass very close to them. Stephen stared, fascinated, thinking of everything he and Matthew and Jeremy had been talking about today, grappling with the disjunction between those things and the appearance of this little grey-haired hunchback who represented them.

'Whoreson papist!' One of the men had shouted the words. The priest did not turn his head, but for a moment his face twitched, a fleeting expression of – of something like contempt.

'Papist traitor!' That was Matthew's voice. And the cries began to fill the air, all of them shouting.

'Bloody papist.'

'Traitor-priest.'

'Bloody Massing-priest.'

'Whoring Spanish spy.'

'Damned murdering papist.'

'Traitor!' Stephen shouted, crying out in protest at this man, who had brought all of *that* – burnings and Inquisitions and massacres and wars and plots – right here into Gloucester high street, and then dared to walk calmly along looking so harmless, *despising* the anger of the men who had brought him to justice.

One of the boys had stepped out and was walking in front of the papist, mimicking his limp and his hunchback and his shambling, shackled gait, and doing it with such liveliness that now they were all laughing, even the guards surrounding the priest smiling.

'Filth!' It was the man, the one who had shown them to the corner, again. 'Papist turd!'

'Filthy turd!' And then someone, either the man or Matthew, had reached out to the dungheap beside them, scooped up a handful of it, and thrown it at the priest. 'Eat shit, papist.'

The man flinched as the dung struck his shoulder. And then they were all doing it, reaching out and throwing as the shackled prisoner drew close, walking too slowly to dodge them. One of the guards stepped back to avoid being struck by the pungent missiles, while the one on the other side gripped the prisoner's arm. The papist had turned his head away to protect his face. Cries and filth and laughter and anger filled the air and filled Stephen's head.

And then as he drew level with the boys swarming round the dungheap, the priest turned his head towards them, and his eye somehow caught Stephen's full on, as the fistful of muck left the boy's hand. Stephen froze still, his eyes staring, his breath stopped, winded as if from a blow by the age of the face, and by the sheer absence of any answering hate.

The second passed, the papist ducked his head to avoid Stephen's handful of dung and failed to, he had walked on limping between his guards, the dung making filthy streaks as it slid and dripped from his cheek. The cries and the shit followed him a little way, and then faded. The boys began to scatter. The men who had led them to the dungheap had gone their way. Jeremy kept on talking, but Matthew had turned rather quiet, and seemed to avoid Stephen's eye even as Stephen avoided his.

The grown-ups had all heard about the trials, of course. Matthew's and Jeremy's father was rather sharp about the papist, and certainly pleased that the judges were determined 'to see it through for once.' Grandam did not say much, except that they must be sure to pray for that man, more than for all the other felons.

Matthew's father said that *that man* had proved himself a pernicious, obstinate papist, and they had best hang him and have done. Even if he did offer to conform, which he would not.

'You speak beyond your knowledge,' Grandam said. 'It could be that God has willed to place him among the elect, as he has done before with the greatest of sinners. His soul may still be pardoned, even if his life is not.'

'I have heard the ministers have been with him before this, and got no very good welcome,' Stephen's father said.

'Then I hope they will try again! There are many of his servants whom God does not call to the vineyard until the eleventh hour.'

Stephen glanced at his grandmother, and knew that after they all departed for bed, Grandam would be on her knees in her chamber praying for that priest. And somehow he knew, too, that at this moment the popish priest was on his knees in the gaol praying for – well, if not Grandmother by name, people like her. And for people like him, Stephen. He picked up his knife and looked at his food. He had washed his hands before supper, of course, but they felt dirty all the rest of that day, and for many days afterwards.

Stephen raised his head and looked round the darkened chamber. He gave up trying to arbitrate the war that filled his mind, of hate against hate, pain against pain, love against love. He did know, at least in part, why he was keeping Hugh's secrets. He did not know whether that made it right. But of two things he was certain: if he did what by law he ought, he would never be able to look Hugh or Bridget in the face again, and his father would be utterly wretched.

*   *   *

Hugh told Bridget about his meeting with Crowe, and when he got back at last he was not surprised to find her waiting.

'You're earlier than you were the last time,' she said.

He nodded, taking off his shoes as she closed the side door quietly behind them. 'I only brought him to where you can see the place, and then came away. Jake said he knew what to take, remember.'

'"Crowe knows which books are for him to take, we expect him at The Raven before month's end, Fowler also".'

Hugh laughed. 'You remember it precisely?'

'Word for word,' Bridget said. 'Do you remember your half?'

'I – if I thought about it. But there's no need. It's done with now.' He yawned as they tiptoed up the stairs. 'I'll wager anything I shall oversleep tomorrow. And I cannot afford to be late for school.'

'Pray a mystery of the rosary before you go to sleep and the Blessed Mary will wake you up. It always works.'

'Unless she thinks my soul needs some good stiff penance at the hands of Mr Lee.'

'Nonsense. Goodnight.'

'Goodnight.'

But Bridget turned at the door. 'Hugh,' she said, 'have you told Stephen about all this?'

'No.' Hugh said, and then added, 'Not yet, anyway.'

Hugh slept deeply and thankfully that night as he had not done since the afternoon Stephen had come tearing across the fields to the willow-flat. And outside in the night John Crowe the pedlar made his way onward with his forbidden load, having first marked carefully in his head the place where the old cot stood, for future use.

XVII

Hugh did not tell Stephen about the hiding-place, and Stephen did not ask him. He did ask once, about a month after that day at the inn, if there had been any trouble, and Hugh said no. In truth, he did not want to speak of it at all, even to Bridget. He was glad it was over.

Autumn blew and rained its way into winter, daylight grew scarce and cold seeped through everything. There had been a letter from Father late in November, but after that the roads were so bad there was no telling how long another might take. Christmas came again to Branton Hall, and with it bad weather. Going away at New Year's was out of the question, and they did not get a Mass until Holy Innocents' Day on the twenty-eighth. On Christmas Day, Mrs Branton, with Hugh beside her, dispensed Christmas cheer as one ought to tenants and parish folk, and the Wilsons and Bridget's parents came to play Christmas games in the parlour while the afternoon faded. The day before New Year's Eve, the Bournes called, partly to exchange courtesies, and partly because there was some business about the parish Mr Bourne wanted to discuss. When they came, Mrs Branton discreetly put away the silk picture of the Virgin and Child with St Joseph that hung among the greenery where the old statue had stood in previous years; and if Deborah Bourne glanced with disapproval at the ivy and mistletoe, she kept her counsel. As they left, Mr Bourne asked Mother if she had heard from Mr Branton lately.

'He wrote a little while before Christmas.'

'What is the news?'

'Nothing of note.'

'Oh.' And then he added, 'It will be good to see him home again... as I hope we shall soon...'

'Yes.'

Late that night, the first clear night there had been since mid-December, Hugh was sitting awake, his stool drawn up to the window and his cloak round him, looking out over the bewintered garden. A snowy night always seemed lighter; even faint moonlight reflected itself in the sparkling, whitened ground, and shadows stood out sharp and blue. It was very quiet.

He saw the horse before he heard the hooves, muffled as they were by the snow and his closed window. He opened the casement, taking his breath in sharply as the cold struck him, and leaned out, straining to get a clear view of the rider coming round the house towards the stableyard. He was almost sure he recognized him. The tall, thin figure with the old hat that perched awkwardly on his head when it was hot or was pulled down hard over his ears against the cold, as now... Ralph Hale. Hugh leaned a little further, and the rider raised his head briefly. Yes, it was certainly Ralph.

Hugh shut the casement, pulled some clothes back on, lit the candle again, and hurried downstairs still wrapped in his cloak. He reached the side door just as Ralph was opening it from the outside and met him on the threshold.

'Master Hugh! I did not think to wake anyone.'

'I was not asleep, Ralph. I saw you ride up and came down. So, you got out?'

'Yes.' Ralph began tugging off his boots and shaking stray snow from them. 'Thanks for bringing the light.'

'It's nothing.'

Ralph stood up. 'Let's stop in the kitchen,' he said. 'I'm famished.'

Hugh followed him. The kitchen held remnants of warmth, even though the great fire was banked up for the night. It was dark. Ralph took the candle from Hugh and lit a lamp with it. He went over to the pantry door and began looking through the shelves.

'Will Jenufer mind?' Hugh asked, with some trepidation.

Ralph Hale looked round briefly. 'No. I am allowed to take food if I need to.'

'I am not sure even my father would dare go through the pantry without her leave.'

'Yes, but I know which things not to take.' He came back with some bread and apples and sat down at the long kitchen table. Hugh sat down across from him. 'I come and go at strange hours often; it's easier thus. Are you hungry, Master Hugh?'

'No thanks.'

There was silence for a while. Hugh wrapped his legs round the stool he was sitting on and leaned his elbows on the table. Ralph ate like a man who has not stopped for food all day. When he pushed the plate aside, empty, Hugh asked, 'what happened?'

'Nothing much. They did not know enough to charge me, so they released me.'

'Did they question you?'

'Couple of times. I do not think I told them much.'

Hugh nodded, and then asked, 'Ralph, had you heard about what happened to the Lockwoods?'

Ralph looked up. 'Aye. I had. The gentlemen that questioned me were good enough to tell me all about it.'

'What do you mean?'

Ralph sighed. 'They had a thought I came from this country, and they've raided a popish house here and not found what they wanted. They'd like a case. They'll question any prisoner who might give them the answers they want. I do not know how much danger Lockwood is truly in, but... well, I must speak to his wife and to Jake. Since they hanged Lampley we cannot -'

'Hanged Lampley?' Hugh said.

'Did not you know? At the last Assizes. Convicted him of persuading to the Roman Church. It's treason by law.' He looked at Hugh again. 'Oh hell. Now I'm going to have to answer to the mistress for telling you.'

Hugh said, 'if you'd rather ride straight back to gaol and face the magistrates again instead, I'll understand.' But he did not know where the words came from, because his mind was filled with the picture of the fiery, sure young man who had dared anyone to put a price on truth. He thought of that young man dying the death of a traitor, of what was left of his head and limbs perhaps looking down from the city gates even now. He thought of how twice in the last three years priests had been hanged in Gloucester, and a name had been added to evening prayers, not to be prayed for but asked for prayer. A name spoken with careful steadiness, and fear-tinged defiance beneath.

Mother had chosen not to speak Lampley's name, at least not before the family, and Hugh knew why. He tried to form in his head the words of prayer one would say, but his mind could not make it real except by making what had happened at the gibbet and under the hangman's knife real. He was frightened, and ashamed of being frightened at the mere hearing of things other people were, it seemed, not afraid to endure. He was also angry.

'Master Hugh, I am sorry. I was not thinking.'

'It does not matter, Ralph,' Hugh managed. 'You were speaking of the Lockwoods?' Or of anything else, it didn't matter, as long as they kept talking a little longer while he crushed the fear down to manageable proportions.

'Well, so long as they keep clear of all – all this work for the present, it may be all right. And I cannot push my luck too far neither. They are watching me, and I must give them nothing to see, and hope that suffices.'

'Well, if they'd nothing before, and you give them nothing now, surely there is no danger.'

'They have some suspicions... It grows very late. I am going to bed, and so should you. I will speak to the mistress in the morning.'

As they left the kitchen, Hugh asked, 'Where will you go now?'

'Nowhere. I shall stay at Branton and act like an honest servant with nought to hide. Perhaps I'll even earn the wages your father pays me for a few months. Goodnight, Master Hugh.'

*   *   *

At the beginning of February, when the roads were becoming passable, Mistress Isabel and Bridget rode out to Norton Court to make a promised visit, with Ralph Hale in attendance. They meant to spend Candlemas there. Bridget set out with something of a sense of relief, perhaps because they had travelled so seldom during the winter, even as far as the town; this would be the first journey she had made since before Christmas. And, much as she loved the Hall, it would be good to have some peace... Not that Norton Court was a place of evident quiet: the great household of a knight and his lady, twice as big as Branton Hall and busy in proportion, filled with people and with comings and goings, often of a more or less clandestine Catholic nature. Full too of gaiety – she remembered well the Christmas festivities of a year ago, but in such a household there was almost always something happening, music or dancing or hunting.

And there was the chapel. It was at the top of the house for safety's sake, but that was its only disguise. When she went in, Bridget could almost fancy herself in one of the Catholic churches over the seas she had heard men who had been there talk of. There were statues, and paintings, and the altar stood always at the east end of the room, covered in a green cloth when it was not being used. Not like at the Hall, where everything had to be moved and put away after Mass. There was a priest who lived at Norton Court and tended the chapel for the household and any other Catholics in the neighbourhood, so that they could have Mass every day and confession whenever they wanted. The chapel held a calm Bridget had seldom known: like being at Mass, only without the sense of danger, the odd contradiction between one's soul so stilled it seemed to sleep like Marian after she had been sung to, and one's ears straining like a deer for the sound of a hunting-horn. It smelled too, an unfamiliar and yet homelike smell of wax candles mixed with the sweet smoke called incense. It was the only place Bridget knew of where they would use anything at Mass that left such evidence behind it, but the Norton Court chapel was a place that simply refused to be afraid.

Mass was to be said in the morning for the feast, candles and all, by the chaplain. Bridget went to the chapel early to make her preparation; but as she pushed open the door she heard a voice praying in Latin, and then another answering. It was not yet six o'clock. Some other priest must have arrived late last night and chosen to say his Mass early. He must be nearly finished by now. She slipped into the back of the chamber, looked up and saw her brother.

Even as she recovered her breath, he finished and turned to leave the altar. He did not see her, of course. But she followed him out of the room with her eyes, while she asked herself beneath the pounding of her heart why he was here. How came it that he was so near home and yet had not visited? Would he stay at Norton Court, or had he come to say Mass so early because he was in a hurry to leave? She pulled her thoughts back to her purpose in coming to the chapel, but she could not keep them there. Eventually she compromised, took out her beads and began reciting the Joyful Mysteries for Richard.

It was not until after high Mass that she was able to speak to him, although he had been there, serving for the chaplain. As they went into the hall to break fast, she passed close to him.

'Richard –' she said in a whisper, suddenly unsure if he wanted his true name or his family mentioned or not.

He smiled and bid her good morning, and added, 'you are visiting with Mistress Isabel, I take it?'

'Yes. We will spend a few days...' But she did not ask how long he meant to stay.

The ladies intended to go out early after breakfast to walk in the gardens, before the morning sunshine clouded over. On her way back from fetching her cloak and gloves, Bridget slipped into the library to put back a book she had taken to read yesterday. As she closed the door behind her she saw, with the strange pang of mingled fear and joy that stabbed her each time she saw him, that Richard was there, sitting at the table and making notes.

'Bridget! Oh – you are going out?'

'Yes. That is, we had meant to –'

'I did not think to find you here.'

It was a year since he had last seen her, but she had changed so much it seemed longer. Only half a child now, he thought. Her eyes still danced, but there was something else behind them; a tune that was no dancing measure had broken into her soul and took possession of it now and then.

He said, 'I must leave directly after dinner, and there is work I have to finish. Are you in a hurry, Bridget?'

'Yes – no – not much.'

'How do you, Bridget – and everyone at home?'

'Did you hear what happened to my father?'

He glanced down at the table. 'Yes, I heard something of it.'

'They arrested him.'

'I - I know. But he is come home, is he not?'

'Yes. Are you not coming home to see them, Richard?'

'I cannot. I am busy – '

'It is so close.'

'Bridget, I cannot take the risk.'

She bit her lip and looked down but made no protest; and that was more troubling than tears. He found himself explaining awkwardly, 'The - the business at the Raven… there is no need for you to know all that – ' His words trailed off, and then he asked briskly, 'how do you like Norton Court?'

'I like the chapel. And the books,' she said. And then, uncertainly, 'It's frightening.'

'This place?'

'Yes… no… No, not this place exactly… being a Catholic. Being here in England. Don't you ever think that?'

To that, of course, he smiled wryly, and said, 'well, just now and then.'

'No,' she said. 'I didn't mean… I do not know what I mean. But last night, they were all talking – about what if the Spaniards had come in, two years ago, or if they came now. Arguing about who you'd be firing at, English or Spaniards, if it came to it. About if England would have become a bloodbath, or whether we'd have had peace for the Church if...'

'Ah.'

'And that if the pope excommunicated the Queen, she cannot be Queen and so it can be no treason to fight her... I think that word must have been thrown about half a dozen times...'

'Ah. I see.'

'What would you have said?'

'I do not have time for politics.'

'No, but how can you stop yourself thinking about these things?'

He laughed. 'Bridget, you can't, not unless you cure yourself of having a mind. But whatever you do, do not pin your life, let alone your soul, to them. Yes, a pope excommunicated the Queen twenty years ago, and yes, there are those on both sides who will say that you cannot, therefore, be loyal to the one unless you are an enemy of the other.' And then he looked at her, and said, 'But what does that mean? That we should bow our heads to falsehood and let the Mass vanish from England?'

'No.'

He spread his hands and picked up his quill again. But she said, 'they were all disagreeing, you know. One of the men was quite fierce about it – about being loyal against the Spaniards.'

'Yes, some of us are.'

'But – you know, I do not think he will go and tell a magistrate that there are people speaking treason in Sir Christopher's house.'

'Probably not.'

'So, is he loyal then? Well, I don't think any of the others are exactly going to raise a troop for the Spaniards either…'

Richard looked straight at her. 'Are you going to tell?'

'I – I do not think I know most of their names.'

'Nice.' And he shrugged, and then sighed. 'England is my country, and I am here – I am saying Mass in English garrets and not in a foreign church because… because a man ought to serve his fatherland, even if it cost him – some danger. Whether I have much loyalty to Elizabeth Tudor, I do not know. But I know that if I am hanged, I intend it to be for my faith, my priesthood, and *nothing* else. The gallows mob are welcome to cry traitor, as long as I can give them the lie.'

He stopped, glanced at her, afraid he had said too much. But she only nodded and stood silent. She was looking down at the table, where he had been Englishing bits of an Italian book of devotion. He followed her gaze, and saw that she was staring at the margins of his note-paper, and at what he had scribbled there. *Dominus illu-*

minatio mea, quem timebo. It was written two or three times, with other verses from the same psalm, while he sat with only half his mind on his task. *Quem timebo... Expecta Dominum...*

Instead of shoving the paper out of sight, he heard himself saying, 'it's from a psalm. It is – The Lord is my light and my salvation, whom shall I fear? The Lord is the protector of my life, before whom shall I shrink?'

She did not look at him. Her lips had tightened, and suddenly she seemed taut as a bowstring pulled to breaking-point.

'It goes on... like that...' he said. 'And then it ends, *Expecta Dominum...* Wait, let your hearts take courage, and wait for the Lord...' He faltered into silence. Bridget was gazing out at the window, very still, giving no sign of having heard him at all.

He cleared his throat, shuffled his papers, picked up his quill again, and then said, 'Bridget, I will be riding after dinner. Would you care to come with me a little way, to set me on my road?'

'Yes. Of course.' And she turned to go. He watched her leave, and ached at the change in her, and could think of nothing he could have said.

They set out as agreed not long after noon. The morning sun had given way to grey skies, and it was a damp February day, of late winter rather than early spring. The snow had turned to slush in the roads, slipping off the trees to mingle with the mud and snow-withered grass. Bridget and Richard rode down the curving road, overhung with trees that in summer shaded it. It was a half-mile to the fork where Richard would take the road northwards, and Bridget would turn back to Norton Court. As they came out of the trees and saw the bend in the road ahead of them, the sun escaped briefly from the clouds, and just for a minute you could see that the trees would be budding with leaves and blossoms in a few weeks, and the grass would be green.

They pulled up their horses. Bridget did not want to hasten the parting by saying goodbye. Then Richard spoke. 'Bridget, look.'

She came out of her thoughts sharply. 'What is it?'

'Not behind you.' He said. 'Out there. Look.'

She looked. They were at the crest of a slope. The fields fell gently away before them, still brown, but with a faint promise of green. She could see the line of the river, reflecting the rays of sudden sunlight; she could see the village by Norton Court, and other villages and farms dotting the fields and hills as they rolled away. Closer at hand, gleaming gallantly in the shadows of dark tree trunks, snowdrops were blossoming hesitantly. And above, the sky was patched grey and blue as the clouds moved across it in the wind, hiding and revealing the sun.

'Beautiful,' she said softly.

'England is beautiful.' Richard said.

He turned, and, disengaging his right hand from the reins, gave her a blessing. Then he let his hand fall on her shoulder and smiled. 'Until God sends we meet again, little sister.'

'Till then.' And as he rode away, 'God be with you, Richard.'

She watched him down the hill, the wind whipping at her cheeks. Halfway, she saw him throw back his head a little and suddenly spur his horse into a canter, heedless of the mud which sprayed up about his boots and cloak. As he rounded the turning at the bottom, he looked back once more and raised his hand, and she saw his smile, the smile that was really a half-finished laugh. She raised her own gloved hand and smiled back, and as he disappeared turned her horse and went back under the still-leafless trees toward the great house.

XVIII

Almost so soon as Isabel and Bridget came back from Norton Court, Mrs Branton started the spring-cleaning. It was rather early in the year, but she said better be ahead than behind. During those days Bridget went to bed so tired she was asleep before the candle-wick was dark, and Hugh escaped almost gladly to school. There was still no money to replace the panelling in the parlour, but the not terribly well-fitting tapestries which covered parts of the walls were scrupulously cleaned.

It was about four hours past noon on the Monday that a man rode up the lane to the Hall. The dogs came leaping and barking as he passed the gate, but quietened when he spoke to them, and went trotting alongside him up to the house. The man halted before the front door and looked up at it but did not knock. He did not call for a servant, but himself turned in the direction of the stables. Having left his horse in the empty stall at the far end, he came back past the gardens towards the house, and went in by the south side-door. Mrs Branton, coming from the parlour, saw him standing in the open doorway and stopped dead. For some moments neither of them spoke.

Slowly, her eyes locked to his, she came down the parlour steps.

'You did not tell me you were coming home.'

'What do you mean? I've ridden post-haste all the way from London to tell you.'

'How comes it?'

'I have leave until the twenty-fourth of July. I set out as soon as I knew I could.'

There was a thud from halfway up the staircase, made by the pile of linen in Agnes' arms falling to the floor as she stopped short in astonishment. As though the sound had cut through her daze, Mrs Branton ran, laughing, into his arms.

Agnes had raced back up to the nursery with her news, and then down again and through the hall, and to the kitchen as well, and soon enough most of the household collected. The little ones followed Agnes' lead, surrounding him in a joyous siege, while Isabel smiled over their heads at her sister, Bridget watched from behind Isabel, and the servants gathered also, spring-cleaning for a moment receding. Hugh arrived last, and saw his father put the little ones off at last and try to greet them by name.

'That is George,' Mother was saying. 'He was still in frocks when you left.'

'Ah. Of course.' He put a hand on George's curls, and then turned and lifted the three-year-old girl in his arms.

'And you must be Marian? And do you talk as well as scream these days?'

She nodded for answer, suddenly shy of this stranger everyone seemed to know. As his youngest daughter squirmed out of his arms and bolted for her mother's skirts, Giles Branton's eye fell on Hugh. The room had gone quiet, as though no-one was quite sure what to do next.

'And this is my eldest son.'

Hugh stepped forward. 'Yes, sir.'

He put both hands on Hugh's shoulders and smiled at him. Their eyes were almost on a level.

It was odd that it should not be more strange, Hugh thought that evening. Father had said prayers in the parlour before the children went to bed exactly as he had always done, while Mother knelt quiet and smiling. After supper, they went to sit in the parlour as they always did; Mother had gone upstairs at her usual hour to make sure the little ones were asleep. Aunt Isabel and Bridget sat at the virginals, practising quietly. Hugh had put his books out in front of him, though he was making hardly even a pretence at studying. His father sat in the chair by the fireplace, one foot crossed over the other which rested on the edge of the hearth. He was not working or even reading, but watching, quietly, the flames dancing within it. The spaniel, Arviragus, had crept in and ensconced itself at his feet, nose on paws, also gazing at the fire, for all the world as if copying him. Father had not glanced at the scarred walls.

The door opened and Mother was standing there, candle in hand. Her face was scarcely visible between the shadows outside and the uncertain light of the candle flame. She said softly, 'Giles, the children are asking if you are still here.'

He turned to look at her and then rose. 'Give me the light and I'll go tell them.' He took it from her, kissing her as he did so, and went out.

The parlour stairs were dark and so was the gallery. The candle threw the same lights and shadows as it always did into the familiar rooms. He recognised the feel of the wall up the stairs beneath his hand and the creak of the fourth step. The patterns and figures of the hangings were lit one after another as he passed down the gallery. He could see some of the marks where they had been mended after the last search. The smell – the smell of beeswax and cloth hangings, smoke, the pomanders she made, and, faintly, Jenufer's kitchen. And the air was dry. It was good to be in a place that smelled of something other than filth and damp and bad cooking.

He pushed open the door of the nursery. One of the twins and Marian had sat up at the sound of his feet, and Agnes had pushed aside the curtains of the girls' bed a little. He stood a moment in the doorway, looking at the six faces which stared back at him, and a voice – which voice? – said 'Father?'

'Yes, I am here.' He said as soon as he could. He went and sat on the edge of the twins' bed, which was nearest.

Harry, leaning up against the wall, smiled suddenly across the room. 'It was awful when you were away.'

'Yes, it was.'

Kit said, 'are you going to stay?'

He had hoped, stupidly, that they would not ask that. He waited a moment and then said, 'I can stay until the twenty-fourth of July.'

'When is that?'

'A month after Midsummer.'

Kit considered the prospect of Midsummer, and a month, from the unpromising rain and dimness of February. 'That's a long time.' And he edged a little closer, dragging with him the covers Tom was still trying to keep pulled up to his chin.

It was not, of course. He tried to recall how unattainably long five and a half months had seemed when he wrote his petition from the depths of a winter in the Clink, and said, 'We must thank God for it.'

George had climbed out from beside Harry now and pattered across the floor. He would have to get them all back into bed before their mother came up again. Kit sat up on the other side of him and whispered, 'I am glad you are come home.'

'So am I.'

*   *   *

The next morning, Hugh, hurrying to leave for school in time, ran down to the library to fetch his schoolbooks and stopped outside the door. His father had always used to rise early, often before the servants. By the time Hugh was leaving for school, well before the breakfast hour, he would be at his desk, and would lay down book or pen to return Hugh's good morning.

Hugh raised his hand and knocked at the door.

'Come in.'

Father was sitting behind the table, the window shutters partly open to let the early light aid the candle near whose flame he held a book. He looked up at Hugh.

'Good morning, sir.'

Father laid the book down. 'Good morning, Hugh.'

'May I have your blessing, sir?'

Father rose and laid his hand on Hugh's head as he knelt dutifully. Then he said, 'You are off to school?'

'Yes, sir.'

'How goes the grammar school?'

'Well enough for the most part, sir.'

'Good lad.'

His father turned to the table and began looking through some papers. 'I am going to ride out to look to some matters over the estate today. I would like you to accompany me.'

'Of course, Father, if you wish it.'

'Good. I have some business to go through with Robson first. An hour after breakfast then.' He looked up again with a laugh in his eye. 'And – I will square it with Master Lee.'

Hugh had not been on such errands before, although he had seen some of the resulting letter-writing and account-entries. There was a place where the fences had come down; there was a tenant's house which had had a leaking roof, and the goodwife was complaining that the repair had not been done well. There was the farmer Blackwood who rented part of his land from squire Branton and had been disputing the rate for three quarters. His father also looked over the sheep-runs, and spoke to the shepherd, and finally rode out as far as the woods north of the town, part of which were Branton land. After that, they rode back towards Branton.

'Well,' Father said as they rode over the hill and came down towards the village, 'it is not near so bad as it might have been, thanks to your mother. I married a woman of sense.'

Hugh said, 'She has written three times to Blackwood in the last four months. She sent Robson to see him too. I was thinking no-one could deal with him.'

Father laughed. 'He's as contentious as a cat and stubborn with it.'

Hugh asked, 'sir, why were you talking about the price of the wool already? The sheep'll not be shorn for months yet.'

His father said, 'no. But I am thinking of selling the wool now.'

'How can…?'

'One could, if one wished, strike a bargain with a merchant whereby he gets the whole wool crop when it comes, in return for ready money now – less than the probable market price, of course. That's his gain.' His father was looking ahead down the road.

'And what is your gain?' Hugh ventured, half-expecting to be told to mind his tongue and his own business.

But his father said, shortly, 'Enough coin to pay a large sum in recusancy fines before I am charged with default-ing.'

Hugh said nothing for a minute and tried not to scowl. His mind went back to the lawsuit he had heard Mother and Aunt Isabel speak of, and for some reason he was quite certain that they were part of the same thing, and that Claydon was behind it.

It was almost time for dinner when they made their last errand. Hugh and his father rode up to the village church and tethered their horses by the churchyard gate, and Father went to knock at the parsonage beside it. 'Mr Bennett says there are some matters that need looking to in the church.'

The parson came out and went with the squire over to the church. Hugh followed awkwardly, and while they stood and discussed the leaks in the roof, the cracks in the chancel floor, and the boundaries of the glebe, he wandered to a chapel by the north side of the aisle with a figure of St George carved into the stone wall above its entrance.

Hugh could probably have counted on his fingers the number of times he had been in the church, but the St George chapel he knew. Father's grandfather had built it as a chantry chapel for the family of Branton Hall and named it for his own patron saint. He was buried there, to the south of the place where the altar had been, his wife next to him. On the other side was the tomb of Father's father, and of Grandmother. Hugh could just remember her, the imperious lady of the manor who had never accepted even for a moment that the new faith had become the established faith of England. He had a recollection of her, once, taking him by the hand into the church, and saying firmly that it might have been taken by strangers, but it belonged to the Lord and His Mother; and so, in some measure, to all folk who kept faith with them. Hugh remembered, too, seeing her lying in the great bed, propped on pillows and her cheeks pale, moving a pair of rosary beads through her fingers. Her face had been as stern as ever, despite its thinness, and her fingers on the beads unwavering. Only there were tears in her eyes, a thing he could not have imagined possible but that he had seen it, and she was not weeping for herself.

He did not know what had happened about the burial. But he was sure that no rites of which Grandmother did not approve had been said over her.

'Hugh? There you are.'

He turned as Father came into the chapel behind him. 'Are you done?'

'Yes.' Father sighed. 'There is a-plenty of work needed in this place. But I think the money can be found.'

Hugh said, 'By you, sir?'

Father raised an eyebrow. 'My grandfather and great-grandfather built about half of this church. And Branton Hall has always been the patron of this living.' He stood a moment by his parents' tomb. As he crossed himself and turned to go, he glanced up at the window above the tomb, through which the trees in the churchyard could be seen, and said, 'what's happened here?'

Hugh followed his father's gaze. Giles Branton had turned back into the nave. 'Mr Bennett, I see you've not been entirely idle about – repairs.'

The parson, who was just leaving, turned back and came over. 'Er – yes. Yes, the old glass was in quite poor shape... and then there were panes broken, what with the weather. Here, you know, and in the south aisle.'

His father crossed the church rapidly towards the large window near the chancel which was, Hugh thought, just over where the lady altar had been. It was filled with clear glass. The other windows, along the aisle, had an odd patchwork appearance: where the old coloured glass had fallen out, it had been replaced with clear panes, so that in some places you had half-pictures of saints, the images broken by holes through which bits of the churchyard peeked. Stained glass images were no more allowed than statues and Masses, and though no-one would expect a parish to pay for a whole churchful of new windows, you could not be making new coloured windows when the old wore out. But the last time he had been in here, Hugh remembered, the big window had still been filled with an image of the Blessed Virgin, and the chantry window had borne St George, his dragon, St Helen and her cross.

'My father put those windows in, I believe,' Father said quietly. 'You never mentioned that they needed repairing.'

'No...but they were quite... At last Mrs Bourne was kind enough to have these two windows glazed new. Else I doubt the parish could have –'

'Oh, Mistress Bourne was the benefactor?'

'Er – yes. Most generous...'

'But I suppose she did not offer to mend the tiles. Well, we had best be going.'

Hugh turned to follow his father out of the church. Mr Bennett said, 'there's a lot more light inside the church now. Good day.'

Giles Branton said, 'take off the roof too and there'll be even more. Good day.'

Hugh's father was silent as they rode back to Branton Hall, as though his thoughts were elsewhere. It occurred to Hugh that his father had sat and knelt in the coloured light of the windows they had not seen that morning through many Sunday Masses when he was a child. Later he had ceased to sit under it for the services of the Protestant Prayer Book. Father had seen the colours of St George reflected on his parents' tomb when they were laid in it, although without the chanted Sacrifice the chapel had been built for. But now Mrs Bourne's glass showed only what was on the other side of it, and no-one would see the coloured light of those glass saints again.

'Well, we're not too late for dinner.' They had reached the house. Hugh's father spoke as though shaking off some train of thought. But Hugh heard him mutter as he dismounted, 'And anyway, who the bloody hell do they think they are?'

*   *   *

'Tell me what happened,' Mrs Branton said, as she unpinned her hair that evening and began combing it out.

Her husband laced his fingers behind his head, looking across from where he lay stretched out on the bed. 'You know, I think your hair's grown longer.'

'Since last night?

'Since last I saw it... You were already asleep when I came in last night.'

'I did not mean to be... but you were in the nursery, and I was so much wearied with the spring-cleaning.'

'Yes, if I'd known I'd have stayed in London another week to be sure of missing it... the children were a long time settling last night. Tough little bargainers.'

'What did they conclude for in the end?'

'Three stories and the *Salve Regina*. Sung twice.'

She laughed.

'The father is a king to his household – humph. I think I'm more the Doge to their Venetian senate.'

She smiled and went on combing. Suddenly she said, 'Giles, did you truly ride *post* all the way from London?'

'Of course. I was here at least twenty-four hours the sooner.'

'It must have cost a small fortune,' she said, with determined disapproval in her voice and her face hidden behind her hair. At last she pushed the honey-coloured tresses back, and returned to the first subject. 'Are you going to tell me what happened?'

'Not a great deal more to tell... It's as I said to you, they have determined to charge me the fines I was hoping had been forgotten, and I made a petition for six months' leave on the grounds that I must go home to raise the money. No loss without some gain.'

'You had to give bond?'

'Yes, and find sureties… Henry Bourne has bet a large sum of money on my yielding myself prisoner, *et cetera*, in due time. And on my not breaking any laws, or not being caught breaking them, in the meantime.' He yawned. 'I must make sure I call on Bourne tomorrow.'

This, she thought, explained Mr Bourne's remarks at Christmas – Giles had asked him to stand surety when he petitioned for his leave. She knew already that if she raised the question of why he had not told her (and, clearly, had asked Henry Bourne not to tell her) that he was seeking leave, she would be told briefly that he had not wished to build up hopes that might come to nothing. So, she did not raise it, and said instead, 'and we won the lawsuit Claydon brought.'

'Indeed. If I'm honest, by the skin of my teeth. But yes.'

'How did Claydon like that?'

'He's not subtle, Master Claydon. He made his offer to buy the land we'd been suing each other over the day after I had the writ for the fines.'

'You'll not take, it will you?'

He laughed. 'Not on your life. Not till I've tried every other way under God's Heaven of raising the money.'

'What are we going to do?'

'That's what I have come home to devise. Mortgage the wool crop. Sell some timber. Sell some leases: Blackwood would make it worth my while to have his farm on terms to his liking. I do not know yet. Perhaps – perhaps, if nothing else will serve, sell some land. Just to any Englishman, Welshman or Scot but Robert Claydon.' And he laughed wryly again, but she sensed his anger.

She put the comb down to tease a stubborn knot out with her fingers. 'But Giles –'

'Yes?'

'Giles, it will not serve, and you know it will not. You can raise some money on a risk now, but you cannot possibly pay over recusant arrears for every month since '86!'

'No, but I can pay enough to buy some time.'

'And then what? Even if we damp all our fires, patch all our clothes, and pay them –'

'It's not that bad –'

'Pay the goddamn Exchequer in full, they can demand the same again next year. And whenever it suits them, they can send in a sequestration commission, and take two-thirds of the estate.'

'That's the point of buying time… there will be a sequestration commission sooner or later, if Robert Claydon knows anyone who can bring it about. But there is much we can do to limit what whoever is granted the lease gains, and what we lose. And, if we have more time, we can also… try to raise the chances that it is granted to someone a little more friendly to our interests than he is.'

'Well, that would be a low threshold to clear, at least. How do you mean to go about that?'

'There are divers ways. But the first task is to raise a convincing portion of what I'm told I owe the Queen's grace. I think I can do it, and perhaps some over and above. There should be money over to take care of some things here – such as the parlour.'

'Giles, if we cannot afford to repair it, it does not matter.'

'We cannot afford *not* to repair it. Not since what happened at the Raven.' He was not referring to the lost panelling.

She was silent, squinting at her hair as she braided it. She had known she would have to tell him, part of it at least. 'We – after that happened – we had the books here for a night or two. I think – I hope – we were not seen. But they are gone now.'

He looked up sharply. 'They were here though? And what now? The Lockwoods are keeping out of that business at present, I take it?'

'Yes,' she said. 'As are we.'

He nodded. 'There are some things we cannot cease doing altogether, I think, but we must be cautious. Claydon did not make trouble here last autumn, did he?'

'No. I was much afraid he would.'

Her husband said slowly, 'You had reason... but he did not do it. He went seeking friends in the Exchequer instead, to drag my recusancy conviction out of the closet. It is curious.'

'Why? Do you think there's any chance he has given up?'

'Not yet, I don't think. But he may... he may be thinking that *he* also has plenty to lose at this game. Not as much I do, to be sure, but – well, how many fruitless searches is his credit good for?'

'I see what you mean.'

Giles was silent for a moment, and then asked, 'Hale is here at present, is he not?'

'Yes, since Christmastide. He had some trouble in Worcestershire last autumn, but nothing came of it...'

'No. It may be fortunate that it was there he was arrested, not some place where more is known of him. I only hope neither he nor his other names will be traced back to Branton. It would, I guess, look worse if he left now than if he stays, but while he lodges here, I cannot have him busy abroad.' He paused. 'It's in the balance; all is in the balance. Claydon will not now attack, unless he can be sure of succeeding – but then he will, with a vengeance. And here am I, on hand to be accused of anything he discovers... and here are all these ends left trailing, to be grasped and followed by whoso can...'

She had finished braiding her hair, and sat with her nightcap in her hand, but making no move to put it on. Her voice was a whisper. 'And if the balance falls –'

'Why, let's be hopeful. If it falls on *our* side, we might be through this with nothing more to worry about than where to find a couple of hundred pounds in recusancy fines.'

She tied her nightcap and crossed the room to get into bed. The only solution to both the nagging fines and the lurking danger which had not been proposed in all their talk lay curled silent between them. Neither of them would take it up, nor even speak of it. Not because to conform in religion was an impossible solution, but because it was so very possible that once named aloud, it might become inevitable.

As she climbed in beside him, she said, 'Dear heart – weighty as all these matters are –'

'Yes?'

'I should be disappointed if your sole and entire aim in seeking leave was to ensure Her Majesty's Exchequer the prompt reception of its dues.'

'Well, perhaps it was not.' He smiled.

'And I should be *very* disappointed if you spent that small fortune on post-horses purely from a burning desire to discourse of bloody recusancy fines.'

He was laughing too as he reached for her. 'Perhaps I did not, beloved.' His lips were where they belonged, pressing against hers; each had returned to the truest home there was, the other's arms. 'Perhaps I did not.'

XIX

Mr Lee had hauled Westby up in front of the school and
beaten him. It was to do with churchgoing; it seemed
Westby had defied orders to file into the parish church on
Sunday with the other boarders once too often that term,
and the schoolmaster had decided to make an example of
him. Example to whom, Hugh thought, seething in his
place. None of the other boarders were Catholics, and it was
not as if there were any other reason to skip church.
Although to hear him talk you would have imagined
Westby was culpably lazy, or some sort of heathen, or had
devised the whole thing simply to annoy Mr Lee.

At the dinner hour Hugh saw Westby slip out of the
schoolyard and into the field beyond. He had never spoken
to Westby before – he was one of the younger boys, and did
not come from Merford – but now he followed him, and
when he came up with him leaning against the fence with
his arms folded on top of it and his head hidden in them,
asked, 'Westby? Are you all right?'

Westby looked up. 'Master Hugh Branton, is it not?'

'Yes.' Hugh leaned against the fence beside him and
wondered what to say next.

But it was the younger boy who spoke. 'It isn't that a beating is that bad, of itself, you know… It is only that you get so – so tired.'

'I know,' Hugh said. 'You never know when something's going to happen, or when nothing's going to happen, or when it's going to stop. Whether you can outlast all the things that could happen, every time…'

'I hate school.' Westby said, quietly, forcefully. 'I want to go home.'

'Where is home?' Hugh asked, and wondered at once if it was the wrong question.

'My parents live in Cheshire.' Westby said. 'But my mother's sister lives in this country… she pays for me to go to the Grammar.'

'Is your aunt a Catholic?'

'Of a sort. Her husband is not. And they are seven miles from Merford… too far to walk. I wish…'

'Why can you not ask your parents – ?'

'Because they're both in prison.' And to Hugh's consternation, the other boy began to cry. He did not cry like the little ones did, because he was trying not to all the time, choking on each sob and trying to blink the tears away because he did not want to concede defeat by rubbing his eyes. But he was crying, and Hugh stood awkwardly silent and waited, uneasily conscious all the while that the time was passing and they must not be late for afternoon lessons.

When Westby had mastered himself enough to speak, he said, 'I am sorry for being such a fool – '

Hugh said, 'No, you're not a fool.' And then, 'My father's been in gaol too, you know.'

'Yes, I know.'

And then for some reason Hugh added, 'and he has to go back there at the end of July.' He had not said that out loud before, and nor had anyone else at home; it was a fact that had been told and then laid aside. But once it was said, the autumn and winter and Christmas when once again Father would not be there seemed very real.

Westby said, 'oh. I thought he had been released.'

'Were your parents arrested when the Spaniards were coming?' Hugh asked.

He shook his head. 'No, they've been there a long time. Since before I was born.'

Hugh turned. 'But where did…'

'I lived with my parents, of course. Sometimes I stayed with my cousins, and sometimes my parents had leave. When there were priests in the prison we went to Mass. You cannot go to Mass here.'

'Why did they send you away?'

'Oh, my mother thought Chester gaol was not a proper place for a child to grow up. And one of the priests – he was teaching me my letters – said I was quick at study and ought to be properly educated. And then just after the priest was gone, there was sickness in the prison, and my mother could not get leave, and we thought my father might be indicted, although he wasn't, and is not yet... So, then my aunt offered to put me to school. Which was a help, because my parents have had hard shifts of late to find money for our lodgings.' Westby looked down again. 'So, I had to come here.' He finished, dully.

Hugh was silent a little while, and then said – suddenly and on impulse – 'You could come to – to serve God at the Hall.'

Westby looked up; his face had changed. 'You have pr- good men there?'

'Sometimes.'

'But I'd never get permission – '

'Well, we would not tell Lee it was for *that*.' Hugh put a hand on the other boy's shoulder with as much confidence as possible. 'I'll ask my father; he will contrive something. Come on, or we'll be late for lessons.'

Hugh never found out exactly what Father said or did, but Westby did get leave of absence. He did not come up to the Hall in the end, for there was a Mass at the Listers' on a Sunday shortly after, so he spent the night and went to Mass there. It was closer, and besides meant that he would not be at school when time came for the scholars to go to church. Westby threw Hugh a smile as he passed him coming into school on the Monday morning, and Hugh realised as he returned it that he had never seen Westby smile before.

Hugh wondered if Mr Lee guessed something of the truth; it certainly seemed as if neither Westby nor himself could get anything right in school all day. He was sure Stephen had guessed, because later when they were conjugating Greek verbs in the parlour at Branton Hall and trying to ignore the first day of real sunshine, Stephen started to say something which looked like turning into a direct question – but then thought better of it and took refuge in his grammar.

*   *   *

Hugh missed the next three days of school, because Father had business to see to in Gloucester, and he took Hugh with him. He had been to Gloucester enough times to know it a little, but not so often it had lost its novelty, and anyway, it was three days without school. They rode in under the city gates and through the streets with their medley of noise and people and colour, towards the house of Mr Ford, with whom they were to stay. Hugh looked up at the gates almost against his will; if Lampley's head and limbs had been put there, there was nothing left of them now. It was almost eight months ago he had been hanged. They passed Gloucester castle too, a collection of buildings behind a dilapidated curtain wall, forbidding and rather ramshackle at the same time. The castle served as one of the Gloucester prisons, and Hugh remembered that Geoffrey Lockwood must be somewhere within those walls.

Just before the supper hour, Hugh stood alone in the guest chamber at Master Ford's house – Father had gone out again – looking into the street. The tide of bustle and noise was ebbing, and people were making their way home. Workmen with their tools on their backs; late travellers searching for lodging; a pedlar coming round the corner tugging a weary horse that looked as though it would like to get lame then and there.

There was something familiar about the man. And as the pedlar chanced to lift his head, Hugh recognised John Crowe. He had almost hailed him aloud before he remembered himself, and, pulling the casement shut, ran out of the room and down the stairs. He was afraid the man would have passed on by the time he came out into the street, but he was still there.

'Crowe!' Hugh called softly, crossing to where he stood trying to coax the horse a few more steps. 'It's John Crowe, is it not?'

The pedlar turned. 'Ah. The lad from Merford who gives his name to strangers.'

Hugh flushed. 'I only wanted to ask whether – if all were well with that business.'

'Aye. Is there any news of the Lockwoods?'

Hugh shook his head. He wanted to ask whether Crowe would be bringing any more books to Merford now, or whether that was finished, but he was not sure that he should. It was Crowe who spoke. 'I am bound for an inn down the next street, if I can get this cursed beast to move. If you wish you may walk there with me.'

They managed between them to persuade the packhorse to stir itself, and as they walked slowly along, Crowe said, 'I will shortly have a pack I could wish to bestow somewhere near Merford. If I go back, will the hiding-place be there still?'

Hugh said, 'Yes. I think it is still safe. Are there – is there stuff to be delivered?'

'Some.'

Hugh said nothing more until they had almost reached the inn where the pedlar meant to stay. Then he spoke. 'When will you go there?'

'Before Easter.'

'If you leave the stuff there and instructions, I will go there the day after Easter and see what can be done.' John Crowe nodded and turned into the inn. And Hugh went back down the street, wondering if he had just done something courageous or merely foolish.

When he came back into the house, Hugh heard his father's voice in the parlour, and another that he knew but could not place. He pushed open the door and Richard Lister turned around. 'Master Hugh!'

'Yes, sir.' Hugh looked from one to the other. He wondered why Richard Lister was here when he was meant to be in the north country, but he had a sense that he would get short shrift if he asked. In the end he said, 'Are you also staying here?'

'No.' He said. 'I have lodging at the inn hard by, but Mr Ford has been so good as to ask me to eat here tonight. And I will return in the morning.' He meant he was going to say Mass.

After supper was done that evening and Hugh in bed, Giles Branton walked back to the inn with the priest. As they left Ford's house behind, he said quietly, 'Mr Woodhill, what are you doing here?'

'An errand that – could not wait.'

'You are not going back to Merford?'

'No.'

'What has happened?'

The priest sighed. 'Very well, come in and we'll speak.'

Once they were alone in the chamber at the inn and the door carefully bolted behind them, he said, 'Perhaps it is as well you have asked me; because it may concern you. I came here to try to see Geoffrey Lockwood.'

'Why?'

'To warn him.'

'Little late for a warning. The matter is rather out of our hands.'

'Nay, he can still worsen his case for not knowing what they have against him…'

'And what do they have?'

'I do not precisely know.' He said. 'But the fact is that a priest I knew has turned informer. It has only lately become known. And he may well have considerable information to give about Lockwood, and the Raven, and all of Merford's Catholics come to that.'

Giles Branton chewed his lip and said nothing for a while. 'Who?'

'One of the names he used was Martin.'

'Mr Woodhill, if this is true, it was dangerous for you to come back here. Why did you do it?'

'I had to warn him. I had to do something. I – '

'Yes?'

'It was my fault. It was I who had sent this man to Merford in the first place, years ago, before I had left Rheims. My fault if he now gives them evidence against Lockwood, or – or any of you. If aught had come of the raid at Corpus Christi last year, that too would have been –'

'And that is why you took the risk of coming here? Could you not have sent a message?'

'Not without delay. Good God, Mr Branton, if you put a man's life in danger, you do not waste time calculating your own risk!'

'Did you see him?'

He leant his head against his hand. 'No, they would not give me permission and they were not taking bribes either. Which is a bad sign –'

'Most certainly it is! Mr Woodhill, you had better get out of here as soon as may be. I know not why on earth you took it into your head to do something so reckless.'

'I tell you, I had to –' he began, and stopped. 'All right, it was bloody foolish.'

There was silence. Then Giles Branton said, 'Father, you must forgive me. I have a habit of losing my temper when I am frightened. Particularly when I have a sense that another man is showing more courage than myself. I will speak to Lockwood's wife; she may be able to get a message to him. And – do not condemn yourself for this other man's weakness. You could not have known.'

'No. But that does not alter the fact.'

*   *   *

Twice that night Hugh woke and saw his father kneeling at the foot of the bed, his head bent over his folded hands. He wanted to ask if something were wrong, and yet was afraid to. The second time he almost spoke and told him about his meeting with John Crowe and everything that had gone before; but he did not. Hugh rose early and was already dressed by the time he heard the priest arriving for Mass. He went upstairs and asked if he might serve.

Afterwards, while they were folding the altar linen and putting things back in the hiding-place, Hugh asked, 'would you like me to take any message home, Mr Woodhill?'

'Oh – yes, of course. Take them all my love, and my duty to my mother and Mr Lister, and they are in my prayers. And I am well but kept busy enough for three.'

'I will.'

'And they are well? Bridget is still at the Hall?'

'Yes, she is. Yes, they are well, I think.'

'And you? You are at the Grammar, are you not?'

'Yes. But I shall be done there soon. I turned fifteen last November.'

'Oh.'

'My father used to want me to study after, at Oxford or perhaps at one of the Inns of Court. Lee says I'm plenty clever enough for the university, but I'm such a papist.'

'Does he? He said much the same to me.' Richard Lister smiled. 'Lee's a decent schoolmaster – not over-severe. Not unless you cross him very badly.'

Hugh thought about school. It was true that the scholars of Merford Grammar did not exactly live in quaking terror. There were certain things that if you did them would get you beaten, everyone tried not to get caught doing them, and no-one succeeded all the time. It was just a pity for Westby that dogged refusal to go to church was one of those things. He thought of the time last year when he had driven Mr Lee into rage, and said, 'But sometimes you have to.'

'What?'

'Cross him badly. If you are a Catholic.'

The priest glanced at Hugh but did not ask a question. He said only, 'Choose your battles. And when you have, fight them through.'

Then Hugh asked, 'You went to Oxford, did you not, sir?'

'Yes.'

'And then to Rheims.'

'Yes.' He laid the vestment he was folding down and looked at Hugh. 'I was sixteen when I went up. Oxford's a strange place: still half in love with the old faith but swearing allegiance to the new. Each man sets the limits for his own conscience there, and I remember that just before I left, a man I knew set his. You are supposed to swear the oath of the royal supremacy, you know, before you proceed Bachelor of Arts. He would not. They would not let it be, and he left. But I wanted to take the degree; why, I could not tell you now – plenty of scholars do not. I doubt I would ever have taken Protestant orders. I did have a mind to be a schoolmaster.' He laughed. 'So, I took the oath and my BA. I went home for the summer, telling myself it did not matter so much, and all that summer I thought, and twisted away from my thoughts, and tried to pray, and did not quite dare – and in the end received a certainty I did not want, and sufficient courage – just – to make my way to Rheims.'

'Do you ever wish you had not?' Hugh said suddenly.

'Roughly once a day. When things go well.' He replied drily. And then he turned away abruptly and began putting the church-stuff back in the hiding-place beneath the floor.

Hugh asked, 'did you hear about the raid last Corpus Christi?'

'Yes. Were you there when that happened?'

'I helped the good man escape to Norton Court.'

'You?'

Hugh nodded. 'He – Mr Foster – said they must have planned it some time. But we did not know how.'

The other looked up at him and said, 'Would you have wanted to know?'

Hugh's stomach tightened, but he answered, 'Yes.'

'It was a priest who had been there. He gave them quite a lot of information after he was taken. You may not have known his true name, though I daresay you met him.' There was a look in the priest's face that frightened Hugh, and he felt that he did not want to know what was behind it. But Richard Lister went on.

'You have seen enough to know what I mean when I say that I am afraid; and that I do not expect to stop being afraid until I'm dead. But you know what frightens me most of all? That I, too, could do more harm than ten spies in half an hour, if I once gave way.'

Then he took the last of the bundles from Hugh, shut the trap door carefully and straightened. 'Well. Good luck at the Grammar, do not give my regards to Master Lee, and

if your father does send you to Oxford - keep your head.'
He turned to pick up his cloak. 'And pray for us, Hugh.
God knows we need it.'

Hugh was at the window as the priest rode away after
breakfast. He watched him disappear through the slowly-
wakening streets toward the city gates and the northward
road with a strange mixture of dread and something that
was almost longing.

XX

'Have you got it fastened yet?' Bridget called. Hugh looked back down at her through the tangle of willow branches and budding leaves.

'Yes,' he said. 'I'm letting the rope down now. See it?'

She watched it weave down through the branches, getting caught several times, but at last hanging beside the trunk. 'Yes. Come down now and we'll try if it works from the ground.'

Hugh and Stephen, with a last tug at the knots, began climbing down. Bridget had already begun to haul at one end of the rope, peering up to see if the white linen was rising to position at the top of the tree.

'Well, it works,' Stephen said.

'Yes. The question is whether you can see it – I am sure we can from the Hall, but – '

Stephen squinted up. 'I think I'll be able to.'

'Are you sure Aunt Isabel will not miss that sheet, Bridget?' Hugh asked.

'Yes. It was in the rag closet. How do I hold it in place?'

'Like this.' Hugh came over and began winding the rope round a branch stub. 'That should stay. But let's take it down now.'

Bridget wandered to the edge of the stream and picked up some stones. 'Mercy, but I am hungry. And Mistress Isabel and I were all morning about the kitchens – that is penance beyond *my* patience.'

'Lent only lasts four more days,' Hugh said.

'And I shall make it up well and truly come Sunday.'

'That's a good Lenten spirit.'

'Oh, drop preaching, Hugh. You've not spent Holy Week preparing for Easter dinner.' She spun one of her stones and watched it skim the water.

Stephen asked, 'Did you hear anything about Geoffrey Lockwood when you were in Gloucester the other week, Hugh?'

'No, why?'

'Nothing – only I heard my father say...' His voice tailed off, and then he added, 'they will surely release him sooner or later. After all, they never found anything, did they?'

'No,' Hugh said. He shut his mouth firmly and did not look like he meant to say any more, but Stephen asked suddenly, 'where *did* you hide them?'

It was Bridget who answered. 'We had a place out in the woods. But most of them are not there anymore. We – have disposed of them.'

'Where to?'

'To them that they were meant for. But, of course, that's a secret: no-one knows but Hugh and I and Jake.'

Stephen said nothing for a minute. He seemed to be concentrating on angling a flat pebble so that it would spin properly. At last, he looked up and met her eyes. 'I am glad,' he said.

Hugh got up from the bank where he had been sitting. 'Bridget, it is time we went home.'

Agnes came running as they neared the house, to say that the work was all done in the parlour and they must come and see. As they went up along the orchard path and through the garden, she said quietly, 'I'm going to do it this Easter. Mother and Father said I know my catechism and I'm old enough, and if the priest agrees, I'll make my confession on Saturday, and then I'll receive the Sacrament at Easter Mass.'

'That's good news, Agnes.' Bridget said.

'It feels odd. That I'll be, you know, properly a Catholic.'

'Yes.' Hugh told her. 'You'll have committed your very own treason.' Agnes looked up at him, and he said, 'it's being reconciled to the Romish Church, after a sort, isn't it? And by the '81 statute –'

'Hugh, hold your peace.' Bridget said crossly. 'It's nothing of the kind. As if Agnes had ever been a Protestant in the first place... Anyway, it's a foolish way to talk, and your father would say so, too.'

For a moment she sounded much like Mrs Branton at her most formidable. 'I'm sorry.' Hugh said. 'Don't mind me, Agnes. Come and show us the parlour.'

The room looked almost as it had done before the raid: the walls panelled again, and over the fireplace intricate carving. Hugh could pick out the coat-of-arms of his mother's family and his grandmother's, as well as the Branton arms, among the shields. The joiner was standing by the hearth, putting away the last of his tools. He had come from a town near Norton Court to do the work at Branton Hall. Father had hired him on Sir Christopher's recommendation.

'It is fine work,' Hugh said. 'Are you leaving now?'

'Come the morning,' the young man said. 'Your father has given me leave to spend the night.'

Hugh nodded. Though no-one said it, he guessed that the young man was not quite done working yet, although the parlour might be finished. Last night Hugh had chanced to wake in the dark and heard sounds at the end of the gallery – very quiet, for the joiner was no fool – but sounds that might have been tools against wood and stone. He had an idea that some clandestine work was going on inside the main staircase too, while Bridget was prepared to wager on the chimneypiece in the great hall. Anyway, Father would probably show him and Bridget, and just possibly Harry, where the priestholes were once they were complete, and then they would know who was right.

In the meantime, preparations went on for Easter. That evening in the repaired parlour Father and Mother talked of the plans they had made for Masses with John Lister and Mrs Wilson. It was important, just at the moment, Father said, not to have too many people visibly gathering in one place, especially not at the Hall. But since a priest was able to come from Norton Court, one could not neglect to mark Easter. They talked of other things too, the estate and the children and Harry's lessons; Hugh supposed that once he had gone to bed they would talk him over, too.

'He does not do so badly, at present,' Father was saying, about Harry. 'He learns well when he wants to.'

'And when is that?' Mother asked drily.

Father laughed. 'When he perceives no alternative. And I do my best to give him none. But something will have to be done when I go back to London if he is not to grow up wholly ignorant. He is old enough for the Grammar; perhaps he should go there.'

Hugh glanced up at that and heard himself say, 'Please do not send Harry to the Grammar.'

Father turned and caught Hugh's eye. He did not ask what he meant, but Hugh had the feeling that it was because he did not need to.

*   *   *

It was Holy Saturday night, and Bridget was standing in her chamber pulling on her gown. Or at least, really she supposed it was already Easter Sunday, but it was so early as still to feel like night. The stars had not even started to fade: Bridget knew, because she had opened the shutters to see when she got up. The gown was new, with bits of blue velvet in its trimmings, and she had worked some embroidery into the bodice. She had also trimmed her best pair of sleeves with what was left of the velvet, to match. Mistress Isabel had helped her, but even between them they had hardly got it done in time – the hem had seemed a mile long. Mistress Isabel came in from the nursery where she had been dressing the little ones and did the fastenings Bridget could not reach, and then Bridget took out her silver cross; she slid the hook over one of the ribands Hugh had given her last New Year's and tied it around her neck. Then she gathered up her skirts and ran, because Mrs Branton was calling her to help get things ready.

On the stairs up to the Mass-chamber she passed Hugh coming down to fetch the altar vessels. 'You look very fine,' he whispered. It was not a question, and she did not try to answer it, but she did look fine. She knew that her gown was beautiful, that her face was clear, that her hair was gleaming golden and that Richard's cross shone on her breast in the candlelight. And she was glad of these things.

She stood next to Agnes, also laced and pinned into her best clothes, turning the pages of the Mass-book they were sharing. Hugh was serving with practised ease and keeping an eye on Harry who had only just learnt how. Since Mass was at home, Mistress Isabel had woken all the children except Marian. It was the first time the twins had been brought to Mass, and they sat round-eyed and utterly silent throughout. Bridget wondered what she had told them to make sure they did not talk about it.

Mr Branton, acting as cantor, intoned the Easter *Alleluia*, the notes soaring loud in one's heart after the weeks of Lenten silence. Bridget had enough Latin to make out that the Gospel was of the women coming to the tomb. They must have got up in the dark to do that, Bridget thought… She could not help wondering if it had been a little like going out in the night to the old cot in the woods. Feeling that it was a little crazy, and listening out for every sound, and wondering what would happen when you got there, and how you would explain if anyone caught you, and in the midst of all the pain, a flicker of gladness, because in the end you could not but be glad to do *something*… But Mary and the others had not found a hut and some books, they had found an empty tomb and an angel… That would be – would be like getting up in the dark to go to Mass; and then, when you stepped through the door of the garret, finding that you were in a great cathedral, and it was broad daylight, and a dozen bells were ringing the Gloria, and no-one was afraid.

At Holy Communion, she watched Agnes go up, her face at once excited and solemn. Bridget stepped forward after her, to where the priest stood with the paten and Hugh and Harry held the houseling cloth and knelt down. Then the priest's voice, '*Corpus Domini nostri Jesu Christi custodiat animam tuam in vitam aeternum, Amen*'. The houseling cloth under her chin, because no particle of a fragment that hid the Divine Body must fall to the floor. Hugh's hand holding the cloth just by her shoulder, and his face in the corner of her eye. She fixed her gaze on the Host. The bread-taste of what was not bread on her tongue, and then she was slipping back to kneel in the corner where she could lean her head against the wall and pray, easily, wordlessly, nothing else mattering for a little while...

'*Ite Missa est. Alleluia, alleluia.*'
'*Deo gratias. Alleluia, alleluia.*'

Bridget ran down the stairs as soon as the priest had left the altar, and for once was at the virginals before Mistress Isabel, playing a tune her fingers had been itching for since Ash Wednesday.

Regina Caeli, laetare, Alleluia!
Quia quem meruisti portare, Alleluia!
Resurrexit, sicut dixit, Alleluia!
Ora pro nobis deum, Alleluia!

When she had finished Bridget sang it again. Somewhere she could hear Mr Branton's tenor echo the tune.

Hugh came through the parlour with his arms full of things which must be hidden away. 'I think you changed key three times from start to end of that.'

Bridget only laughed, scarcely even tempted to rise to Hugh's bait. She got up to open the door for him, since his hands were full, and as she did so said suddenly, 'Hugh – '

'Yes?'

'Are you going to do it?'

'Do what?'

'Go back to the old cottage and see what is there.'

He stopped, looking at her as they stood in the doorway. 'I shall go tomorrow morning, early. Are you – will you come?'

'Of course.' There was no time for further conference because Mistress Isabel was coming down the stairs. Bridget turned back to the virginals, and Hugh went to put the altar vessels away.

They made the journey out to the woods together early on Easter Monday and found a note from Crowe suggesting that someone should come on or about the sixth of each month, and anything that was to be delivered he would leave there. On this occasion there was a packet directed to one of the priests who came sometimes to Merford. That would not be too difficult.

Hugh tore a blank leaf from one of the books and wrote a reply to the effect that they would do their best for as long as they could. He did not sign it, and Bridget tore John

Crowe's note into tiny fragments and ground them with her heel into the earthen floor of the hut.

*　　*　　*

It was Ralph Hale who brought the news to Branton Hall, two days after Easter. He brought it from Norton Court, having accompanied the priest returning there on Monday. Mrs Branton, fifteen minutes later, took it to the Lister household, Bridget with her. Hugh heard it that evening, from his father, and in due course all the Catholics in the district, and after that their Protestant neighbours, heard it. Mrs Lister's son had been arrested in Staffordshire on Good Friday, on suspicion of being a popish priest.

They did not talk about it much; there was little point in speculation. The Catholic women went to the Lister household at various times to offer their sympathy. A few of John Lister's Protestant neighbours and fellows in business mentioned it, and relations were soured with one or two in consequence. There was some gossip about the town, but there was very little to say. No word yet of a trial, or of the likelihood of his being condemned. Bridget did not come back to Branton Hall, because her mother needed her at home. Hugh did not really know what he could have said to her in any case.

The Friday after they had heard about Richard Lister, Hugh was sent over to the village on an errand for Father, and, returning, lingered on his way back from stables to house. He decided to go the long way round, through the orchard. As he came through the gate, he heard a movement among the cherry-trees, and turning saw Bridget there. She was leant, half-sitting, against the sloped trunk of the little old tree, staring at nothing.

'Bridget.'

She turned. 'Hugh.'

'What are you doing here? That is, I thought...'

'I don't know. Everyone at home seems to keep on crying, except my father, and he is not there very often.'

'But 'tis nearly four miles! Have you walked all this way?'

'No. Yes. I just went out of the garden and started walking and kept on... and got here.'

'You've not been up to the house?'

'No – oh no. I – I should go. I know not why I – I just –'

'Bridget, I am terribly sorry.'

'Thank you – I – I – ' And then she was crying, quietly, putting her hands up to her eyes as if to stem the tears, but failing.

'Bridget, don't cry – '

'I'm sorry, Hugh – I'm sorry...'

He fished for his handkerchief, but it was hopelessly dirty, of course.

'I'm sorry.'

'It doesn't matter,' he said, and put his hand gently on her shoulder. Her head went down to meet it.

'Oh God – oh God…' He let her cry like that, her face hidden against his shoulder, for a while, feeling how wretchedly little it was to be able to do. At last, she choked her sobs into sniffs and raised her head.

'I've stopped being foolish now,' she said, smiling ruefully. She reached into her pocket for her own handkerchief, dabbing it carefully over her tear-blotched face in order to dry it without rubbing it even redder.

Hugh said, 'You ought to go home now. Your mother will be wondering where you are.'

'Yes. Oh dear.'

'Come. You can borrow Silver. I'll ride with you.'

He did not tell the others that Bridget had been at the Hall. He came back well before the supper hour, riding Gilian with Silver on a leading-rein. It would save Bridget the inevitable explanations had she had to bring her back.

'Hugh, I am terribly sorry,' was what Stephen said when they met. Hugh did not reply, and the next thing he said was 'Have you seen Bridget? How does she?'

'How do you think?' And then, relenting, 'she's well enough.'

Stephen said, 'I saw… I saw Mrs Lister in town the other day. But I did not know what to say… She was – she looked as though every hour was a torment, and yet you'd cling to it for fear of the next.'

'Her son's been taken as a priest.' Hugh said coldly. 'How else would she look?

Stephen said, 'it may not turn out so bad...'

'They can hang him. They can do worse than hang him – they can gut him for a traitor.'

'But surely, there is no treason against him, is there? I mean I don't believe Bridget's brother is a rebel.'

'He is a priest,' Hugh repeated, still more coldly. 'There does not have to be anything else against him. There's a law which says if he was made priest and then returned to Her Majesty's realm, that is treason and they can have him hanged, drawn and quartered any time they choose. Of course, they may not; sometimes they only banish them. Sometimes they have them in prison for years and do nothing at all... But that is the law, and they do not have to prove that he so much as spoke against Her Grace, nothing but that when they ask him under oath, are you a priest, he cannot deny it. And that's treason.'

'I know – I know that is the law. But come, Hugh, if that is all they cannot actually hang him for a traitor... it is not the same thing as – as real treason.'

'Tell that to the bloody Privy Council.'

'But I do not believe it.' Stephen said stubbornly. 'I do not believe that they will hang Bridget's brother when there is nothing but religion against him...'

'You know nothing about it. I'm going back to the house.' And he rose and left the willow-flat, walking fast with his head down.

*　　*　　*

Stephen watched him out of sight, and then got up himself and wandered toward home. But when he got there, he did not go into the house. He went straight round to the stables and, without quite knowing why, saddled his horse and rode towards the town.

It was not until he reached the Listers' house on the far side of town that he realised he had no idea how to introduce himself and ask to see Bridget. Or indeed why precisely he needed to do so. At last, he dismounted and led his horse round to the back of the house. It was built in the shape of an 'L', and a wall enclosed the square space formed by the two inner sides. There was a gate in the wall, and through a gap where one of the planks had broken away, he could see a garden. Even as he looked through, a door opened from the house, and someone came out. 'Bridget!' he called, as loud as he dared.

She turned, and then walked quickly across the garden toward him. 'Stephen! What on earth are you doing here?'

'I – I – wanted to ask – how you did.'

Bridget smiled. 'I am well enough, thank you.'

And then he said, 'Bridget, I am sorry.'

She said nothing.

'About your brother. I am sorry.'

She smiled at him again, a calm, distant little smile. 'It is not your fault, Stephen.'

'I hope – all will – be well.'

She said, 'It is better not to, if you can help it. Then if the worst happens, your heart is already settled to it.'

'And if it does not?'

'Good news was never the worse for being unlooked for.' And then, as though in concession to him, 'I do not know how much hope there is. I do not suppose Richard knows... It depends on so many things. I know there is nought against him but his priesthood, and I do not think he has been taken before. But his priesthood is enough in law.'

Stephen said, 'I am going to pray – that the worst will not happen.' There was a kind of defiance in his tone that surprised him.

Bridget said gently, 'do that.'

Someone called Bridget's name from the house. 'I should go now,' he said.

She nodded. 'Goodbye.' And then, as he turned away from the gate to mount his horse, she added, 'Stephen – thank you.'

*   *   *

'And that is all you know?' Giles Branton asked.

Ralph Hale shook his head. 'It might be better not to tell Mrs Lister this, but – I had this from the man who was with Woodhill when he was arrested, and but narrowly escaped himself. That day, the day they were raided, the altar-things were not all that were found.'

'What else?' Mrs Branton said, sharply.

'A lot of Catholic books he was carrying.'

'Such as?'

'Everything. Missals, catechisms, controversy… I suppose the ones they'll hate the most will be Southwell's *Epistle of Comfort,* and a couple of copies of Allen's *Defence.*'

Mrs Branton took in her breath; her husband said, 'No, that's not going to help him.' And then, 'Hale, there's something more.'

'Only that – well, too many things have happened this year.' Hale said. 'Lockwood's in trouble. Crowe, that pedlar Lockwood kept in touch with, was questioned and released very quickly when he was arrested just after Candlemas, and I do not trust that.' He glanced up at Mr and Mrs Branton. 'Richard Lister knew – knows – Geoffrey Lockwood. He has been in Merford. They may know that; may even know he comes from here. I would say, we must be careful, but we all know that much. It is not as though we would ever be aught else. The truth is, there is nothing at all we can do.'

XXI

The spring days continued to lengthen. After Easter, the scholars no longer needed candles during the first lessons at school and found themselves released well before dusk. Hugh was no longer asked to drag Harry to his schoolbooks when he reached home, but he would often come into the library with his satchel to find his brother ploughing dutifully through a lesson under their father's eye. He saw little of Bridget, although he knew Aunt Isabel had called on them more than once. She said Mrs Lister was doing better as time went on.

One Sunday in May, the Bournes came to dinner, walking up after service was finished at the church and morning prayers at the Hall. Most of the conversation during their visit was kept up by the gentlemen; Mrs Bourne and Mrs Branton made short remarks about the likely fruit crop and the children's health, and Hugh and Stephen talked little in front of their elders. It was only later – much later – that it occurred to Hugh to wonder why he had not felt more awkward sitting across from Henry Bourne, justice of the peace, because that same morning he had quietly left the house before light and gone to the hut in the woods to find out what forbidden goods he might be handling this month. But he had not thought about it. It was as though he had placed all that in a distinct compartment, a priesthole within his mind. One did not forget it existed, but one did not tend to think about it as part of the rest of life.

Later, Mr Bourne and Mr Branton excused themselves, having business to discuss, and went together towards the library. As they left the parlour, Hugh heard both of them laugh at something or other, and somehow it sounded like the way he and Stephen felt when they escaped from school or from their parents' houses and ran out to the stream or the hillsides where nothing mattered more than they chose it should. Suddenly it struck him that thirty years ago, their two homes had stood the same mile apart that they did now, with the same stream running between them, dotted with places where two boys might play or climb or sit and talk.

Two days afterwards, Bridget and Hugh stood at the willow flat, arguing. Bridget had managed to get away from home, where she was still staying, to ask Hugh what had happened when he went back to the old cot as agreed. There had been a packet meant for Fowler as well as some bundles to be stored in the hut for the time being. Hugh had intended to deliver the packet in Merford when he went to school; but now Father wanted to take him when he visited his land holdings in Herefordshire, and he would have to miss school. Bridget wondered aloud if she might go instead, and Hugh pointed out that a young maid could not slip into the Unicorn alone without people taking note of it, which would defeat the purpose. They had reached the point where neither of them wanted to be the first to admit that they would have to give up, when there was a sound behind them, and Stephen was standing at the top of the bank.

None of them spoke. Stephen climbed slowly down to the flat and joined them.

'Stephen –' Hugh said, 'we were wondering when you...'

'No, you were not.' They were standing side by side, facing him, uneasy, as though they were afraid. 'You need not worry,' he said, almost sullenly. 'You know perfectly well I am not going to tell.'

Bridget said, 'it's all right, Stephen. It is just – you might have been anyone.'

'Well, I wasn't.'

Hugh said, 'we did not see you coming.'

'Well then don't stand with your backs to the path. I thought you two were better at plotting than that.'

For a moment Hugh looked angry. Then Bridget laughed. 'There's no harm done after all,' she said. But there were still shadows of that startled look in both their eyes. Stephen opened his mouth to utter some superfluous reassurance, and heard himself say, 'you know, I could take them.'

'What?' Hugh said.

'I could take that packet into Merford tomorrow. Since you will not be here and Bridget can't.'

Hugh looked at Stephen without speaking. And then Bridget said, 'would you know the man?'

'Yes. At least, I know the man. Not his name.'

'Well, that would solve the difficulty,' Bridget said. She picked up the satchel which lay beside the willow-tree. 'If you're sure.'

Stephen looked at Hugh, who still said nothing. 'I'm sure.' He turned back to Bridget and took the pack out of her hands, and she smiled. A smile not of kindness nor even friendliness, but of kinship.

They had not realised how much that secret had mattered until it ceased to matter. But though they rarely spoke of the affair – there was no need – it was different now that it need not be avoided. As the evenings grew longer, Hugh or Stephen sometimes ran down after supper and hoisted the signal, and they would spend half an hour trying who could carve his initials highest up a tree. Sometimes they would see Hugh's parents or Stephen's father and grandmother go past on an evening walk, and be called at to come in before the light failed, or not to break their necks, or some similar injunction. During the Whitsun holiday, they spent days scrambling and scraping themselves in the willows and beeches, and in Hugh's case once tumbling from a branch into the stream. He had clambered dripping to his feet, to see both Agnes and Bridget laughing from the top of the bank. Bridget did not stay at the willow-flat that time; the girls were out walking with Mistress Isabel.

One Tuesday in late June, they were all three down at the willow-flat. Bridget and Stephen were spinning ducks and drakes; Hugh was sitting against the great tree-trunk, whittling. The shade of the willow and the cool of the stream were welcome now that it was past midsummer and often hot.

Bridget had not come back to the Hall since the news of her brother's arrest, for three weeks afterwards Elizabeth, her father's daughter by his first marriage, had arrived. She was with child, and the birth of her last baby had resulted in dangerous disputes with the churchwardens of her husband's parish as to whether he would or would not be christened, and his mother purified, in the parish church. So, now her stepmother had invited her for a well-timed visit, as her affairs were no business of Merford's church-wardens, and Bath's would be a long way off. John Lister maintained that he could not see what all the fuss was about: a baptism was, after all, a baptism even if the minister were a heretic. But he did not object, even to the arrival of his two older grandchildren, who could not be left to run wild in their mother's absence. The Lister house was, if anything, noisier now than the nursery at Branton Hall, and Mrs Lister could not do everything while her stepdaughter had to spend more and more time in her chamber. So, Bridget stayed at home to wash and dress and scold unwilling infants, and help with the household in between. But she found ways nevertheless of escaping to the willow-flat; today Mrs Lister had sent her to the Hall to ask for some receipts from Mrs Branton, and afterwards she had not gone straight home, but quietly down the meadow path to the stream. Hugh and Stephen, riding back from school through the summer dust, had seen the grubby white shape of their signal hoisted among the willow-branches.

'I do not know how you make it work every time, Bridget,' Stephen was saying, referring to the pebbles and the water.

'My brother taught me.'

'Your brother?'

'Before he went away.' Bridget smiled. 'He taught me to whistle too.' She wiped her hands on her handkerchief and curled up against the bank, resting her chin on her knees. 'What is that to be, Hugh?'

'A fox,' Hugh said. 'If I can make it right.' He had done a lot of whittling this spring and summer. It had started because of the stray bits of wood that lay around while the work was being done on the parlour. Things like a bird that he had given to Agnes (his father's comment had been that if any bird shaped like that flew it would be a miracle), or a little cross. He had bored a hole in the cross and started wearing it strung on a cord beneath his clothes. Most of the time he forgot it was there, but sometimes when he turned his head he felt the cord rub against his neck and remembered.

'Hugh,' Bridget said, 'which of us is going to the hiding-place next time?'

'Next time is not until next month.'

'All I meant to say is that it might be better if I went. You have done it twice now, thrice if you count the time we went together. Suppose someone takes note?'

'Well...'

'It is quite as near my parents' house – nearer.'

Hugh turned his half-formed bit of wood over, scrutinising it. 'Very well.'

'I'll take at least as much care as you, never fear.'

'There is another thing I was thinking,' Hugh said, his eyes still on the bit of wood. 'It was – you remember Westby?'

'I've heard you speak about him.'

'It was just – it is hard on him, being at school. I'd like – I'd like to give him one of those books.'

'To keep in *school*?' Stephen said. 'Hugh, Lee would skin you both alive.'

'You know, I was not going to tell Master Lee.'

'Well, no, but if he finds out?'

Hugh said, 'There is always a risk.'

'What book did you want to give him?' Bridget interposed.

'I am not sure yet. Perhaps that thing of Persons that my mother has. The *Christian Directory*.'

'Would Crowe mind?'

'I do not think so. There are so many. Some are addressed, but the rest are for – well, anyone who wants them.'

Bridget picked up a stone, examined it, and discarded it as the wrong shape to throw. 'Well, if you can find a way that is safe, I do not see why not.'

'*If* you can find a way that is safe,' Stephen said. Hugh frowned and went on whittling, and for some time no more was said.

'Have you heard aught of your brother, Bridget?' Stephen asked suddenly.

'My father tried to see him last month, but he could not. Richard wrote though. He heard my father was there and got a letter to him.'

'He wrote?' Hugh said. 'What news is there?'

'None, really. They have not examined him since he was first taken, and he thinks there'll be no trial this session at least. For the rest he knows no more than we... But there are a fair number of Catholics in the prison, he says, and many other poor souls in more need than they know, and he is well-nigh as busy as he was outside.'

'Well, all is well then.' Stephen said. Bridget said, 'Perhaps', and Hugh said nothing.

* * *

June had passed into July. Harvest and the end of school were approaching. The sheep grazing the dusty summer grass were starting to lose their newly-shorn look, while on the roads great cartloads of wool could be seen making their way to London and thence to the weaving looms of the Low Countries. Hugh's father spent even more time out on the estate, determined to set all in order by the twenty-fourth of the month, and Hugh sometimes went with him. Harry was to be spared the Grammar school: the household at Norton Court had begun employing a Catholic tutor, and Father proposed to send Harry there. He would not go at once, not until the autumn, which, Father said, left just time to teach him enough not to disgrace himself. Nothing definite had yet been said about Hugh, but Father was spending almost as many hours guiding Hugh through the business of the estate as he was on Harry's lessons. Ralph Hale was no longer at the Hall. He had gone down to Herefordshire, ostensibly to look to the maintenance of his master's estate in that county.

On Tuesday the seventh of July Hugh woke early. He and Stephen would – hopefully – be meeting Bridget this afternoon. They would hear if she had managed to get to the old cot in the woods, and whether she had found anything. Hugh was not sure what to do if Crowe had left any books; there were still several hidden inside the mattress of his bed which he had failed to pass on last month. When he met Stephen, neither of them said anything, but they both were thinking the same thing.

'Stephen,' Hugh said, 'I am going to give Westby that book if I can.'

'Which book?' Stephen asked, uneasily.

'You know. I put a copy in my satchel this morning.'

Stephen said only, 'well, if you want to.'

They arrived at school early for a wonder, and Hugh managed to slip the volume in among Westby's schoolbooks as he passed him, whispering, 'if you had rather not, give it back at noon.' At noontime Westby caught up with Hugh and thanked him for the gift.

The afternoon was hot and heavy, and Hugh, who sat wishing it was safely over, was not the only person counting the hours. The scholars were longing for the sunshine, the room felt close, and no-one – either master or pupils – wanted to be working. But when Mr Lee left his chair and began walking about the schoolroom, Hugh felt there was going to be trouble. He could see Westby's back stiffen, even though Lee was only making sure his scholars had their minds, or at least eyes and hands, on their books. Lee drew almost level with Westby and leaned over to look at the copying of the boy just behind, Westby shifted awkwardly in his seat, his elbow jerked, and the small pile of books beside him fell to the floor.

The whole room, including Mr Lee, turned at the sound. Westby froze.

'I – I beg pardon, sir. I'm sorry, I – ' His eyes were fixed in fright on the schoolmaster's. Hugh wanted to leap across the room and gather up the books himself before anyone else saw what he had seen – that the unbound volume at the bottom of the pile had fallen face-up, its title page in view.

Mr Lee grunted. 'Well, pick them up.' Hugh almost breathed. And then, even as Westby bent with feverish haste to obey, Lee frowned suddenly, stooped, and picked up the *Christian Directory*.

He did not say anything at once. He stood still for a second, while pens fell idle all over the room as the scholars stared, and Westby stared not at the master but at the book in his hands, as though by willing he could change it into a Latin primer, and Hugh prayed desperately in his head, *O dear God, O God...* Mr Lee said, in that quiet voice which meant he had already decided you were not getting off lightly, 'What is this?'

'I – I...'

'Well, I suppose I can see what it is. *The Christian Directory guiding men to their salvation... set forth now again with many corrections, and additions, with reproof of the corrupt and falsified edition of the same book*. Robert

Persons of the Society of Jesus, if I am not mistaken. The question is, how did you come by it?'

'I – cannot tell you.'

'Indeed.' He had grasped Westby's shoulder and pulled him to his feet. 'Indeed.'

Hugh had risen too, vaguely aware of Stephen's strained whisper, 'Hugh, no…'

'Sir, it was my fault.' He almost shouted it. 'Let Westby alone, it – '

'What was that, Branton?'

'It was my fault, sir. Westby does not know anything about it. I gave him the thing only this morning. He does not know. It was all my doing…'

*   *   *

After school, Hugh felt he ought to apologise to Westby. Westby shrugged his shoulders and said, 'it's nothing. My fault for dropping the thing on the floor like an ass.' Which did not make Hugh feel any better. And then Westby added, in a sudden rush, 'I would not have told him. If you had not spoken, I mean. I am nothing like you, Master Hugh, but I was not going to tell, honestly.'

Hugh said 'No – no. Westby, that was not why…'

Westby said, 'well, it's done with now.' He grinned suddenly. 'I hope Mr Lee enjoys reading the *Christian Directory*.'

Stephen was waiting for Hugh. Bridget would be at the willow-flat. As they rode away, he asked, 'you all right, Hugh?'

'Yes.'

'Is Westby?'

'Yes.'

'Hugh – what in God's name possessed you to do such a brainless thing?'

Hugh turned on him. 'I could not sit by and watch Lee beat hell out of that child for shielding me. Even if you could.'

'Well, what good did you think you were doing by playing Sir Launcelot?' Stephen demanded. 'How was that to help Westby?'

Hugh scowled and told him to shut up. They were both still smouldering when they neared the willow-flat. Late already, they tethered the horses by the road and went straight across the meadows to the stream. The signal had not been raised, and Bridget was not there. Perhaps she had not been able to get away. They waited at the top of the bank, looking toward the road, and just as Stephen opened his mouth to wonder where she was, Bridget came running up and drew level with them. 'Someone's been there.'

'What?' Hugh said.

'At – the place in the woods. Someone has been there.'

'How do you know? What happened?' Stephen demanded.

Hugh glanced back towards the road and said, 'come on.' They scrambled down, close to the stream and under the shadow of the willow. 'Bridget, tell us what happened.'

Bridget spoke almost in a whisper. 'I went out there before first light this morning. And – well, someone's been there. The first thing I noticed was the door – it was shut. You remember how it is almost off the hinges, you have to sort of lift and pull it carefully – well, someone had not, and it was sort of jammed – I did not realise I had noticed at first, but when I got it open there was a great rut on the floor where it had been dragged to. They must have made ten times more noise than we ever do. But then I saw the chests had been opened. And it was not Crowe. He just puts his packets inside the lid, but someone had gone through the whole lot, and some of them had been put back in different places.'

'What did you then?'

'Left everything as it was and came away.'

'Well,' said Stephen. 'Now what?'

'I do not know. Should we go and take the things, before anyone else does, or leave it in case of making them suspect the more?'

'Most likely safest to leave them,' Stephen said.

'At least, they do not know who it was put them there.' Bridget said hopefully.

'Well, they damn soon will, now Hugh's shouted it out to the entire grammar school.'

She looked at Hugh.

'I gave Westby a book and he dropped it on the floor in front of Mr Lee. Lee was going to beat him, so I told him it was not Westby's fault.'

'Oh Hugh.' Bridget's voice was exasperated, but he caught a glint of sympathy in her eye.

'Anyway,' Hugh said, 'there's no reason Lee or anyone else should think there was any more to it than one book and the two of us. Why should anyone put together that and...?'

'Then why did he keep both of you behind all that time?' Stephen demanded. 'Must have been near half an hour. What did he want to know?'

'Mostly he just lectured us. In any case, I told him nothing. I said the book was mine, and I knew not where it came from, I gave it to Westby, and Westby had not asked for it. Not much to go on. And Lee's hardly a magistrate.'

'But he can tell them, can he not? And Lee's always giving Westby hell over not going to church. He only leaves you be as much as he does because you are not a boarder and your father's Branton squire. Oh God, Hugh, what have you done?'

'Well, what was I supposed to do?'

'Keep your mouth shut?'

'I could not.'

'Didn't stop Westby getting beaten, did it?' Stephen said. 'Just landed both of you in trouble – and all of us in a lot more.'

'Not *all* of us.'

'Oh, for heaven's sake!' Bridget cut between them sharply. 'The question is, what's to be done?'

Hugh let his folded arms fall and kicked at a tree root. 'There is nothing to be done. We cannot go back to the place, that's certain. All we can do is wait, and try if we can find out what they know, and if they mean to – do anything.' He turned. 'Stephen, do you know if your father…'

Stephen said, 'my father's got nothing to do with this,' and shut his mouth in a tight line.

'But – that other time, you told us…' Bridget pointed out.

'That was different.'

'Stephen, it cannot do any harm –'

'There's no need for me to spy on my father.'

'Leave it, Bridget.' Hugh sighed. 'Well, then there is nothing we can do, except pray like you've never prayed before.'

XXII

Jem could not help feeling, as soon as he entered the kitchen, that something was going to be discussed. Jane and William were there. Bess looked subdued, as though she knew she must not interrupt the grown-up conversation. Mother looked solemn. And after they had finished eating supper, when grace had been said, Mother looked at Jem, and said, 'How goes it at school, Jem?'

'Very well, Mother.'

'Your master says you are clever and do very well.'

'You went and asked Master Lee?'

'A woman's entitled to enquire if she's getting a good bargain for her money, is she not?'

William Hudson said, 'you must have more book-learning than any tradesman in Gloucestershire tucked away in that head of yours by now, little brother.'

Jem said nothing. It was a long time since he had wanted to be a shopkeeper. But then his mother spoke again. 'Yes, you've profited plenty from your schooling by now, and many boys your age are glad to be 'prenticed in a good trade.'

He looked round at them all. Even Bess was staring at him. 'Do you want me to leave the grammar school?'

'Listen, Jem. You know I've done my best with the shop, and we don't do so badly. But I cannot run it all quite alone, and we cannot keep paying for all this hired help forever. If – if your father were still alive, or if Tom had come back, it might be different. But you are old enough to be a great help to me now, and being so bright, you – why, you might do very well for us.'

William said, 'my father and I wish we could help more, Mother.' He had first called Mrs Carter 'mother' after Jem's father died, and since the bad news about Tom he had made a habit of it.

'You do as much as anyone could expect, and then some,' she replied. The Hudsons were no wealthier than most tenant farmers.

Jem remained hopelessly silent. He did not think there was any point in telling them about the dreams he had begun to dream. If he could stay at school only a little longer – only a couple of terms, to master the Rhetoric class – he could, perhaps, convince Lee that he was scholar enough for the university. He might go up to Oxford as a sizar, or perhaps find a way to study at one of the Inns of Court. If he could do something like that, he might become a schoolmaster, or a clergyman, or – if he could go to the Inns – a lawyer. He might be called to the bar. Then – *then* – he would help all of them ten times more than by being quite a good cordwainer. But Jem did not think they wanted to know about what he might do in a year, or five, or ten. They wanted the shop to do better and cost less now. When at last he spoke, it was only because he had to, because he would never get another chance.

'I want to stay at school.'

Jem's brother-in-law sighed impatiently. His mother glanced at him and said, 'well, we can talk of it again another time.'

There would not be anything new to say, though. While Jane stood up and began clearing the dishes, Bess decided a change of subject was due and started to ask Jem what had happened at school that day.

'Did Lee get in a temper?'

'Yes,' Jem said. 'Not at me though.'

'Who then?'

'Westby, as a matter of fact. And Branton. It was – it was crazy, really.'

'Why, what happened?'

'Well, Westby's a papist. That's not really a secret. But this afternoon, Lee caught him in school with a Jesuit tract.'

'Jesuit tract?'

'Yes. A book of some kind written by Robert Persons. You've heard of *him*, Bess. Anyway, Westby dropped it on the floor – I mean, of all the foolish – and of course Lee jumped on him...'

'How did Branton come into it? Which Branton is this?' That was Will.

'Well, Hugh Branton. Squire Branton's son. Westby – listen to this – had the book from him. Lee was in the middle of raging at Westby, trying to get him to say, and Branton stood up and said Westby had it from him.'

'Where did Hugh Branton get it from?'

Jem looked over at Will. 'I do not know. Lee tried to get it out of them, I think, but that was after school. He beat them both – well, they'd pretty much asked for that – and after school he kept them in...'

'Where are you going, Will?' Jane said, for Will had risen from the table quite abruptly.

'I've some things to see to. Thank you for supper, Mother. Jem, you'll see your sister home when she's ready? I need to take the horse. I'll see you later, my dear.'

'Will, where are you going?' Mrs Carter asked, for Jane merely nodded and turned back to washing dishes.

'Oh, not far, just too far for an evening walk. Goodnight.' And he picked up his hat, kissed his wife, and left.

Jem took his books out into the shuttered-up shop for some quiet, and sat over them thinking of school, and of his father, and of futures that could never be, and of the things he would like to do to the particular Spanish papist who had landed Tom Carter in a pestilence-trap of a prison.

*　　*　　*

When Hugh reached home, almost at the supper-hour, he went straight up to his chamber, lifted all the covers from the bed, and dug out the books he had hidden in the mattress. He looked at them for a minute, as though wondering if there were anywhere safer to put them. But there was not. After he had hidden them again, and smoothed the bedclothes, Hugh went downstairs, took a deep breath, and knocked on the library door.

His father was there. 'Hugh. I was about to send for you. There is an errand I want done over to Norton Court, and I have not time.'

'Yes, sir.'

'It will mean losing another day or two of school… I am sorry, but I must leave in the next fortnight and there is still much to be done.'

'Yes.' Hugh said again. And then, 'when will you be coming back again?'

'How can I possibly answer that, Hugh?' Father said, and then relenting, 'that I got leave is a good sign. I cannot say when I shall obtain my release altogether, but I can certainly seek leave again, perhaps before this winter.'

'This winter?'

'No promises, Hugh. But there is no reason why not, provided there is no trouble. We were lucky at Easter, but we must continue to be careful.' And then he picked up the papers in front of him. 'And now to the business at Norton Court…'

'Yes, sir.' Hugh pulled the stool up to the table and sat down. But before he went into explanations and instructions and letters and deeds, Father said, 'Hugh, was there aught you wanted to say to me when you came in?'

Hugh looked down at his hands. 'No. No, there is nothing.'

He left early for Norton Court the next morning, and stayed the night there, coming back on Thursday after dinner. He reached home hungry from the journey and thought he would go to the kitchen and beg some food from Jenufer. But Mother came out and met him at the door even as he dismounted.

'Hugh, there you are.' She seemed almost relieved.

'What is it?' he asked.

Mother said, 'Come inside.'

And she reached out to put a hand on his shoulder, as though she would shepherd him indoors like one of the little ones. As they went into the parlour, Hugh's mind flew at once to the books under his mattress, and he wondered how much he could or should explain if Mother had found them. But what Mother said was, 'Hugh, they have arrested Bridget Lister.'

'They have – ?'

'Bridget is in custody; we understand, in Gloucester gaol.'

'But why?' he said desperately. 'What reason can there be to…?'

'I do not know. Her mother has been here, wondering that, but how can any of us know what to think?'

Hugh shook his head and sat down on the windowsill. 'Tell me what happened.'

All that was known was that Robert Claydon, the justice, had summoned Mrs Lister and her daughter to see him, over an accusation of recusancy. A summons to herself Mary Lister might have risked ignoring, since answering any questions of Mr Claydon's could only increase the chance of a recusancy conviction in the end. But indicting Bridget as well was a different matter, so they had gone, armed with a deposition from Bridget's godparents to the effect that she had not yet turned sixteen and therefore was not liable under the recusancy statute. And then Bridget had been questioned alone by Claydon; and two hours later her mother had been sent home without her, and told that Bridget had been sent to Gloucester, where the gaol was.

Hugh listened until there was no more to be told, and then he left the house, hunger forgotten, and ran out past the gatehouse and on toward the road. He had almost reached the bridge when he heard a voice behind him and turned.

It was Agnes. 'Hugh?' she said as she came up with him. 'Hugh, where are you going?'

He stood still, looking down the road which led to Stephen's house – to Mr Bourne's house – and said, 'I – do not know.'

'Hugh, please do not do anything foolish. It'll not help her, you know.'

'What do you mean?' Hugh said, caught by something in her tone.

She looked at him, half-frightened and half-relieved to be speaking aloud. 'Hugh, you know what I mean. What should I think, when you and Bridget are talking in whispers in the long gallery and stop when anyone comes near? When Mother goes away and a pile of books appears at our Mass? When I can hear Bridget creeping through the nursery in the night, and you come down in the morning with muddy shoes?

'Agnes...'

'*Something* must have been happening. I know not what, but I am sure you do.'

Hugh sighed. 'Please, Agnes, not another word of this to anyone – even anyone at home. It is not fair to Father and Mother – '

'I know.' And then her voice grew small as she said, 'Hugh, I hope nothing happens to you.'

'I hope nothing happens to Bridget,' he said, staring away across the stream again. There was a silence, and then Agnes put her hand in his. 'Hugh, come back to the house now.'

What was left of the day passed in painful normality, except for an anxious, unspoken petition hanging in the air at household prayers, and a whispered conversation between his parents that Hugh heard from the dusty garden but caught no words of before the library window was closed. After supper Hugh went straight up to his chamber, and on Friday morning set out for school. It seemed terrible to do so, as though it were any ordinary day, but there was nothing else to be done. When he met Stephen, whose face was all fear and concern and confused guilt, he said briefly, 'I've heard.'

Stephen said, 'My father's from home. He left yesterday, after I did for school. He's not come back yet.' He paused. 'Grandmother said he'd gone to see Claydon over some business of – of the Queen's peace.'

Hugh turned. Stephen looked away, not wanting to admit the import of what he had just said. After a minute he asked, 'Hugh, what do we do now?'

'Nothing. There is nothing we can do now.'

At school they went to their seats, got out their books, and tried to work as they always did. It was during the morning's lessons (Hugh could not have said precisely what hour, because time had stretched wholly out of its accustomed shape that day) that there was a forceful knock at the schoolhouse door, and then it was opening before Mr Lee had time to enquire as to the identity of the intruder.

The constable had a man with him, and he himself was holding a paper with a seal attached. Afterwards Hugh reflected that it was a fairly foolish thing to do, although in another way it did not matter in the least because anyone in the room from Master Lee down could have told them who he was; but when the constable said his name, he got to his feet without thinking, and heard himself say, 'that's me.'

He did not remember much of what followed; his brain was whirling too much. But he heard distinctly the scrape of the bench against the floor as Stephen stood up to let him pass, and he saw Master Lee march up to the constable and scrutinise the paper he held, and then nod and stand back. He remembered that Westby's face was all eyes as he passed with the constable's grasp tight on his shoulder, and that Robert Wilson looked up, caught his eye and whispered just audibly, 'God go with you.'

It was not until the end of that day, when he was standing alone in a chamber in the Northgate gaol in Gloucester and putting his satchel down on the stool, that Hugh realised he had carefully put all his schoolbooks back into it and taken them with him. He looked down at his Latin reader staring up at him and laughed. The sound fell into the prison cell and died.

Stephen stayed in his seat only until noon. Then, as soon as the dinner-hour began, he ran out of the school-yard, fetched his horse from the inn and was riding back along the road to Branton, digging his heels into the horse's flanks mercilessly. The beating he would doubtless get tomorrow for being absent paled into insignificance beside the thought of telling Mr Branton and his wife what had just happened to Hugh; but clearly it had to be done. As for going home and facing his father…

The thing was, that he himself was almost certainly quite safe. He had never been to the hiding-place in the woods, and so he could not have been seen there. He knew he had not been seen that one time he had spoken to Fowler at the Unicorn, because he had checked carefully. And besides all that, Stephen Bourne was above suspicion. He was the son of a magistrate, and he was a Protestant. Oh yes, he was safe.

Stephen was not foolish enough to pretend to himself that he was not glad of that, but at the same time it was horrible.

XXIII

They had been having something of an argument before the boy was brought in.

'They're children,' he had told Claydon. 'We must have no cruelty – '

'For heaven's sake, Bourne. Who is talking about cruelty? We have questions, and we will ask them.'

'And suppose they will not answer? You saw the girl yesterday... you think she's about to accuse anyone of popish crimes?'

'Bourne. We both know there is popish sedition going on here, and I hope we both know our duty as servants of Her Grace. Lockwood kept his dealings so close even his partners can give us little of use, and he himself surely will not... but these little plotters might be able to tell us all we need – about the Raven, and Branton Hall. It would not surprise me if Giles Branton had been behind all this knavery for some time.'

Mr Bourne fidgeted uneasily. It would not surprise him either; but he hoped to God that he might on this occasion be surprised as much as ever a man was. If he had known – or allowed himself to know – sooner that Claydon meant to arrest Hugh Branton next... but what could he have done, short of leave Claydon's house and his investigation, and hasten back to Branton to warn them? Did he indeed wish he had done that? Time and again, he felt, he had acted to limit the harm that came to the Brantons for their recusancy. And Giles Branton could not keep himself from trouble-making for six months, to honour a bond for which he – Henry Bourne – had pledged surety. Had he not stood between Giles and the consequences of his law-breaking enough times? Only it was not Giles facing those consequences today, it was a boy of fifteen.

Hugh was brought into the parlour by the constable, who released the boy's wrists and withdrew, leaving Hugh to stand in the middle of the room. The shackles had not been strictly necessary; but they might, Claydon had said, serve as a useful reminder.

Claydon had commenced the examination. 'Hugh Branton.'

'Yes, sir.'

'Were the seditious books you hid in the hut in the woods near Merford the same as those Geoffrey Lockwood had kept in his inn?'

The boy seemed taken aback by the direct question. When he found his tongue, he lied outright. 'I know nothing of any seditious books.' Except that a well-taught papist would argue that 'popish' and 'seditious' were quite different things.

'Perhaps you would like to see a list?'

'Please.' Claydon took up a paper from his writing-desk and gave it to Hugh, who studied it carefully while the magistrates studied him. It was a full list of everything that had been in the old cot, drawn up by the two of them after the search. Hugh chewed his lip hard as he read it, but he gave no other sign. And as he handed the list back, he said, 'I see nothing seditious about any of those, sir.'

'Do you not? It is the greatest load of popery I ever came on.'

'That,' Hugh said, and suddenly there was an edge to his voice too, 'Is not the same thing.'

'Listen.' Now Claydon's voice was ruthlessly quiet. 'We know you had to do with the hiding of these books; we know you must know at least something of whence they came. And, mind, boy, this enquiry will not desist until we know the whole matter.'

'And I will tell you nothing.'

'Then it looks to be a long enquiry, does it not? We shall see who wearies of it first.'

They went little further that day. Claydon told Hugh curtly that he was committing him to gaol in Gloucester. Henry Bourne passed the notes he had made to Claydon, who glanced over them. Both magistrates signed the paper, and then Claydon beckoned Hugh forward. 'Sign here.'

The boy hesitated and looked up into Mr Bourne's eyes. 'It is a record of the examination.' Henry Bourne told him. 'It must be signed by all the parties.'

Hugh looked down again and scrutinised the paper, word by word. Claydon shifted impatiently.

'Give him time,' Henry Bourne said. Hugh picked up the pen, and wrote carefully beneath Henry Bourne's signature, *per me* Hugh Branton. He looked up again as he laid the quill down, but Henry Bourne looked past him at the armed men in the doorway and nodded to them to take the prisoner away. It was a long enough journey to Gloucester.

*　　*　　*

It was cold in the Northgate gaol, even on a summer night. Cold enough at least to make it difficult to sleep, unless you were more tired and less apprehensive than Hugh was. As he twisted about trying to find a position which kept all of him warm, he wondered with determined thankfulness what it would have been like in December. His mother had come in just as it was growing dark, trailed by a keeper who possibly should not have let her in at all. She had brought a bundle of his things with her – a spare shirt and doublet and his winter cloak, and a blanket, money and some food. They had not said very much – he could not have said anything of importance anyway because the keeper was there, and for the rest, he knew she was worried, and she knew he was afraid, and nothing would be made better by dwelling on those things. When she left, Mother had put her hand on his head, tracing a cross on his forehead with her thumb. She had said, 'God keep you, my son. Trust in God and have your wits about you.'

Hugh had replied, 'yes, Mother. Goodnight,' which sounded better than goodbye. But he found it difficult to meet her eye, though he made himself do so.

He was glad of the winter cloak and the blanket, but they did not keep out the damp chill left behind by God knew how many fireless winters that had passed through here. He had eaten all the food she had brought, partly to prevent the mice or rats from taking it, and partly because he had last eaten at breakfast. By the time Mother had come, he had begun to wonder if anyone even remembered that he had been brought in.

It was cold. Mother had given him a rosary – sewn into the lining of the spare doublet – and he went round it at least five times and still was no more than half asleep. He prayed one decade for every intention he could give words to concerning this business, and then he prayed one for everyone at home, and then one for the Holy Father, for the souls in purgatory, for the Queen, for England, for the heathen... About halfway through the first glorious mystery the Resurrection for the third time, he fell asleep. But the cold awoke him three times during the night, and each time he was half-glad because his dreams were worse than waking.

It had taken him some hours to grow afraid. At first, the facts of his surroundings swallowed all his attention, leaving none for taking in what happened. Stone walls partly covered with cracked plaster. The sounds, not strange in themselves, of distant voices and people moving in other parts of the building, the scratching of rats and mice, the barking of dogs in the town; but all strangely coloured, muffled and yet made louder, by the brooding air of the gaol. The smell of damp, and of filth, and rust from barred windows, and old food, and underneath everything the smell of fear. Hugh closed his eyes against it all and tried to believe his own weakness was making it worse than it was. He wondered where in this God-forsaken place Bridget was, and whether he would be able to see her if he asked, and if perhaps she too was lying awake.

Bridget was asleep in a chamber not many yards from his own, with a blanket and her winter cloak wrapped tight around her. Her father had come and left them for her, but he had not been let in. Bridget had had a couple of days' start on Hugh in learning to sleep despite the cold and the place, and she was tired. Tired by very sleeplessness, and with worrying and fearing, and wondering what questions they were going to ask. If only they had worked out something beforehand, a lie they could both tell consistently. At present the only thing she knew was not to tell the truth.

It did no good speculating on what would happen when she found herself in front of Mr Claydon and Stephen's father. In a way, the latter was the more terrifying. Claydon she hated quite simply, and if she could fight him to any effect whatsoever she would be glad of it. But she did not know how she was going to face the plea in Mr Bourne's voice, the weariness in his eyes…

That was what had been so frightening when they arrested her. There had been no real questioning, only Claydon saying that they were conducting an investigation into the bartering of seditious books in the district, and they had reason to believe she knew something. Bridget had asked why they thought she should know anything, and thought she was doing rather well, because that was not a lie and yet it hid the truth nicely. And Claydon had said, coldly, that if she would not tell the truth now she could wait in gaol until either she was prepared to tell them, or they found it out. But then Mr Bourne had come in. Claydon had looked up and said, 'you received my message, then.'

Mr Bourne had said, not for Bridget to hear, 'I suppose this is absolutely necessary?'

'Yes.' That was all.

And then Mr Bourne had spoken to her, had made her look at him. 'Bridget, if you can be honest with us now, I promise you it will be less pain for us all.'

He was quiet like Stephen, and like Stephen many of the things he did not say had a way of crowding into his eyes. And the pity and fear she had read in Mr Bourne's eyes terrified her.

When thinking got too much she prayed. Even without beads, the Aves of the rosary could be counted on one's fingers, ten for each decade. And Bridget prayed countless decades during those day-long hours. For Hugh; for Stephen; for herself. When prayer became indistinguishable from fear, she would untwist her hands resolutely, and change tack, and pray for Richard instead. Of course, that hurt too, but then it always had.

*   *   *

It was late when Mrs Branton, sitting in her chamber too tired to work and yet unable to go to bed, heard the dogs bark and a horse coming up towards the house. When Giles did not appear, she knew he had gone into the library.

She herself had gone to Gloucester as soon as the news came yesterday, leaving a message for her husband, who had been out and not expected back until late afternoon. When she had returned home today, he had already set out as she had known he would, to try to glean some kind of explanation from the justices.

Mrs Branton slid the grey cat gently off her lap and went to the library. The chair behind the table was empty; he had sat down on the little backstool that stood in front of it. He was leaning on the table with one elbow, his head resting in his hand. She noticed, as she had avoided doing since February, how much more grey there seemed to be amongst his brown hair, and how very weary the stoop of his shoulders was as he sat. He did not seem to hear when she came in.

'Well, Giles?'

He looked up but did not turn round.

'What happened?' She crossed the room towards him.

'They'd tell me nothing of Hugh or Bridget, except that they were both committed to gaol in Gloucester. Mr Bourne said he was sorry matters had come to this pass, and for his part he would hold no one longer than his duty required.'

'Good God. And of yourself?'

'They will endorse a request to be excused returning to the Clink until the fourteenth of next month as opposed to the twenty-fourth of this as first stated, Henry Bourne to take custody of me in the interim. Bourne has been very decent.'

'Indeed.'

'Aye, indeed. He need not have gone out of his way to stand surety for me in the first place, and he certainly need not do so again now.'

The room was stuffy in the July heat, even at night; Mrs Branton put her candle down on the table beside his, went and eased the window-catch out of its rest and pushed the window open.

'Did you see him?' Giles asked from behind her.

'For a few minutes.'

'Did he tell you anything?'

'He could not. There was a keeper stood in the corner.'

'I see.'

'Giles, what are we to do?'

'I do not know. It has been heard of, when they are trying to bring charges against someone. Children may know, and tell, more than they think sometimes. And yet I did not think Henry Bourne would consent to such a thing.'

'Well, he has.'

'I wonder. Hugh is near sixteen.'

'Still a child, for heaven's sake!'

'No – I only meant to say that he is reaching the age when there may well be things you and I do not know about him.'

'What do you mean?' She half-turned to look at his face, dimly lit in the candleflames.

'I am not sure. But I do not think Henry Bourne would have permitted this if he could help it. He is a good man.'

She swung away from him again and stared out at the moonlight. The leaves of a shrub moved as some small animal hid in them, rustling loud in the silence. It was all wrong, silence between them, and even worse was the necessity of speaking just to break it. She said,

'When will you leave Bourne's for London?'

'As late as I can without missing my day.' And then he added quietly, 'I promise you I will not leave for London until Hugh is at home again.'

She made no reply, and in the empty pause his words rang with their hollowness. It was a relief when she spoke again.

'And you are sure they will do nothing but keep you in his house and send you back to the Clink next month?'

'No,' he said. 'I am not sure. Whatever they think they can get out of Hugh and Bridget, it cannot be but that…'

'It is your life in the balance. I know … I know.'

He took a breath. 'There's no call to despair now. They have not charged me with anything yet; and if they do, we will fight the case every inch, and fight to win.'

'And if we lose?'

'Then we will fight that battle too.'

She did not answer.

XXIV

'What were you doing at Ford's house in Gloucester last spring?'

Hugh said nothing. He felt he had been standing in front of them for hours, but perhaps that was only because he was tired, and hungry. It was late afternoon, and he had not been brought food since noon the day before. Hugh had thought of telling the justices so, but then, they probably already knew, and besides it was all he could do to keep his mind on his answers and his tongue in check. Claydon went on, and on, and never explained a question, and sometimes Hugh did not even know whether he had denied or admitted something. He did not know how much he had told them.

Claydon had grown impatient and was pacing the room. Hugh went on looking at the table. His eyes were too weary to follow Claydon's movements.

'I was there with my father.'

'And what was his business there?'

'You had best ask my father,' Hugh said, and immediately wished he had not.

'What does your father know of these dealings?' That was Mr Bourne.

'Nothing!' His voice sounded suddenly even more desperate, and he repeated firmly, 'nothing.'

'Did he send you to speak to John Crowe?'

'What?'

'You spoke to John Crowe the pedlar in the street. What was your business? Or was it your father's business?' Mr Bourne's voice was sharp with a strange mingling of relief and dread.

He was recovering his wits. 'John Crowe is a pedlar?'

'So, he gives himself out.'

Hugh shrugged with over-studied nonchalance. 'I may have bought something from him, I suppose. I do not remember.'

'Did you also buy something from him when you saw him at the Unicorn in Merford?' This was Claydon again.

Hudson, Hugh thought. But he said again, 'I do not remember.' It was all he could think of. And then Claydon asked, 'do you know this writing?'

Hugh looked up. Claydon was holding a paper, thrusting it towards him. He knew it, and he knew what it said. It was the note he had written to Crowe and left in the old cot. Somehow, they had found it. The letters on the paper in front of him ran into a blur. He realised he was swaying on his feet, and he folded his arms across his stomach.

'It is useless to deny your own hand. You will please tell us why you wrote it, and who gave you your instructions.'

'I – I do not know.'

'Hugh, who else was part of this?' Mr Bourne asked, almost as though he were begging. 'Who else, apart from Bridget Lister, helped to hide and to disperse these things?'

Hugh looked at the magistrate, and for one burning moment longed to tell the truth. But the thought was foolish. He dropped his eyes again, and lied, 'I do not know.'

'We know what dealings you had with Crowe.' Claydon again. 'We know he had dealings with Lockwood. And with Branton Hall. There are others we can ask, if you will not say, but it would be better for you if you did not make that necessary.'

'I do not know. I do not know.' It was not defiance any longer; it was more that he was so giddy with racing fears he could barely have given his own name, let alone the string of events last spring they wanted him to tell them about.

It was only at the end of the examination, after he had signed his name to a sheet of paper that he was too weary and too sick to read properly now, that the words jumped out at him. Crowe. The note. Nobody – even Hugh – was stupid enough to leave a note like that undestroyed. *We know what dealings you had...*

'When did you make Crowe a spy?'

'What?' That was Mr Bourne.

'He *gave* you that note. You cannot have arrested him and taken it, he would not have kept it. Who else told you I was speaking to him? Who told you my name, that I met him in Gloucester, that - ?'

Claydon looked up sharply. 'We are asking the questions. You may go.'

But it did not matter. He knew, now, who had been watching them. And yes, he was a fool, and no, he did not know who to trust. But he did want to know *when* – whether he had trusted a liar right from the beginning, when he first met the man with his piercing eyes in the stable at the Raven, or whether they had taken and bullied him later so that when he came back to Merford it was to give them what they wanted. There was no use in hiding anything anyway. Crowe would tell them – except that he had not, or he and Bridget would not find themselves here, struggling not to answer a thousand questions. Perhaps Lockwood had not been so stupid, had not trusted Crowe – or anyone – so much that his evidence was sufficient. But Hugh and Bridget were weak as well as reckless enough to know and to tell all Claydon wanted. If Hugh knew what it was they thought he could tell them that Crowe could not, he might be able to deny it. But if he did not know, he would not be tempted to tell.

Only he had not been a fool trusting Stephen, from the day he agreed to take him to Mass until that last afternoon at the willow-flat. It was the people you never thought to mistrust that you had to watch. He was cursing himself for signing the paper at the end of the examination. His father would not have. But then his father would not have got into this situation at all.

*   *   *

There was no more fight in Bridget, or even any denials. It must be the third time she had stood before them now, and the notion of trying to answer well, or cleverly, or courageously seemed to belong to another world. She had pressed her lips together, fixed her eyes on the floor and wrapped her arms about her waist, and concentrated grimly on standing upright. And on not hearing what the magistrates were saying. She tried to think of Richard, but that hurt too much now. She could not think of him without remembering her father's accusing face after she had played her fool's game in St Martin's church, could not think anything except that if they hanged him she would never forgive herself. She could not have said now exactly why; it was all mixed up in a fever of shame and self-contempt and fear...

'Bridget, do you know this book?'

Claydon's tone had changed. She looked up at the volume he held in his hand.

'Come here and look at it.'

Slowly, uncertainly, Bridget walked to the table until she was close enough to read the words on the title-page Claydon had opened. *A True, Sincere and Modest Defence of English Catholics that suffer for their Faith both at Home and Abroad; against a False, Seditious and Slanderous Libel Entitled: The Execution of Justice in England.*

Mr Bourne said, 'A copy of this book was – er – found in St Martin's Church the autumn before last. Do you know who put it there?'

Claydon said, 'I think perhaps you do, little maid. We know you are somewhat familiar with the trafficking of popish books; we know your parents' house is near St Martin's. This business goes back a little further than this last year, perhaps?' Bridget shook her head. It was as though she had been watching a rock tremble on a cliff-edge for a long time, and now it was falling towards her and she could not move. 'Do you not know what it means to spread traitorous, poisonous writings by that arch-traitor Allen? To insult the Queen's majesty and the Church by placing it in the very chancel? Are you utterly foolhardy, or merely ignorant?'

'It is not. That book is not traitorous.'

'So, you have read it, then?'

Mr Bourne interposed. 'Bridget, listen. Perhaps you were not aware of what you did. We know you have been brought up wholly in popery, and you are not to be held responsible for that. But by your own acts you have made yourself culpable, in some measure. And so, you understand, we must have an answer from you.'

'There is no treason in it! There is no treason in maintaining that if you hang a man because he is a priest, he is a martyr of religion and no traitor! There is no treason but that you make – '

'Are you sure, Bridget?' He had the book open and was looking down at it. '"Christ… hath right in his Church over all kingdoms, to plant and pluck up, to build and to destroy…" Can you tell me this has *nothing* to do with sedition?' She made no answer. '"…kings be received of the bishop that in God's behalf annointeth them…their people may and, by order of Christ's supreme minister, their chief pastor on earth, must needs break with them" … Bridget?'

'Who gave you Allen's book?' Claydon again.

Bridget shook her head. She could hardly move it, for it seemed to be filled with stones, and her throat was dry.

'Was it your brother? We know he is a popish priest, and we know he was in Merford. If you tell us the truth about this matter, we may not say any more about your parents having harboured him in their house.'

She almost looked up at that, but did not because they would read her parents' guilt in her face. 'You cannot prove that,' she said desperately.

'Can we not? Your brother is in prison at this moment. Think you he has not been questioned, even as you have? Think you he has not spoken of - ?'

'That is not the matter in hand.' Mr Bourne said, 'we are more concerned to know whether he carried this tract of Allen's.'

'And if he did not, who did. Could it have come from Branton Hall, perhaps?' Claydon again. 'Come, you will not have your own brother presumed guilty if you know who is truly to blame?'

'I don't know – I don't know…'

Claydon strode round the table and seized her by the shoulder; grasped her hair so that her head came up and she had to look at him. 'I think you had better know, little maid. Because that brother of yours cannot afford to have much more dirt to his name.'

'Mr Claydon –' came Mr Bourne's voice.

'Did you get that thing from Branton?'

'*Yes.*' And then she had wrenched herself free, not in defiance but sheer terror, and backed away, blindly, across the room. Her eyes were smarting with pain and then overflowing into tears and she let herself cry. She kept backing until she was against the wall, and then she let herself fall to the ground and went on crying. Crying for Richard; for Hugh; for her parents; for herself. For every-thing… crying until there was nothing in the world but her tears, her sobs, and the grey-blue folds of her skirt with her fist clenched into it – always afterwards cloth of that particular shade of blue sickened her…

Someone was slapping her face, shaking her so that her head knocked against the wall. Claydon was still talking, still asking the same question and demanding the same answer. But you cannot talk and cry at the same time, if you only do it hard enough, so she cried until there was no room to speak.

A voice that for a moment sounded like Stephen's but was really Mr Bourne's was saying, 'for God's sake, the child's frightened out of her wits – you cannot call this evidence... Stop, for God's sake...'

Bridget did not really remember how it ended, or how she got out of that room. She hazily recalled a paper she was ordered to sign, and Mr Bourne putting a hand gently on her shoulder as she stumbled on the stairs. Later, she woke in her chamber in the gaol, with her head aching and her throat sore as it often is after one has been crying too much. She lay quite still for a while, wondering what time – or for that matter what day – it was now, gathering her thoughts, remembering. And as her stomach tightened against the recollection of what had happened, Bridget thought of Branton Hall. She thought of the way the sun fell onto the parlour table, and the orchard with the children's voices dancing between the trees. She thought of Mr Branton's voice reading aloud in the parlour in twilit evenings this last spring. She remembered coming to live at the Hall, and finding Mistress Isabel, and Mrs Branton, and Agnes, and

Hugh. It was as though she had walked into a shrine and destroyed it.

A sentence ran into her head, a voice from a long way away. *The Lord is my light and my salvation, whom shall I fear...* A long way from the darkness and the sickness in her stomach and the smell, the unbearable stench, of betrayal.

*   *   *

Hugh was sitting with a book open before him when he heard the footsteps go past the door. He had never thought he could be so glad of his schoolbooks, or spend so long studying at a stretch, but it kept one from thinking about the wrong things.

It was the heavy feet of a keeper he heard, and the rustle of a skirt. And something else; it sounded like sobbing –

He did not even stop to wonder whether the skirt belonged to some other girl or woman. He was tugging at the door before he remembered that it was locked. Then he pressed his face against it, searching for even a crack, trying to look through the keyhole, and all the time hearing her tears and seeing nothing.

'Bridget – Bridget...'

They had passed up the stairs. Hugh slid to the floor, his back against the door and his head dropped forward onto his knees.

He did not know how many hours later he raised his head at the sound of the keeper unlocking the door, stood up and followed him as bidden out of the chamber and down the stairs. It was a room within the buildings of the Northgate that they went to, that Hugh thought was usually the warden's.

Claydon was there, and another man waiting – not the under-keeper, but a servant of Claydon's. Hugh realised, as the keeper left, that on previous occasions Mr Bourne's presence had somehow made him feel safer.

The magistrate had Hugh's note in front of him again. 'You have acknowledged your hand in this paper. Now tell me why you wrote it, who gave you your instructions, and what other letters you wrote or delivered.'

Hugh did not reply. A dullness had spread through him, the shame and sick fear replaced by a terrifying calm.

'Look, we hold Lockwood, and the girl Bridget, and your father also. We would, of course, rather hang the guilty than the innocent, and we would prefer not to be harsh in collecting the information we need. But if you will not comply...'

Your father. Lockwood. Bridget. The sobbing in the corridor. The possibilities sickened him, and yet the turmoil did not return. Hugh heard himself speak. 'No. You do not have evidence against my father, or anyone except me: that's my hand you have there. That is why you are questioning me and Bridget, and not anyone else.'

'And you are deeper in this even than I thought. Up to your neck, indeed.'

Hugh's voice was starting to shake, but he got the words out. 'That still does not give you a case against anyone else.'

'Oh, you have a lawyer's tongue from your father! But you will tell me the truth, you damned brat, if I have to have it scourged out of you. And I promise you I will not spare the girl either.'

Hugh's eyes slid to Claydon's man watching quietly from near the door, and to the cords of the whip he held, and he knew that no mere beating was meant. Why had Bridget been crying?

'You can't do that to her!' It was not what he had meant to say at all.

'By God, you think yourself brave. So, you are not going to confess, and you are going to save your popish friends from justice? You do your father no good by shielding him anyway, little hero, and you're not helping yourself either.'

Hugh looked up, and now he was shaking, and that infuriated him. 'I am not shielding my father,' he said, his voice as clear as he could manage without it cracking, 'because he had nothing to do with it. And no, I am not going to tell you anything.'

The magistrate rose. His face had reddened. 'In that case,' he said through gritted teeth, 'I will beat every ounce of information you have out of you; and afterwards, if you're still set on making a papist martyr of yourself, we can go and find out what the judge and jury have to say.' Hugh felt his cheeks flame at the sneer. 'Or,' Claydon added, 'you can stop quivering like a leaf there and tell me now where you got this dungheap of popish sedition and what you did with it.'

Hugh forced himself to meet his look. When Claydon merely smiled – a smile of scorn and unmistakable triumph – he stepped forward, right up to the magistrate, and silently undid the button at the throat of his doublet. His fingers were shaking, but he no longer knew whether with rage or fear. He had opened his doublet, let it fall to the floor, tugged back his shirt. And all the time his breath was coming in gasps and his stomach was churning and Claydon's face alternately loomed close and glared from far away.

Suddenly Claydon swung his fist, a box on the ear that sent Hugh spinning against the wall. He tasted blood in his mouth as his face crashed against the plaster and saw stars. He heard the magistrate shout an order, but he was still angry; at the first blow he braced himself against the wall, his fingers scrabbling for something to grip. He must not give in, but nothing – nothing – he had ever known at home or even at school could have enabled him to imagine this. He never knew afterwards whether he had been crying aloud or only in his head. He remembered that he bit his lips to shreds, because if he made any sound at all he would start talking and he must not do that. But he was sure there were ugly, groaning cries in his ears, and he did not know who else could have made them.

XXV

Giles Branton was tired, wary and irritated. He had arrived at Henry Bourne's house that morning to yield to his custody according to agreement and had been dismayed (if not altogether surprised) to find an armed escort under whose charge Mr Claydon proposed to send him to Gloucester. He spent the dusty, sweaty journey trying to think clearly if he had to think at all, concluding only that if he knew what Hugh had been up to, he might be able to defend both himself and his son. But that information was unlikely to be forthcoming.

They had brought him to the Northgate gaol when they reached the city that evening, for two reasons, he thought: firstly, the Castle might well be full of prisoners, it being so near the Assizes; secondly, Geoffrey Lockwood was in the castle, and Claydon did not intend that Giles Branton have any chance to confer with Lockwood. But they had barely stopped at the Northgate long enough to give the prisoner's name to the keeper, and then he had been taken to the Boothall, the great building belonging to the burghers and aldermen, but used for Assizes and Sessions and other matters of the Queen's business. In a small chamber near the hall, both Claydon and Bourne were seated behind a table, waiting for him, although he had the impression that Henry Bourne had not had much more warning about this examination than he himself. Claydon, on the other hand, looked like a man who has seen all the cards, and only needs to play the game through, watching the prisoner constantly with piercing, calculating eyes.

Giles Branton was calculating too. They had still told him infuriatingly little, but it was clear that the point under question was trafficking in Catholic books. They seemed convinced that popish literature was still being conveyed all over the county from somewhere in Merford, and they had turned their eyes from the Raven to Branton Hall. Crowe had turned informer when he was arrested last spring, as they had feared, and he had told something of Hugh and Bridget. What else they had learned, and from whom, he had yet to deduce.

'Mr Branton,' Claydon was saying, 'you must understand that these facts have placed you under grave suspicion. We must have some answer from you.'

'When you bring charges against me, I will answer them. As for these books, I am afraid you will have carry out your search for unlicensed literature without my assistance.'

'When we bring charges it may be a little late to begin clearing yourself.'

'I rather thought that was the purpose of a trial.'

'You're a proper lawyer. But the law has a way to deal with traitors, Mr Branton.'

'Do you think you are talking to a child?' he said with sudden anger. 'There's no statute makes it treason to deal in Catholic writings and we all know it. Search my house if you like, question me till kingdom come, but even if you could prove all this you cannot hang me for it.'

Mr Bourne spoke rather wearily. 'The statutes do not, as you say, expressly prescribe this offence treason, but that trafficking in popish books is against the law you cannot deny. Her Grace's Proclamations forbid it. And the spreading of seditious writings that defame the Queen's grace is a felony, and men have hanged for it.'

'You will need to prove that there was sedition, and not only what you refer to as popish superstition, in any of the writings concerned in order to make that charge stick. And further, that I handled and spread abroad those particular works.'

'What makes you think we cannot prove that?' Claydon said. 'Furthermore, Mr Branton, the statutes most certainly prescribe death for other offences of which I fancy you would find it hard to acquit yourself in any court of law. Harbouring and assisting of priests, for one, is a felony. To be reconciled to the Romish church is treason; and so is it also treason to persuade others to reconcile…'

'You have strayed from the point, Mr Claydon.'

'Not entirely. You say these matters in question cannot be accounted treason, but I would say that so constantly and perniciously to spread abroad popish writings, even including the seditious work of Doctor Allen, *is* to persuade men to the Church of Rome. Which, as a lawyer like yourself will know, is treason under the statute of the year 1581, the twenty-third of Her Grace's reign.'

Was that what Claydon meant to do?

'Thank you, I am aware of the clauses of that statute.'

Could they make a case out of that?

'Listen,' said Mr Bourne. 'We have no wish to be more severe than is necessary, but the popery in this district has gone on too long, has become too flagrant. We have sought to punish only the persons who are truly at the heart of it – and I warn you, it can be done. I swear to God I have no desire to see – but all that we can find out points to Branton Hall. Are we correct? Or where else must we look?'

'In other words, you want to make an example, and if I will not put a noose round some other man's neck, you'll put it round mine.'

'Put it in any words you like, the matter is whether you clear yourself or whether you hang and forfeit for treason.' Claydon again.

This is working out remarkably well for you, is it not, Claydon? Though I'm damned if you get your hands on Branton this or any other way. But he went on looking at Henry Bourne.

'For God's sake, Gi – Mr Branton. If you are not guilty, then tell us – '

'I will accuse neither myself nor any other, Mr Bourne. You know that. Do not ask me for help.' He knew he should have left it there, that to make anything that sounded like a plea was always a mistake, but he heard himself say, 'but leave the children alone, will you?'

* * *

It was dusk when Mr Bourne came into Hugh's cell and sat down on the stool. Hugh drew his cloak about him and did not move from the corner where he had curled up. He still felt as though every nerve he possessed was shot with pain and he kept having to grit his teeth, and yet for some reason the presence of Mr Bourne made him more uneasy than anything else.

'Hugh,' Stephen's father began, and then stopped. 'For Christ's sake, what is that bruise on your face?'

Hugh looked away. Part of him would have liked to tell Mr Bourne, and dare him to side with Claydon, but he did not want to think about it again. He muttered, 'I made Mr Claydon angry.'

'I'm sorry.' Mr Bourne said. 'That should not have happened.' And he could not see Hugh's back.

The magistrate was speaking again. 'Hugh, I need you to listen to me. Mr Claydon is determined to know the truth of this matter. And, you know, if you will not tell us we will have to deduce it from the information we have.'

Go on then, Hugh said silently.

'Mr Claydon believes that what is most likely, given his record, his being in Gloucester last spring, and the finding of these books, is that your father is behind this.'

'My father?' His thoughts went back, reluctantly, to Claydon and his questions. That, then, was where they had been driving him all the time. Was that the truth they thought he was biting back, all the time he was trying not to betray Bridget and the Lockwoods – and Crowe?

'Can you clear him, Hugh?'

'He did not do this. I swear he did not.'

'Then who did? Where did you get all that popish writing from?'

We would rather hang the guilty... 'You have to believe me.'

'Hugh, I want to believe you. But you are not making it easy, and you are making it even less easy for me to convince Claydon. He's searched the Hall itself now and found books there. You shield your father, of course you do, but all the evidence...'

'But if I tell you...' Hugh stopped, bit his lip, and spoke carefully. 'But what if I did know something, and it was other people who I –'

'Yes, I know,' Mr Bourne said, 'There are other names you are hiding. Bridget, and so on. But it still seems that –

well, in Mr Claydon's words, it is clear there is a web of sedition here, but the spider at the heart of it is Giles Branton.'

'And you? What do you think?' Hugh looked straight at Mr Bourne, and then wished he had not. He looked for a moment so like Stephen, and so wretched that it was frightening.

'I know what I do not want to think.'

Hugh swallowed hard. 'If I told you everything you think I know, what would you do?'

'I do not know, Hugh. Mr Claydon speaks of sending the case to the Assizes – I do not know if there is matter to make a charge. I hope not. I do not want hangings. But this trafficking in popery does have to stop.'

Hugh said nothing. His back was throbbing again, and Mr Bourne's words and Claydon's and the terrifying threat in both were spinning through his head. He remembered William Lampley. He remembered the priests hanged in Gloucester; how his father had gone each time to the city to witness it and come back tight-lipped. He pushed that thought away.

'Hugh, please listen. If you can clear your father, for God's sake do it. Give me something to tell Claydon, because he'll not drop the case for mere denials. But you are going to have to do it quickly, because the summer Assizes begin very soon.'

After he had gone, Hugh shut his eyes and let himself fear. *Father arrested. My mother. The children. The Hall raided. The Hall taken. Father arrested. Father hanged – my father…* At last, to stop himself screaming then and there, he got to his feet and paced the floor, trying to think.

If he told them nothing, they would believe Father guilty. Father did not know what had happened, but he would guess that if he was not responsible, Hugh and Bridget were. If he told them the truth, they would see that Father had known nothing, but they would have a case against Geoffrey Lockwood, and also Jake, and even Mrs Lockwood. And in the end, the spiders at the heart of their 'web of sedition' were only himself and Bridget.

If I tell them nothing. If I tell them the truth. The thoughts chased each other round his head, losing all meaning as they melted into nightmare and hardened again into waking fear, all night as he tried to sleep, and all day as he tried to keep awake. Another dusk and another night crawling through the gaol, and still all he knew clearly was that the only thing that would help was to undo the past, and God himself could not do that. He must have slept a little, because when early next day the key again turned in the lock, he opened his eyes at the sound.

Hugh sat up painfully and rose uncertainly to his feet. His hand curled around the stones of the wall behind him as though that would protect him from having to go out and face the magistrates again. But the door opened only enough for his father to slip into the chamber, and then was locked again.

His father. Hugh stared, his eyes wide with fear and his chest bursting with relief. Father strode over and seized Hugh's hands. 'Hugh. I am not supposed to be here – I had to bribe the keeper.' His voice was matter of fact and his face calm, but his hands gripped so tightly that the fingers dug into Hugh's palms. 'It does not make much difference, but I had rather I told you than they did.'

Hugh could not speak.

'I have been charged with treason. I expect a trial at the summer Assizes.' And then he caught Hugh in his arms and held him there so he would not collapse to the floor.

It had happened; the nightmare was real, the question answered. This was what he had done.

His father laid a hand gently on the tangled curls of Hugh's hair. 'Hugh, your face is all bruised.' And then, as Hugh winced involuntarily at the pressure of his father's arm around him, 'you've been beaten too. Badly. What...?'

'Nothing I did not deserve.'

Hugh did not know if his father heard the words, muttered into his shoulder, but he said, 'Hugh, listen. I do not know what has been happening, but I do know that you have done nothing I cannot forgive.'

At that, Hugh tore away and flung himself into the corner of the cell. 'I should have told them the truth,' he said aloud. 'I tried so hard to – but I should have told them the truth.'

Father came and sat down beside him. 'Suppose you tell me the truth.'

When it was all told, between halting explanations, gentle but firm questioning, whispered answers, neither of them said anything for a little while. Father leaned his head back against the wall and closed his eyes a moment. In the silence the horror of what he had done came flooding back over Hugh. Why had he not known this would happen? If danger had crossed their minds at all, it was only as a risk to themselves, and even that had never been quite real, through that heady spring and summer of drumbeats in their souls and fire in their hearts and Bridget's eyes dancing in a way he would never forget.

'But –' he said, 'it's like I told them – the evidence is against me, not you or – or anyone else. That is why they questioned me and Bridget in the first place. Why do they not…?'

'You told them that?' Father almost smiled. 'You are a Branton all through, aren't you?'

'But why?'

'In theory, they could,' Father said. 'The law makes no exemption for your age, and if the charge will stand against me it would stand against you… But a boy not sixteen, in a matter of religion? Not a good story. Besides which, you have nothing to forfeit which anyone wants to gain.'

Hugh made himself meet his father's eye. 'In that case,' he said, 'we should tell them the truth.'

'Hugh, I don't know. If we do that, firstly we give them a case against the Lockwoods at least as good as the one they are making against me. Secondly, I'm not minded to put you and Bridget in danger, however lessened by your youth. And –' He sighed. 'I am not sure how much difference it would make, even if you told them everything you have told me. They need not believe you, that I had no part in it. It is not only this business... There are other things, Hugh. Things which perhaps if I had told you... and there is also –'

'Claydon.'

'Quite. So, it seems we have much to lose and perhaps nothing to gain from speaking.'

'But we cannot – I cannot let...'

'I think perhaps what we cannot do – or I should say, what neither of us is entitled to do – is to inform on other Catholics to spare our own danger.'

'I don't want to be spared,' Hugh said.

'I do. But it will not be that way.'

The unbearable silence fell again. Father spoke softly into it. 'At the least they may send you home soon.'

Home. The word bit into him like a fish-hook. He had not thought of going home. To Mother who would try to keep loving him in spite of everything. To a house that would always have an emptiness now, an empty place in every room to accuse him. The children – Marian and the twins would not remember having had a father and it would be his fault. Home, where he would have to wake day after day to the knowledge of this, and carry it always, forever.

There was a quiet knock at the door. Father said, 'I must go... Hugh, do not look like that. I've not lost this case yet, and even if I do, there are several obstacles I can put between that and the sentence. It – it may well be all right.'

'But if it is not?'

He rose and laid a hand on the boy's head. 'Hugh. You are still forgiven.'

Hugh did not answer. Perhaps they both knew that the bitterest of curses could not have stabbed more deeply.

*   *   *

After that there was nothing to do but hate himself. He was not questioned again and heard nothing more of the case. He was not sent home.

He gave up counting days. Waking was the choking realisation that his nightmares were true as daylight, and sleep was a thing he avoided desperately because each night his father's head lay severed before him, or his mother gazed at him from under a widow's coif with heartbroken, loving eyes, or Branton Hall was burning to ashes in front of him and instead of flames crackling he could hear only the children sobbing in the dark. And sometimes Bridget was there, her eyes no longer dancing but burning with tears in her chalk-white face. He knew she was blaming herself, and he wanted to tell her that it was his fault, but he could not speak.

Sometimes, in spite of what his father had said, the thought flickered like a hope through his mind that he would be charged, if not instead then as well. At least that would be some sort of justice. At least then he would not have to go home. He did not know what it would mean for the others if that happened, but none of that would worry him because he'd be dead. Hugh believed in purgatory and Heaven, but most of all dead meant not having to think any more, not having to see anyone or go anywhere. Dead was being able to curl into a soft darkness and never come out as long as the world was still here.

It ran through his thoughts also that it would not be particularly difficult to die. All you had to do was not eat the food that was brought and eventually you would be dead. But that would be suicide and you would go to Hell, and Hell, unlike life, did not have to end.

He did not stop eating and drinking, even while he sat hoarding the pain in his back which had become the closest thing he had to comfort. Each throb gave him a dark satisfaction, akin to that of smashing his fist into Jem Carter's face when Carter had been throwing his cheap, stinging little barbs. He did not stop praying either, going mechanically, desperately, round the string of rosary beads. He forced himself to say the names of the dead priests, Rowsham, Sandys, and Lampley's name also, praying for the miracle he did not deserve but his father surely did. Not because there was a grain of comfort in any of it, but because it seemed like the only thing left.

Some words drifted into his head, of someone else who was in prison now, three counties away. *I could do more damage than ten spies in half an hour, if I once gave way...* But Hugh had not given way. It was not cowardice that had made him kill his father, only – folly. Pride. Thoughtlessness. Vanity. And he had thought – no, he had not thought, he had simply assumed – that he was doing right. That if he was taking risks, it was all right, because one did take risks for the Faith.

He remembered the talk he had had with Richard Lister that had both frightened and drawn him. The priest riding away, and the longing that had risen in him – and risen again and again, never without fear, but never quite quenched by it either. Until once or twice Hugh had almost thought he might tell his father that it was there... Hugh clenched his fingernails into his palms almost enough to draw blood. He wanted to slap the boy who had stood by that window, daring to fancy that he had anything to fear from the perils of Richard Lister's calling.

*   *   *

Mr Bourne had come to the gaol with a sinking heart in answer to Giles Branton's message. It sank still further as he waited for a keeper to show the way, rose very slightly when he saw that they had given him the driest of the upper chambers, and retreated into numbness as the key turned in the lock.

Giles Branton rose at once. 'Mr Bourne, thank you for coming.'

'It's nothing,' he said.

'Have you washed your hands of this case?' There was no trace of irony or reproach in his tone, only urgency.

'Well –' Mr Bourne said, 'you know it is Mr Claydon who has taken charge of it. I hoped it would not come to this. When he told me he had got the case put up before the Assizes, I – but you will understand it cannot be withdrawn now.'

Giles seemed uninterested in his explanation. 'Listen. If you can, I want you to keep my son safe, at least until after the trial. Do not let them question him again. Do not let him see anyone. Anyone at all. Please.'

Henry Bourne stared. 'I – I can try. I think – I do not think he was going to be sent for again… Why?'

'It is safer – for him, and others.'

'Does he know something more that could damage you?'

Mr Branton paused. 'You could say that.'

Mr Bourne thought of the last time he had seen Hugh, and said, 'you do not trust him very much.'

'I am trying to protect him.'

Mr Bourne was suddenly cross. 'A little late, is it not? You might have thought of that before you made use of him to commit popish crimes. Not to mention John Lister's daughter.'

Giles Branton looked up sharply; but he only said, 'Will you do this for me?'

And, because one does not really have a right to be angry with a friend whom one has helped to bring to the gibbet, Mr Bourne said, 'I will do my best.'

After he had gone, Giles Branton stood still for some time, staring at the door which had closed behind him. It was Claydon's best card, after all. It might have been a weakness, to have so much of his evidence depending on children. But it was the card he would play against the prisoner's character, against the sympathy of upright, honourable men. Yet telling the truth need not make that any better; to begin with, it might not be believed.

The slur of traitor meant rather less to him now than it might have when first he encountered it, but he should have known that for every man there is some slander he cannot bear to die with in his ears; some accusation which will tempt him to tell everything, do anything to silence it. Something with which his enemies will taunt and his friends reproach him, which will send the blood rushing to his face no matter how many times he hears it.

His wife came in later. He said as little as he could of the case; he did not want, even to her, to repeat what he had heard from Hugh.

'I have sent a message to Jake Lockwood to tell him what has happened,' she said. 'He has gone on business to Bristol. I do not know if it will reach him in time.'

'There is little he can say that would not harm more than help. And good God, I cannot ask him to accuse his father –'

'Perhaps not. But he has some right to decide on the matter, do you not think?'

There was an edge of reproach in her voice which he understood. But one did not accuse other people of Catholic crimes, whether truthfully or not. And the meaning placed on one's silence was simply outside one's power. He moved away from her and sat by the table with the papers he had asked her to bring. 'Listen, there are some things I must talk with you about. This case – it is going to be complicated.'

'Yes.'

'You see – and this is important – they have not charged me with sedition: with setting forth seditious writings, and so on, which is a felony under a statute of the year '81. They have charged me with treason. Now, I've not seen the indictment, but I understand they are using the treason statute of that year, the same Will Lampley was hanged under last summer. The proposition is that all of this dealing in popish books constitutes persuading men away from their allegiance to her Grace, and to the Church of Rome.'

'And - can they do that? Is that within the law?'

'That's my point. The felony charge is the simple one. They only need a couple of witnesses to depose that I handled whatever works they pick out as seditious, and I'm a dead man. Well, a convicted man at least. The treason charge is, I think, tenuous. It is without precedent that I know of. It should be far easier for me to defend myself against.'

'Well – good, I suppose. But if they – if Claydon and Bourne know that, then why... ?'

'We can leave Bourne out of it, I think. But Claydon – well, I'm not in his confidence, but I can hazard a guess.' He put down the papers he was holding, but he did not look up at her. She remained standing, one hand touching the wall behind her.

'The goods and lands of any convicted felon are, of course, forfeit, and those held *in capite,* direct from the Crown, may be sold or granted to whomsoever the Crown thinks fit. That is the law. But the statute against seditious speech and writing makes the lands of felons guilty under *this* law forfeit only for the life of the felon. When he dies,

or is hanged, his heirs may claim. So, if they'd charged me
with this felony and then hanged me –'

'There'd be no gain for anyone.'

'Precisely. They could, of course, pardon my life and
keep the forfeiture until I died. That would be gainful, for
whoever sued for the grant, and a bloody nuisance for us.
But it would be a temporary gain only and would be limited
to those lands found to be tenure *in capite*. And I think
someone wants more.'

She said nothing, since it was obvious who was meant.
He was talking quite fast, in low clipped tones, his fingers
moving quickly through the papers he was looking at. She
was standing still, even her lips barely moving when she
spoke.

'Do you see, dearest? A traitor's goods and lands are
forfeit to the Crown in their entirety, and for good. If I'm
convicted of treason, there is a chance to take both life and
land.'

'But...' She took a breath. 'This is what I meant to say.
Can we not use the entail? Land that is entailed can be
forfeit only for the life in any case, because the traitor or
felon is not, in lawyer's terms, the absolute owner. As once
you explained to me...'

'That is true, as far as it goes. But you know about the
little war Claydon has been fighting with me in every court
he can think of. And in the latest campaign – he began this
just recently – he has raised questions about the land

settlements my father and grandfather made. Points to put the entail in doubt.'

'And is he right?'

'No, I do not think so. But if he can cast the matter sufficiently into doubt, and if I stand convicted of a crime which carries forfeiture...'

'I see.'

'Robert Claydon, I think, has decided to play for all or nothing.'

Her fingertips were pressed against the wall she was leaning against. 'What do you want me to do?'

'We have to make the case that the entail stands – and find someone to plead it for us. If I lose the case at the Assizes, we ask for a reprieve, and use the time both to defend the entail, and to try to get the forfeiture granted to someone who – who will use us well. If we cannot get a favourable lessee, then we have to convince Claydon that he cannot both hang me and have my land, and he had better settle for confiscation during my life. But I need to go through all this with you before – in the next few days. Because if we cannot get a reprieve, you still have to fight the case over the lands on behalf of the children.'

She forced her lips to obey her. 'Yes.'

He rose and began straightening the papers against the table-top. 'It all hangs on – Claydon's interest in my death turns on whether the entail stands. Though I have now and then thought that Robert Claydon would rather enjoy seeing my quarters adorning Gloucester gates quite regardless of any material gain thereby. But since such a speculation is neither useful nor charitable...'

'Stop that *now*.'

He did glance up at her then, for a moment. 'It's all right. I may well be able to drive a devil's bargain to have my estates spoiled and wasted for the rest of my life. If not, then –'

'Then?'

'I'd better convince that Assize court.'

And then he put the papers down and held her very close for some time.

XXVI

There were noises in the prison. Feet up and down stairs; sounds like metal scraping and clinking. Hugh listened, sitting in a corner of his cell bolt upright. He thought he heard doors opening, perhaps the main door. He glanced across at the barred window, but he knew already that very little was to be seen through it. If he could have screwed himself up to look.

The sounds died away, but Hugh was still listening, the limp blackness replaced for the moment by this tight, still watching. He was both relieved and afraid when the keeper came in at last and he could ask a question.

'I had almost forgot you, it's been that busy,' the keeper said. 'You hungry?'

'What is happening?'

'Happening? The Assizes is happening. The judges came into the city last night. We've had to get all the prisoners down to the Boothall to be ready.'

'For what?'

'For the pleadings. Every one of them's got to be there when they start taking the indictments. And we've to get them there. Then we've to make sure each one's at the bar to say guilty or not guilty when he's called to trial. Then we've to bring them that the jury votes guilty back to the gaol, and have the next lot ready when they're called. Then when they're all done we've to bring all the guilty prisoners back for the sentencing. And then…'

'That was why the chains this morning? And all the footsteps?'

'Yes, we took them all down for the arraignments.'

'My father too?'

The keeper looked at him with pity as he turned to go. 'Yes, lad. Your father too.'

*   *   *

Three weeks after the day he had run out of school at noon and ridden in miserable haste to Branton Hall with his news, Stephen Bourne was riding home along the familiar track. It was the end of July, and there would be no more school until the middle of September. He had taken this road alone for eighteen school days now, his mind divided between worry and confused guilt and the last fight he had had over it at school. At first there had been endless open-mouthed speculation, and Stephen had fought Carter and two or three of the other boys. Later they had found other things to talk about. But then today as he was going out through the schoolyard, Stephen had heard the name Branton unmistakably. He tried not to listen rather than hear anything he would feel obliged to pick a fight over, but he was hungry for news... The boys saw him and lowered their voices very slightly, and so he had to ask outright, 'What has happened?'

Jack Taylor answered, awkwardly. 'Mr Branton is going to go on trial. It's going to be tomorrow, at the Assizes.'

A claw of fear gripped him, and he had to force out a question. 'What for?'

'Spreading popish books. They're making it a treason charge.'

'They can't,' he said. 'They cannot – he will not be found guilty – they...'

'My father reckons he might well.' Taylor was almost apologetic.

Treason. Hugh's father. 'It's not true. You do not know what you are talking about. None of you –'

And then he had fled. When he came out of the stables at the Unicorn, he found that Jem Carter was at his elbow.

'Bourne...'

'What?'

'You're very troubled by it, are you not? About squire Branton.'

'Yes.'

'I – why? Why do you...?'

'Hugh Branton is my best friend.' How cowardly, Stephen thought, that he hoped Carter would believe it was no more than that.

'I know. But maybe it's fair enough, in the end. I mean nobody *likes* it, but what if he really was – what if he is a traitor?'

'He's not. Oh, go to hell, you –' Stephen was too desperate to notice that Carter's face was streaked with misery.

'If he's not, they will not hang him, will they? Nobody is trying to – to be cruel. And if he is a traitor, then – I mean, they *are* papists, and we *know* Branton was plotting about Jesuit books, and England has to be kept safe, does it not?'

'Good God.' Stephen exploded. 'What is *wrong* with you?'

He swung into the saddle and escaped as fast as his horse would carry him. He passed the turning to Branton Hall and found that he could not look round.

*   *   *

Henry Bourne was halfway through perhaps the most wretched journey he had made in his life. It was hot: sticky, dirty, heat, in which the only thing worth having was the next patch of shade across the road. The sun was unforgiving, even in the late afternoon, glaring and ruthlessly bright. He had been with the other county officers to receive the judges. He had sat through the Assize sermon and the opening of the court. He had been at the Assizes many times, of late sitting among the Justices of the Peace below the bench; before that, at least once, among the spectators with Giles, a young Gray's Inn student with a new-grown interest in all things legal and a compulsion to explain them to Henry at every opportunity.

The court moved briskly – Assize judges had not time to waste in any county on their circuit – through the list of indictments, and he had heard the grand jury return a *billa vera* against Giles Branton. Claydon had spoken for the bill; he could not have done much about it. Claydon had drawn up the indictment and arranged for Giles Branton to be added to the list of defendants for the summer Assizes. He had not known until it was too late. There was nothing he could have done.

They began taking pleas as soon as the indictments started coming back from the grand jury, so that the first trials could commence. He saw Giles, standing somewhat incongruous among the assortment of criminals shackled before the bar waiting to answer to their names. He heard Giles Branton, esquire, late of Branton near Merford, required to hold up his hand. He heard the charge read, heard him plead crisply *not guilty* and request to be tried by God and his country according to form. The clerk said, 'God send you a good deliverance'. The clerk's pen scratched on the register. Giles stepped back among the prisoners and gave place to the next. He gave no sign of having seen Henry Bourne. Perhaps he had not.

Mr Bourne learned from one of the under-clerks that the case was, in fact, to be held over for the next morning's trial jury. It was better to start a weightier case at the beginning of the day. Henry Bourne left soon after. He wanted no further part in it.

There was nothing he could do. There was no gain from staying. And yet as he rode home, he was burning not only from the sun. It was as though there was – ought to be – something he could do. He had never wished it, he had never asked Giles to be such a bloody idiot, he had not started this enquiry nor drawn up the charges. It was not as though anything were being fabricated, in any case: the facts were clear. He did not like them, but they could not be gainsaid. Yet he could not stay, which meant he was running away.

When he reached home, after even the late summer dusk, he found Stephen waiting for him in the doorway to the parlour.

'Is it true?' Stephen demanded. His father looked at him, the answer written all over his weary face. 'Is it true they are going to try Hugh's father and hang him?"

His father walked past him into the room and sat down heavily. 'So, you've heard.'

'You have to stop it!'

'Stephen, if I could I would have already. But –'

Stephen gripped the edge of the table. 'You have to stop it. He is innocent. I know, because – because we are guilty.'

Henry Bourne looked up. 'What?' And then he said not one word more while Stephen told it. He held his son's gaze, his eyes unmoving and his face expressionless. At one point, his fingers began playing with a quill which lay in front of him, his thumb brushing its fronds up and down, and the tiny swish pulsed under Stephen's words all the rest of the time he spoke.

When Stephen had finished, the rasping swish repeated itself once or twice more, and then Henry Bourne rose and walked away towards the window. At last, without turning round, he spoke. 'Stephen, go to your chamber.' Stephen unclasped his fingers from the table-edge and went.

The only thing he really resented was that Stephen did not look like her. There was a portrait, that hung on the parlour wall, but that did not look like her either. You could collect from it the information that Alice had had brown hair that curled where it escaped from her coif, and light blue eyes, and was slender and not very tall. That was as far as it went. He had half-hoped that in the son that she had left him he might have the bitter comfort of a true portrait, but Stephen, dark-haired and long-legged, took almost entirely after himself, with echoes of his grandmother. Indeed once or twice Mother had been heard to call him Henry by mistake.

But today... today Stephen had stood here in the parlour, and it was in that split second when he reached out and gripped the edge of the table as though he were hanging on for dear life that he had seen Alice's hands. The hand he had slipped a ring onto at Branton church, looking at it because it was the most perfect hand God had ever created, and also because there was a cloud shadowing the light blue eyes that he had not wanted to see.

He remembered those hands, too, gripping the edge of a table, thumbs pressed white, hanging on as though for dear life while the birth pangs that became her death throes seized her. He remembered standing down here in the parlour, the day after the little girl-baby had been born, waiting. Giles Branton had been there. He had come bringing a physician, not the usual man from the town, but someone Alice had said Mrs Branton could send, and had somehow desperately wanted to have look at both her and the frail infant. And Martha had said it was better to humour her, even if there was nothing more anyone could do.

At last, the strange doctor had come in again; and he had asked him, 'well?', it being all he could trust himself with, and the other man had said gravely, 'I think you had best go upstairs.'

And he had gone up to the lying-in chamber and stood in the doorway. He had known as soon as he opened the door, by the way her breathing sounded, that he had lost her. He did not know if she knew he had come in, because she had not the strength to turn her eyes to him. Her head was turned to gaze out of the window, and looped over her hand was a string of beads. The pale child was beside her now, quivering a little with each unpractised breath, the minute head wet with sweat (it must have been sweat) that looked like splashes of water. He supposed he must have gone over and sat beside the bed, because he distinctly remembered the scrape of the chair as he got up to leave after it was all over, but that was his last memory of Alice: lying in the great bed the other side of the room, looking away from him towards the window; her face drawn tight around her sky-blue eyes, her hair limp and damp around her whitened forehead, and over the whole a terrible tranquility that contrasted oddly with her laboured breathing. And the rosary in her hand.

Mr Bennett had been there when he came downstairs, leaving Alice's body to the care of the women who did these things best. Giles Branton had turned to leave, but he had stopped him. Mr Bennett was a good parson, but he had hardly been six years in the parish, and Henry Bourne had known Giles Branton since they were boys.

They had buried the older and the younger Alice three days later, in the same coffin, and Mother had come to take over the household and bring up Stephen, who was not yet three years old. One would not expect to grieve over an infant who had scarcely lived long enough to open her eyes as one did for a wife... he remembered how pitiably small the new-born corpse had been; how achingly wrong it seemed that such tiny limbs should rot to dust under the earth instead of growing. He remembered feeling that it was unfair that Alice had lost her life to bring this infant to birth, and it could not do her the courtesy of living.

And this – this was unfair too. It was not as though he had enjoyed doing his duty in this matter; it was not as though he had asked Giles Branton to mix himself up in such a business, let alone a pair of children. Was that not enough, without Stephen walking in and twisting his hands, Alice's hands, around the table, and handing him the worst confession he could have imagined receiving? Dear God…

The room was too stuffy to breathe in. He pushed open the side door and went out into the garden, which was only a little cooler. He walked up and down, clenching his hand around the handkerchief he held so that the beads wrapped in it pressed into his palm. The only shred of comfort was that it seemed Claydon had been wrong about Giles Branton, on this score at least. But the evidence of that was Stephen's confession – and what Hugh and Bridget had refused to tell. And, God, the trial was tomorrow, and Giles would stand there and let them condemn him before he would allow suspicion to fall on his son. What did Stephen expect him to do? What, come to that, did God expect him to do? What would Alice…? Slowly he unfolded her handkerchief and stood there a long time looking down at her rosary beads curled in his hand.

It was late in the night when Mr Bourne at last went and knocked at Stephen's chamber. He got no answer. Perhaps the boy was asleep. Nevertheless, he went quietly inside. 'Stephen?' But there was still no answer, and the bed was empty.

He ran downstairs again. He looked in the parlour and peered into the hall. He did not want to wake his mother for a foolish scare. But he knew it was not a scare. Stephen had gone.

XXVII

It was early, but the August sunlight was already streaking through the windows of the Boothall, lighting up the faces of the men and one woman who stood before the bench. A small cluster of jurors and five prisoners wearing their shackles. The clerk spoke.

'These good men that were last called, and have appeared, are those that shall pass between our Sovereign Lady the Queen and you upon your lives and deaths. That therefore you or any of you shall challenge them or any of them; you may challenge them as they come to the Book to be sworn, before they be sworn, and you shall be heard.' Twelve times he called a name, and twelve times a man stepped forward, placed a hand on the bible, and swore to well and truly try, and true deliverance make, between his Sovereign Lady the Queen and the prisoners at the Bar, according to the evidence, so help him God. One of the prisoners, the one whose good clothes and the folded notes he carried stood out, watched them carefully. He did not challenge any juror, but he looked as though he were considering it each time.

The twelve jurors stood lined on either side of the bar, the prisoners between them, and the clerk took up another list of names. 'Giles Branton, esquire, late of Branton near Merford, hold up your hand. Look upon the prisoner, you that be sworn, and hearken to his cause...' As he read the first indictment, people were beginning to trickle into the courtroom, friends and enemies, lawyers and clients, witnesses and bystanders. 'Upon this indictment he has pleaded not guilty, and for his trial has put himself upon God and the Country, which Country are you.'

When the preliminary business was over, the clerk sent the jury to their place and the waiting prisoners to one side and began the first trial of the morning. Giles Branton unfolded his notes and turned his attention to the first witness for the Crown.

*   *   *

Mr Bourne did not know exactly when Stephen had left. They rode hard, but presumably he had too. The boy could have been just round each bend in the road, but he and Carson never saw him. Why had he done this? Did he believe his father would do nothing, or just that he could do nothing?

The man at the outer north gates, already sweating in the morning sun, did not especially remember seeing a boy of Stephen's description, but he might have forgotten. The gates, he said, had been open between two and three hours.

'What now, sir?' Carson asked.

'Follow me,' Mr Bourne said. He knew where Stephen would have headed. The Northgate gaol, when they reached it, looked much as usual, but in front of the wall near the gate a boy was sitting. He was slumped to the ground, his knees drawn up to his chest and his head buried in his arms. The horse standing patiently beside him looked as dejected as its owner. Henry Bourne dismounted quickly.

'Stephen. What in God's name possessed you to run off like that?

His son looked up.

'They would not let me in,' he said. 'I begged and begged but they would not... I had to see Hugh. I had to...'

'Stephen, what have you done this for?'

'I had to do something! I had to try...' There was a ring of desperation in his voice. 'It is our fault, don't you see? Mine and Hugh's. And now they are trying to hang Hugh's father... he is in that courtroom now and...'

'Now? Already?'

'I saw him. I saw them taking the prisoners to the Boothall. I don't know if he saw me. It's too late.'

'When?'

'Oh, it must be two hours ago... it is too late.'

'It is not too late. They cannot be half done yet. Not if I know anything about Giles Branton.' And his father pulled Stephen to his feet and knocked peremptorily on the prison door. He spoke even more peremptorily to the keeper who answered it, almost pushing him aside. Stephen had never heard his father give anyone orders in such a manner before; within a minute, he had an under-keeper running to fetch Bridget Lister from the chamber where she was lodged, and then marched both her and Stephen towards another door, still barking commands at the keeper fumbling with his keys.

Hugh Branton stared in disbelief as the door opened. Stephen's chest tightened at the sight of him. It was not just that Hugh was thinner, that his face was grubby and his hair rather untidy and his clothes unwashed. There was a pallor about his face and a deadness in his eyes that was frightening.

'Hugh, you are a bloody fool,' Henry Bourne said. 'But your father does not deserve to hang for that, I think. The trial will not be over yet. If a witness appeared now with fresh evidence, he might be heard.'

Hugh said, 'Stephen has told you.'

'And I am wishing to God he had never met you. But if you are prepared to tell the court what you would not tell me, you can do so.'

Hugh looked at Bridget Lister, who stood beside Henry Bourne, suddenly tense with a new hope and a new fear.

'Well?' Stephen's father said.

'It's not too late?'

'I hope not. I am going to overrule your father's wishes, Hugh. You and Bridget are free to go and do whatever you think you must.'

*   *   *

'If the prisoner has done questioning,' Lord Justice Manwood said, 'I understand this completes the evidence for the Crown. Has the prisoner any further witnesses to call?'

'No, my lord.'

'If you wish to address the jury in summary of your case, you may proceed.'

'Thank you, my lord.' The defendant bowed courteously to the bench and turned to the jury. 'The charge you have heard against me...'

And then a voice near the back of the courtroom interrupted him, a voice that rang across the jostling hall and silenced other talk. 'My lord, you must wait!'

The defendant looked up and started. The clerk half-rose to his feet. The judge leaned forward. 'What is this?'

Henry Bourne walked towards the bench, bystanders stepping aside for him. 'My lord, forgive me, but there is a witness in this case I think you ought to hear.'

The judge frowned. 'I thought we had concluded the evidence for the Crown.' He shot a glance at the defendant. 'And I think the prisoner has taken ample time to present witnesses in his defence.'

'I understand that, sir. But this is a witness whose evidence is – is irreplaceable. I am sorry I was not able to bring him before the court earlier; but I do earnestly request you to hear him before you proceed any further.'

'Who is this witness?'

Henry Bourne drew forward a boy who had followed him through the hall. 'This is Hugh Branton, of Branton near Merford, my lord.'

From among the little knot of spectators came a low, wordless cry, and a woman made to rush forward, while the man standing nearby tried to hold her back.

The defendant stepped right up to the bar, his voice sharper and more urgent than it had been all morning. 'My lord, at this I must protest! You cannot call this witness…'

The judge turned from Henry Bourne to look at him. 'For what reason?'

'This is my son!'

The tall woman, her face drained white, was struggling past one of the marshals to reach the boy. 'Hugh – for God's sake – God damn you, you will not…'

'I will have order!' Lord Justice Manwood raised his voice. 'And I will have arrested anyone who lays a finger on this witness.' Then he turned to the boy. 'Come forward.'

Uncertainly, the boy obeyed. His face was dirty, and pale beneath its dirt except where a heavy bruise was spreading. He was biting hard on his lower lip, and he looked neither right nor left as he came up towards the bar.

The defendant tried again. 'My lord, he is scarce more than a child. You cannot take…'

'I will determine that.' He turned to the witness. 'Look at me. You are Hugh Branton, of Branton near Merford.'

'Yes. My lord.'

Again, there was an interruption. Robert Claydon had risen from his place among the Justices, and was saying, 'My lord, this does not seem necessary. We have heard all the evidence, my lord, and this boy...'

The judge shot a glance at him, and repeated, 'I will determine that. Hugh, how old are you?'

'I'll have sixteen years come November.'

'Who brought you hither?'

'Mr Henry Bourne did, sir.'

'And has any instructed or sought to compel what you should say?'

'No, my lord. I want to tell you the truth, that is all.'

Lord Justice Manwood leaned forward. 'Do you understand that the prisoner – your father – is here answering a charge of treason, to which you are presented as witness?'

'Yes, my lord.' Hugh was dimly conscious of what everyone – from the judge to Mother to the casual bystanders – thought he was doing. This was why he could not look at any of them, at the pity and contempt and sheer curiosity in the eyes that were fixed on him.

'Do you want to do this?'

'I must.'

The judge sat back and spoke to the clerk. 'Give him the oath.'

The clerk rose to offer Hugh the book. Hugh heard his father's voice scarcely a yard from him. 'Hugh, this is madness. You are not to – '

'Enough!' The judge barked. 'You can examine the witness after the court has heard him.'

And Hugh laid his hand on the heavy bible and, prompted by the clerk, swore to tell the truth, the whole truth, and nothing but the truth, so help him God.

Then he started to speak. He accused himself of treason. He accused Bridget. He accused Stephen. He accused the Lockwoods. He told the story of the old cottage and the popish books, and he cleared his father of any knowledge of it.

He spoke on and on, aware all the time of the eyes on him. He could not look at his father, nor at Bridget or Stephen, hovering behind Henry Bourne. Mother was there, standing tall and white among the little knot of spectators, but to look at her was out of the question, and to meet John Lister's eye would have been nearly as bad. The disapproving almost-sneer on Claydon's face was unbearable, but far more frightening was the expressionless gravity of the judge. So, in the end he fixed his gaze on a panel in the wall above the bench and told his tale.

So intent was he on getting through what he had to say without crumbling that he had no leisure to notice how it was heard. Once or twice the judge interrupted him, pressing a question, and Hugh stopped and tried to answer, but he could do no more than glance at the questioner. He did manage not to say that the books from the Raven had been at Branton that night last autumn, and he did not mention the list Jake Lockwood had written, but he could not avoid saying that Jake had known about the hiding-place. The other times the judge only seemed to want him to repeat again that his father had not known, and that was easy. It was what he had come to say.

When he had finished, Hugh lowered his eyes at last and looked down at his hands, waiting for something to happen.

'Well,' came the voice from the bench. 'This was quite some evidence from the Crown's witness.'

'I am only trying to tell the truth.'

The judge turned to the prisoner. 'Mr Branton? What have you to say? Did you know the substance of this – testimony?'

'By your favour, my lord, the court insisted on hearing the witness.'

'And does he speak the truth?'

There was a silence. Hugh at last turned to look at his father, wordlessly pleading.

'Do you say he speaks the truth?'

Giles Branton turned his eyes away from his son and back to Lord Justice Manwood. 'If he speaks the truth, then by what he speaks, I cannot vouch for any of it.'

Hugh allowed himself one choking breath of relief. His father had not given him the lie to shield him.

'My lord, if I may,' Robert Claydon rose to his feet. 'Sir, surely this is an outrage – a witness on oath to thus make mockery of the court... will you have the jury find on this boy's tale?'

'He was put on oath to speak the truth. For the time, the truth of his words is all I or the jury need determine. The judge and jury, mark you.' He leaned back again and looked at them in turn, prisoner and witness and magistrate. But before he could speak again, one more voice cried out to be heard.

'Please, my lord.' It was Stephen Bourne. 'Please, sir…'

'Now what? Another papist schoolboy?'

'No, my lord. I am Henry Bourne of Merford's son, and whether or not the court will hear me, I swear as God's my witness that what Hugh has said is true.'

XXVIII

Hugh stood at the window of his chamber, putting on a clean shirt rather carefully and awkwardly. It was evening, a hot, summer evening still. The room around him showed traces of having been searched while he was away – there were crisp new sheets on the bed, the furniture had all been dusted and polished afresh by whoever had tidied up afterwards, and inside his linen chest the clothes had been re-folded more neatly than Hugh ever kept them.

He had been at home nearly an hour. They had been through greeting the little ones, who did not really understand why they had been away, and also Aunt Isabel and Agnes and Harry, who did. Hugh found that he could not quite meet Harry's eye; but Agnes ran up and hugged him until he winced. He had gone up to his chamber to wash, had submitted to Mother's treatment of his bruised face and his back, and eventually been left alone until supper. The supper hour was in fact long past. Aunt Isabel was downstairs giving orders to have the table set afresh for the master and mistress and Hugh.

Even as he stood by his window, trying to make his mind grasp the events of that day, he could recall very little of what happened after the murmuring which followed Stephen's words had died down. Claydon had stood up and started talking. Then his father had joined in, and so had Stephen's father, until they seemed to be all three conferring with the judge at once. Hugh still stood in front of the bench, not knowing what else to do, until one of the court ushers touched his arm, and he followed the man out of the hall. Then there were hours, he did not know how many; he spent them in a small room, somewhere in the Boothall he thought, watching the diamond-patterned patch of sunlight from the window stretch and move across the floor.

At noon, when the light fell square in front of the windowpanes, Henry Bourne opened the door. 'Hugh, can you come with me?'

Hugh had stood up, a wave of fear lurching through him. Mr Bourne said, 'the verdicts for the morning's trials have come in. They've acquitted your father.'

Hugh did not remember what he said in reply, but he grasped at those words and clung to them fiercely, as he followed Stephen's father out of the little room, still afraid, still not understanding. The great hall was almost empty now: the judges were at dinner, the defendants from the morning's trials had gone home or back to gaol to await sentence, as the case might be, and those for the afternoon's trials had not been brought in yet. Outside, in the street, both of Hugh's parents, and Bridget and her father, and the two servants from Branton, were ready to ride away. Hugh did not ask a question. He did not know what to ask. And none of the others spoke either, while he mounted the horse that was waiting for him, and they set off.

At the Northgate gaol they stopped, and Giles Branton went inside to settle their charges with the keeper and to retrieve his possessions and Hugh's.

Hugh found himself next to Bridget. He glanced at her, and she at him in the same moment, and at once they both looked away. Her mare shook its head suddenly, and she absently stroked its neck. He wanted very badly to say something to her, but he hardly knew what. At last, it was she who spoke.

'Hugh...'

But at that moment, Hugh's father, with Fletcher behind him carrying things, came out of the prison again. As he turned to mount his horse, the squire said, 'yours, I think', and put into Hugh's hands the satchel of schoolbooks he had carried with him from Merford grammar that last day. Hugh stopped to sling it over his shoulders, and then spurred his horse after the others.

They rode out of Gloucester towards Merford. A few things Hugh did remember of the journey: the fierce, hot blue of the sky; the way the sweat started to dry on his forehead with each patch of shade they plunged into and then rose out of; the sounds of the scythes and the labourers' voices each time they passed fields in harvest; the smell of the dust of the road and of the grass at its edges. And the look on Aunt Isabel's face, as they reached Branton church and she came running from the Hall to meet them, shaken with sudden hope.

Hugh opened the window and leaned out. The air was heavy, threatening a downpour later. He could see out past the house and the herb-garden, over the stableyard and the meadow that ran down to the stream and the willow-flat. He reached for his doublet, and as he stuffed his arms through the sleeves half-fancied he saw something move in the branches of the willow. But the signal, the old sheet they had rigged like a flag among the branches last spring, did not appear.

He wanted to go down there. In his head, he could see Bridget waiting under the tree by the water, waving as he came up. He dreaded talking to her of what had happened, and yet it seemed to him that to each other they could perhaps have told everything, or as easily remained silent, together among the green and the familiar sounds. They might have looked at each other and faced down the shadows and shame that had been too much for them in Gloucester this afternoon.

But the night was falling, Bridget was in Merford facing her parents, and at that moment one of the maids knocked at the door to tell Hugh he had to go down and face his, over the supper table.

*   *   *

That evening, Mrs Branton lay in the great chamber, the covers of the bed folded back to its foot in the heat, and the bedcurtains open. She was staring up at the canopy of the bed above her, every muscle in her body still tense, not quite daring to believe that the horror she had been steeling herself against had receded.

Her husband was still downstairs. After they had eaten, just as she had sent Hugh up to bed, Henry Bourne had come to the Hall. Giles seemed to be half-expecting him; they had immediately disappeared into the library together, and she knew there were things which had to be said, and perhaps (as it were) unsaid, that were better known to as few souls as possible. So, she had gone upstairs, and un-pinned her clothes, washed and dragged on her nightshift and combed her hair, all of it still in this taut daze.

Giles Branton came up the stairs slowly, and slowly entered the chamber. His eyes met his wife's, and yet neither of them spoke. He sat on the edge of the bed, pulled off his shoes, and began unlacing his doublet. A little time ago he had forced himself to contemplate taking off his clothes for the hangman.

As he drew the curtain and lay down beside her, he realised that she was crying, noiselessly, without words or sobs, the tears she had not permitted to form when they needed each other's strength slipping from her eyes and down her temples into her hair.

He was silent, not turning his head, not closing his eyes. At last, he moved his hand until it touched hers. 'Lucy,' he whispered. 'Lucy.'

She curled her fingers around his, and lay still listening to him breathe, the most beautiful sound in the world.

XXIX

The weather broke that night with a thunderstorm that brought two trees crashing down in the orchard and woke the little ones. Hugh heard the shrieks of mingled fear and excitement coming from the nursery, followed by Mother's voice as she went in to restore order. It rained again the next day, and he wandered uneasily from room to room, trying to feel relieved that they were home, and the danger was over. There was still a knot in his stomach, an unquiet feeling that a great part of it had yet to be faced. And, unbidden, the dreams that he had been quietly nursing for the last months – no, for the last year at least – kept coming back to his mind. Even though he knew, with a wry self-scorn, that they were never going to be more than that. This was the truth his recent folly had taught him: that he was not fit even to think about such a thing as the priesthood. That afternoon, his father sent for Hugh in the library.

He was seated behind the table. Hugh came in and stood in front of him, waiting. Father looked up. 'Hugh.'

'Yes, sir.'

'I am leaving at the end of the week, Hugh. I have still to return to the Clink, and I cannot afford to miss my day.

And there are a couple of matters I must speak to you about, before I leave.'

Hugh nodded. He was trying to formulate the words of an apology, and failing to find anything adequate, when his father spoke again.

'Hugh, do you know…?' He stopped, as though he were also searching for words. 'Do you know who it was that told them what they found out?'

Hugh glanced up in surprise before looking back down at the table-edge again. 'It was Crowe – John Crowe. He told them what I told him.' And then, doggedly, 'it was me, too. I think I must have told them – many things, although I – I thought I was trying not to. I should – I do know, now, that I should never have…'

'Did you hear of anyone else? Or anything else, that they found out from – not from Crowe?'

'No, sir. Apart from that man Hudson –'

'Did Bridget?'

'I do not know… but you could ask her. She would not mind, very much. What is it, sir?'

'Oh, nothing. One should always work out, as far as one can, how these things happen… The Listers have had no news, have they? Of the Lister son?'

'I do not think so, sir,' Hugh said, taken aback by the abrupt change of subject.

'No. No. Well.' He picked up a quill and examined its nib carefully for some seconds, and then said, 'you know,

Hugh, it is not the evil that is done by wicked men that is hardest to forgive. It is – it is the evil that good men are sometimes brought to do. To forgive where you wanted to find no call for forgiveness...'

Hugh merely nodded. He had not really thought about forgiving or not forgiving anyone else. It would be strange enough if he could ever again contemplate Hugh Branton without loathing.

'And yet one must. One must, because everyone tells them something. There are those that turn and tell everything; but even men who will endure anything rather than do that, do not tell them nothing.'

Then his father put down the quill and looked at his son until Hugh looked back at him. 'The other reason I sent for you is that we have to decide what you are to do.'

'Sir?'

'I had thought of sending you to study, either the law or at one of the universities, once you are finished at the Grammar. I believe it is a good thing for a gentleman to be more than simply lettered. But this that has happened makes the question rather more urgent.'

'How, sir?'

His father leaned back in his chair, looking at Hugh. 'Because of that long tale you told against yourself – and a few other people – at the county Assizes.'

Hugh felt sick. He had known it was not over. 'What will happen?'

'Possibly nothing. Robert Claydon, let me tell you, was not keen to turn you and Bridget loose without further question. Bourne and I spoke to Manwood, the judge, during the dinner hour, after the verdict came in... There are unlikely to be any charges against either of you.'

Hugh nodded and waited for his father to continue.

'However, Geoffrey Lockwood is still in prison, and your evidence in court has incriminated him fairly decisively. Now, I do not know of anyone who has any interest in Lockwood's ruin. But if there should be any such attempt, *you are the witness.* If they can summon you, there could be a case.'

'If?'

'If you are not here, you cannot be questioned again, nor summoned, nor – of course – punished on your own account. So, the question is where to send you. It must be out of Gloucester County, and preferably at some useful employment.'

'Yes, sir.'

'But we have very little time. I wish to see you settled somewhere safe as soon as possible, before I leave. I have thought hard of who I might ask to do me such a favour; I think some good household where you can stay, be of some service, and not lose your education entirely is our best course.'

'Yes, sir,' Hugh said again.

'I have written, this morning, and sent in haste a letter to a Catholic nobleman, with one or two of whose people I have some acquaintance since my being in London. I hope to have a favourable reply before I leave, and if so I will take you with me and bestow you there in my journey back to London.'

Hugh was silent for a few seconds, trying to take this in. 'Where is it? The place I'm going? Who am I going to?'

'In the county of Northampton. You'll know the name as soon as you need to.'

Hugh nodded. He kept looking down at the table. He was thinking it was better this way. It was better if he did not have to avoid his little brother's glance, wonder how to ask his mother's forgiveness, choke with shame when he saw Bridget, face Stephen or his father. It was better for all the others if they did not have to worry about what imbecile thing he would do next, or what further trouble he could cause. His father dismissed him then, and Hugh went out and down to the stream and the willow-flat, for the first time ever hoping that neither of the others would be there.

But as he drew near, he saw that Bridget was standing by the tree. He waved, but then realised that she was facing away from him down the stream. He called her name, and she turned. Hugh began to run.

'Bridget...' He pulled up short as he reached the bank, and his voice died away on his lips. She stood looking up at him, and her face was white. Hugh, unable to drag his eyes away from hers, scrambled down the bank as they had done so many times, grasping ladder-rungs of grass and tree roots to keep himself steady. 'Bridget, tell me.'

Her voice was still, controlled, dead. 'Richard wrote – that is, he sent a message; another man wrote it down for him –' She paused and took a careful breath.

'What did he say?' But he knew.

'Only that he was sorry he could not write it himself, but that he is now in custody in London, and his case will be heard there soon. The indictment will be only on the '85 statute, he says, but he thinks it certain – there will be no reprieve. And then he said he prayed for all of us, and asked our prayers in turn. He signed it himself, Richard Lister, his own name...' And then, only just catching her voice, 'the signature was all over the place.'

Bridget's face twisted up as though it hurt too much to cry. Hugh said nothing. It was not only his being tried, but the darkest of fears that lay behind those last words, the thing too frightening to say... Feeble phrases drifted into his brain and disappeared again before he quite found them, as though there was anything he could have said anyway. He could not bear the look on her face, and yet to turn away would have been the last unkindness. So, they stood and looked one at the other, and the only sound was that of the stream.

'Hugh! Bridget!' Stephen's voice, ringing with pleased surprise, broke into the silence. 'I was going to put the signal up if you were not here, but see, you've beaten me to it…Why, what's amiss? Bridget?'

Bridget turned and fled, put the willow tree between herself and the boys, standing with her back to the trunk and one hand pressing against the bark as though she would crush the pain out.

'What is it, Hugh?'

Hugh told him as quickly as he could. Stephen said nothing, standing shocked and disbelieving. At last, he turned as if to go to Bridget.

'Leave her be.' Hugh said.

Stephen did not reply for a minute, and then turned back to Hugh. 'I could not blame her if she did not want me to speak to her.'

Hugh knew he ought to say something kind to Stephen. But suddenly he could not bear any more and turned without another word to escape back to Branton Hall and his own chamber. Stephen stayed where he was, looking after Hugh and back to Bridget. But there were no words to say, there was nothing he could do, and there was no comfort for him here or anywhere. He went away, tears pressing against his eyelids, hoping only that he could get home without being spoken to. And Bridget stood leaning against the tree, staring unseeing across the stream with burning-dry eyes.

XXX

Father presumably had a favourable reply to his letter, because Mother set to packing Hugh's belongings, and he set out with his father on Friday morning. Fletcher went with them, riding the packhorse with most of the baggage. They went a day earlier, because bestowing Hugh in Northamptonshire would mean a longer journey and Father could not afford to be late returning to London, and so the loss of one more day at home was Hugh's fault too. They said goodbye, both of them, to Mother and Aunt Isabel and the little ones. Hugh did not see Bridget or Stephen again. He had been given to understand that his going away was not to be generally known, and he supposed that meant he could not start saying goodbyes.

But as they came towards the village from the Hall and passed the road that led over to Henry Bourne's house, they saw that a figure was standing at the verge. Giles Branton frowned as they drew close, and he recognised him. The boy spoke.

'Mr Branton.'

Hugh's father pulled up his horse. 'Good day, Stephen.'

'Good day, sir.' Stephen was glancing at Hugh, obviously surprised to see him, but he spoke to squire Branton. 'Sir, I – I heard you were leaving today.'

'That is correct.' He followed Stephen's eyes toward his son. 'Hugh is leaving home also, for a little while.'

'I – I see.' Stephen did not ask for any further explanation, and nobody offered one.

'Can I do anything for you, Stephen?'

'I meant to... wish you godspeed...' Stephen muttered. 'I – Mr Branton, I –' Hugh knew what Stephen was struggling to find words for. So, perhaps, did his father.

'Stephen.' He spoke quietly and waited until the boy glanced up at him. 'Stephen, thank you.'

Still looking more at his shoes than at his friend, Stephen said, 'goodbye, Hugh, and godspeed.'

'Goodbye.' Hugh replied, and then added, 'you'll have to bid goodbye to Bridget for me.'

At that, the memory of the meeting by the stream flashed through both their eyes, but Stephen managed to meet Hugh's and answer, 'Yes.'

Then the two riders spurred their horses again, and Stephen watched them out of sight before turning for home.

Hugh and his father made a good journey and passed Saturday night at an inn. The Sunday was agonisingly empty, with very little to do, after prayers, other than hope nobody noticed whether they went to church or not. Hugh was unspeakably relieved when Monday came and they could travel the last miles to his destination. That morning, his father gave him some instructions.

'My lord Vaux is a Catholic and a recusant and has been troubled enough for it in his time. But they live quiet enough at Harrowden these days. You will find it in all respects like many another Catholic household. We are much beholden to my lord and his lady for this kindness and must take care it brings them into no hazard.'

'Yes, sir.'

'To be the more safe, you are not to use the name Branton. Your surname is Heath, and your father is the younger son of a gentleman in Herefordshire. If anyone wants to know more than that, inform her ladyship. You ask no questions neither of anyone else in the household; most especially not of any good men that come. You will obey my lord and my lady as you would me and your mother, and I will have you go nowhere beyond Harrowden without their knowledge and permission, nor make acquaintance of any but that they approve. Clear?'

'Yes, sir.'

'You must write home, but you will have to address your letters Mrs Branton at Branton, so take care as few people see the superscription as possible, and do not write too frequently. You may write to me at London under the same conditions.'

Hugh nodded. 'Sir, how long do I have to stay there?'

'I do not know. Six months; perhaps a year. We shall see.'

'And then what?'

'Then you will come home. Hugh, you have to understand that I may be kept away from home more often than I am there for some time hence. I need to know that you are at Branton to act with competence and discretion in my absence.'

Hugh nodded. It was all so painfully clear, the way he had proved unequal to every duty and every obligation.

His father said, 'now, we had best be riding. There are some miles yet to Harrowden.' And then, as he picked up his gloves and Hugh stood up slowly and drew on his, 'oh, for God's sake, Hugh, please do not look as though I were consigning you to prison.'

Hugh's father stayed for dinner at Harrowden. Hugh sat at table in the great hall with the others, trying desperately to remember his manners and his name and only vaguely taking in the rooms and people and furnishings of the house in which he was going to have to live for however long. His father sat opposite, courteous as ever, and answering to an *alias* without a hint of unease. Lady Vaux, a grey-haired, tired-looking lady, played the deception with equal gravity – she knew, of course, who her guests really were. Lord Vaux seemed even older than his wife, with a kind but oddly absent look, and Hugh was not sure he had really noticed the new arrivals at all. Most of the talking was done by another gentleman, who sat on Lord Vaux's other hand, and was witty, genial, big with a voice to match, and firmly *decided* about every matter you could ever need to hold an opinion on, from the quality of the Harrowden game to the Scottish king's foreign policy. His name was Sir Thomas Tresham, and he was Lady Vaux's brother.

He showed a friendly interest in the guests without being unduly inquisitive; for all his genial loquacity, Tresham was a Catholic of many years' standing. He talked about bits of general news he had heard from Herefordshire, commiserated over the necessity of returning to the Clink, and at one point, asked, 'Have you heard aught, in your way, of that strange case in Gloucester County? Some Catholic gentleman bloody nearly done for treason over, for all I can make out, trafficking in Catholic books...'

Hugh wondered if everyone was looking at his suddenly scarlet face. Without turning a hair, Hugh's father said, 'I think I heard something of it.'

Tresham continued. 'It happened just now, it was all the talk at the summer Assizes. Indicted under the '81 treason statute for *persuading*, because there'd been a lot of missals and tracts kicking around the damn country. I lie not. Old family. Hold a fine manor up in the Cotswolds. I ask you, what in flaming hell made the godless knaves imagine they could do that?'

'It does seem a – an unusual extension of that statute. Know you what happened in the end?'

'He was quit, I think. Better have been. Bloody lunacy. But here's the crazy part: I heard that what came out was that all the mischief was done by his son. Boy of about fourteen. The man hadn't known. They say.'

Hugh wondered whether, if he wished it hard enough, the floor of the great hall would open and swallow him. He could live indefinitely in the cellar, he thought, as long as he could not hear Sir Thomas Tresham's voice.

'I suppose that's a reason for acquittal.'

'Still a god-damn fool, if you ask me. If a man cannot govern his sons, that's the kind of bloody cock-up that's going to come his way.'

'You may be right.'

Hugh did not know if his father looked at him as he spoke, because he could not raise his eyes.

Lady Vaux broke in. 'Thomas, not to interrupt, but I have been meaning to ask your advice about selecting fruit-trees...'

Sir Thomas had plenty of advice to offer on the matter, and the talk turned to orchards.

After dinner was over, Father said goodbye to Hugh, blessed him, and left. The youth he was to share a chamber with took Hugh upstairs to unpack his belongings, and offered to show him around the house and its grounds. It rained while they were on the way back from the horses' paddock. Hugh had an interview with Lady Vaux, who was kind, and asked no questions except about his schooling and the quality of his penmanship. After they went to bed, the boy Rob chattered in a whisper until Hugh wondered if he ever meant to sleep at all. It was amazing how much he managed to talk, without telling Hugh any actual fact about himself or where he came from or requiring similar information from his companion.

At last he did sleep, though, and left Hugh with his thoughts and Rob's snores for company. When he could not endure either any longer, he climbed out of bed and felt his way over to the window in the dark. It was shuttered, but he got the shutter open and stood in the faint moonlight. The floor struck cold on his bare feet, and the windowpanes cold as he leant his head forward against them. He was thinking of the home he had forfeited, of the father he had betrayed, of Bridget, of Stephen, of Bridget's brother waiting for death, of how he would get through the months he had to spend in this place. But most of all he was thinking of how things might have been. It was strange. The other path – the one he could not take, the one he had no right to – had never thrust itself so clearly on his imagination. He might, instead, have been taking a false name in order to go to some London port and board a ship. He might have been worrying about journeying to Rheims through foreign countries. He might have been preparing for lectures and study, and years in the college... One day, he might have said Mass. Hugh stood against the window a long time, learning the misery of knowing exactly what he wanted at the moment he realised that he could not have it.

Instead, there was this place – Harrowden – for six months or a year. In that time, Bridget's brother would have been hanged. Harry would have gone to Norton Court to school. Stephen might have left the Grammar. And then Hugh would go back to his home – a home relentlessly the same and yet changed beyond recovery – and he would try to get by and not serve his father worse than he already had, that was all. Everything else had slipped down into the past and could not be drawn back.

He was quite alone, exiled more completely than by merely leaving places and people. A barrier of shame stood between him and the past; the future he had lost; the present was shapeless. There was only Hugh in his nightshirt at the window looking out at nothing, no other presence whatsoever unless it was almighty God's. When the grey fingers of morning began to search the room, he was still there.

*   *   *

Bridget Lister sat at the willow-flat in the shadow of early evening, throwing stones into the stream. She was not spinning ducks and drakes but casting them straight so that they hit the water and sank the way Hugh's always did. The shapes of the pebbles, and the dirt on her fingers from picking them off the ground, and the dull splashes as they fell, these were all she could fill her mind with, all the thoughts she dared allow. There was a sound of footsteps behind, and Stephen came up. Bridget did not look round, but pitched the pebble she was holding into the water.

Stephen said nothing either. He sat down on the bank a little way back and to one side, and both of them watched the ripples from the pebble vanish into the stream's flow, while he waited for Bridget to turn round.

Afterword: historical note

All the central characters in this novel are fictional and are not based on historical individuals. I have tried to portray the context in which their story is set as accurately as possible, according to the surviving sources and current historical scholarship. All the laws mentioned under which Catholics were prosecuted were, indeed, on the Elizabethan statute books (and remained on the statute books until the eighteenth century). They resulted in the executions of about 187 Catholics during the reign of Elizabeth I (r.1558-1603), and 70 more from 1604 to 1681. Historians continue to piece together the evidence of other ways in which the proscription of Catholicism affected people's lives – imprisonment, financial penalties, the various aggravations associated with enforcement of religious laws, sporadic quasi-official harassment. I have tried to create fiction that is consonant with what we know.

Some real people appear briefly or are mentioned in the story. Edmund Campion, SJ, executed in 1581, was probably the best-known Catholic martyr of the period; it would have been impossible for my characters not to have heard of him. His Letter to the Lords of the Council is a real, and surviving, text. William Lampley's martyrdom in Gloucester, 1589, is recorded in a contemporary Catholic report, as is the incident involving the priest Stephen Rowsham in 1587, in which one of my fictional characters is involved. The other people named as Catholic martyrs were also historical people; all of them have since been officially recognised as martyrs by the Catholic Church. William, Cardinal Allen was the founder of the first English seminary overseas and his *True, Sincere and Modest Defence* (1584), and the quotations from it, are real. John Hooper, Protestant bishop of Gloucester, was burnt for his religious beliefs in Gloucester in 1555, one of 286 executions under heresy laws during Mary I's reign (r.1553-1558). Sir Thomas Tresham, and his Vaux relatives, were also real people. Sir Thomas deserves to be remembered for his wonderfully idiosyncratic building projects, the amount of money he paid in recusancy fines without allowing it to cramp his style, his peculiarly bloody-minded combination of religious dissidence and vocal loyalism, and his generosity to historians in leaving behind a large number of gloriously evocative, at times hilarious, personal papers. For more on this, see Katie McKeogh (D.Phil Oxon.).

There is a great deal of scholarship on Elizabethan Catholicism. Unfortunately, there is not currently a really good single-volume introduction to the subject. The relevant chapters of Peter Marshall's *Heretics and Believers* (2017) give some material. Gerald Kilroy's *Edmund Campion: a scholarly life* (2017) brings Campion vividly to life, though its assessment of the wider subject of Elizabethan religious policy has limitations. My own work has explored the lives of Catholic children and young people (Lucy Underwood, *Childhood, youth and religious dissent in post-Reformation England,* 2014). *Catholics and the 'Protestant Nation'* (2005, edited by Ethan H. Shagan) collected essays by some of the best scholars on the subject, while Alexandra Walsham's work on Catholic topics is collected in *Catholics in Protestant Britain* (2014). T.M. McCoog's three-volume tour de force (*Our way of Proceeding* (1996), *Building the faith of St Peter on the King of Spain's Monarchy* (2012), and *Lest our Lamp be Entirely Extinguished* (2018)) deals with the Society of Jesus in the British Isles from 1541 to 1606, while Michael Questier's *Catholics and Treason* (forthcoming) is a comprehensive, and compelling, history of Catholic martyrs and martyrology.

For a voice from Elizabethan England itself that tells the story of its Catholic communities, read the autobiography of the undercover missionary John Gerard SJ (translated by Philip Caraman). It represents one person's experiences and point of view, and there is plenty Gerard does not tell us. But there is also plenty he does, and he is certainly not dull.

I am grateful to the fellow historians who helped me to double-check my historical accuracy: Simon Healy, Michael Questier, Krista Kesselring, and Katie McKeogh. The flaws are all my own.

Printed in Great Britain
by Amazon

86814730R00241